GW01018387

City of Dreadful Night

LEE SIEGEL

City of Dreadful Night

A TALE OF HORROR
AND THE MACABRE IN INDIA

THE UNIVERSITY OF CHICAGO PRESS *Chicago & London*

The University of Chicago Press, Chicago 60637
The University of Chicago Press, Ltd., London
© 1995 by Lee Siegel
All rights reserved. Published 1995
Printed in the United States of America
04 03 02 01 00 99 98 97 96 95   2 3 4 5

ISBN: 0-226-75688-2 (cloth)
0-226-75689-0 (paper)

Library of Congress Cataloging-in-Publication Data

Siegel, Lee, 1945–
City of dreadful night : a story about horror and the macabre in India / Lee Siegel.
p. cm.
1. Indic fiction (English)—20th century. 2. Horror in literature. 3. Death in literature. 4. Vārānasi (India) in literature. 5. Indic literature (English)—History and criticism. I. Title.
PR9492.5.S54 1995
823—dc20   95-9750
CIP

♾ The paper used in this publication meets the minimum requirements of the American National Standard for Information Sciences—Permanence of Paper for Printed Library Materials, ANSI Z39.48–1984.

For Noreen
who read and told me stories
when I was a child

The City is of Night; perchance of Death,
But certainly of Night; for never there
Can come the lucid morning's fragrant breath
After the dewy dawning's cold grey air;
The moon and stars may shine with scorn or pity;
The sun has never visited that city,
For it dissolveth in the daylight fair.

. . . .

The phantoms have no reticence at all:
The nudity of flesh will blush though tameless,
The extreme nudity of bone grins shameless,
The unsexed skeleton mocks shroud and pall.

JAMES THOMSON, *CITY OF DREADFUL NIGHT* (1874)

Straight as a bar of polished steel ran the road to the City of Dreadful Night; on either side of the road lay corpses disposed on beds in fantastic attitudes—one hundred and seventy bodies of men. Some shrouded all in white with bound-up mouths; some naked and black as ebony in the strong light; and one—that lay face upwards with dropped jaw, far away from the others—silvery white and ashen gray. . . . "Will the Sahib, out of kindness, make room?" What is it? Something borne on men's shoulders comes by in the halflight, and I stand back. A woman's corpse going down to the burning-ghat, and a bystander says, "She died at midnight from the heat." So the city was of Death as well as Night after all.

RUDYARD KIPLING, *CITY OF DREADFUL NIGHT* (1885)

In the City of Dreadful Night men tell stories of a Glorious Day. What else can they do? How else could they endure? . . . Take it as a sign then that all is well, that you are safe, when you hear tales of horror and the macabre, when you find yourself taking pleasure in what is terrible and gruesome. Take it as a sign!

MARY SHERIDAN THOMSON, *CITY OF DREADFUL NIGHT* (1911)

City of Dreadful Night

I

Ay, I was once a famed teller of stories when I was begging on the road between Koshin and Etra; before the last pilgrimage that I ever took to Orissa. I told many and heard many more at the rest-houses in the evening when we were merry at the end of the march. It is in my heart that grown men are but as little children in the matter of tales, and the oldest tale is the most beloved. . . . A tale that is told is a true tale as long as the telling lasts. . . . All the earth is full of tales to him who listens and does not drive away the poor from his door. The poor are the best tale-tellers; for they must lay their ear to the ground every night.

GOBIND THE ONE-EYED, IN THE PREFACE TO RUDYARD KIPLING'S *LIFE'S HANDICAP* (1891)

A local legend . . . tells of an old Indian known as the Father of Stories, a man of immemorial age, blind and illiterate, who uninterruptedly tells stories that take place in countries and times unknown to him. The phenomenon has brought expeditions of anthropologists and parapsychologists; it has been determined that many novels published by famous authors had been recited word for word by the wheezing voice of the Father of Stories several years before their appearance.

ITALO CALVINO, *SE UNA NOTTE D'INVERNO UN VIAGGIATORE* (1979); TRANSLATED BY WILLIAM WEAVER as *IF ON A WINTER'S NIGHT A TRAVELER* (1981)

The spell of the story has always exercised a special potency in the oral-based Indian tradition and Indians have characteristically sought expression of central and collective meanings through narrative design. . . . The preferred medium of instruction and transmission of psychological, metaphysical, and social thought in India continues to be the story. Narrative has thus been used as a way of thinking, as a way of reasoning about complex situations, as an inquiry into the nature of reality. . . . Whenever an orthodox Hindu wishes to prove a point or convey what the world is like or ought to be like, he or she is more than likely to begin his exposition with that shift in the register of voice that is a prelude to the sentence, "Let me tell you a story."

SUDHIR KAKAR, *INTIMATE, RELATIONS: EXPLORING INDIAN SEXUALITY* (1989)

21 May 1991

(Eighth lunar day of the light half of Vaishakh, Samvat 2048; Durga's Eighth)

Naked, Chitralekha is standing in front of the mirror, pouring coconut oil into her palm, rubbing her hands together gently; she massages the oil into her scalp, extending her fingers through the long, pliant cords of hair to draw the lusciously shimmering dressing down through the locks, undoing twists and tangles, pulling toward the curling ends; tugging and squeezing, massaging and stroking, rubbing and rolling, then tying the tresses back to rest and drink up the oil as she bathes.

Breathing deeply to savor the smell of her fragranced hair, she looks at the photograph, the corner of which she has secured under the dark, warped wooden frame of the polished mirror. Moving her head, adjusting her position so that the reflection of her own face is close to the face in the photograph, she already feels that she's near him. She moves closer and ardent breath clouds the silvery glass.

She's perspiring from the heat and nervousness and her lower lip trembles as she swallows and, feeling her throat dry and her empty stomach churned, she takes another deep breath to calm her heart. She dreamed of him last night, a dream in which he softly touched her cheek with fingertips no less warm, eager, or uncertain that her own. She sucks in another gasp of air and with the back of her jittery hand wipes the perspiration from her dark brow as real eyes fix onto the wide and anxious stare of those in the mirror. "Chitralekha," she mutters her own name in deep whisper, imagining it is his muffled voice that speaks to her as she strains to envision herself through his eyes.

People at home, in Chavakcherri village in Jaffna, consider her plain, uninteresting, and unlikely to ever possess a man. She's already twenty-five years old. They're unaware of the exquisite passions, carnal ache, and distillates of desire that move and intoxicate Chitralekha. But soon they'll discover the woman of grace and power; she smiles at his face in the photograph; and with teeth so white, straight, so perfectly formed, he beams back. Her face will soon be close to that face, that flesh and blood.

The ceiling fan wobbles above and behind her, and over the din of it she can barely hear the sounds of the Madras street: honk of a horn, tinkle of a bicycle bell, low whine of a motorcycle, drone of a machine, bark of a dog, caw of crows fighting over refuse, laughter of children, a vegetable vendor calling out, and faintly, faintly she can hear a song, a woman's voice, sweet Tamil words crackling as they're strained through the metal screen of the speaker on Nalini's transistor radio: milk from a magic cow, sweet rice pudding from the kitchen of a king, and a golden child . . . la la la . . . leaves of betel, pierced with clove . . . la la la. . . .

The drumming sound of water gushing from the tap into the large bucket drowns out the song and the random melody of the street outside where the setting sun appears as an enormous blood-engorged tick on the flushed and luminous body of sprawling sky. In the crimson darkening, the black silhouette of still coconut palms is redolent of home. She turns from the window to see the disconsolate movement of solemn shadows, she among them, across the dappled, graying green wall as she returns to the cool, unremembering mirror.

Although the hungrily coming darkness does not diminish the wearying heat, crystalline water from the iron bucket is balm and solace as she rubs the new bar of Mysore sandalwood soap between her hands to lather flesh that's anxious to be clean and fragrant for him, uncorrupted for the midnight to come. The soap was a gift from Nalini, the confidante who comprehends the passion and the transport, the fear and the desire.

Again in front of the mirror, she tries to dry herself and bites her lip to still the quiver. For a moment unsure that she'll be able to muster the courage to go to him as plotted, she shakes her head, spraying droplets of oil and water from her hair and face, and allays the impulses of weakness of nerve in desire. Touching her lower lip with her finger, she then touches the finger to the lips in the photograph, leaving a slight trace of oil there.

Lush, coconut-fragrant, oiled hair clings to wet skin, forming wild clutching curls and serpentine swirls on swollen cheeks and a sweating forehead, on her neck and rounded shoulders, her back and breasts, a wet black labyrinth of hair through which glistening droplets of water and oil roll and purl like crystal beads and precious pearls.

Nalini said tonight's auspicious: this is Durga's day, and surely that splendidly powerful goddess understands, condones, and even sanctifies Chitralekha's desires. Tonight she'll welcome Chitralekha, perfected and beautiful, into the pantheon of goddesses. The lizard on the wall promises consummations.

Although she continues the effort to dry herself with the clean white towel, the heat is so insistent that her perspiring prevents her from accomplishing it. Everything is wet and hot. Her skull throbs from the heat and her legs ache with it. Dusting herself with talcum powder—her neck and under her breasts, her stomach and down across the plot of hair to the flexed thighs—blowing the powder across her arms, she remembers the dream again: he had parted his lips over her breast, lingered with his breath, and he had wept. The perspiration on her body in sleep had been transformed by dream into his tears.

Before pulling them over her legs, she unconsciously touches the new Lyril panties to her cheek as she rehearses in her mind again what she has envisioned a thousand times, and she asks herself, as she has done again and again for weeks now, if he will think her beautiful. With all her heart, she yearns to ravish and enrapture, to take his breath away.

"I bow, bend, touch his feet, then make him mine, giving him all of myself, more than his wife or any other woman ever has or would or could, giving my life, every fiber of myself in a perfect, all-consuming exploit of passion that obliterates all that has kept us apart until now, binding us in higher realms, together forever, merged by a carnal feat of deliverance from physical limitations."

Dabbing her skin with precious attar, the extract of kewra, lifting her finger to her nostril to smell the delectable fragrance, she touches a trace to her upper lip, smears a line on each breast, around each nipple, and on her belly, just above the top of the panties.

After fastening the bra that she has bought in Saidapet bazaar expressly for this illicit meeting, she separates her hair, now glossy and alive with the coconut oil that it has absorbed, using the narrow edge of the black comb to make the part, her hand quavering with persistent anxiety, then combing, then dividing the hair into the three thick, luxuriant twisted vines, separating and then intertwining the heavy cords, weaving, braiding, and then finally coiling them into a tight and ordered knot of dark splendor and fragrance.

Helping her pick the salwar kameez, the green pants with the matching scarf and the orange top, Nalini had joked about the colors (the green and orange of the Indian flag), had made a risque Tamil pun that equated sex and patriotism.

Freeing the anklet that has snagged on the green pants, she then pulls the shirt over the vest and sees her face come through the opening to greet itself in the mirror: "I've never been beautiful until tonight. But I'm beautiful now. I am. I have his radiance now."

Powdering her face as she scans the other pictures of him around the room, she stops to gaze at the largest one, taped to the green wall: he's so fair, she thinks, and she so dark—dark but comely.

Carefully extracting the stick from the little bottle of Shringaar kumkum to stamp the bright crimson circle on her forehead, she has to hold her right hand steady with her left to make the mark perfectly round for him.

She pulls her lower eyelid down with her finger, wipes the dark kaajal around the eye to make seductive the glance, softening the edges of the mascara with her finger after lightly licking it. She sticks her tongue out at herself and laughs: "Kali!"

The eyes are all the more enchanting once she touches the dark pencil to her brow. She reddens her lips with the lipstick that, without clashing with her orange kameez, will make the lip look ripe and swollen, passionate and moist. Then she blots it, softens it— "not too much, not too strong, not too noticeable."

His large deer eyes, soft, dark, and sensual even in the photograph, watch her prepare for him. The sweet, pliant mouth seemingly so full of smiles and whispers, kisses and promises, is poised as if for her alone. She considers the thinning of his hair and the new wisps of gray as she fixes the jasmine flowers in her own hair for him and the bouquet of it—enhanced by the coming night, blending with coconut oil, kewra perfume, and the aroma of the sandalwood flowers that she'll drape around his neck—utterly intoxicate her. Sweet, sweet, so sweet they'll smell when she touches him.

Removing the silver ornament in her nose and replacing it with gold, then slipping the gold bangle—not her usual glass ones—over her hand and onto her wrist, she wishes that her toe rings and anklets might be studded with clear diamonds and blood-red rubies. Nothing is too fine for him, as everyone knows, but tonight nothing is too fine for her either.

As a child, she suddenly and for no meaningful reason recalls, she had watched lovely Mala dress, apply her make-up, and wrap her sari, and she had dreamed then of being beautiful like her someday, of feeling men's eyes voraciously gazing at her. She turns before the mirror as if to show herself to Mala, as if to inquire if she's done her toilet properly, as if to ask, again and again, "Am I beautiful?"

The earrings and necklace had belonged to her mother—if only her mother and Mala could know what Chitralekha is going to do and become tonight, but, no, no, it's a secret, a great and wonderful secret. And that's the most terrible part for her, that she can't tell others about her and him and what will become of them tonight.

That they are bound together by destiny and feeling, by desire and suffering, is her consolation, and that this is illicit intensifies her passion.

"Am I wicked?" she asks the self in the mirror with a sly smile. "No, no, beyond the law, beyond propriety, there is a truth, an obliterating ecstasy, a meaning. Flesh merging into flesh, soul into soul. Perfect, holy sacrifice." He is, she knows, at once her victim and her destruction. She'll overcome her fears, take what she desires, and he'll not be able to resist her.

It suddenly saddens her to put her glasses on. "Do they make me unattractive? Do I have to wear them?"

"Are you ready?" Nalini calls from the other room, and the wall lizard with bulging eyes scampers behind the mirror. "You'll be late. You mustn't keep such an important man waiting!"

Surely Nalini, whose feelings for him have been confessed, must envy her; and certainly Shubha must be jealous that he's all Chitralekha's tonight.

Tonight: the culmination of oaths and promises, sighs and whimpers, a thousand proofs and protestations that she was willing to die for him: "His heart is mine," she whispers to herself. "His soul is mine, his flesh and blood. . . . I'm ready to take him. Ready to give myself, all of myself. I'm ready. Nalini, I'm ready. Now."

She has waited anxiously for tonight—passion has no patience. Moved by Chitralekha's faithfulness and ardor, Nalini, dressed in a clean white choli and a golden sari, smiles sadly at her ardent friend and clutches her hand lovingly, with both pity and envy.

Gently she goes to him this hot night, carrying the sandalwood flowers for his neck, and he is dressed immaculately in white.

She looks into his eyes and he into hers, greeting, and there's surrender in the split second as she bows to touch his feet, whispering words he cannot hear, and then, then she touches it, touches it gently, so gently with such ease, touches the switch, the toggle switch on the denim vest hidden underneath her kameez, touches it, and there's the blinding, deafening, obliterating blast, the terrible detonation all at once of the grenades containing the C-RDX explosives imbedded with steel pellets, ripping apart Chitralekha's body, evaporating her midriff, hurling her limbs, making her head a cannon ball blown from her neck through Rajiv Gandhi's stomach, cleaving him in half, and at the same instant the pulverizing impact of the explosion dissolves his face, effaces it, and as the shrapnel of mutilating metal and depredatory fire, bone and flesh, mangles his entourage and devotees, splatters the ground and sky with gore, and it rains blood and fat, chunks and morsels, the slag of human beings, hair and clothing, the wood and cloth of banners, flowers, and bodies, blood oozing through cracks in charred crusts of skin, are strewn around and amidst the remaining scraps of Chitralekha and Rajiv, smoldering flesh merged and scattered, split, spilled, and splintered, twisted and contorted and, as the horrendous echo of the extirpatory explosion subsides, there's the faint sound of moaning, an instant of silence, and then, then there is a great shriek, a horrifying collective scream that reverberates through the vastness of this dreadful night.

We arrived unaware of the assassination that had taken place six hours earlier; the door of the plane was opened with mechanical ceremony and, as we passed through it into the heat and night, trudging tiredly, as I have done many times before, down the fluorescently lit corridor toward customs and immigration, we began to sense that something was wrong. The chaos and confusion that characterizes the hall where the corridors converge are usually tempered by an uncanny Indian cheerfulness. But there was, that heated night at Indira Gandhi International Airport, a palpable dread in the air, a feeling of panic, a sense of senselessness, a distinct despair, the source of which was subsequently explained to us by the immigration officer: "Rajiv Gandhi was assassinated tonight. Killed by a human bomb in Madras." He looked at our U.S. passports and, as if in an attempt to transform his shame into our guilt, he added: "The CIA is suspected to be involved."

Lugubriously perusing our documents, he shook his head with what seemed disdain as sorrow-reddened eyes read the official supporting letter from the Indian Ministry of Education and Culture: "I am directed to inform you that the Government of India has approved the research project entitled *City of Dreadful Night,* a study of horror and the macabre in Indian literature to be undertaken in Varanasi by Professor Lee Siegel."

"Welcome to India," he said perfunctorily, with a pained glower.

I took a deep breath of conditioned air, cool, scented, and disinfected, before stepping out through the exit into the unconditionally dark flames and toxic fumes, through doors swinging into the incinerating furnace of a wicked night.

A crow pecked at the window while we watched the cremation on television in the late afternoon two confused days later: "As the body of the slain leader sets off on its final journey from Teen Murti, a horrified nation mourns." The roar of wind and the growl of helicopters made an eerie whir and howl, a desperate, wordless litany, behind the voice of the Doordarshan reporter: "Yes, here come the mortal remains
of the ex-prime minister of India." The helicopters were mythic birds scattering flower petals over the reassembled corpse, the body dismembered, now in anguish and procession remembered. "And here come the mortal remains of Rajiv Gandhi. . . ." Funeral fire transformed the entire city into a bier, made the air seethe, and, looking out through the window, I saw the crow's beak cocked open but emitting no sound. "You are looking at the mortal remains of forty-seven-year-old Rajiv Gandhi as the body makes its way to Shakti Sthal."

The skull did not need to be broken by the son; the explosion had already done that. The foreign wife placed a garland of tulsi on the pyre. A pot was broken and left behind. The mutilated corpse burned. . . .

"Another Scotch?" my old friend, seemingly unphased by the assassination and unmoved by the cremation taking place on the television in the corner of his living room, asked with a smile. "Look, you'd better drink here. You won't be able to get anything at the hotels. The country's dry. They say it's out of respect for Gandhi, but it's not. It's never what they say. It's because the government's terrified that whiskey will unleash the horror, that the whole country will go raving mad like we did after his mother's assassination. Everyone's afraid that there's going to be a repeat of the riots, the murders, the suicides. We're becoming almost as violent as the United States. So, come on, have another drink, and tell me what you're doing here this time."

"I'm off to Varanasi in a few days, as soon as I can get a plane reservation. I need to see Pandey, the Sanskrit literature man at BHU, do you know him? No? Consultation with him justifies the grants. I've been working on a book on horror and the macabre in India, thinking about the ways in which fear and disgust, as universal emotions, are specifically and particularly resolved in Sanskrit literature. And I want to hang out around the cremation ghats, to try to collect some of the death lore."

"Horror and macabre! Haha! You know, I re-read *Dracula* a few years ago, and it wasn't half-bad. But there's something rather disconcertingly puritanical about it, don't you think? Well, I'm not the one to talk about all of that. Frankly," my friend laughed, "I can't stomach that sort of thing—blood and bones, ghouls and goblins, musty crypts and haunted houses."

He stopped for a moment. "Let me tell you a story," he smiled then, pausing to toast me with a welcome to India, and then downing a gulp of scotch in my honor: *Some years ago, just after the assassination of Indira, I was in Varanasi for my father's funeral. After the ceremonies I went to visit a former student of my father's, not so much to get condolences as to give them. The man's a householder Aghori. You know the Aghoris? They meditate in cremation grounds, eat human flesh from skull bowls, and wander around naked. Well, the householder Aghori does none of that—he's a rather ordinary, conventional chap whose religious practice consists in giving alms to the real Aghoris who do all those terrible, disgusting, and forbidden things. So when you're at his house, you're likely to meet some horrid Aghori sadhu who's come for the free meal. They say they eat human flesh and excrement with the same relish as if they were eating curd and kebabs, that they'd drink human blood as soon as cow's milk, and yet you can bet that it's something good to eat that lures them to the householders' doors. It's a blessing to have had an Aghori in your home; they leave behind remnants of the merit they've accrued with their horrific, anomian practices.*

At any rate, I was there to assure my father's former student that I was doing just fine and that, more importantly, the rites had been properly performed to prevent my dear father from being reborn as a crow. I was about to leave—it was getting very late—when a man arrived. I thought he was an Aghori because of the eccentricity of his appearance and because of the hour at which he had chosen to arrive—it was almost midnight. Yes, I was certain he must be an Aghori. The ones who don't go naked, who appear in town, often wear outrageous attire, garlands of bones and that sort of thing. And indeed, this man presented an extraordinary spectacle: for one, he wore a top hat, an old, battered English top hat that he had adorned with peacock feathers; he was bedecked with amulets, a garland of little skulls—of birds and rodents I presumed, and that seemed typical of what one would expect from an Aghori—and dangling over his heart, amidst cylindrical metal charms, some small cloth bags containing god only knows what, and bits of strange twisted roots and twigs, was, much to my amusement and surprise, a crucifix. Who knows where he came by that. The old man was naked from the waist up, and he wore a black lungi and was barefoot. He had a gnarled walking stick, a sort of ominous shillelagh that could have been well used as a cudgel.

But no, no, my host explained to me, no, he was not an Aghori, not at all. He had arrived with another man, some sort of jewelry merchant or some such thing, who was introduced to me as another householder Aghori. And the strange visitor in the top hat was introduced as a storyteller and an exorcist, an ojha, a sort of wandering bard who told ghost stories and, on occasion, if necessary, used such tales to exorcise spirits. I can't, for the life of me, remember his name. But the sight of him remains vivid in my mind. His stories, I was told, kept malignant spirits away. He used fear to frighten fear away, dread to fight dread, terror against terrors, horror to dehorrify. He tells Aghori stories, my friend said, terrible and wonderful stories about what goes on in the cremation grounds at midnight.

My host seemed delighted by the storyteller's arrival and his children were no less jubilant—they too apparently knew the old storyteller and they begged him to spin a tale for us.

"Yes, yes, tell us a story!" everyone pleaded with bright and expectant smiles.

He seated himself on the floor, cross-legged in ascetic posture, and they offered him tea and sweets and he talked of his travels, explained that he had just come in from the villages to pass the rainy season in Varanasi.

Finally—it was just after midnight now—he was ready to begin. "And now," the storyteller, said, closing his eyes and then opening them to smile almost sadly, "let me tell you a story, a true and terrible story." One of his eyes was clouded over, filmy, milky, and that gave him a rather macabre presence, but that was balanced by the warm sparkle of the other eye. His smile too was warm, friendly, inviting, but he restrained it, to take on a somber, almost fearful look, to create, I suppose, a mood for the story. But, before I tell you his story, let's have another scotch."

We discussed the recent improvement in Indian whiskey, and I asked him what he thought about the girl who had murdered Rajiv. Who was she working for? LTTE? How did they convince her to blow herself up? Uninterested in talking about that, he was anxious to return to his story and the story within his story. It began with a businessman from Delhi, named Janak, taking a train to Orissa. One train led to another and then the man was staying in a Dak Bungalow in some fairly remote place from where he was to get a bus that would take him into the tribal regions. It was arranged that he would get off the bus at a spot where a tonga, sent by a certain chieftain whose tribe had recently, all except him, died out. The jungle potentate, who had amassed a good deal of gold, the legacy of his extinct tribe, had sent for the businessman to make arrangements for the purchase of a large house in Delhi.

The very mention of the tribal lord's name—Betul Rajo—terrifies the manager of the Dak Bungalow: he and his wife adjure Janak not to go, warn him that it's not safe in that part of the jungle where Betul Rajo lives. The beginning of the story was ominous—you could tell that terrible things were about to transpire. But I was puzzled—the whole thing sounded vaguely familiar to me. He described the bus ride through the darkening countryside. When Ja-

nak tells the bus driver where he wants to alight, the driver and the passengers become anxious, nervous, inexplicably upset. No, the driver says, it's not a good place to stop, not a safe place—it's near a cremation ground and this is amavasya, the darkest night of the month. Janak insists that a conveyance sent by the tribal lord will be there to meet him and that he will be safe; but when they arrive at the designated spot, no one is there, and it is very dark, as rolling smoke-black clouds have covered the delicate sliver of a fully waned moon. Still Janak insists on stopping. The bus driver pleads with him not to leave the bus; the passengers argue with him, and, feeling a bit of their contagious fear, he momentarily reconsiders. But at that very instant a tonga, pulled by a coal-black horse, emerges from the forest and approaches the bus. At this point I was still trying to figure out where I had heard this story before.

The headlights of the bus fall upon the face of the driver, illu-
minating a hard-looking mouth with very red lips and sharp-looking teeth, as white as ivory. The driver, darkly draped, vague in the murk of night, takes Janak's luggage from the top of the bus and directs our hero into the tonga.

Suddenly, with the arrival of Janak at the place where the tribal lord lived, I realized how I knew this story. Betul Rajo lives in an old jungle ruin, once a flourishing temple ornately embellished with erotic friezes, now engulfed by forest, overgrown with creepers, the couples united in the infinite postures for sexual union which the imagination has invented for flesh to try, are corroded, disintegrating, stone flesh eaten away by time and weather, must and rot, vine and root. Of course, jackals are howling in the shadows and bats are circling in the darkness above as the tonga driver motions Janak out of the cart and then disappears into the night. Our hero's heart is pounding wildly as, slowly and fearfully, he approaches the decomposing, moldering temple. Then suddenly he sees him, there in the entrance, a large man, not dark as one would expect of tribal people but very pale, tall and wan with long white hair blowing wild in the brusque winds that augur a coming storm. He's wrapped in a black shawl and he speaks to Janak: "Welcome to my home."

He said it in English! Haha! That's when I realized it and, much to the dismay and embarrassment of my host, I laughed out loud and could not restrain myself from interrupting this preposterous tale "Dracula! Dracula—you're telling us the story of Dracula. This is neither a true story, nor an Indian story. It's Dracula! *Janak is Jonathan Harker. Orissa is Romania. You're telling us the story of Count Dracula."*

The storyteller was unruffled by my intrusion into his narrative. "I'm telling you a true story," he said with composure, without a bit of defensiveness and, astonishingly, in English. He smiled slightly: "The English story of Dracula is a true story. It truly took place in London. And this story, the story I'm telling you now is true as well. It truly took place in Orissa. Dracula, the Vetala Maharaja, after he was slain in Britain, reincarnated in India, the land where he had lived thousands of year before."

16 With an incredulous laugh I interrupted my friend's story of his interruption of the storyteller's story: "You're making this up. I don't believe you. You're the liar, the storyteller."

"No, no," he laughed back. "It's true," he insisted with a devilish chuckle. "I swear it's true."

"If I were to write about this, to describe you and what you just told me in the book I'm writing about horror and the macabre in India, no one would believe me. It is, to use your word, preposterous."

"Come on, another sip of scotch," he said as he refilled our glasses. "No, no, Lee, you don't understand. Listen. Go ahead and write it. If I believed the storyteller and you believed me, then your readers would not believe you; but since I disbelieved the storyteller's story and you disbelieve my story of the storyteller, then your readers will believe you. The real trick would be to make your readers believe the storyteller—that's the hard one. Oh god, let's finish the scotch."

He pointed to the muted television on the screen of which dignitaries were filing past the funeral fire of the former prime minister. "Do you believe that? Do you believe the horror story of the girl who killed Rajiv?" And he laughed. "Believe, not believe, half-believe, believe a little . . . haha! . . . It's a fine game isn't it. Sorting out truth and lies, fact and fiction. That's what storytelling is all about, isn't it? It's what writing, whether storybooks or scholarship, novels or newspapers, is about. It's what psychology and philosophy are about. It's what everything's about! The ghost stories, what you refer to as tales of horror and the macabre, are moves in the philosophical game. India, of all cultures, of all civilizations, has the best stories. Our religion is nothing but stories; our history is nothing but stories; damn if our lives aren't anything but stories."

He suddenly stopped, stared at me and then laughed again: "I've gotten so carried away that I've left out the reason that I began to tell you this story in the first place. I'm trying to help you with your project. I'm going to give you the address of my father's student, the householder Aghori in Varanasi, and I'll write a letter of introduction for you. I think you ought to visit him and have him introduce you to the storyteller. You need him for your work. The rascal tells horror stories after all, tales about ghosts and goblins, ghouls and vampires, all sorts of spirits and demons—bhuts, prets, vetals, pishachs, churels, all that sort of thing, just the kind of 'death lore' you'll probably want to collect for your study. Wonderful stories, ancient stories! True or false? I don't know—that's your problem, or the problem of your readers. Forget about Pandey and the rest of the professors—what do they know that's interesting?—try to meet the storyteller. Encourage him to take you with him to the villages so you can listen as he sits beneath the village pipal tree telling his ghost stories. Then you'll understand something about horror and the macabre. Or maybe you won't; but you'll understand something about India, about storytelling in India, and that's much more interesting. The soul of India is in her stories. The truth is, by its very nature, embedded in fictions."

"He's drunk," his wife said as she entered the room with my wife. "He always gets drunk when you show up, Lee. And when he gets drunk he thinks he's a poet or a philosopher."

Insisting that he was not drunk, that he had never been drunk except once when he was very young, he quite soberly invited us to stay for dinner, and his wife nodded her endorsement of the invitation.

Later, bidding us goodnight at the door, he spoke in mock-sinister tones: "Be careful tonight. Be very careful."

"Why," I asked, "do you think there might be riots over the assassination?"

"No, no" he laughed, "no, I think there may be hungry ghosts and vampires—the heat stirs them up just as it does the mosquitoes. Yes, there may be ghouls and goblins out to get you, anxious to stop you from writing about them. They like to keep their world secret." He yawned, then laughed again and "maybe I am drunk after all," he said as he closed the door.

Reading the newspaper on the plane to Varanasi, I stared once again at the picture of the "human bomb," the vaguely reassembled body of the figure they were calling "the dark woman from the South" in the article linking her to the women's wing of the LTTE suicide squad, the "Cyanide Warriors" whose goal was "to strike terror in the hearts of their enemies and to spread horror throughout South Asia."

When we emerged from the plane into the record heat that was causing deaths throughout the country, the taxi drivers who had no doubt kept their gaze skyward in anticipation of planeloads of customers, were waiting for us and, like crows over carrion, they began to fight amongst each other for our money.

I opened the back door of the car closest to us and we pushed into the back seat. As the triumphant taxi driver pulled out of Babatpur airport at full speed, I told him our destination, the house that had been arranged for us near Durga Kund, in Kabir Nagar, New Colony.

No, he insisted, he couldn't take us there. Deaf to my persistent argument that there and only there was where I wanted to go, he refused. Assuming that he didn't know where I meant or that it was confusing to him that we, as foreigners, didn't want to go to a hotel, I changed my strategy: "Okay, Diamond Hotel, take us to the Diamond Hotel," from where I planned to get another taxi to our house.

No, no, absolutely not, he couldn't take us there. Where, I asked, could he take us? "Nowhere. Curfew. No Banaras. Curfew."

Not believing him, assuming that it was a ploy to deposit us in some hotel outside of the town where he'd get a kickback, I asked where he was going.

"Cantonment. No Banaras—curfew. Cantonment."

When we arrived at Clark's Hotel in the cantonment, the desk clerk confirmed the taxi driver's assertions: there was a shoot-on-sight curfew in the town; we'd have to stay at the hotel until the curfew was lifted.

"When will that be?"

"One week? Two weeks? One month? Who knows? How long will you be staying sir?"

"If the curfew's not over in a day or two, I'm going to try to get a flight back to Delhi. There's no point in staying here."

"There are no reservations for flights to Delhi. Everything is booked up, sir. Relax, sir. There is a point in staying here—you can enjoy yourself. What greater point can there be in life than enjoyment?"

"No reservations? You mean, I'm stuck here?" I asked with genuine consternation. "I'm a prisoner here?"

"If that is the way you would like to put it, sir," the desk clerk responded cheerfully, "although I personally would use the word 'guest' rather than 'prisoner,' the difference being that guests enjoy what prisoners do not. Please sign the guest register. We are thoroughly five-star and fully air-conditioned for your comfort and enjoyment. With this heat, it is better if you do not go out anyway. Why risk sunstroke? Enjoy the swimming pool! Enjoy the air-conditioned bar! Enjoy the air-conditioned shops where you can buy all the products for which Varanasi is famous—brass, copper ware, ivory, handicrafts, jewelry, silks, and brocades—shopping in the comfort of your own hotel without having to haggle or fight your way through crowds. Enjoy the excellent programs of the closed-circuit video that we have piped into each five-star air-conditioned room on our own exclusive cable system. Enjoy yourselves! Welcome to India, to Varanasi, and to Clark's!"

There were hardly any other guests in the hotel except a tour of Japanese who had come to visit Sarnath, the site where the Buddha is said to have preached his first sermon after his awakening, his victory over fear and desire. Perhaps it was because there were so few guests that I was shown the list, marked "Viewing Menu," of the hotel's videotape collection and asked to make any requests that I might have. I was rather surprised and amused by the irony that there were, among the hundreds of titles on the list, a number of horror movies: *Nightmare on Elm Street, Friday the 13th, The Exorcist, The Omen, The Howl-*

ing, Carrie, Cujo, and *Lair of the White Worm.* When I commented on it, the desk clerk smiled proudly: "Yes, I am personally responsible for this aspect of our collection. I am, you see, somewhat of a connoisseur of horror films, and of American films and books in general. I am a great fan of the inspired writings of Mr. Stephen King. And yourself?

"I'm not much of a connoisseur, but I'm very interested in why people like such books and movies, why people would want to watch or read something that frightens or revolts them."

"That's the fun of it precisely."

"Yes, but why?"

"Why? It's just human nature, I suppose."

The first night he showed *Nightmare on Elm Street* over the closed-circuit television. Neither my wife Cheryl nor I could quite stomach the site of the mutilated Freddy Krueger, his fingers for some unknown reason sporting razors, terrorizing American teenagers. The second night was no better: *Nightmare on Elm Street II.*

"How did you enjoy Freddy?" the desk clerk asked in the morning. "Our Japanese guests were quite enthusiastic about it."

"Excellent," I answered politely, despite the fact that we hadn't watched it.

"It's not as good to see these films in the cinema. It's much better to see them in the privacy of your own room, just you and madame. It is very good for a marriage. Madame becomes terrified and she throws her arms about your neck for protection. Haha! Fear arouses female passions. She feels the instinct to turn to a male for security—god placed that instinct in woman purposefully. Horror is good . . ." He hesitated with an innocently prurient smile: "Do you understand?" Looking to the right and the left, making certain we could not be overheard, he continued: "Let's face it, horror is an aphrodisiac. Isn't it?"

"More than the news," I answered and turned to join Cheryl at the swimming pool where we were spending our days drinking beer and reading books, magazines, and newspapers purchased at the hotel's air-conditioned shop. I bought the latest edition of *India Today,* and there again was the grisly image of the reassembled body of the "dark woman of the South," now called "Thanu" in the magazine and "Dhanu" in the papers. There were photographs of her comrade, Nalini, standing next to her as she waited to garland Rajiv Gandhi. And there was a man with them who had been identified as One-Eyed Jack, so named because "one of his eyes, damaged in an explosion has been replaced with a glass prosthesis." One newspaper called him "One-Eyed Jack the Tamil Ripper."

I purchased a paperback copy of an Indian edition of *Dracula* in the shop, amused to have found it there; thinking that as long as I was stuck here and unable to get on with my research, I might as well give the seminal horror story another read. I showed the book to the desk clerk as we passed him on our way to the pool. "Excellent!" he smiled, "I have seen many versions of the film: *Dracula, Wife of Dracula, Daughter of Dracula, Son of Dracula, Return of Dracula*. Excellent one and all. Unfortunately we don't have any of these in our video collection. I sincerely hope, however, to find and purchase some of them in the future."

"I am interested in Indian versions of horror, not English or American horror movies or books, but Indian ones. Do you know anything about that? Is there such a thing?"

"I've seen these films of the Ramsay Brothers, feeble Indian attempts to imitate Western horror. *Dak Bungalow,* the Indian version of your *Psycho,* is not bad. But it is not too great, either. Not frightening enough. Not very good actually. In fact, it is terrible."

"But what about stories, novels, books?"

"India has not yet given birth to her own Bram Stoker or Stephen King, I'm afraid. I cannot think of a great horror writer from India."

"But there are storytellers who tell horror stories, ghost stories, vampire tales, storytellers who go from village to village. I've heard there are such men."

"That is the past," the Clark's clerk said with a certain mannered nostalgia. "These people are no more. Now it's films and video. When I was a child, yes, there were storytellers who came sometimes to our village, and there was one I remember, an old, man, who told stories that would scare you to death, make your hair stand on end, and give you nightmares. But these fellows are dying out. They don't exist any more."

"It's uncanny," I explained to Cheryl. "Every time I write something about India and come here to do research, everybody—I mean everybody—I meet in India is a self-styled expert on whatever it is I'm writing about."

I was afraid that the desk clerk might be right, that I would never, even if we were released from the hotel and permitted to go into Varanasi, be able to find my storyteller, that the itinerant bard, together with the ancient tradition, was dead and buried in the past or burned away by the pyrotechnological fires of the present. I tried to picture him as my friend had described him, starting with the English top hat festooned with peacock feathers, moving down through my imagination over the body seated in ascetic posture, to focus upon the amulets dangling from his leathery neck, then to follow wrinkled arms waving gracefully as he told his stories.

That night, the last night of the light half of the month of Vaishakh, May 28, was the Buddha's birthday, and the day of his death too, his nirvana and his parinirvana. Because of the full moon I expected a werewolf video to be shown on our closed-circuit television but discovered rather *Nightmare on Elm Street IV,* and then switched the channel to Doordarshan National Television which was broadcasting an operatic dance drama based on the life of the Buddha. "Because Lord Buddh taught us, India and the world, the way of ahimsa," the announcer said as outside the tanks and trucks of armed soldiers rumbled through the streets, "we celebrate this day with pride."

It was difficult to choose between the channels, between Freddy Krueger and the Buddha, and I felt claustrophobic in the room; so, despite the heat of the night, I went outside to the garden, found and unfolded a deck chair, and, seated in it, I looked up at the full moon, trying to envision my storyteller. I closed my eyes, opened them, closed them again and I could see him sitting under a pipal tree in a nearby village. The terribly real image of the "dark woman of the South," of her body dismembered by the explosion and reassembled by the police, kept intruding on my attempt to visualize the storyteller.

I opened my eyes and looked at the moon. My friend in Delhi had probably made the story up. Was there really a man in a silk top hat out there somewhere telling tales of horror and the macabre?

In the distance a dog barked, and there was a siren. Someone, perhaps a chowkidar or some other hotel worker, was moving in the shadows. The dark form stopped as if surprised and perhaps frightened to discover me there. I shut my eyes again, and when I opened them the figure had disappeared. I closed my eyes and again tried to see the storyteller. I strained to hear him.

Come close, let me tell you a story, a story about horror and the macabre, a story about stories, a story about India. Come close, let me tell you a story, a true story. . . .

2

"This, my son, is the skull of a man which is burning in the pyre." Then the boy in his recklessness struck the skull with a piece of wood lighted at the top, and clove it. The brains sprouted up from it and entered his mouth, like the initiation into the practices of the Rakshasas, bestowed upon him by the funeral flame. And by tasting them that boy became a Rakshasa, with hair standing on end, with a sword that he had drawn from the flame, terrible with projecting tusks: so he seized the skull and drinking the brains from it, he licked it with tongue restlessly quivering like the flames of fire that clung to the bone. Then he flung aside the skull, and lifting his sword he attempted to slay his own father, Govindasvamin.

KATHASARITSAGARA OF SOMADEVA (ELEVENTH CENTURY); TRANSLATED BY C. H. TAWNEY AS *THE OCEAN OF THE STREAMS OF STORY* (1880)

Concerning the factors of silence, solitude and darkness, we can only say that they are actually elements in the production of that infantile morbid anxiety from which the majority of human beings have never become quite free.

SIGMUND FREUD, *DAS UNHEIMLICHE* (1919); TRANSLATED AS *THE UNCANNY* BY ALIX STRACHEY (1925).

The horror story makes us children. That's the primary function of the horror story—to knock away all of this stuff, all of the bullshit we cover ourselves up with, to take us over the taboo lines, to places we aren't supposed to be.

STEPHEN KING, *BARE BONES: CONVERSATIONS ON TERROR WITH STEPHEN KING* (1988)

19 May 1991

(SIXTH LUNAR DAY OF THE LIGHT HALF OF VAISHAKH, SAMVAT 2048; RAMANUJAN'S BIRTHDAY).

"And now," my storyteller, Brahm Kathuwala, softly speaks, hesitating, closing his eyes and then opening them to smile almost sadly and begin. "Now, come a little closer, come now and let me tell you an old, old story, yes, a true story, the terrible tale of the boy who became possessed."

Cross-legged in ascetic posture on the platform under the pipal tree near the now dry bed of the stream, the dais constructed of stones covered over with sun-fired clay polished smooth by centuries of sweeping, the vagrant storyteller is at home. His stage is ornamented with a black shivalingam and the bright bouquet of marigolds that has been placed before him not so much out of respect as from cautious hospitality, a tentative welcome to the small farming village. Despite the infernal heat of summer, this is a time of work; paddy fields must be readied for imminent rains. Once the downpour comes there will be no visitors, no movement, and even the ghosts will be impounded in whatever dark refuges they might find from the merciless torrents of the torrid season.

"Who's this man?" they ask each other and themselves, with the vaguely fearful curiosity that is the natural prerogative of people unaccustomed to strangers, as he solemnly unrolls his tattered mat—"some sort of sadhu perhaps . . . a magician . . . maybe a tribal priest or shaman . . . who knows?"

Other storytellers have come to sit on this very platform and recount the raffish pranks of playful Krishna or the wondrous deeds of righteous Ram, scenes glorious and heroic, full of mirth, wonder, and terror. That's happened again and again over the years. The great and ancient tree has soaked up tales and recitations as its trembling leaves have shaded the innumerable wanderers who have arrived, alone or in troupes, with stories, songs, and inevitable sermons. But specialists in tales of horror and the macabre, stories of ghosts, ghouls, and goblins, are scarce these days. And this old man ("Just how old is he?" several wonder) is peculiar. His hat is strange—an English hat, a silk relic of the Raj, the black top hat festooned with peacock feathers. Beneath its flat brim an odd earring, a small skull fashioned out of silver, catches the gleam and glow of the kerosene lamp set near him, beside the walking stick of dark gnarled wood, near the old book, foreign like the hat, its green cloth cover and cracked leather binding stained and worn, frayed and faded. Clusters of amulets dangle from his leathery neck and wrinkled wrists, both of which have a watch upon them: one has a face and hands ("Half past eight," it says), the other just electronic lines ("7:19 PM," it argues). Among the periaptic charms there's a Christian talisman, a necklace of beads holding a small silver crucifix over his heart.

Brahm Kathuwala has positioned himself so that the lamplight makes bright his clear right and youthful eye; the shadowed primeval left is clouded, glaucous, and mysterious. He has insisted that the electric lights of which the panchayat is so proud not be used; though he has explained that it's because of the noise of the generator, it is, in fact, that smokeless bulb light and the shadows it casts are wrong for horror stories. You need real fire to awaken the spirits.

"He'll tell some ghost stories," Mitu, the tired, rawboned village carpenter, explains to his son, wide-eyed Nishad. "He passed by here some years ago, before you were born. I remember the hat. I heard him then and it almost scared me to death," the father laughs, pleased with the prospects of an evening of stories, a distraction from the spiteful weather, a pounding heat that makes it insufferable even to sleep. "He'll make your hair stand up on end. He might give you nightmares." Mitu can't help looking back to make certain that his wife is there with the other women. Only a few women have come, and no young girls.

"Nightmares," Mitu repeats the word to himself. "Nightmares: fear-dreams," he thinks. "Why do they come? Why, when we need rest and peace the most, do we have bad sleep?" He's been troubled all day by a terrible dream from the night before: he had been alone in the fields, searching for something lost (he can't remember what), and it was viciously dark and brutally hot. Suddenly the ravening form, darker than the darkness of the night, all darkness except for small flames that were its cruel eyes, pounced upon him, snarling and biting, scratching at his face with razor claws, trying, it seems in memory of the dream, to rip away his face as if it were a mask. Mitu had awakened trembling and sweating with terror. His wife was asleep next to him; his son, also asleep, was curled up on the nearby mat. Had he screamed? No—that would certainly have awakened them. Or perhaps he had, and they had absorbed the shriek into their own dreams, dreamed of him screaming in fear. And in their dreams did they help him or did they watch as the skin was peeled from the screeching skull?

The carpenter had tried to resist going back to sleep for fear that he'd fall back into that malevolent dream, that the nightmare was waiting for consciousness to yield, and it would suck him into it, and that the demon was waiting silently, patiently and hungrily, there. Waiting for him to close his eyes. Inescapable. Malignant. "Protect us, Lord Ram!"

Now Mitu can't remember sleep having overcome him again nor any other of last night's dreams but, this morning, looking at himself in the fragment of crackled mirror that he had found long ago and fixed to the choice wooden beam that supported his roof, he saw, much to his bewilderment, that he had a scratch on his face—a delicate red line from his hair, straight down the right side of his forehead, over his eyelid, and halfway down his cheek. "I scratched myself in sleep," he thought and looked for the small knife to trim his work-dirty fingernails short. "The demon is only myself!" He laughs disgruntled, "Protect me from myself!"

Pleased to have found a place so close to the platform, sitting cross-legged like the storyteller himself, cradled between his father's bare and bony legs as he listens to the beginning of the story, Nishad's eyes survey Brahm Kathuwala's props—the weathered monkey skull with iridescent vermillion streaked upon it as on the forehead of a bride, the animal bones Nishad thinks are human, the drum and flute, and the bound bundles of fragrant faded herbs and dried grasses.

There was then, long ago, but it seems like yesterday, a drought in the land, the storyteller begins: *sky and earth had become bitter and ascetic; the river had receded, crawled back to her mother Ganga, writhed and slowly squirmed away in pain from her children, lovers, and devotees, those people of the village. They had devised their homes of mud and wood, woven them out of strong and fragrant thatch, arranged them on what had been the clean sprawl and generous stretch of the river's once moist bank. Now she was wizened and the land was cracked, earth and river racked with fever, sick and dying and dirty, and the hyenas' fitful barking—yap, yap, yap—was mad lamentation. The villagers made offerings to their febrile goddess, that infected river, too listless to take them to her lips. Her smokey waters were meager and putrid.*

With withered branches, leafless trees were skeletons reaching in supplication to indifferent heavens. Bark skin cracked. Dust. Wooden limbs ached and brittle fingers trembled. Dust, dust. Dogs barked and death whispered invitations. Disintegrating cadavers of village cows, oxen, and buffalo were strewn as a fly-infested banquet for crows and jackals on the dark dried mud where once a fecund flowing river was luminous and cool. Mahars were sluggishly dragging the cumbersome bodies away. . . .

The storyteller seems to sing his tale, rocking and swaying to the rhythm of it, transported by dreams or memories of his own life or others' tales heard long ago. He finds the current in the river of stories, catches it, and lets it carry him along. From its source, far away in an ancient time and place, here the river rushes while there it's calm and quiet. Brahm Kathuwala knows each bend and turn and gracefully he glides through the story. The destination is a great ocean of silence, the black sea of oblivion, the white shores of which are death.

This is not his tale; rather he belongs to it. Its beat and cadence, merely tapped and released by him, still the village crowd, open eyes and ears and hearts. And the storyteller feels it. He sits lean and shirtless before them and strangely, despite the heat, he doesn't perspire. This is no ordinary man. The unsewn black cloth that covers his loins suggests an ominous pact with terrible Bhairavi. The one misted and murky eye makes the other seem to glisten, sparkle, opalescent black, all the more. His soft gray beard is clean and his arms move as gracefully as the words that, like flocking birds, fly from his lips. They soar and circle, rise and fall, and the patterns change and shift again.

The language isn't what you hear everyday, not in the village at least. Neither is it the Hindi of radio or films or of the government officials or salesmen who occasionally come to the village from Varanasi. It sounds old, like the tongue of ancient saints or like the language of sacred hymns. Maybe he's from Assam or from the mountains. Or perhaps it's a Kinnara dialect. Whatever the sources of its enchantingly lyrical distortions, its magical intonations and mysterious inflections, Nishad feels he understands the words. He knows the storyteller is speaking just for him.

There was a brahmin, good Govindaswami, in this village, my very own. I never met the man myself—he died, you see, died before my birth. Oh, but my father knew him and he told me the story. Everyone in our village had some account of the terrible tale of that brahmin Govindaswami and his two sons, Sanjayadatta and Vijayadatta. It's a story dreamed and told and told again, told by fires in the night, told no less in times of abundance than in times of famine, told now no less than then, told and retold differently at different times, for different ears and hearts, but told and told and dreamed again. And now, let it be told again. Listen to our story.

It was the very worst of droughts, he murmurs with a storyteller's loud whisper, *and in the fierce, flushed night of famine you could hear ceaseless sobbing, cries of hunger in those who lived, unresigned to die, and cries of sorrow for those who'd given up and departed. And there was fever, malaria, cholera, and plague. Human moans welled through the heated drone of cicadas and the thirsty high-pitched hum of mosquitoes, and the jackals' nasty yelping was terrible exultation. Cowering, cringing, crouching in the murk and gloom of hot night and shadow, they cried out for the fleshy spoils of the raging fever and famine: "More bodies! Bodies! Gives us bones to chew!"*

The desolate, gruesome words are uttered with such relish and delight that they seem not so horrible or ghastly but rather thrilling, almost mirthful as they tease the ear and make the leaves of the pipal quiver.

As if human touch might inspire rains to come, Govindaswami embraced his wife, not the anxious caress of passion but the softer cling and sadder clutch of woe. In her arms he gently wept for her, his wife, and for his distant mistress, the languishing river. He lamented for the people of the village too and he wept then for the earth. The women, like the river, sighed and, like the earth, did not, could not, speak. There was nothing to say. Words would be obvious and horrible. In such times one feels it—that words are a presumption. They violate the silence that is truth. Storytellers listened but did not dare to speak.

Our Govindaswami had been a wealthy man. The storyteller's tone is modulated, becomes matter-of-fact: *Before the epidemic and the famine he had owned a hundred cows and there was a parrot caged in his window. When the bird chewed through the bars and flew away, the brahmin had taken it as an omen.*

It was not what Govindaswami had lost that pained his heart and made him weep, but what remained. Strange as it may seem, he lamented the supplies he had still stored—pulses, flours, spices, oils, pickles, honeys.

"It's intolerable," he told his wife and he taught those sons, Sanjayadatta and Vijayadatta. Now the storyteller's tone is pious: *"It's wrong. Everything we have deprives another of that very thing." He took a brahmin's vow and made a noble offering, piously gave everything he had to the destitute of the village, divided it up as fairly as he could, deciding after some deliberation to give equally to all. It was not for him, he concluded, to judge who needed what; it was not their need to have but his to yield up that dictated the terms of offering. That was how brahmins were in those days of righteousness.*

Squatting on the ground, Sanjayadatta listened, and Vijaya-

datta, the younger boy, cradled in his father's lap, fidgeted as Govindaswami explained renunciation. "What was ours is theirs now, theirs to pass beyond them in time. We may try to hold to things, but finally we must let them go, let all things pass by and on, through others, into oblivion. In the end there's nothing, and in that, there's rest." The brahmin smiled sadly. "Let us let go and go. We'll take only what we can carry, each bearing only what's essential. We'll learn from that, discover exactly what we need and just what we do not. The pilgrimage is good. It itself is prayer, lesson, purification."

The expressions on the storyteller's face had been those of the father; now they become those of the son: *As his father spoke, Vijayadatta saw it—the dusty black serpent's head waving from beneath the bed, so near his mother's foot—and his gasp froze them. The mother closed her eyes, held her breath. Vijaya's were wide open. Sanjaya slowly rose. The snake, silently uncoiled, swayed, swerved, curved its way across the floor, hesitated, raised its hooded head, and in the shiny black beads of death—its fearless eyes, sparks of cold fire—the room was reflected.* The storyteller's arm undulates to transform itself into the snake, his hand its head, his thumb its jaw, playful and frightening in the light of the kerosene lamp. The shadow of it clings to the trunk of the great pipal tree, slithering up into the branches as a real serpent might. The head, horrid and exquisite, arches and turns. *The supple cobra's eyes, glittering with menace, sought Vijaya, then Sanjaya, anything that moved.* They seek Nishad as well. *Like this, like this. The split needle of tongue waved and wagged through the front of the fatal, lipless mouth to taste the vapors that laced the heated air. Like this the snake head lowered, came to rest with terrible grace on the floor, and the lithe, scaled body curled up behind it, flexed, pushed forward, and the serpent rhythmically essed its way away. Like this. Like this.* Nishad's eyes are fearfully fixed on the storyteller's hand.

Vijaya's mother opened her eyes. Sanjaya, who'd been frozen still by the icy glare of the cobra, slumped down. Vijaya could not take the breath of relief in too deeply for he sensed he'd meet that snake again.

Nishad senses that he'll meet it too. He leans and turns his head to look around his father for his mother squatting with the several other women in the back. They whisper among themselves and cover their mouths with thin shawls to hide insouciant smiles. "What are they talking about? Why aren't they listening to the story?"

Vijaya was not an unusually fearful child—no more or less than you, or you, or you, or you. The storyteller points directly at Nishad and, curiously, it pleases the boy. *But what child does not know fear, does not know of things that are there but can't be seen? Vijaya knew them well, had felt their presence more than once—those things neither living nor dead, invisible nor visible, those uncontrollable phantasms of night.* And Nishad knows them too.

And in the morning, with the villagers weeping obeisances as their good-byes, Govindaswami led his family across the barren field to the dry and desolate road that would take them to Varanasi. The villagers see themselves.

Along the route to the holy city then as now there were pilgrims and traveling merchants, monks and mendicants, sadhus and sannyasis; there were thieves and tricksters too, and, of course, the sick and dying and the beggars. Of course. Then as now. Nothing changes. Same fields, same goats, cows, and oxen, same mango trees, heavy with fruit at this time of year. Always the same. That's why old stories don't seem so old.

They were gathered at a roadside stall. But Vijaya could hardly see it until they were very close, because a wind—not the cool sandal scented breeze of the south but the rancid hot bluster of the west—had risen and rushed to them; they were its prey, and they covered their faces for protection. Holding his mother's hand for guidance through the dry, sour, gray-brown, storm, Vijaya trembled. Growling dogs announced their approach.

Suddenly the stall, alive with the restless bodies that had swarmed to it for refuge, appeared in the dirty haze. Cloaks and cowls, masks and veils—black, brown, white, gray, and ocher muslins, waving and flapping—kept eyes, ears, mouths, nostrils almost free of dust. They looked like corpses sheet-wrapped for cremation, dusky cadavers moving to and fro, some silent, some talking, some coughing or laughing, some standing, some sitting, some going for food or drink. A hand suddenly emerged from a cered form to reach for a battered, rusted cup or dry, dirty roti and pull it back inside the funereal shawl where the shape of it could be seen to move up, toward the face, the skull within; a skeleton seemed to struggle and writhe, lost and tangled beneath skin stretched loose and shapeless.

Since lepers only passed by the village, never daring to advance so close, the details of their horrible disease were unfamiliar to Vijaya. So when the chalk-white finger stumps of the coal-black hand emerged from the wrapping of dark and oily rags that approached them, Vijaya, gazing out through the gauze that covered his face, shuddered. He could smell what was concealed by blood and pus-stained tatters.

Govindaswami, who had given all he had to the village, made no attempt to offer up any more to the leper, and Vijaya's mother tightened the shawl around her head. To expose his need to them, to wrench their hearts with the horror that is the foundation and essence of pity, the leper threw off the rag that draped his dark night of a face. A single open eye was a hideous moon in the murky visage, more smeared than stretched across the battered skull, a slab of night blotched and stained with large white, fumy clouds of disease. Drool dripped from the hole out of which the moans of supplication bubbled and rolled over a sore and greenish tongue. A pearl of yellow pus had pushed its way through fused eyelids. All the putrefied fluids of the body, seething exudations, ached to burst through cracks in the desiccated skin, stretched taut by the rot within: organs liquefying into a soupy ichor, rancid human seepage laced with filaments of blood. The crusty slough and gluey ooze of the disease that sabotaged his flesh, cankered, ulcerated carnage corroded, rusting like metal, burnt like wood, and ashen white. Vijayadatta wanted to vomit up a scream, but he held it back and buried his face in his mother's side.

He could feel something quite impalpable, but quite real somehow, clutching him, squeezing his neck, running its hand down his stomach toward his groin, as if the leper wanted him, something in him, lusted even to wrap those rags around him, envelop him with sickness, engulf him and take him, encoil him like a snake about its prey, to swallow, dissolve, and absorb him, to merge with him. And suddenly it happened. "Bhooo!" the storyteller shouts. "Bhooo!" and his audience flinches, gasps, and then they laugh at themselves for being so frightened by the sudden roar. Nishad and his father laugh. And the storyteller joins them in their laughter.

Something touched the boy's shoulder. Terror snapped open his eyes and he caught his breath. The grip tightened. It was the hand of his father; it must have been—the leper's hand, the storyteller darkly laughs again, *was fingerless.*

"Come, come, let's go," Govindaswami said, and they passed by the stall and Vijaya looked back at the cinder-gray wrapped bodies, dust- and haze-swathed, moving as if in some slow, spasmodic dance for the dead. The leper seemed to hobble after them at a distance. And Vijaya would have sworn he could hear a pained and muffled laughter from inside the filthy wrap of the leper's rags.

As you get closer to Varanasi, paths converge. Who's been to Varanasi? Who's traveled those roads? There are, you know, the pilgrims and renouncers, beggars and robbers, salesmen and who knows what else; there are those who hope they'll make it in time, those who long to die in the place they call Kashi, the City of Splendid Light. But I call it Ugraratri Nagar, the City of Dreadful Night. Varanasi is a great cremation ground, and we flock to it. It pulls us there, yes, yes its invisible fingers tugging us. And, no, no we can't resist the invitation to die.

Suddenly, in the instant he hesitates, Brahm Kathuwala senses it. *He* is there. Yes. It's certain. It's *him*. Betul Rajo, the Vetala Raja, the Vampire King, Lord of the Un-Dead. Is *he* behind Brahm, hidden by the great trunk of the tree? Or is *he* above, in the branches, looking down at the storyteller and at them, watching, listening, waiting? Yes, *he's* there again. Why? The storyteller slowly picks up the hourglass drum, holds it still and silent for a moment, looks up into the branches sprawling out between him and the infinite darkness of the heavens. Nothing to be seen. But the storyteller can hear his words in what is silence to the others: *You think you have left me without a place to rest, but I have more. My revenge is just begun! I spread it over centuries, and time is on my side.* Why is *he* here now? Why? Lowering his eyes, then closing them as he raises the drum, stretching his arm above his head, with sudden, violent twists of the amulet-wrapped wrist (the other hand touches the crucifix around his neck), he makes the drum thrum, rattle and clatter, the clamor of it covering his whispered words: *phrum phuh phuh prah phat phrah phat namah*. He wills *him* away—*stay away, at bay, away, away*. The drum still rattles, and he remembers the words: "Stories have the power to control *him;* tales of terror drain and sap *him* of what is terrifying about *him;* they deplete *him* of his power. Tell the stories. Tell them wherever you go. *In the roadside camps,* the storyteller, lowering the drum, steeling himself against the power of *him,* concentrating with all of his strength, begins again, *people, in fear of thugs and thieves, or ghosts and ghouls, kept and still keep, to themselves, huddled in groups—families or circles of friends. Then as now. Owls and jackals laughed at those who slept at night, closing their eyes at the hour most suitable for finding prey. Still now they laugh*. And the Vetala Raja laughs too: *"You think you baffle me! Haha! You think you have left me without a place to rest?"* The storyteller covers the terrible, faint echoing utterance with the rattle of the drum and the rolling words of his story: *Vijaya watched his father eat one of the chapatis that his wife had prepared for the melancholy pilgrimage, biting into it with lips curling back, then tugging, ripping it, pulling off a piece, then wrapping his lips around what remained in his teeth, chewing slowly, and as the jaw rotated with purpose, his eyes, reflecting the fires of the camp, fell upon his wife, then his older son, Sanjaya, then Vijaya, and he offered the boy a piece of the bread. It was refused as if in fear of poisons. The child expected the serpent to appear at any time, any moment now. Even if it did not, he knew it was there. If not the serpent then the leper. He trembled. There in the shadows, animated by the flames, obscured by the smoke, protected by the night, both of them and others too. Over there. There in the blackness, the formless beings, ravenous and cruel, knew Vijaya's every thought. He tried not to think of anything. That would make them go away. Fear would draw them close—they could smell it and it made them hungry. Think of nothing; think no thoughts. Then they'll pass you by.*

The storyteller's walking stick, dead still on the platform, casting a twisted shadow, is, as far as Nishad's concerned, the story's deadly serpent.

Lost in the story, not thinking of what he's doing, Mitu runs his fingers gently across the fine scratch on his face. The slender line of scab cracks at one place on the cheek and there is a glistening droplet of blood. And the Vetala Raja smells it.

Sanjaya's tongue licked the yellow-brown daal from his lip as he dipped the chapati again, sucked more sauce from it, forced it into his mouth, and chewed like his father. Vijaya couldn't eat; the smell of meat cooking in the distance nauseated him. This boy of ten or eleven, delicate and small for his age, felt sick. A dizziness. Something vague gnawed at him. He fell asleep with his head upon his mother's lap, slept and shivered in fevered dreams of cobras and corpses. The dream was a story, an ancient tale that had once had some meaning, but was now, to Vijaya, ill understood. The leper came to his dream, entered it by force like a thief into the brick house where his mother had once slept. And the leper touched her, pulled back her shawl, breathed upon her neck, her breast, her stomach . . . and he laughed.

The storyteller breaks his whisper with a frightening laugh of his own. It startles Nishad. The storyteller laughs again, laughs triumphantly because he knows that it's working, that the story, the cadence of its images, are lulling and weakening *him*. He laughs in the face of the Vampire King.

Mitu wonders why there's a small blotch of blood on his shawl. His wife, not listening to the story, yawns. An old keeper of goats suddenly remembers the storyteller: "Yes, he's been to our village before. I'm certain of it. Several times. Yes, he told this very story before. How did it end? I can't remember." He scratches his head trying to recall it, the first time the man had come to their village almost half a century before. He scratches the white stubble on his chin. It was the year of Independence, the year his wife died of malaria, a year, despite self-rule, of terrors and sadnesses, of riots and madnesses, of bad crops and diseased goats.

"Vijaya, wake up! Wake up!" his father said. The village schoolmaster, slumping into a doze at the back of the gathering, opens

his eyes and sits up attentive. *And as the boy opened his eyes, he gasped in fear at the sight of him, seated there by the fire with them, with Sanjaya and his mother—the Skullbearer, an Aghoribaba.*

From the prongs of the trident, staked into the ground, hung a drum formed of two inverted skulls across which skin had been stretched, a drum shaped like this one. By the rattle and din of the hourglass drum that threatens the Vetala Raja, the storyteller escapes by transforming himself into the Skullbearer and he turns Nishad into Vijaya. *The man, perhaps Vijaya's father's age, was naked, smeared with ashes, white as a corpse. Ashes too were caked thick and chalky in the hair around the swollen genitals and under the arms raised above his head where his hands joined in some mystic mudra as he recited the magic syllables: "Phrum phuh phuh prah phat phrah phat namah."*

Around his neck, under the beard of serpentine tresses, there was a garland of rat skulls, a string of rudraksha beads, and the sloughed skin of a krait. He wore a skull ring. His sacred thread was a black weave of human hair. Two ominous skulls of crows ornamented his ears and there were other skulls as well—the cranial alms and eating bowl and, resting at his side, the jawless human skull, its forehead painted with mystic signs. His hair was thickly tangled, dirt and cinder matted, entwined with twigs, bits of string, and unidentifiable debris. That there were no ashes on his face made it seem as if a decaying cadaver carried a living head around upon its shoulders. There was a scar emerging from his scalp to crawl down his forehead, over his right eye, across the cheek, and burrow into the tangles and brambles of his beard. He sucked the red clay chillum and Vijaya could smell the sickly sweet ganja.

"He'll tell our fortune," Govindaswami said, taking his boy's hand in his and tugging it toward the mendicant magician. "He's here to read our fortunes, to tell us a story, our story." The father still held Vijaya's hand as the fortune-teller took hold of Sanjaya's.

"Like this," the storyteller suddenly says, grabbing the hand of the boy nearest him at the edge of the raised platform, and the boy's shoulders flinch, throat shuts, heart quakes, and the wanderer laughs. Nishad envies the boy, wishes it was his hand that the storyteller had magically touched. Vijaya's face is his own face, his fear his own fear. Nishad gulps as *Vijaya's throat shut and his heart quaked, and the wanderer laughed.*

Forcing the small hand wider open, the Skullbearer licked his finger and wiped the hand with saliva. Sanjaya smiled and winked at Vijaya whose teeth chattered in fear and whose stomach flexed and waved queasy. The taste in his mouth was acrid with the fumes of his nausea.

"Good boy," the mendicant said. "Good boy. Good man. Strong man. This boy will be a hero: a warrior like Bhima, a wrestler like Hanuman. Virtuous, righteous, wealthy. So much gold! Great success. Always close to his father, helping father and mother in every way. Helping everyone in need. There will be challenges, difficulties, betrayals, but all of these will be overcome by physical strength and mental cleverness. One wife. Two sons. So easy to read, so easy to see—it's all here, all very clear." He laughed, dropped the hand, swiveled around and reached out for Vijaya who instinctively pulled back.

Govindaswami coaxed and urged his child to extend the hand in which a destiny was inscribed: "Don't be afraid. Do just as your brother did. There's nothing to be afraid of."

Under his breath, Nishad repeats the words, a mantra against evil: "There's nothing to be afraid of." The storyteller, glancing around, looking up, then closing his eyes, repeats them too. "Don't be afraid."

Against his will, too weak to resist being obedient to his parent, Vijaya yielded. The Skullbearer squinted, blew on the febrile hand, wiped it clean, stretched it flat open, looked more closely at it, grunted, and twisted his lips in consternation. The boy was aware of the bones of the Skullbearer's fingers. He could feel them pressing against the bones in his own hands. Through the Skullbearer's cold, translucent skin he could see the network of bluish veins and white arteries woven through the cartilage, tendons, and ligaments that held the bones together; he felt the blood pulse in those vessels and the current in the nerves. He felt the muscles move the bones as he looked at the cracked and dirty nails that forced their way through the fingertips as if trying to escape the insides of the hideous body.

Vijaya could hear dogs yapping in the distance. Nishad hears them too, the village dogs barking, incorporated into the story so that what might have distracted and detracted from the eerie mood adds and enhances instead. "Why are they barking so?" Mitu wonders. "What do they smell in the air tonight?"

The storyteller contorts his face, deepens his voice, and stiffens his posture so that his audience can more clearly see the Skullbearer before them, seated beneath their dark pipal tree. The Vetala Raja sees him too.

"Also good boy," the Skullbearer whispered with a smile. "Also good man. But problems. Problems." He hesitated with a frown. Govindaswami's heart beat wildly with fear for his child. "Strange things." The Skullbearer dropped the small hand and reached out for that of the father, read it carefully, dropped it, and
40 *took the boy's hand back, pulling it close to his madly gaping right eye. He dropped it again, snatched Sanjaya's hand once more, then, mumbling to himself and sticking out his tongue, he seized Vijaya's hand again, as if trying to divine a story, a part of which was inscribed on each of them. Each hand held a fragment of some version of some larger plot. The mendicant nodded, turned to Govindaswami and spoke: "You're destined to be separated from your younger son. It can't be helped. But through the strength, courage, and wit of the older boy, you'll be reunited. The young one's hand is hot—there's a fever coming on." And that was all he would say. He wanted to be paid. You have to pay for stories. Everyone's got to pay.*

In fear of that foretold separation, Vijaya grasped his father's hand tightly as they made their way, the next day, into the crowded bazaar in Varanasi. When his father freed his hand from his son's to pay the merchant for their food, the boy quickly clutched the more delicate arm of his mother and followed her to a stall where silks were sold. As her trembling fingers touched the luxuriant softnesses of the delicate weaves, as her quivering hand disappeared into the soft pleats and rolling, dappled folds of it, she longed for the life that they had left behind. There were tears in her eyes.

Some older boys looked at Vijaya and grinned. One spat and, though it landed far from him, the child knew it was an insult and a challenge. Vijaya wanted them to see Sanjaya, to be warned and kept at bay by his older brother's size and strength, but Sanjaya was with their father. Although he has not been to the city, Nishad is afraid of the boys who live there—the closer you go to holy Varanasi, the more cruel are the children.

The storyteller falls silent for a long, unnerving moment. A disturbing hesitation. . . . Silences, no less than words, divulge the story, form verbal darknesses haunted with inscrutable images and spectral fears.

Suddenly again he sensed it, Brahm Kathuwala begins again in softer tones, *something much more frightening than the hostile children of the city: the leper was there in the bazaar. Although Vijaya couldn't actually see the man, he was sure of it. He was there. Dead sure. He heard distant laughter over the cries of the hawkers, the chanting of priests, the arguments of customers at the stalls ("Fifty rupees and not an anna more!"), the shouts of devotees ("Har, Har, Mahadev!"), and he recognized the leper's hideous laughter ("Haha! Haha!"). He was hidden in the clamorous crowd that shoved and pushed their way through the galis—sick and holy people, frightened and desperate, cunning and devout, animated by bloated miseries and delicate hopes, interminable greed and love, and their incalculable fears and desires—students, merchants, brahmins, pilgrims, young, old, all kinds of people, but, above all, those who had come to Varanasi to die.*

When Govindaswami returned from buying the food—the succulent, fleshy, heart-shaped mangoes of this hot season—his family pushed forward, deeper into the bazaar where they stopped to purchase sweets and marigolds to be offered to the goddess.

"Mother, look, look! There he is!" Vijaya cried out in sudden panic. "There! There!" the storyteller shouts, points, and the audience looks. Heads turn. But there's nothing.

"Who, my child? Where? What are you saying, my son?"

"No, no, he was wrong," the storyteller laughs, *"there was nothing threatening to be seen. Haha!"*

"There's nothing to be afraid of," Sanjaya, his older brother,

said, and again Nishad, looking around once more into the darkness, mutters it to himself.

"You're hot, burning up," the mother sighed with a hand on her child's cheek, turning alarmed to her husband to alert him of the fever. They were afraid of malaria. Taking Vijaya into his arms to carry him the rest of the way, Govindaswami bounced him slightly, cradled him with reassurances—everything would be alright, he'd be protected—and the boy buried his head in his father's neck, hid from the horrors of the holy city, blocked his nostrils from the stench of filth, shit, and vomit laced with incense and cooking fumes; he put his fingers in his ears to keep out screams and laughter, chanting from the shrines and arguments from the vendors' stalls. He ached for their village, a village like this one, with a pipal tree like the one up above us, protecting us, with a well like that one over there. The boy thirsted for clean, cool water, for familiar things, for a childhood left behind. And he began to cry.

The sun in hot twilight crawled slowly down the mottled gray bank of sky, slowly crawling down, seeking darkness beneath the chafed lip of earth as if unaware of the cold-hearted hunger of that darkness. The night waited for the sun; the hidden panther waited to ravage and ravish its prey. Then the sudden splash of pent-up blood, the brusque burst of flames that precedes extinction, and the sun was gone, devoured, snuffed out in rapture. The panther rolled over in dark ecstasy. The stars were punctures on the night; white scabs and scars of needled light.

The mother and father and the two boys, camping by the temple of Bhairavi, devised a clearing in the crowded huddles of refugees who had staked out bits of ground for rest.

A fevered vesper flattered and intoxicated the black exquisite goddess. Screaming crones, possessed by her, voiced the delirious bliss that energized her brutal dance upon the corpse of God, cold and pulpy his stomach and thighs, but still hot and rigid the sex. Desire stubbornly, desperately, vainly, persisted in his death.

"Are you still listening?" Brahm Kathuwala asks the Lord of the Un-Dead under his breath. "Are you still here?"

The chanting—the moan, grunt, warble, and sorrowful sigh

of sex, and the shriek, hiss, and sorrowful sigh of death—grew louder in Vijaya's ears, reverberated in his skull, seeped down into this throat and made him gag. He tossed and whimpered and burned in sleep, dripping with sick sweat, saturated with sick fire, infused with the heat of the camp and cooking fires, the fires of sacrifice and cremation, and though the flames illuminated his dream, their oily smoke, at the same time, made it murky: mother and father, brother and snake, leper and Skullbearer, goddess and corpse, all confused, scrambled in the gloomy conflagration, indistinguishable, their words, screams, and laughter garbled into a horrible choke and hum.

It was the cold that awakened him: he sat up shaking, teeth chattering, limbs out of control, and called out to his mother, his father, called for help, help, anyone, "Help!"

Govindaswami wrapped his own blanket around Vijaya, held him to warm, calm, and quiet him: "Shhh, everything will be alright."

But the boy begged for the heat and light of fire.

"No fires here," the father said, "not by the temple, not by the shrine. It's hot enough tonight. Everyone's asleep. We can't have fire here."

Nishad wipes his brow with the edge of his father's light shawl. Mitu gulps anxiously. The fine line of scab on his face itches and instinctively he scratches it. The storyteller is resolute. The dogs no longer bark.

"There, over there," the boy begged. "See the fires there—there, take me there; warm me by those fires." He was so cold that he felt no fire could burn him, that he could walk on coals or dive into a sea of flames and not be melted nor consumed.

"No, not those fires, my son—over there's the cremation ground, the city of dreadful night. Those are the fires that feed on corpses and deliver them."

But the boy shivered and trembled, cried and begged—"please, please, please, I'm dying. I'm cold and dying"—until the father, moved by devotion to his son, would not say no again.

"It's the cemetery, the arena of jackals and hyenas, mourn-

ers and death, not the place for a child. I'm afraid you'll be afraid, my son."

The boy persisted: "Take me there. Hurry, please, I'm dying of cold." He insisted: "I'm not afraid." Nothing, not the boys in the bazaar, nor the Skullbearer in the camp, nor the leper at the road stop, nor the cobra under the bed, could frighten him right now. Nothing. His fear, perhaps by the malarial fever, had been strangely inverted. The crematory fires crackled a call to the shivering child: "Come, come and we shall warm your heart. There's nothing to fear. Everything will be alright." And the boy answered: "I am not afraid."

Mitu whispers in his son's ear: "Brave boy. Like my boy, brave boy. . . ."

Sanjaya and the mother slept as the father carried his younger son away from the dark temple of the goddess and toward the blazing site of death. Nishad is familiar with their own village cemetery, the pyres by the river, several furlongs away, where his grandfather had been cremated and the adjacent graveyard where the casteless ones are inhumed. Three Muslims are buried there; there are haunting stories about them and why they had been in the village. Fearlessly Nishad has played near there; he had even run after a ball batted into the graveyard during a game of cricket, but never, he thinks to himself, never would he venture there at night or by himself. Never. During the rains he has thought of the bodies in earth that turns to sog—waterlogged, bloated, and doughy remains, souls trapped by the dark mud ooze that fills mouths and nostrils. And he has pitied them for not being burned. "I want to be burned . . . so the bugs don't get me."

"I'm not afraid," the child moaned again and again. And the storyteller repeats the words for the Vetala Raja.

Not believing his son, Govindaswami imagined that the shudder was as much from fear as from the chill into which fever had turned: "No, no need to be afraid. Though storytellers speak of prets and bhuts, of ghouls and goblins, spooks and specters, this is all nonsense, phantoms of human imagination, the rotten fruit of fear, not something for us, if we are righteous, if we are wise, to be afraid of. Men, I suppose, have heard the howls of hyenas in the night and imagined the language of the pishachas, have seen fires reflected in the eyes of scavenging jackals and imagined the faces of vetals. They see smoke on funeral pyres and envision the disheveled hair of some hungry rakshasa or rakshasi. There's really nothing to fear." And, indeed Govindaswami was not afraid, neither for himself nor for the boy. That good, kind man, that righteous brahmin, could not imagine that he might have any need for apprehension. That's one of the many dangers of virtue.

Holding his son close to him, repeating tender words of reassurance— "there's nothing to fear"—it startled him to hear the child faintly laugh. Mitu holds Nishad just as close. He suddenly, for no reason, thinks of his dream and remembers now that Nishad had, in fact, been in the nightmare: yes, he was running away from his father and screaming. That was how Mitu had ended up in the dark field where he had been attacked by the demon. "I won't hurt you! Come back to me! Come back to me," he had screamed. He had been screaming when the dark form pounced on him. "Was it an animal or a man, or maybe a woman, a witch, some demon or rakshasa?" he wonders now. "And my wife, where was she? Did she come to the gloomy field?" The carpenter, momentarily distracted from the story, looks back again for his wife. The storyteller looks for *him*. Nothing.

Smoke in spirals rose in whirls and ghastly curls, reached with dark and ghostly fingers through branches overhanging, fruit bats there the ripe and heavy fruit; smokey fingers passed through scorched trees into blacker, bleaker, nearly moonless night. Fat-fed flames flickered on the flesh of cadavers strewn and jackals yelped a hunger for the oily lumps of roasting rancid meat. Black was the smoke gushing from white fat and grayish gristle. Putrid flames blazed in Vijaya's eyes. He saw the shadows of a man, the Skullbearer sitting in meditation by the crackling corpse and cackling: "khphrem mahachandayogeshvar . . ." They passed close by him. Was it the same mendicant they had met on the way? You can't tell—the same skulls and ashes, identical signs, ferocious nakedness, and frightful poise. They're all the same. They're all death in life.

Having gorged all day on human flesh, the vultures slept deeply in the highest branches of the trees above, dreaming vulture dreams. Our most terrible nightmares are their sweetest reveries.

Finding a place away from him, Govindaswami set his son close to a fading fire that jackals had abandoned. There the bones were fleshless, all meat charred or chewed away, tendons and ligaments all severed by teeth or beaks or flames. Picking up a stick, sharpened at the end by fire into a spear, black-pointed and still warm, the boy began to poke at the red embers, uncovering them from the white ashes, letting them breathe, gasp bright, and flare. The chills began to ease. Brahm Kathuwala holds up his walking stick, a poker now jabbed into the fire conjured up and seen by the village audience, now a stake brandished to menace the unseen King of Vetalas.

"What's that?" the boy asked his father as he prodded it. "A skull," a toothless, jawless skull, rolled over in the cinders. The holes—eyes, nose, and that aperture like an eye, underneath, and all the smaller orifices, grooves, slots, fissures, and cracks—were encrusted with a tar of melted viscera and candied juices—brain, eye, tongue, muscle, fat, marrow, skin, nerves. The skull itself was black, not white as they're depicted, more stone than bone, rocking back as the boy poked at it again. The empty sockets of the eyes looked at the boy and he, staring back at it, saw something ooze from the nasal cavity to burst at once into flame. Vijaya poked the skull yet again, rolled it, poked once more. His father's arm, wrapped about him, felt the shuddering slowly fade. Warmer now and more steady, the boy raised the stick high up, brought it down hard upon the skull, and then again he clubbed it. And once more. Crash! Crash! The cranium cracked and splintered. And as the bone was smashed, a roar exploded from the skull, shook the heart of Govindaswami, and echoed through the wooded cemetery. It woke the vultures from their dreams. They screeched and screamed as if in fear of the night. And falling back, our brahmin witnessed a thick and dark, sticky, stenchy, acidic vapor rise and engulf them.

Jumping up, Vijaya, transformed by demonic powers, leapt laughing onto the pyre, seized the shard of skull and drank the brains that sizzled in it. Possessed! Dark jellied juices bubbled and dripped down his chin as his mouth gaped wide with convulsions of gleaming laughter. Licking the hot bone, lapping up its treacle and gravy, he then threw it down, and laughed again to show the sudden tusks that rimmed his mouth. Hair on end, eyes now burning coals, the poker in his hand was now a flaming bludgeon raised above his father, lifted for the kill. And eyes wide with horror, betel-red stains on his teeth, gums, and tongue made apparent by the gaping of his mouth, Brahm Kathuwala shakes the gnarled walking stick in triumphal fury. *Laughing again, laughing loudly, releasing in that laughter an energy unknown, boundless, all-powerful, all ecstasy, Vijaya felt the strength in all his limbs, strange, new potencies and fires. Vast, uncontainable power. He could see in darkness and hear in silence. He could laugh aloud in the place of death. Haha!*

The furied words blast fast from the storyteller's crackling mouth like a torrent of flames fanned by the hot season's most fervid winds. Language booms, explodes, and the velocity with which the shrapnelous words penetrate the ears stuns the village listeners.

He sensed their presence: the leper, the serpent, and the Skullbearer—they'd be his obeisant attendants now and they'd laugh with him. Haha!

Trembling on the ground, Govindaswami called weakly to Vijaya—"Help! Help!"—flinched, writhed, gasped for breath, and begged for the recognition that might bring forth the mercy of his transformed son. "Help! Help!" The man whimpered and pleaded like a child.

Knowing now that he'd absorb the power of anything he slew, Vijaya laughed again, blew upon the smoldering spear to sharpen it: it would enter flesh like a heated spike into butter; it would bring the blood in the heart to a boil. Raising the stake, he aimed at that heart and let laughter yield to scream as he summoned up the strength to bring it down, to twist and force it in and through.

Knowing it was the end, the father, good Govindaswami, closed his eyes and cried out to God: "Jay Ram! Jay Ram!"

Brahm Kathuwala suddenly stops, and there's not a sound. No

one in the village audience stirs. Mouths and eyes are wide open. The storyteller listens to the silence, strains to hear faint stirrings, distant sounds. Nothing. The story has been effective: *he* is gone. The Vetala Raja has retreated. Stillness. Silence. Nothing. Safe.

Placing a bidi between his lips, the storyteller hesitates and then the strike of the match violates the silence. The sudden flame illuminates his face and the insides of his cupped hands. He takes a deep puff and blows out the match with the smoke. "That's enough," he announces without expression. "It's late. I'm tired and I'm hungry. That's enough of the story for now. There's still a lot to tell. But not now."

"You're teasing us," the toddyman laughs, and his laughter prompts others to laugh, and their laughter bestows relief from the sheer terror of the tale. "It's your game with us," the schoolmaster shouts: "Come on, get on with it, finish the story."

"No," the storyteller smiles. "No," he yawns and rubs his belly. "No, I'm afraid that's all of it for tonight. I could finish it tomorrow night, but I'm on my way to Varanasi. If you want me to stay tonight, to stay here until tomorrow night so that I can finish the story, I'll need a place to sleep—nothing too shabby, of course. I'll also need food and drink and, of course, paan and tobacco too."

"You'll have all this," Mitu boasts. "You'll stay in my house. Well-constructed wood house. You'll share my food." He looks back for his wife among the women. "Bihari cooking. Best food. Will that suit you, Mr. Storyteller? Then you'll stay tonight?" Nishad, unlike his mother, is delighted by the proposition.

Brahm Kathuwala remembers being in this village before by himself, but also with Mena. In his stories all villages are the same, and each village stands for all others in the world he knows, but in his experience each village is different and stands for nothing but itself. He remembers this tree, this riverbed, that house, that field, and he recollects that there's always something to eat in this village.

Mitu has decided that he'll ask the storyteller about nightmares. "He's a specialist in this sort of thing. He knows about ghosts and demons and terrifying stories and bad dreams. Maybe he can figure it out, explain what it means, tell me what that dark form was. What was it? Who was it? Maybe he has some special amulet or ring to keep dreams sweet. Or some herbs or powders for me to take. I'll follow his advice. Why not?"

"And tomorrow night," the Lingayat breaks in, "after the work is done, after our meals have been taken, you'll continue this story? Is that our arrangement?"

"That's the arrangement," Brahm Kathuwala smiles as he positions the silk top hat on his head, and the betel vendor tosses an unopened packet of ten Charminars to him, not bidis but real cigarettes. The storyteller picks them up and touches them to his head in a gesture of gratitude.

"Does the boy kill his father?" Nishad hollers. "Just tell us that." The boy's father uneasily laughs, caresses his son's head, and awkwardly laughs again. "Come on, Mr. Storyteller, just tell us that everything will be all right in the story."

"I can't tell you anything else tonight," Brahm smiles.

"Please, just give us some hint or idea—will it be all right? What will happen to the older brother?"

"He'll save the father," another boy, the tailor's son, cries out. "The older brother will save the father from the younger brother. I know this story already. I've heard it lots of times."

"But every time a story's told," the storyteller chides with a smile, "it's different. It's different if it's good, good only if it's different. Don't you know that? It has to be that way. We'll have to wait until tomorrow night. Maybe I don't even know yet what happened to the brahmin," the storyteller says. "Maybe I too have to wait until tomorrow to find out."

"This is wrong," an old man, the keeper of goats, complains with genuine anger. "How can you stop a story just before the end?" He could not for the life of him remember the end of the story he had heard almost fifty years before.

"Real stories have no end," Brahm Kathuwala tells the crowd under the pretext of answering the old man. And it's true. None of the storyteller's stories have a beginning or an end—the story he has just told is but an interlude in a larger story, the ghost-filled adventures of a certain renouncer, the older brother of Govindaswami the brahmin.

And that story is told by a bard to his king in yet another, still larger tale. Though the weaver of tales often stops with *but that's another story,* there are no other stories, no separate, discreet tales. There are no borders. All of the stories are intertwined and overlapping: characters from this one inevitably walk through that one, change this one, which suddenly gives new significance to the events in some other one. A bird migrates through this one to roost in that one, its call echoing across the interludes; a tiger pouncing in his one lands in that one, is killed in this one and is reborn as some man or woman, good or wicked, in that one; those men and women, transmigrating from story to story, connect all ages of the past, great ages of story, with the present; some tributary of the Ganga flows through all of the tales; the wind carries the dust of one story and lets it settle in another. Stories stitch time and space together and give them structure. All of the stories, each one having limitless versions, each with infinite recensions, are interlocked and interlinked episodes of a greater, amorphous epic, and each contains the whole in a mysterious, unexplainable way, and the more stories the storyteller hears, learns, changes, or imagines, the more clear and certain that becomes. Every termination has countless possible beginnings fused into it; and every beginning can lead to an infinite number of endings. Every story is embedded in the middle of this great, circular epic. There's no way out of it.

"What seems like an ending is always and inevitably the start of another story," he announces and that, Brahm Kathuwala feels, keeps him alive. He fancies that immortality would be possible if one knew all the stories, the epic in its entirety. But eternal life doesn't interest him. Rather, and what gives him a sense of strength, is that he feels he controls the span of his life, that he can determine the time of his own death: he will die only when he has finished his story, when, and only when, he says, *the end*. The Vetala Raja cannot get him as long as he tells the stories.

To live, he has been convinced, is itself to make a story, happy and sad, full of fear and desire, courage and cowardice, love and disappointment, wonder and shame; and men, women, and children, he's certain, tell stories for the same, untellable reason that they live. "You can stay alive as long as you can keep the story going. That is why our *Mahabharata* is so long, why Vyasa lived so long; that's why our *Ramayana* is so long, why Valmiki lived so long. Tulsidas didn't live as long as Valmiki because his *Ramayana* wasn't as long as Valmiki's."

"And you, how old are you?" Mitu asks, in hopes of generating the sort of personal conversation that will make it possible for him to ask the storyteller about the terrible dream, as they enter the carpenter's small, but carefully constructed, house. It's too soon to ask him about the nightmare. Later, when he's eaten.

The storyteller evades the question by lighting a cigarette from the fresh pack he has been given. It adds power to his stories if he seems ageless: he could be old or young, at once ancient and youthful—40? 60? 80? 100? or, if you really appreciate stories, 1000 years old or more. He heard this story from Vyas, that one from Kalidas, another from Kabir, yet another from the poet Jagannath. His accent and phrasing, the perfect voice of itinerancy with an inflection from here, an expression from there, an idiom from here, a dialect word from somewhere else, suggest that this ageless man is from nowhere and that he has been everywhere. Whenever he tells a story, in whatever place, there is a feeling of timelessness and placelessness.

"You are from which state?" Mitu asks despite the storyteller's disregard for his first question, and Nishad answers for Brahm: "A village on the banks of the tributary of the Ganga. Don't you remember? He told us. He said the brahmin, Vijay's father, was from his own village."

"How," Brahm suddenly asks the carpenter in a dispassionate voice, "did you get that scratch on your face?"

"Why do you ask me that?" Mitu snaps with inexplicable annoyance and seemingly inappropriate emotion. "Why don't you answer my questions? Answer me first? Then I'll answer you. How old are you and where are you from? Are you really from that village in the story?"

"What interests me is that the line goes over the eyelid, indicating that your eye was closed—lucky for you—when you were scratched. It reminds me of a curious story I once heard. That's all. Don't let it get infected. Put some salve on it."

Flustered, mildly exasperated, ashamed of the scratch for some reason that he did not himself understand, he sarcastically addressed his guest as "doctor," and directs him, the visitor whom he has invited not only to question him about his dreams but also for the sake of the prestige it might give him among the villagers, to be seated outside on the charpoy while his wife prepares the meal. Mitu tries to calm himself. "You may admire the construction of my house while you await a delicious meal. And after dinner we can continue our conversation."

Nishad squats at the feet of the storyteller, fanning the old man, and feeling more annoyed than embarrassed or ashamed over the commotion of his mother and father arguing inside the house.

When Brahm offers Nishad a cigarette, the boy refuses it with a laugh: "I don't smoke." And the storyteller smiles: "You should smoke. If not now, then someday. Smoking is good."

"What's this book," the boy asks the old man as he picks up the antique volume with the tattered green cover and the cracked leather binding that the storyteller has set on the ground by his stick.

"English book. *Dracula*. A fine old story about the Maharaja of Vetals. A woman, an English Memsahib that I knew many, many years ago, gave it to me."

Nishad opens the book and looks at the inscrutable marks that form the cryptic words. "It's a good story?"

"Very good story," Brahm smiles.

"You can read English?"

"Memsahib taught me. She taught me by reading this book to me and explaining as she went along."

"I like stories," the child says. "I'm learning to read now. The schoolmaster says I have some talent for reading. Maybe I'll study English so that I can read *Dhakula*. I like stories about rakshasas, vetals, bhuts, prets, and the like, very much. Very much! My father's not much good at telling stories. I don't think he knows any ghost stories. When I was younger, sometimes mother told me some of the stories about Krishna and about Ram. There was a story about a crow I think. Yes, a man died and, because he didn't have a son to perform the rites, he became a crow and had to scavenge for food. Something like that. I don't remember it very well. I'd like to be storyteller, to travel from place to place like you. Or maybe if I learn to read and write well enough, I can write some stories."

"What would you write about?"

"I don't know," the boy mumbles, puzzled, and then his face awakens with excitement: "No, I do know! I could write about you. I could follow you around, from village to village, and to cities too, to Varanasi, and I could write down your stories. A book about you with your stories in it! *Once upon a time there was a boy named Vijay. He became possessed by a rakshasa.* Yes, that's what I would like to do. Why would I want to stay here? Why would I want to be a carpenter or a farmer? Was your father a storyteller?"

"No," Brahm Kathuwala smiles. He lights another one of the Charminars and, instructing the child to remember it for his book, he begins to make up a story: *My father was a carpenter like your father. And, like your father, he wasn't very good at telling stories. In fact both my mother and father scolded me for lying every time I told a story. But my uncle, dear Chachaji, Bhutnath Kathuwala by name, would laugh and even give me sweets as a reward for any good story I'd invent. He was a storyteller. "Don't listen to your father," he'd say. "That's my advice to every boy. Don't listen to your father or your mother. Be devoted to them, but don't ever pay any attention to what they say. If you do pay attention, it will, in fact, be all the more difficult to be devoted to them. Personally, my little one," the man would laugh again, "I believe your lies completely."*

I adored Chacha and spent all the time I could listening to the intricate melodies of his beautiful voice, watching his graceful hands dance stories in the air. He seemed to know every tale that could ever be told—he was an ocean of stories, such wonderful stories of love and courage and folly and fear. Mother said he was a wastrel and a rogue. He could make me tremble with horror or laugh uproariously; he could make me want to be good or feel sorry that I had been bad. Chachaji knew the Puranas *by heart, the* Mahabharata *and* Ramayana *of course, but not only every great and famous legend, in a myriad of versions, but also every little homespun story, every joke and anecdote. My favorite tales were those of fear and dread, violent and terrible, riveting and wonderful to the child's ear: Bhim drinking the blood of Duhshasan, Ram firing arrows into the hideous body of Tataka until the sky rained with her blood, Narsingh plucking off the arms and legs of the demon king Hiranyakashipu, tearing open his gut and sucking out the entrails. Haha! I loved ghost stories, tales of bhuts and prets and vetals and rakshasas, the hosts of the Un-Dead, best of all. When he told me the story of the boy who became possessed, I was so frightened by it that I would wake up screaming every night. After a few nights of this, my mother scolded Chacha fiercely and admonished me not to listen to him any more. "They are just stories, just so much nonsense," she insisted: "They're not real. They are nothing." In whispers, outside the house, Chacha warned me not to heed her: "Stories have great power. They are magic. Of course, as everybody knows, magic can be very dangerous. Stories, you must realize, you must be warned, can kill. But the magic can also be used to cure, to heal, to purify, to deliver, to do so many things. Do you understand? Stories have the power to save us."*

"And you, Nishthi-baba, do you understand?"

Nishad gestures that, yes, he does; although he knows that he would not be able to explain what it means, he does feel that, yes, yes, he understands.

Removing the top hat and setting it next to him on the charpoy, the storyteller lights another cigarette with the butt of the one he's smoking, takes a puff, exhales, and, in the moments of silence, he and the boy listen together: the argument inside the house has been muffled into angered whispers and venomous hisses; there is the very faint cry of a baby in the dark distance, the less faint chatter of an old woman too, some distant laughter, the low of a cow (strange at this hour of the night), the bark of a lone dog. All the murmurings of the night are woven into the fevered hum of cicadas; no owls cry tonight. Nishad yawns.

I remember saying good-bye to Chacha; we had to leave our village during the great famine. The Ganga had receded and, though the villagers made offerings to her, she seemed too weak to take them. Chacha and his wife came out that morning to watch us leave, to make our way across the barren field to the dry and desolate road that would take us to Varanasi.

Mitu interrupts the story with the announcement of dinner, and Nishad falls asleep on the ground while Brahm Kathuwala eats. Thus the storyteller doesn't continue the story of a storyteller's childhood. And he doesn't have to talk with Mitu. The carpenter feigns a yawn and, with the excuse of fatigue, he goes into the house because his wife has demanded that he come to bed. They argue in embittered whispers.

Brahm remembers his first encounter with *him* in the great house, dark and empty. It was hot like this. It was the month of Jeth. He smiles over tonight's resistance of the Vampire King. He lights another Charminar. It's safe now to let thought adrift.

He ponders the untold story of a village childhood as later he lies there on the charpoy, alone, outside. Nishad sleeps inside near his mother and father. The storyteller wonders what the story would have been, where it would have taken them, what ghosts and spirits would have haunted it.

Brahm Kathuwala feels that his audience authors the stories: he watches them, reading their expressions, postures, movements, letting those signs of what they want or need, what they fear and dread, spark his words, construct the story, command the teller what to tell. He had received clear signals from the child's wide eyes, eager smile, and hands held together. It was Nishad's story, and it would have been a good story too, Brahm Kathuwala reflects with an affectionate smile. It would not, in any case, have been anything like the actual facts of the storyteller's childhood. He never speaks of that childhood. He never tells true stories; truth imposes too many restrictions.

There had been no Chachaji, no village, no famine that he remembers. The Chachaji of the story, however, looks in Brahm's mind, very much like Bhutnath Kathuwala, the man from whom Brahm has received a name and borrowed many tales, an itinerant storyteller who had come one evening to the home of Dr. Thomson, the house in the cantonment near Varanasi where Brahm's mother had been a servant when Brahm was a child. Dr. Thomson allowed the old storyteller to stay and entertain the family and a few friends on the veranda each evening after dinner.

The night tonight, despite the heat and moonlessness of it, is beautiful, so exquisitely vast that it makes the storyteller ache with joy. Each star, sparkling in the infinite blackness, is a memory. He smiles. *He's* far away now. *Him!* The story has kept *him* at bay. The magic has worked once more. The storyteller, still smiling, closes his eyes and lets his mind meander from *him* to her, coast from that to this, here and there, back and forth he floats.

More and more all the time these days he suddenly remembers things from so very long ago. Memories of those days come more easily now: finding one buried deep within his heart, hidden away for so many years, he brings it out, turns it over, scrutinizes it, cherishes it, and smiles. He smiles even over the sadnesses that he has known. Everything is now sweeter to recall. "In old age, ghosts become our friends," Bhutnath once said. He remembers.

He can see the old man in the shadows: *and now,* the storyteller, the awakened ghost of Bhutnath Kathuwala, softly speaks, hesitating, the glistening silver ornament, a little skull dangling from his earlobe, closing his eyes and then opening them to smile almost sadly and begin: *now, come a little closer, come now and let me tell you an old, old story, yes, yes, the terrible tale of the boy who became possessed. . . .*

And vividly, as clearly as if she has risen from her distant Christian grave to come to him, he can see the woman: *Manlike, they have told me to go to bed and sleep,* the English Memsahib, Mrs. Thomson, reads from the book, it's green cloth cover bright, the leather binding shiny new. Each night she read aloud the stunning story, *Dracula,* in a voice that was clear and sweet: *as if a woman can sleep when those she loves are in danger! I shall lie down and pretend to sleep, lest Jonathan have added anxiety about me when he returns.* Leaning close to him and closing the book, she whispers: *That's quite enough for tonight. Tomorrow night we'll turn from Mina Harker's Journal to Dr. Seward's Diary. We'll go once more to the Un-Dead home of the Vampire King, Count Dracula, the Vetala Raja. But now, my darling Brahm, my little Brahm Stokerji, it's time for you to sleep.*

The storyteller sleeps and dreams of a distant childhood, a great house in the cantonment outside of Varanasi when it was called Banaras. *But that's another story.*

3

There are, in India, ghosts who take the form of fat, cold, pobby corpses, and hide in trees near the roadside till a traveller passes. Then they drop upon his neck and remain. There are also terrible ghosts of women who have died in childbed. These wander along the pathways at dusk, or hide in the crops near the village, and call seductively. But to answer their call is death in this world and the next. Their feet are turned backwards that all sober men may recognize them. There are ghosts of little children who have been thrown into wells. These haunt well-curbs and the fringes of jungles, and wail under the stars, or catch women by the wrist and beg to be taken up and carried. These and the corpse-ghosts, however, are only vernacular articles and do not attack Sahibs. No native ghost has yet been authentically reported to have frightened an Englishman; but many English ghosts have scared the life out of both white and black.

RUDYARD KIPLING, MY OWN TRUE GHOST STORY (1888)

Three natives in my employ were introduced into an ill-ventilated, well-screened room which was furnished with all sorts of materials infected by malaria patients from the hospitals—the clothing they had worn, mattresses on which they had died their wretched deaths, the pillows, pillow cases, and blankets upon which they had vomited in their fitful sleep. These materials were further encrusted with the feces of malaria victims as well as, in one case, with the blood of a patient who had cut his own throat (in a fit of the melancholia that is frequently a symptom of the disease under our scrutiny). In these filthy surroundings my men lived for two weeks and, despite these horrible conditions, none of them contracted malaria.

DESMOND THOMSON, REPORT ON MALARIA IN THE CENTRAL PROVINCES OF INDIA (1903)

"Ah, but how lovely!" she said. "I delight in having my blood curdled. Go on with your ghost-story, Mr. Urcombe. I adore ghost stories."

"It wasn't a ghost story exactly," said he. "I was only telling our host how vampirism was not extinct yet. I was saying there was an outbreak of it in India only a few years ago."

E. F. BENSON, MRS AMWORTH (1912)

May–June 1919

(Vaishakh-Jyeshtha, Samvat 1862).

"And now," Mrs. Thomson softly said, smiling as she lifted the mosquito netting, coming under it to settle in on the bed next to the child. "Now, come a little closer to me, yes, that's it, pull the covers up around you, be warm and comfortable and safe, and I'll read you more of *Dracula,* the terrible tale of the Vetala Raja. The story is true. Come closer to me, closer, yes, that's right."

Chapter three. Jonathan Harker's Journal (continued), she began in her Jonathan voice: *When I found that I was a prisoner, a sort of wild feeling came over me. I rushed up and down the stairs, trying every door and peering out of every window I could find; but after a little the conviction of my helplessness overpowered all other feelings. . . .*

Eyes wide with wonder, limbs trembling ever so slightly with delight and fear, heart enchanted, little Brahm, cradled warm and softly sheltered in clean billows of down-stuffed pillows, bulky but light and bright white and silk-soft as only English things were, listened to the creamy voice and smelled the sweet minty breath that fragranced the odd English words that it carried serenely and airily into his ear. Lush green mint mingled with the misty pink perfume of English roses from English gardens overgrown, all pastel green and muted pink, flurried with powdery pollens, a pale pink haze of overlapping haloes glowing with the golden sunlight of a distant land. She read smiling: *I am beginning to feel this nocturnal existence tell on me. It is destroying my nerve. I start at my own shadow, and am full of all sorts of horrible imagining . . . .*

Closing his eyes, then opening them, closing, opening, the delicate, lacy tendrils of those faraway, fantastic gardens wrapping slowly around his limbs, caressing, he summoned the courage to respond to the warmth of her breath and flesh with tentative touch. He rested his arm against her side and looked at his dark hand near hers, so very light. Amber lamplight was finely filtered and delicately dimmed by diaphanous cascades of the soft, fine, clean, white mosquito netting that formed a cloth bower for their nightly rendezvous. Occasional languid rustlings, slight and silent, were traces of a breeze through a window barely opened to the infinite night. Varney, the Irish Setter bred in Burma, there at the window, reached his moist nose up to the almost imperceptible draft that he might smell what could not be seen. "If only he could speak," Memsahib would say, "he'd surely have some stories to tell, tales of invisible, slightly scented spirits that would set your hair on end."

Even when Brahm's eyelids were closed, he could see her: the high white collar, dark velvet bows beneath and the pink curve of graceful neck above, wisped with strands of hair, ruddy-red like Varney's, locks bound back, but from a bow then flowing free and soft in soft curls and purls of soft, soft hair, fragrant, soft, soft, the softest hair that Brahm had ever seen or smelled or wished to touch. And her strange eyes, above round pink cheeks, liquid jewels glimmering green. Everything about her was tongue-pink or egg-white or pipal-leaf-pale green—feathery and powdery, soft, soft and sweet, silk and cream. His tenacious vision perched to rest on the little pillow lips, soft, that would softly graze his forehead when she'd finish. They'd part tremblingly to leave warm moist breath, the delicate dew of dreams, on his skin. Sometimes, if he promised playfully solemnly (as was his part in their ritual) not to tell Dr. Thomson or his mother, she'd give him Irish whiskey mixed with warm milk and a swirled dollop of Irish honey gathered up by drunken Irish bees from fragrant Irish flowers far away. "It was," she smiled, "Mr. Stoker's customary bedtime libation.

It sweetens dreams." And she'd join in that drink: "Irish bees are angels disguised and flown down to earth to make candles for the Mass, our puja—that's what my own mother used to say. Ah, but that's another story."

Sometimes, especially after a cup of honeyed milk and the burly whiskey that made the throat warm and even more hypnotic the story of the dread Vetala Raja, the boy savored the delicious, goodnight kiss, the silk-soft and rose-sweet assurance, the velvety "sweet dreams, my little Brahm." Custard-sweet the words, the breath, the honeyed sigh in darkness. Honeysuckle sprays and invisible jasmine bursts, the indelible kiss and unintelligible whispers, the soft-glistening lips puckering to blow out the bee's wax candle, the red glowing wick in the darkness, all conspired to melt him away in each night's climax to the reading of Bram Stoker's *Dracula*. Then sleep, sleep, and honeyed dreams so transient and hard to remember.

Still at the window, transfixed by mysteries the night possessed, Varney made a sound, part growl and part whimper, grumble and sigh, and, "Shhh," Memsahib commanded both to warn him against causing further distractions from the story and to comfort him: *And there are bad dreams for those who sleep unwisely,* her voice deepened into Jonathan Harker's. *Be warned! Should sleep now or ever overcome you, or be like to do, then haste to your own chamber or to these rooms, for your rest will then be safe. . . .* "These rooms, my little Brahm, be at home here and sleep and dream safely here, near me."

Memsahib looked up smiling from the book, the moist purse of rose-pink lips velvety petals opening to reveal cream-white teeth, her eyes sparkling childish fun, naughty and sweet, all honey and milk and whiskey late at night. Brahm's real mother was dark, dry, and thin, barefoot and bareboned, smileless and overworked, persistently tired and tearful. "She's asleep by now," the boy thought and sadly yawned and could see her thin hair tied tight, the aching arch of her spine, the jutting curve of the bony shoulder, the angular spindle of legs, feet turned out beneath the hem of dark blue but fading sari. She took cold baths from a rusty metal bucket and wore a shiny silver ring upon her toe. Her teeth were red from the betel that was her only solace in this lonely place, our world. It's too sad to notice or speak of the pox that marked her skin.

Dolorously, with taciturn grunts and reticent gasps, she swept and swept and swept and swept with the reed broom, thrashed and flogged with thin dark arms the wet rocks with clothes that she'd never wear. There were silent lamentations and melancholy meditations as she balanced bulky bundles atop her head, and there was no man to make her smile, to tease, to ease the dull pain, to cradle the tired head in his arms and rest a gloomy face against a deep warm breathing breast. In the evening, resisting the stir and sweep of salacious memories, she patted the dung between her hands into patties and slapped them against the wall to dry. It was not her wish to be sorrowful, but neither did she fear her vexations. At night spirits of vagrant lovers growled in her sleep. But still, despite it all, Brahm sometimes, in midnight stillness, in twilight rustlings, early in the morning, before first light, heard her sing. Fragile fragments he remembered, shards of song: *milk from a magic cow, sweet rice pudding from the kitchen of a king, and a golden child . . . leaves of betel, pierced with clove . . . la la la . . . all the gods of Kashi and the lonely sweeper woman . . . la la la la. . . .* The song, some sort of story, for no reason almost frightened him. Sweep, sweep, sweep—that was how he would always remember her—alone and sweeping the dust here, then there, then back again, then pausing to wipe the sweat from her unmarked brow, sweeping as if to assist the god of wind. Kalyani, the luckless, sweeping servant, was deeply devoted to Dr. Thomson: he had treated her bouts of malaria, and he had given the blue sari.

Brahm had no father, not in memory, nor in dreams, nor in stories. No one spoke of him. There were spectral siblings, two dead (were their ghosts crying out to Kalyani through the beaks of crows on the roof?), two sent away to a sister's husband's uncle's friend (or something like that—does even Kalyani know what's really happened to them?)—colicky babies, an older brother run away, an older sister disappeared (was she such a bad girl as mother Kalyani said she was?). Maybe dead. Murdered? La la la. No father. La la la la. Neither alive nor dead: nowhere a father. "That's why you're named Brahm," his mother said with a protracted ache and her perpetual sadness: "Brahm the creator. How can the creator have a father?" It was not said frivolously, nor ever with a smile. "Brahm the creator," she whispered as she took her remaining child in arms strengthened by labor and rocked him gently, surely, and with all of the grace of her rhythmic sweeping.

Memsahib smiled often, smiled when she called Brahm "my child, my son, my little one." And the boy reflected: "No father—who cares? Two mothers: one, two." He couldn't help but laugh: "Light pink and dark brown; cheerfully plump and sadly scrawny; Britishi and Hindustani . . . haha! . . . rich and poor; one tells stories, one sweeps . . . la la la. . . ." The list was endless, full of rhymes, and, if he couldn't sleep, he'd start it and on and on it would go until he drifted into dreams and spirit worlds.

Bless that good, good woman, the good, good woman read, *who hung the crucifix round my neck! for it is a comfort and strength to me whenever I touch it. It is odd that a thing which I have been taught to regard with disfavor and as idolatrous should in a time of loneliness and trouble be of help. Is it that there is something in the essence of the thing itself, or that it is a medium, a tangible help, in conveying memories of sympathy and comfort?* Brahm clutched it, more to display his gratitude to her than to give himself comfort, put it in his mouth, sucked the thing around his neck, the rudraksha-like rosary with what she called a "crucifix" attached, a British superstition, a charm just like the one that protected Jonathan Harker from the Maharaja of Vetalas *(his hand touched the string of beads which held the crucifix and it made an instant change in him . . . the fury passed so quickly)*, the silver cross ornamented with the scrawny little man or boy, lungi-clad, hands spread and mercilessly pierced, head tilted to the side, the sadhu Brahm called "Inri," Memsahib's little Irish god.

Varney ambled toward the bed, sniffed around it, peered through the mosquito netting, slumped down, his tongue curling in a yawn, and then he dozed with ears perked up as if to hear the story or to listen for intrusions.

"Here comes a good part now, a shock, a thrill," she whispered grinning: *My feelings changed to repulsion and terror when I saw the whole man slowly emerge from the window and begin to crawl down the castle wall over that dreadful abyss, face down,* she read with a frolicsomely eerie relish and mock-ghoulish delight, *with his cloak spreading out around him like great wings.* Sometimes she'd pause and follow the English words with whatever Hindustani equivalents she knew: "repulsion—*ghrina;* terror—*tras;* abyss, abyss, let's see, what's Hindustani for abyss? What is an abyss? How does one describe it? A chasm—no more than that—a profound void. An abyss. Infinite, terrifyingly infinite. A bottomless pit, as they say, a yawning gulf of endless space, reaching out forever and ever and ever, tempting us to peer into it, deeper and deeper into its darkness, and then inviting us to lean, lose balance and fall, tumbling head over heels forever and ever. 'Come, come,' it murmurs, growls, moans, sings. Beware of it—it can open here or there or anywhere. Beware the beckoning. Beware the song. Beware the yawning abyss." She smiled, thought, and whispered: "'Who shall tempt with wandering feet the dark unbottomed infinite abyss and through the palpable obscure find out his uncouth way?' or something like that. That's Milton. He knew his abysses. Abyss. I'll ask Dr. Thomson for the Hindustani. Abyss."

The little boy could repeat the English words for her—"Abyss. Repulsion. Terror. Dreadful, infinite abyss." He could remember and recite in his version of her version of Jonathan's voice after a single hearing: *I am in fear,* he smiled, *in awful fear,* he giggled, *and there is no escape for me,* he laughed louder and, smiling profoundly, she joined in: *I am encompassed about with terrors that I dare not think of.* And "bravo," she said, "*shabash,* my little Brahm, my extraordinary child."

"Absolutely wondrous," she told her husband excitedly. "It's uncanny. It's not like he is learning English—no, not in the way I'm trying to learn Hindustani—it's rather as if he's remembering it. And the truly curious thing is that it's connected with the book. *Dracula.* He knows the book. He can recite passages from it." And what she had read that night from chapter three, he was, indeed, able to repeat in the morning for Dr. Thomson, mimicking at first Memsahib's Britishy Transylvanian accent and playfully grotesque gestures, laughing through his display of histrionic horror. *He is young and strong; there are kisses for us all,* he quoted in a suddenly high and girlish tone and then cleared his throat to switch into the voice of Jonathan Harker: *I could feel the soft, shivering touch of the lips on the supersensitive skin of my throat, the hard dents of two sharp teeth, just touching and pausing there.* The boy uttered the words with the same stress, the ghoulish, infernal delight, that Mrs. Thomson had used the night before: *I closed my eyes in a languorous ecstasy and waited,* the boy closed his eyes too and spread his arms like Inri sadhu, *waited with a beating heart.* Ears twitching, nose quivering, the pupils of his suddenly open eyes dilating. Varney, as if beguiled by the play, growled uneasily.

Dr. Thomson offered a scientific explanation of the phenomenon to his wife: "Illiterate peoples have a remarkable capacity for memorization. Because we, as the beneficiaries of civilization, have the ability to record words with writing, our memories have atrophied like a limb that goes unused. This is true both in us as individuals and in us as a race. The Hindu has long exercised his memory, memorizing rather than reading his sacred texts. Mnemonic proclivities are characteristic of the race."

For the purpose of demonstrating to his wife that the boy was merely, by means of a uniquely prodigious recollective prowess, parroting her words without understanding them, he turned to the boy and asked him the meaning of the word "languorous." Brahm blankly, shrugged his delicate shoulders: *"Mujhko malum nahim."*

"No, no. The reason he remembers the words is that he knows English already," Mrs. Thomson argued. "I'm convinced of it. He's merely remembering it. Don't you understand? He spoke English in a previous life."

Mrs. Thomson's theosophical reveries and occult speculations (energized over the past few years by a mutually rhapsodic correspondence with Annie Besant) concerned the physician: "The child is gifted. There's little doubt of that. But really, I dare say, you are making quite a bit too much of it." He looked very despondent. The doctor feared that life in the Colony, despite the protective insulation of the cantonment, despite the comforts of the Club, had taken its toll on his dear wife. "The weather. The deprivation. The children," he thought to himself as he gazed lugubriously at Mary Sheridan Thomson: "She's not been right since we sent the boys back to England for their education. My God, that was over twenty-five years ago—they're adults now and yet it's as if she's still mourning the departure! Time is so grotesquely distorted in India." With a tired sigh he recollected the words she had muttered the day they left for the Tonbridge School: "We have empire, yes, but these people have family, large sprawling families that do not separate. Who, I often wonder, us or them, which one of us has real power, real dominion?"

There was a vivid picture in his memory: one evening, about four years ago, like a little girl clutching a golliwogg doll, his wife had held little Brahm in her arms and wept: "We should never have sent the boys away to school. We should have known they'd never return." Brahm's real mother also remembered the scene: from the crying woman's arms the child had looked to Kalyani for a signal—should he pull away from the Memsahib or surrender to her? The servant woman turned away and continued her sweeping.

"Most often in India," Dr. Thomson began with a rather academic air to Inspector Weston and Mr. Sanders in the Billiard Room at the Club, "it's the ayah who usurps the British mother's role, who becomes the mother of the white child, feeding him, putting him to bed, scolding and indulging him, disciplining him and giving him affection. In our home it's been just the reverse—my wife has become the white ayah for this brown native child. In the usual case, the British mother is rarely resentful and cannot imagine raising her child without the ayah. But in our case, I fear that poor Kalyani, rather than being grateful for the favors and luxuries lavished on the child, feels deprived somehow, considers her nest robbed, her child kidnapped. And as far as my wife is concerned . . ." Thomson hesitated and the shadows of colonial melancholy fell across his face: "I'm concerned, very concerned, about my wife. The boy has become a surrogate for Nigel and John, for Nigel more than John, rather for her memory of him as he was back in '91. Nigel, you must understand, was mad about vampire tales, keen on books like *Carmilla* and *The Monk* and *Frankenstein,* on supernatural fictions full of crumbling castles, ghost stories with rattling chains, horror stories and macabre fables replete with crypts, skeletons, corpses, worms, and all that—the bathetic Bulwer-Lytton and the puerile Poe, that awful Wilkie Collins and the unreadable Elizabeth Gaskell—you know the sort of book I'm talking about. In order to recapture the nights when she read those stories to Nigel, she reads to the servant boy now, reads Stoker's *Dracula* to him from the first edition that Nigel sent to her for her birthday in '97. It's obvious. Of course. She's comforting herself. That awful book! This is the third time she's read that same damn book to him! Horror and the macabre. It's a genre meant solely for little boys and old women, or for Hindus and Catholics. They're the only ones who actually savor the stuff. One has to be a little Hindu boy or an old Catholic woman to really understand horror, I suppose."

"Your wife is hardly old, Thomson," Weston turned from the bar with a raised glass of brandy shrab to interrupt his friend's elegy with a bit of good cheer: "She's a vital, handsome woman, if you don't mind my saying so; and she's quite a talented raconteuse, a favorite at the Club. My daughter adores her."

The physician set down his own glass and shook his head: "India is making all of us old. One ages a year for every month spent here. Antiquity is a contagion here." He gulped his whiskey rather desperately as he watched Sanders try his shot and miss. The snooker balls, red and white like the corpulses in the malarial blood on the slides under Thomson's microscope, ricocheted in crisscross paths across the green felt. "Dear God, what is India doing to us and why? It's getting to all of us. Is this their subtle revenge?"

That night, like a cuckold spying upon a trysting wife, the doctor stood next to the slightly open door listening: "*Are we to have nothing tonight?*" Mrs. Thomson asked in her own voice, *as she pointed to the bag which he had thrown upon the floor and which moved as though there were something living within it. For an answer he nodded his head. One of the women jumped forward and opened it. If my ears did not deceive me, there was a gasp and a low wail of a half-smothered child. The women closed round, whilst I was aghast with horror.*

Brahm listened as she read, and when she came to the last line of the chapter he finished it for her, remembering it with a great, proud smile: *Then the horror overcame me, and I sank down unconscious.*

She clapped her hands for joy and in congratulations—*"shabash!"* and Dr. Thomson withdrew whispering, "Poor woman, my poor, dear Mary." The last image in the child's eyes after she had blown out the lamp, so different than the image in the physician's eyes, was a radiant smile, the lips of Lakshmi, the golden idol in the temple, all magic and beauty. The goddess blessed the child, and the vision persisted, pulsed, and glowed in the darkness. "You are good, so very good, my child." In the unlit night of the room in which she invited him to sleep, he felt the movement of her breath upon him. Sweet it was, honey sweet and whiskey mellow, and it sent the same tingling through his nerves as her voice. There was nothing bitter in that dulcet breath or voice. "Goodnight, my little Brahm," she whispered as she lightly kissed his cheek, "My little Brahm Stokerji. Goodnight and sweet dreams."

Although Dr. Thomson dismissed her reincarnation theory as a symptom of the nervous strain caused by life in India, Annie Besant had written back encouragingly and certain ladies of the Club, aficionados of the Gothic who had formed a literary group, "Our Ladies of Otranto," thought it quite original and even plausible.

Frequently they gathered on evenings when, after a jackal hunt, polo match, or some other manly exercise in distraction, the men played billiards or cards (whist or the recently fashionable game of flinch-fright) while they smoked themselves dizzy with Burma Cheroots or drank themselves stuporous on Devil's Milk or Rum Blood Punch. An almost aromatic, smoky blend of exultation and despair, camaraderie and loneliness, bravado and sadness, filled the Billiard Room, Card Room, and Men's Library. It hung in the sepulchral hallways where the servants, like skeletons in a catacomb, stood at fatigued attention in mute anticipation of commands. The mood in the Ladies' Library was less complicated; there was simple, highly jasmine-scented resignation in the air.

It was Mrs. Thomson's turn that night and she'd worn black for the occasion. Facing the fireplace for the effect—a fandango of flames on her face, flickerings of fire in her eyes and on the gloss of her berry-round lip, a danse macabre—she'd tell a ghost story or a tale of terror, something she'd read or heard or something new, or one of her own compositions, written for the occasion or improvised on the spur of the moment. Her fame as a renderer of macabre stories was so great that, in clubs throughout the United Provinces of Agra and Oudh, "telling a Thomson" had become a euphemism for recounting any truly grisly or ghastly event or tale, true or false. Her credentials for this activity were impeccable. Mary Thomson, née, Sheridan, born in Calcutta in 1860, belonged to the Old John Stock Company. Her father, the late General Robertson Innes Sheridan of the Bengal Calvary, his flame-red eyebrows like blazes above his coal dark eyes, his swollen ruddy lip wet with precious Irish whiskey, used to tell his young daughter gruesome stories of how he had personally decapitated seven Indian insurgents in Delhi in retribution for the deaths of British civilians during the Mutiny of 1857. He'd roar with laughter and tell her to take pride in the rich red blood that flowed in her little Irish veins.

General Sheridan sent his daughter to England for schooling where she developed a lasting friendship with the exquisitely beautiful Miss Florence Balcombe, daughter of Lieutenant-Colonel James Balcombe (serving in India and the Crimea), dear, delicate "Florrie," who, in the years to come, was (and it had made Mary envious, even, she might admit, jealous) to become (after a reputed intimacy with Mr. Oscar Wilde) Mrs. Bram Stoker.

Mary Sheridan returned to India at the age of twenty-one to marry Dr. Desmond Thomson, a somewhat distinguished medical officer in the Indian Civil Service. He became district supervisor of quarantine regulations during the outbreak of bubonic plague in India in 1895; and he had begun to conduct malaria research in collaboration with Major Ross in Secunderbad in 1896 when the monsoon failed and the resultant famine diverted government attention and money from tropical diseases to starvation. Thomson, author of "Report on Malaria in the Central Provinces of India" (*Lancet,* 1903) and "Infection of Bats with Proteosoma by the Bites of Mosquitos" (*Indian Medical Gazette,* 1911) was currently continuing his research on malaria; and he had been for some years, with the assistance of Mr. Godfrey Sanders (Fellow of the Asiatic Society of Bengal, professor of Post-Vedic Sanskrit at the faltering Queens College of Banaras, and member of the Legislative Council of the United Provinces), compiling a sort of demonological dictionary and reference guide to the superstitions of India: *On the Ghosts, Ghouls, and Goblins of Hindoostan*. While Sanders' interest was philological, Thomson's was medical, was in the ways in which the uneducated saw a causal relationship between diseases and spirits of the dead.

Mrs. Thomson's own literary endeavors included the publication of her translation of Théophile Gautier's macabre *La morte amoroureuse* which had been serialized in the *Weekly Sun Literary Supplement* (London, 1900–1901) under the title *The Impassioned Lady of Death;* her ghost story, "The Vampire of the Varana," had been published in the *Civil and Military Gazette* in May of 1908. *City of Dreadful Night,* the florid Gothic novel set in India that she had written in 1911, however, remained unpublished these eight years later. The title for the novel had come from the popular poem of the same name written by her husband's second cousin, a drunkard whose very name brought embarrassment to Dr. Thomson. "A poetaster, a dipsomaniac, and a Thomson—a most untoward combination," he sighed more out of despair than wit.

Mary Thomson's girlhood friendship with Florence Balcombe Stoker was renewed, after a ten-year separation and silence, when Mrs. Thomson received a letter from Florence (postmarked "Bocastle, 12 June 1892"): "My husband would be most grateful to you for any information on vampires in India with which you may be able to supply him. He has studied the quaint, but obviously unreliable tales written by a certain Bhababhuti in old Sanscrit, entitled *Vikram and the Vampire,* as translated by his acquaintance, the disreputable, iron-countenanced Richard Burton, and he has questioned Mr. Burton extensively on vampirism in the East Indies, but he is not able to entirely trust much of what Mr. Burton, aflame as he is with fancy, says or writes on any Oriental subject. I have assured Mr. Stoker that you, my dear friend, are to be trusted in all matters."

Given a correspondence with Bram Stoker (mostly through Florence at first) that had, after all, lasted almost twenty years, Mrs. Thomson had been confident that the famous and influential author would certainly have been eager to assist her by placing her text with his own publisher, Archibald Constable and Company of Whitehall

Gardens, London. She was thus more than disappointed to receive his comments (not conveyed by Florence but direct from the hand that wrote *Dracula*): "How is it, that you, reputedly one of the most upright of the fair sex, can have so brazenly allowed yourself to have written a document that is in its every existence a flagrant breach of both moral law and aesthetic propriety. There is, Madame, corruption on these pages. I was unable for the life of me to read beyond page forty-six. I would heartily suggest that you return for inspiration to the somber and sublime Ann Radcliffe. She knew what to make explicit and what to leave to the imagination. For there is where the horror lurks—in the imagination. You have left nothing, I'm afraid, to the fancy of your reader."

She had imagined that the page in question would certainly have caused Bram Stoker, author not only of *Dracula* but of the new

and even more deliciously terrifying and disgusting *Lair of the White Worm*, immense delight: *The natives were chanting their diabolical dirges in the distance, and beneath the shroud-like netting that protected her from the mosquitos thirsting for their share of her blood Francesca writhed in ecstasy*, she had proudly, excitedly, and exultantly written. *The servant must have fallen asleep, or fled, or died (murdered?), for the punkah did not move. The air was hot and still. There had been an excruciating pain when the needle-sharp teeth pierced her white breast but, as he sucked her blood, she felt a curious wave, undulating and tingling, in her loins, up her spine, a pulsing in the base of her skull. Her mouth opened in rapture. Pain and pleasure merged into uncanny ecstasy, a state beyond pain and pleasure, good and evil, and in that languorous trance, she was, with the terrible dark vampire, the very Maharaja of Vetalas, at her breast, like a mother nursing an infant. The madonna's blood was milk to feed the demon to whom she, through some private passion, felt she herself had given birth. She gasped and moaned, wept and smiled, as the vampire sucked her blood, her love, her soul, from her, and as he sucked, she could hear the rhythmic chanting of the heathens outside, down by the river, on the ghats, louder and louder, louder the gruesome litanies to Kali Ma, Mater Diablorosa with the garland of skulls around her neck. Their song sustained him.*

Bloated white, half-charred black, corpses floated down the murky Ganges past the shadowed singers, and Francesca, weak and wan, fainted away.

Why had Stoker been so cold? she wondered—the women at the Club, members of the Our Ladies of Otranto group, had relished every lurid work of it. Perhaps, she reasoned, something in the text disturbed or even terrified the master. Her male protagonist (a physician whimsically modeled on Major Ronald Ross), infatuated with the beautiful Countess Francesca Dionisi, explained his discovery in a scientific notice (for which, later in the novel, he is a made a laughingstock of the medical community and goes mad) on page 47 that the very vampire who had traveled from Romania to London in July of 1887, he who some thought to have been slain on a Friday in November of that year, had not died at all but had feigned death, risen two days later, and fled to India in 1895. The actual plague and malaria epidemic of that year was thus explained by her sensational fiction.

Did Stoker mistake her patent homage to him as some sort of churlish literary theft? Why did he feel none of the pleasure that her friends at the Club felt upon reading it? What bothered him so? Florence apologized in a brief note: "He has been very irascible of late. He is unable to concentrate. Please do not let his importunate reaction discourage you. I am afraid to say more."

Among the anxiously smiling members of the women's Gothic Literary Club, Mrs. Sanders fanned herself more from the heat of excitement than the bake of the season. Mary Thomson looked at each of them in turn and then began: "There's an evil in this world. Sometimes I can feel its palpable presence. That's what I am going to tell you about tonight. I can contain it no longer. This is no gothic tale, no spectacular romance, no macabre fancy. No. Tonight, though I suspect that some of you will not believe a word of it, I want to tell you a true horror story. I have, O Ladies of Otranto, made a haunting and harrowing discovery. But first let me read something to you, a sort of epigraph to what follows."

Places in the book with the bright green cloth cover and the shiny leather binding were marked with folded papers, envelopes, and news clippings (all of which were supplemented by the documents in a full leather satchel). She knew exactly where to open the book: *You think to baffle me,* she read, explaining that Count Dracula, "Lord of the Abyss," has turned to his pursuers to say it: *You—with your pale faces all in a row, like sheep in a butcher's stall. You shall be sorry yet, each one of you! You think you have left me without a place to rest, but I have more. My revenge is just begun! I spread it over centuries, and time is on my side. Your girls that you all love are mine already; and through them you and others shall yet be mine—my creatures, to do my bidding and to be my jackals when I want to feed. Bah!*

There was a delicious moment of dramatic silence through which the women continued to smile with the pleasure of savoring it. "I don't accept this as fiction though it appears in fiction," Mrs. Thomson stated with a defiant tone born out of repeatedly futile attempts to elucidate her theories to her husband. "This is not fiction. Not at all."

Where shall I begin? she asked and then spoke: *With birth or with death? Let me start with death.* She smiled. *Death always marks the beginning of something. The death in question took place eight years ago, in 1912 on the 20th day of April, in London. The death of a real man of flesh and blood. The body remains in the ground at Golders Green. The death certificate oddly, eerily I think, explains that the man died of "exhaustion." The man of whom I speak is none other than Mr. Bram Stoker, celebrated author of* Dracula, *husband of my dear and beautiful friend Florence Balcombe Stoker. Poor Florrie, how disconsolate she was those last months. She wrote to me from Cruden Bay: "It is sometimes as if he has become possessed by that Count of his creation, tormented by his own imagination or literary conjury. . . . I confide this in you* ('and I confide it in you,' Mrs. Thomson looked up to say). *It frightens me sometimes. And Lady Arabella. She has become all too real in his mind. He fears that she'll come for him. He hardly has the strength to fight whatever it is that he is fighting. He vacillates back and forth between extreme fatigue and a frightful restlessness no less immoderate, an unbounded restlessness, an uncontainable excitement, an almost maniacal egotism. He is struggling with something unspeakable. At night he paces—I hear him in his room speaking to himself. There's such anger and fear in the voice, such confusion, desolation, and an-*

guish. I do not know what to do. Then, in the morning, there's the morbidity, melancholy, and the horrible listlessness. Doctor Browne has diagnosed it as locomotor ataxia, tabes dorsalis, or some such thing; but naming is not curing—he cannot discern or fathom the cause of it. Dear, dear Mary, my friend for so many years, what am I to do? I am afraid. Perhaps Dr. Thomson may, even from afar, have some advice."

The next time I heard from Florence was after the funeral. A note to inform me of her husband's demise included an announcement that I had been named in his last will and testament: a crate would arrive containing all of his notes and research on vampires, spirits, and other occult and religious matters. I could not help but think of the crate on the ship Demeter that had carried the coffins of the Count in Mr. Stoker's great novel! After the fiasco with the manuscript of my own novel (an event which terminated all direct *correspondence between us), I would not have suspected that I might, in any way, be his beneficiary. Perhaps, I reasoned, it was because of my novel that he sent his notes to me. Perhaps he had not found my literary endeavors so dreadful after all. I was ashamed that I had not had the humility to have continued writing to him despite his appraisal of my talents. Florence suggested that "perhaps it's because you're Irish—like Le Fanu, Maturin, and himself. 'The Irish understand monsters best of all,' he said once. The will indicated that you would know what to do with the documents, to whom to disperse them when the time came."*

The collection was extraordinary. A Gothic theater piece complete with ribbon-bound, loose-leaf manuscripts, lots of good English dust, pieces of burnt-edged paper with wonderfully indecipherable scrawl upon them. I set the documents around me—books, magazines, papers, notes, letters, drawings, maps—and marveled just to look at them as physical objects, magical items. The books, what lovely books. Oh the sight and smell and touch of the books that had been in his hands and no doubt in the once trembling hands of others also dead by now. Each book a coffin of sorts and yet a womb ready to burst open and spill spirits into the world. I smelled each book and sheaf of papers, smelled ink, sea, blood, and, I imagined, the musk of vampires there. I am certain Mr. Bram—Abraham—*Stoker was speaking through Van Helsing,* Abraham *Van Helsing, when the passage I read to you, the epigraph to my story; was written. The same with this,* she opened the book again: *"I have studied, over and over again since they came into my hands, all the papers relating to this monster." And now, I too had those documents, and I too have studied, over and over again since they came in my hands, the papers relating to a very real monster.*

Allow me to give you a clearer sense of the contents of that crate that arrived in Bombay by ship from England: there were countless (she paused, struck by the irony of the word, and began again by repeating it) *countless books of course, the underlining and marginalia in which have proved crucial to my understanding of the terrifying situation at hand: books on vampirism, spirit lore, secret histories, magic, and many speculative texts, both scientific and occult, on reincarnation and the survival of the personality after the death of the gross body. Also other books, just what you would expect, novels and such:* The Italian, The Monk, Melmoth, Udolpho *and of course Prest's and Polidori's books. And many lesser known. And there were many articles and stories on the same topics. I was pleased to find my very own "Vampire of the Varana," and my translation,* The Impassioned Lady of Death, *among them. But what was most astonishing and utterly flattering was that I found the manuscript of my own* City of Dreadful Night *and, from the markings throughout, I discerned that he, despite his claims to the contrary, had read the whole with ardent interest.*

Also within the crate were boxes of letters that Mr. Stoker had received, including all of my own epistles to him. Imagine the delight I took in reading his notations on my letters, seeing the ink of the master mixed with my own. "India," he had written on the bottom of a letter I wrote to him in July of 1910: "India next. Is it safe? Confirm with Burton. Write to L. S. Ask F. to write, to inquire at once."

The bulk of the correspondence came from Dr. Arminius Vambery, distinguished professor of Oriental languages at the University of Budapest. The first one is dated April 1890. Listen, let me read a bit of it to you: “He must, indeed, have been that Voivode Dracula who won his name against the Turk.” She stopped, looked up to confirm that she had their attention: *“We know him in history as Vlad the Impaler. That mighty brain and that iron resolution went with him to his grave, and are even now arrayed against us. The Draculas were a great and noble race, though now and again there were scions who were held by their coevals to have had dealings with the Evil One.”*

There are literally hundreds and hundreds of newspaper clippings. What I believe to be the first, though certainly not the oldest, document in the collection is from the East London Advertiser dated 10 November 1888: “It is impossible to account, on any ordinary hypothesis, for these revolting acts of blood that the mind turns as it were instinctively to some theory of occult force, and the myths of the Dark Ages arise before the imagination. Ghouls, vampires, blood-suckers take form and seize the excited fancy.” This refers to the atrocities committed by the one who, during the period in question, in London, you will certainly recall, called himself Jack the Ripper. And it is appended with probably everything in the newspapers of the period about that evil monster. The reading is grisly, there are children decapitated, blood-drained corpses of young women, a man whose face is peeled from his skull. Bound with this, from the early years of the century, are more clippings, both originals and handwritten copies, about a very similar murderer known as “Spring Heel Jack” who is repeatedly identified as having “fiery breath” and “eyes of flame.” There is the letter of a certain police inspector, with whom Mr. Stoker seems (from the warmth of the salutations) to have been a close friend: “We know the identity of the Ripper. Be certain of that. But it cannot be revealed and he cannot be arrested. No one, I can assure you, would believe what we have discovered. Not even you.”

There are older news accounts still, reports from the period of 1727 through 1735 chronicling a flare-up of vampirism in Europe. These are often associated with eruptions of plague and invariably with inexplicable outbreaks of malaria. There was also a box of clippings from newspapers in America, collected during his visits there: the first, from the New York World, *is headed "Vampires in Rhode Island—Dead Bodies Dug Up and Their Hearts Burned." Note,* she said, holding the clipping, marked and underlined with red ink, *his cryptic notation here, along the side of the article: "Shigalov visited Providence. But when?" We shall return to that.*

There are also the copious—dare I say "laborious?"—notes that he, in the manner of his own Jonathan Harker, made from the collection in the British Museum. It was in the halls of that venerable institution, within that mausoleum of culture, going through newspaper accounts from earlier in the century, that Mr. Stoker had copied out this news story from an American journal of 1847 which begins to insinuate the identity of the above: "A Mr. Lev Shigalov, visiting our country from Oriental Russia, was found dead under mysterious circumstances today. The skin of his face was peeled from the skull and the blood was drained from his body through the fingertips. Mr. Shigalov, a Jew, was here lecturing on various occult subjects. The police suspect fowl [sic] *play, but no clues have been found."*

Mr. Stoker became immediately fascinated with this nebulous figure. The bottom of the page has this: "Acquaintance of Edgar Poe. Listed in the newspapers as being in attendance at the funeral of Virginia Poe, Fordham, 1847." There was an obituary from a Russian newspaper published in Vladivostok together with a letter from a certain Professor Afanasief: "I enclose my hurried copy of the following obituary as requested. It was no easy task to unearth. But I spared no energy as I very well understand and appreciate the urgency of your request. I am sorry to say that I have, as yet, been unable to locate the book, presumably some sort of novel; nor have I been able to discover any further information on Shigalov. The search, I assure you, continues. Vade retro me Satana! *In the meantime, I am sending you my other notes on the vampire legend in the Ukraine and among the Kashoubes." These are also found in the box. The obituary (translated by Afanasief) reads as follows: "Leopold Shigalov (22 July 1799–27 October 1847), folklorist and fabulist, author of Upir ("The Vampyre"), a Jew, died unexplainably in the Americas whilst doing research on the funerary practices of the*

Indian natives of California. He will be missed by those who knew him."

There were numerous letters referring to Shigalov, none of them containing much of interest, most of them merely apologies to Stoker for the particular writer's inability to secure the information he had requested. One of them, the last in the bundle, is, however, curious: "Dear Stoker, Everything you suspected about Shigalov is correct. Be careful. I am afraid, truly afraid. Yours, L. S. (Moscow)."

What concerns us here, however, is simply this, Stoker has marked the date of Shigalov's demise with red ink: "27 October 1847" and noted: "13 days before my own birth!"

She held up the clipping rather ominously, and the women smiled as they nodded knowingly. "Let's see it," Mrs. Sanders asked demurely, and it was passed around for their inspection while the story continued.

Further references to Shigalov are scattered throughout Stoker's notes: "I know this man. I have, in some sense or way, seen him." These random jottings, made with red ink on quarter-size sheets of paper, are of great interest because they contain much of what is actually in the novel, verbatim, word for word like the epigraph with which I began this true and bizarre tale. This suggests—if not proves—that the novel was not so much a novel as a report about actualities. This for example—chapter eight, Mina Harker's Journal—the storyteller opened the book to page 212, *a text ascribed in the novel to Van Helsing: "Let me tell you, he is known everywhere that men have been. In old Greece, in old Rome. He flourishes in Germany all over, in France, in India,"* Mrs. Thomson looked up meaningfully, perceptibly shivered, and then purposefully returned to the text: *In India, even in the Chersonese; and in China, so far from us in all ways, there even is he . . . ,"* her voice faded, faltered and then rose dreadfully: *"The vampire lives on, and cannot die by the mere passing of time."*

There are many passages that do not appear in the novel but well could have. For example: "The monster must be destroyed. He knows that I am looking for him. He knows it." Van Helsing could certainly have written or recited that.

Among these notes are scraps of paper with scribblings upon them in Pitman shorthand, a script I've struggled to master in order to decipher what follows. On the back of a program from the Lyceum Theatre is this interesting catalogue of villains: "Pontius Pilate, Attila the Scourge of God, Vlad the Impaler, Pharaoh Ramses (?), Antiochus, Nero, Elizabeth Bathory, Giles de Rais, Jack our clever Ripper (What 'appened ta yer spring 'eels, Jacko?)"—and some that aren't legible, and then there's the scribbled comment also in Pitman: "Not the most terrible, the most famous. The unknown ones, the most dangerous. Anonymity, evil. Here? There? Where are you? Where?"

The following note, written in regular letters but by a frantic hand may or may not better explain the above: "Who is he? Is he really Vlad the Impaler? No. Hardly! He has no name but has gone by many. I'll call him Dracul or Nosferatu, Upir or Vieszcy. Prince Dracul? Baron Upir? Count? No matter. Each time he's decapitated, the spike driven through his heart, he leaves that headless, blood-drained body to find a new birth, a new form. Killing him is worse than not doing so. It releases him! Out there somewhere. He's here. Lord of the Un-Dead. I've got him. But, of course, to the degree that I've got him, he's got me. He's after me. Careful, Stoker. I am afraid, Is my fear a madness, or is it sanity itself, a perfect comprehension. . . . What can I do?"

It's clear, is it not? Mrs. Thomson said as if the story were finished. *I'm sure you understand. Let's think it through. Mr. Stoker, intrigued by the events surrounding the so-called Jack the Ripper murders, looking into that mystery, discovered the true identity of that figure. He wrote his great novel to reveal the identity. Jack the Ripper was a vampire, none other than the Count Dracula of Stoker's novel.*

The Ladies of Otranto were delighted with the tale. "But, why didn't Stoker just come out with that? Why didn't he go to the police, the newspapers, the authorities?" Victoria Fitzpatrick (a newcomer to the literary group) asked as she returned the circulated clipping to Mary Thomson.

No, no one would have believed him. But if you write a novel, a story, then people can believe you without having to believe you. Had he told the story as a truth, people would have laughed at him, dismissed him as a clown or a Tom o'Beldam. But telling it as a novel, he made people afraid and afraid they should be. Afraid we must all be, for Dracula, Nosferatu, Vlad, Upir, Jack—whatever he is called now—lives: "You think you have left me without a place to rest, but I have more. My revenge is just begun! I spread it over centuries, and time is on my side." And he had his revenge on Stoker. He, the King of the Un-Dead was the cause of the fatal "exhaustion," to use the pathologist's euphemism.

"A thrilling sequel to the novel," Bithia Croker, as Irish as Mary, and no less capable of spinning a sumptuous horror story or a chilling tale of hungry ghosts or thirsty vampires, smiled. "Yes, you must write it, Mary dear—*The Return of Dracula*."

This history, my dear Bithia, is a sequel to history, Mary
Thomson said urgently, almost angrily, *and history by its very nature continues without end, or at least until some apocalyptic day of judgment. Only then will the evil rest. The sequel remains not to be written but to be acted out, to be feared, endured, overcome perhaps, perhaps, I don't know. The king of the Un-Dead lives—of that I am certain. The spirit that was in the flesh of the so-called Ripper, that Bram Stoker described in the body of a Romanian Count, lives and thirsts, lives here in India now. Here, he is here. The Betul Rajo of the tribals. Lord of the Abyss. He arrived in India eight years ago. Do you remember the malaria epidemic and the so-called outbreak of vampirism in Bombay, the spread of terrible reports throughout the Northern Provinces, the wild narratives of hideous crimes blamed on Thuggees and Tantrics? They mark his arrival. I've researched it all. Listen: the maritime office of the Bombay Board of Trade Registry records indicate that a ship named the Demetra from London docked in Bombay June of 1912. Is it a coincidence that the ship in Stoker's text is called the Demeter and that it was a Russian ship?*

"Why did he come to India," young Christine Weston, home for holiday from the convent school in the hills, asked with an almost salacious grin, relishing the mystery and eagerly playing along. As the daughter of a chief inspector in the Indian Imperial Police, she had perhaps inherited a taste for crime and mystery, horror and the macabre.

It was clear to all of the Ladies of Otranto that there were no loose strands in Mary Sheridan Thomson's tale: *he* came to India in search of his nemesis, in search of the one who knows *his* secrets, in search of Bram Stoker or rather the spirit that was in the body called Bram Stoker, the same spirit that had animated the body of Mr. Lev Shigalov. And, after Stoker's death in 1912, after the burial of his mortal remains, his frightened spirit fled England and came here, to be born again in India: *Yes, Stoker's spirit's here in India now, here in Banaras, as if seeking refuge from the Evil One amidst the Hindu gods and powerful magicians of India. They are, perhaps, his only hope against the Lord of the Un-Dead. He has come to me! Having read my* City of Dreadful Night, *he realized that I would understand, that I would know, that, while others would be incredulous, I would try to protect him.*

The women were startled and thrilled by the turn in the story that brought both hero and villain home. *Yes, he's come to me. I'm guarding him, preparing him. If only I could tell Florrie without her thinking me quite mad for asserting it; I know that it would please her immeasurably to know that I am taking care of him for her.*

"Where is he?" Christine asked excitedly, playing the game, make-believing it. "Let's meet him."

Mrs. Thomson presented the denouement: *Yes, he is here and I am protecting him, trying to protect him, although I'm frightened that I am not able to do so well enough. His name is Brahm, the child of Kalyani, the maid-servant in my employ. The Vampire King is looking for him. I'm certain of it.* He *could be anywhere.* He *could have entered and animated any corpse. We have no idea or conception of what* he *looks like now. Bram Stoker has come here intentionally to hide from* him, *and this explains why he willed the documents to me, to instruct me, so that I'd care for him, know what to do, so that I'd teach the boy exactly what to know and do. I have the obligation to teach the boy English so that he may study, when the time comes, the documents in my possession. Bram Stoker willed the documents to me for the boy, which is to say, he willed them to himself.*

Little Brahm, Brahm my Bram. At first, wondering whether or not the name was surely a coincidence, I asked Kalyani why she had chosen that name and she answered that she didn't know: "Mujhko malum nahim."

You need only look into those eyes to witness the spirit there, using those eyes, those ears, that innocent heart, that child's delicate body. Yet, it's Bram Stoker, not Bram Stoker the great, tall, burly, ruddy Irish man, but the spirit that was in that red-haired Irish giant. The same spirit again and again, each time having to relearn the horrible truth it already knows. Where was the spirit before he took on the form of Bram Stoker. The Russian Jew, Shigalov? I believe that. But, before that, across the centuries? Who knows. The spirit must be tired, so tired.

But of course it wasn't just the boy's name. My suspicions lead me to read Stoker's Dracula *to him. One reading and he can recite the passages. Not all of them. But of course Stoker himself wouldn't be able to do that. But he knows what's coming with each turn of every page.*

But this is not the sort of thing that constitutes proof. Listen to my case. This little boy was born in 1912, on the third day of May—another coincidence? Exactly thirteen days after Bram Stoker's death in London. And there's more than that. The third of May is the day on which the narrative of Dracula begins, the day that opens Jonathan Harker's Journal! It can hardly be a coincidence that there are so many coincidences.

"Have you told the boy?" Bithia asked excitedly. None of the women really knew whether or not Mary was being sincere, whether she actually believed this marvelous story, or if it was just another parlor game, another Gothic composition. "I don't think it would be a good idea to tell the child," Bithia continued almost nervously. "It could scare him to death."

Christine, whose father had investigated the "outbreak of vampirism" of 1912, not much more than a child herself, disagreed: "You must tell him. You must warn him!"

"Yes, of course I've warned him," Mrs. Thomson announced with what seemed a genuine fear and urgency. "He willed the documents to me just so that I would do so."

The ladies applauded.

Mrs. Thomson, as if she believed the story, as if to prepare the boy to face an invincible and very real enemy, had indeed warned him: "Read this book, your book, read it again and again. The answers are within it. Your answers, your messages to yourself. And tell stories of the Maharaja of Vetals. Tell stories of ghosts and vampires, ghouls and goblins. These stories have the power to control *him;* tales of terror drain and sap *him* of what is terrifying about *him;* they deplete *him* of *his* power. Tell the stories. Tell them wherever you go." She repeated the story that night after the reading of chapter three.

Brahm and Varney had fallen asleep, and Dr. Thomson had withdrawn from the door and returned to his study. Mrs. Thomson had closed the book and rekindled the lamp and was staring lovingly, fearfully, sadly at the boy. She leaned forward and kissed his cheek. "Bram," she whispered in the ear of the sleeping child. "My dear Bram, remember what you wrote? *'We want no proofs; we ask none to believe us! This boy will some day know. . . .'* You were speaking to me then, at the end of your prophetic book, were you not? Were you not?"

Inspector Weston, having been endlessly and piteously beseeched by his young daughter to take her to the Thomson residence, finally yielded and arrived with her in the morning. He announced it rather lackadaisically: "There's been another Tantric murder. The head of a servant child has been found in Ballia District. It was mounted on a stake and placed at a crossroad. The body remains to be discovered. We're rounding up the priests. But there's not much hope in finding the killer. We can expect such things at this time of year, at the beginning of the hot season when they're getting ready to prepare the paddy fields. The nefarious holy men sacrificially decapitate a child, bleed him, and soak iron nails in the blood. These magic nails are then sold to the farmers who believe that if they're planted with the seeds and shoots, the crops will be good. This is our responsibility here—isn't it, Thomson?—to teach these people the folly of their terrible superstitions, to enlighten them for their own good. But sometimes it seems so hopeless. Perhaps we'd be better to pack up and go home, let them suck each other's blood without our interference."

"There must be vampires after all," Thomson sighed, "demons, ghouls and goblins, zombies and nosferatus, vetals and prets, and the devil only knows what else. How else might we account for the evil in this world? Surely human beings of flesh and blood could not, in their own interest, perpetrate such evils, such crimes as we see all around us, everyday, everywhere, violations of life itself. Though we might, unwittingly, or because of some petty blinding fear or desire, become instruments of the great persistent force of evil, no, no, I refuse to believe that we as human beings could design it. And surely if there is a god, he could not be responsible for such horrors as we encounter here."

The boy had come the door to greet them. And the girl, only a few years older than he, smiled: *"Namaste Brahmji, mai Christine hum. Tum kaise ho?"*

Opening his eyes wide, stretching out his arms, curling back his lip, he answered her in the English of the book: *"Welcome to my house! Come freely. Go safely; and leave something of the happiness you bring."*

"Yes," Christine gasped with delight, "It's him!" And the boy ran off to hide. She asked permission to search for him: "And when I find you," she called out, "you'll be sorry little one. I'll suck your blood!"

"What language, Christine!" her father chided and then turned back to Mrs. Thomson. The inspector's report had chilled the woman. It was as if she was afraid that the Vetala Raja was in the area and that he was looking for Brahm.

Inspector Weston and Christine stayed for tea and were still in the Thomson house when Varney's ears perked up. He growled at first, then began to bark wildly, and then they heard the damaru drum rattling its plaintive announcement and call from the road that passed the house.

"Who is it?" Mrs. Thomson asked Kalyani.

"Kathuwala, storyteller, Memsahib," the servant answered. "Storyteller and ojha, some sort of sadhu, a magician, a tribal priest or something like that. Crazy man."

"Yes, I recognize him," Inspector Weston remarked from the window. "We questioned him last year as a suspect in some case of theft or other. He's a vagrant storyteller and exorcist, an itinerant bard and shaman who makes his living reciting passages from the *Ramayana* and *Mahabharata,* telling stories of the gods, saints, and heros. Quite harmless, I think."

"Let's ask if he knows ghost stories," Mrs. Thomson suggested, and the prospects thrilled young Christine. The woman, her servant, and the girl replaced Weston at the window as the men descended to talk to the storyteller.

The old man, gray-bearded, clusters of amulets dangling from his neck and wrists, salaamed them and responded to their questions in a Hindustani dialect that was barely intelligible to the British. Little Brahm translated for Mrs. Thomson: "Yes, ghost stories he knows. He

says every story is a ghost story. In a story of Ram, the ghost of Ram comes to haunt or help us if the storyteller knows what he is doing. If he knows what he is doing, the storyteller gets possessed. 'I don't make anything up,' he's saying, 'I invent nothing. I remember from so long ago.'"

"Yes, yes," Dr. Thomson cut him off in formal Hindustani, "but do you know the stories of ghosts and ghouls and vampires?"

The old teller of tales, a black twine of twisted hair worn over his shoulder, across his chest, as if to parody the twice born, waved his peacock-feather fan, and salaamed again with the native suppliants' perfunctorily and eternally pitiful look in his eyes. "Is my name not Bhutnath Kathuwala, Mr. Ghostmaster Storyteller?"

What manner of man is this, Brahm burlesqued the reading of *Dracula, or what manner of creature is it in the semblance of man?* Christine joined Mrs. Thomson in appreciative laughter. And they laughed over the artless cunning of the storyteller's pitch and received him into their company with a certain excitement. He was to wait in the servants' quarters until after dinner and then entertain them on the veranda with some terrifying story of his choice.

"You can understand why we questioned him," Inspector Weston said as they withdrew to dine. With that earring, a small skull fashioned out of silver, with that gnarled wood walking stick, the clusters of amulets, and the peacock-feather fan, lean and shirtless, wrapped only in that unsewn black loin cloth, the old storyteller was an ominous presence.

Emerging from dinner, the foreigners discovered that he had set the stage for the tale: the damaru and bone flute, a monkey skull with vermillion streaked on it, the bones set out on the cloth before him. There were dark jungles in his eyes. Amidst the amulets around his neck, bundles of herbs and grasses rested on his chest beneath the serpentine tangles of an ash-gray beard. He sat in the posture of a yogi patiently waiting for them. And when they were gathered, smiling, he began by excusing himself for not knowing more of the English language. "More?" Thomson broke in in English, in what was clearly a jibe, "What can you say in English?"

The storyteller closed his eyes, took in a deep breath through his nose, spread his arms as if to recite some magnificent ode, and smiled the words: "The grass is green, the rose is red, and night is dark. I am a poor man but I have a pair of legs and eat with a right hand. How many hands do you have? What are you by caste? How do you do? What do you do? Are you afraid? Do not hurt me for I am regular in the habits. Always speak a truth. The hog jumps the log. Peoples are afraid. He is a lame man because of the leprosy. I have a malaria fever. She fainted because of the hot and could not get out of a bed again. I have a diarrhea and a vomit and a nose that runs. Don't be afraid. Goodbye."

"It's a poem! A wonderful, wonderful poem!" Christine giggled and clapped her hands and they laughed both at her and at him, and Mrs. Thomson mused that that must be what she sounded like in Hindustani and her husband assured the old man that, while they were all amply impressed by his linguistic and poetical proficiencies, he could proceed in Hindustani. "But slowly for the ladies."

Let me tell you an old, old story, yes, a true story, the terrible tale of the boy who became possessed, he began, and at once Christine, Mrs. Thomson, and Brahm were entranced.

There was a brahmin, good Govindaswami, in this village, my very own. I never met the man myself—he died, you see, died before my birth. Oh, but my father knew him and he told me the story. Everyone in our village had some account of it, some version of the terrible tale of that brahmin Govindaswami and his two sons, Sanjayadatta and Vijayadatta. It's a story dreamed and told and told again, told by fires in the night, told no less in time of plenty than in times of famine, told now no less than then, told and retold differently at different times, for different ears and hearts, but told and told and dreamed again. Whoever tells this story will never become possessed. Whoever tells this story will never become a hungry ghost, even if he has no sons—he will not become a bhut or pret. Listen to my story.

He told the tale, and his gruesome words, as gnarled as his stick, were uttered with such relish and delight that they did not seem so horrible or ghastly, but rather thrilling, almost mirthful, as they teased Brahm's ear. He had no less a knack for horror than Memsahib. She too knew how to twist terrible words into wonderful diversions. Telling and listening became a kind of pact, a game with rules; there was a complicity between tongue and ear. And Mrs. Thomson felt a natural affinity for the old man—they were both tellers of ghost stories. He was the Indian, male, a low-class manifestation of what she was, the British, female, upper-class equivalent. "Stories unite us," she reflected; but there was something unnerving in that, a bit frightful, the uneasy but tantalizing feeling of being seduced against one's will.

His bardic Hindustani was difficult to understand. The melodically echoing vowels (Sanja*ya* rather than Sanjay, veta*la* not vetal) sounded sacredly archaic.

Mrs. Thomson asked Brahm to retell the story to her in English later that night, before their ritual reading of *Dracula: The boy with eyes like blazing coals laughed as he raised up the stick, aimed at the heart of his trembling father, the brahmin Govindaswami. The man closed his eyes and, knowing it was the end, he cried out to God: "Jay Ram, jay Ram."* That was where the old storyteller had stopped, had said he was tired, but if they'd give him food and a place to sleep, he'd stay and continue the story the next night. Christine begged her father to let her attend.

"Jay Ram!" Govindaswami cried, but it was not Ram that saved him, no, not God nor any amulet, the old storyteller began that

next night. *No, it was, believe me or not, a rakshasa who interceded. He came for Vijaya. There he was. These rakshasas can take on any form, you know: dark, velvety black or luminous, leprous white, or painful crimson, or stale green, or the color of you, or you, or you.* He pointed at Brahm, and it pleased the boy; he felt the storyteller was speaking just to him, just for him, showing him something, teaching him something. *Immense monsters with tusks studding blood-red rims of dark, cavernous mouths or minute, two-legged insects with needle-teeth, bristled skin, and minuscule dots of fire in their eerie eyes. They change from this to that, from a beauty that beckons to an ugliness that sickens. In the cremation grounds they are ghastly, for there, there in the city of dreadful night, the horrible is beauty. There monstrosity is perfection. And there he was: gray skin, dry, pocked and peppered with wet sores, encrusted with molds and spores, bone revealing, barely covered by filthy shreds of burnt cere* *cloth, glassy, eyelidless eyes rolling, lips eaten away, nose disintegrated, scaly scalp issuing sparse wisps and tangles of long gray hair, fine like threads of spiders' webs, and, his body trembling with shooting laughter, the rakshasa cried out to the boy, "Come, my boy, come away, into the death that is our life."*

It was as if the boy in the story was alive, alive in and as Brahm. The child reveled in the story; it was like *Dracula* but better, easier to understand because it was in his own language and about his own people. The blood that dripped in that story, that was lustily drunk by vetals, was Indian blood.

Again the storyteller stopped mid-story: *The king, Sanjaya's patron, became very ill. He was dying. And the only way to save him was by performing a magic rite in the cemetery. And for that a corpse had to be found and used to heal the king. Ah, but that's another story, a terrible, horrible story. And it's a long one too. And it's late now, and I'm hungry and tired. Perhaps you would like for me to stay another night?*

Terror was this man's livelihood and sadhana. Where did he hear those stories? He claimed (and this made Mrs. Thomson tremble) that he had not heard them, not in this life, that he had been born knowing them, and that in this lifetime he merely remembered them.

"We're all born with stories in our souls, but for so many of us, it's too hard to recollect them."

The old storyteller found particular pleasure in frightening children. "They understand fear better than we do," Mrs. Thomson had written in her novel, *City of Dreadful Night:* "When we're afraid, my dear Francesca, it's the child in us who shivers."

And so he stayed, and stayed, and stayed, and after a week, more and more members of the Club were in attendance. Mr. Sanders took notes as the storyteller told the tale of Narasimha disemboweling the demon Hiranyakashipu: *Narasimha growled and shrilled, hissed ecstatic laughter in the twilight (neither day nor night!), clutched the throat of the Asura and dragged him, wiggling and writhing, screeching terrors, to the threshold of the hall (neither inside nor out of doors!), lifted him up, upon his lap (neither on the earth nor in the sky!), then, then—haha!—he gouged into his bloated belly with those lion claws in human hands, sharp and golden nails ripping and wrenching, and razor tooth trailed barbed claw into the guts to cleave, rip and rend, and then, oh then, he sucked out the gore, disgorged the vitals, unraveled the demon's entrails, delicious and putrid, laughing to bare white teeth dripping with demon blood, lion's mane flecked with flesh and frizzles of fat, blood-raw, blood-sweet meat rended and dripping bile, and he laughed, sucked, cleaved, growled, as the Asura shrieked his last and fell limp. Thus did Lord Vishnu triumph over nonvirtue and establish righteousness on earth. Haha!*

He told the story of Bhima drinking the blood of Duhshasana: *On the sixteenth day of the great battle, blaze-eyed Bhima, his hair like black smoke from the fires of revenge burning in his skull, having knocked Duhshasana from his chariot with his terrible blood-stained mace, morsels of warrior flesh still wiggling upon its spikes, leaped from his own chariot to pounce upon his enemy as the lion upon the elephant. Mercilessly, pressing his foot into the throat of Duhshasana, choking him, breaking the bones of his neck, Bhima thunderously laughed, and the gurgling in Duhshasana's throat made him thirsty. He roared his laughter as he drew the sword, howled as he swung, growled as he sliced into the chest, cracking the ribs, twisting out the succulent heart. Falling to his knees, still laughing, howling, growling all at once, he gouged his fingers in, pulled open the chest and thrust his head into the gaping breast of his enemy, burying his face in it, sucking, sucking, gulping the hot, pulsing blood, swilling the spurting crimson liquor. He threw his head back, smacking his lips and the blood from the chest was a fountain of nectar splashing up and Bhima drank more of it, laughing still, his face streaming with the luscious red rivulets, spurting glistening fresh and hot, and he belched his triumphant laughter with scorn and ecstasy: "The blood of my enemy is more delicious to me than the milk of the mother to her baby, than Soma to Indra, than the sweetest mead, more refreshing than nectar, delicious, delicious, haha!" And the troops, seeing the gruesome spectacle took flight, screaming, "He's been transformed into a beast or demon, or been possessed by some terrible vampire who subsists on blood." And even the brothers who loved him trembled in awe at the sight of him as he drank and drank more, laughed louder and stretched wider the wound and sucked and sucked, and then threw his head back again, spitting, gargling, gurgling, laughing, and then dug his head again like a drunkard into a ripped skein of wine. He howled hyena cries. He wiped his lips with the back of his blood-drenched arm. He bit off a fingertip, spit it out, then sucked the blood from the finger, then another fingertip and sucked that finger dry. He did that with each of the ten fingers as if they were ten bottles of rum. Then, drunk with the glorious bliss of vengeance, he cracked open the head of Duhshasana with the ease of a parrot cracking a nut, squeezed the brain like a sponge over the inverted top of the skull and, just as Lord Bhairava drinks blood from a begging bowl made of skull bone, he lapped up the now clotting blood of his enemy.*

He told the story of Rama slaying the demoness Tataka: *Cloud-clusters were burst asunder by her quaking breasts, adorned with entrail ornaments, and her hair was undone by the flapping wings of the vultures, greedy for the meat sticking to lips stretched wide with hysterical laughter. As she attacked, the sky resounded with the cacophonous din of her rattling adornments. Wild with lust, her terrible body, its swollen breasts shaking, beaming with the horror, cov-*

ered with the filth and blood that she has drunk and vomited up again, she circled above them. And Vishvamitra cried out to Lord Rama, "Night is coming. Slay her quickly, before the darkness conceals her. Slay the witch well versed in dark magic, slay her without delay." And Lord Ram drew an arrow from his quiver, stretched the great bow, and with one winged shaft both of her hands were severed from her arms. With the second twang of the bow, her intestines burst forth, unraveled, flowed out, spewing black juices. Her liver, ripped from her side and green, gushed with dark and pungent blood. And, drenched by the scarlet rain, Lakshmana and Rama rejoiced.

Inspector Weston arrived and he too had horror stories to tell, less mythic and differently terrible. He announced the news of the massacre at Amritsar. General Dyer had sent his troops to the public meeting in the Jallianwalla Bagh, the square surrounded by high walls, and then ordered his soldiers to open round after round of deadly fire. Screams echoed across the subcontinent. "My men think the murders here in Banaras are in retaliation for all that. I don't know quite what's going on. But I do know one thing—that I am afraid. There's been another murder, another decapitated child," Inspector Weston continued. "Christine, my wife, and the baby will stay tonight as usual, but I must be excused. We must unearth the source of these horrors as soon as possible, not simply the perpetrators but the motives if there are any. This time right in Ramnagar, so near the city. Abominations abound in this cruel land. I don't think it's revenge because for revenge you need a sense of justice. This is simply evil. It's the evil of this land of Bhairava. It turns even Christians into savages. There's misery and chaos ahead. There is real horror in the world. There are real draculas, nosferatus, wicked people, and satanic spirits. We need metaphysical detectives, some sort of cabalistic police, for this crime, I'm afraid. This whole business is no good. I'm afraid, Thomson, really afraid."

Christine was sitting next to Brahm, holding his hand, turning to him to smile occasionally, bound to him by the mutuality of their avid appreciation of the storyteller's tales.

Distressed by Weston's report, Mrs. Thomson was too nervous that night to concentrate enough to follow the archaic, colloquial Hindustani. The Dyer incident had upset her terribly; she envisioned the bullets piercing the flesh, nicking the walls behind the lines of panicked people, and around each bullet notch an ominous crimson aureole of real blood. The more she tried not to think of it, to find diversion in the story, the more vivid the visions of Amritsar became. She could hear the screams.

The old wizard smiled at Sanjaya and Sanjaya was unnerved by it, Bhutnath Kathuwala continued the story he had begun the night before. *It did not seem to be the cruel, unnatural smile of the Skullbearer but the kinder, known smile of his deceased father, Govindaswami.* And the old storyteller smiled at Brahm. He spoke the wizard's speech, and as he did his breath seemed fiery and he had eyes of flame: *"Not far from here there's an ashoka tree, its leaves singed by the flames of the funeral fires, and suspended upsidedown in its branches is a corpse. There, in that direction—follow that dark path until you see the light. Fetch the body. Bring it here. Go now. And hurry. Hurry! Bring that flesh to me."*

Varney growled with simultaneous menace and qualm just as he had done on the afternoon when the storyteller first arrived. Mrs. Thomson looked at the dog, then at the storyteller, back and forth again, watching the animal watch the man and the man look at Brahm. "Why has he stayed here so long? What does he want?" She felt a shiver of terror, a rush of premonitions, a lump in her throat, the devastating distress and sentimental riot that overwhelms a woman who suddenly realizes that she has been deceitfully seduced, betrayed and deceived by a heartless lover. Her pulse quickened. Varney growled again. And Mary Thomson, suddenly jolted by her suspicions, leaped up screaming, "Get him out. Dr. Thomson, send him away! At once! At once!"

The physician tried to calm his wife. The impetuous outburst of hysteria startled the old man, frightened him and Christine and Brahm.

"It's *him,*" Mrs. Thomson gasped, still trembling, unable to stand steady, and her husband put his arm around her for support as he tried to escort her from the room. "No, no," she cried desperately. "Don't leave them together. It's *him!* Don't you understand? Bhutnath, 'Ghost Lord,' *him*—of course, of course, why didn't I realize it earlier? Oh dear God—the Maharaja of the Un-Dead has come. The slaying of the children in the area! The horrible deaths! The blood! God, it's *him!* Call Weston. Hurry! *He's* after Brahm. *He's* here for the child. We must protect the boy." She tore away from her husband's arms, cried out, lunged forward reaching for the child, and in the style and spirit of Francesca Dionisi, the heroine of her own *City of Dreadful Night,* she fainted.

When she began to emerge from the delirium, coming up out of it like a drowning woman suddenly floating up from the depths of a calm but treacherous sea, the doctor, her tired and distraught husband, was at her side. "Where's the child?" she moaned and mumbled. "Is he alive? Where's Brahm?"

He tried to calm her with more laudanum and soft, soporific words, "Yes, my dearest one, yes, the boy is fine. He's with Christine."

"And the storyteller? Where is he?" she murmured, the panic, itself a horrid demon, swelling again to choke the words from her throat: "*He's* after the child. I'm certain of it."

"I've sent the old rascal away," Dr. Thomson explained with a forced smile. "Here now, take another spoonful of the medicine. It will help you sleep. Sleep, sleep, my dear Mrs. Thomson, sleep and dream sweet dreams, dear Mary, and be calm. There, there . . ."

He had had enough. His wife was falling to pieces. Enough of this horror and the macabre, enough of ghosts and ghouls, demons and vampires, enough of superstition, reincarnation, and Bram Stoker. "Enough of these books, these stories, these obsessions with the horrible. And this heat is no good for her. I'm taking her to Almora," he explained to Weston and Sanders. "We'll leave Kalyani and little Brahm behind in the house. It's for her own good. She's become too attached to the boy. The fangs of affection! And soon, God willing, we'll be going back. I'm anxious, especially after this Dyer business, to return home. Hopefully my request to return to London to work with Dr. Manson at the Seaman's Hospital will have been approved by the time we return from the hills. Ross is all for it. Still lots of mosquito work to be done. She's going to want to take the boy with us to Almora. I know it. But I'll draw the line and stand firm. I've got to cut the ties. I'm afraid for her."

Mrs. Thomson wept of course, but all her protestations only

strengthened her husband's resolve to separate her from the child. Her terror was genuine, her anxiety all consuming. On the eve of their departure she settled down on the bed next to the boy, tenderly wrapping her arm around him, gently holding him, and, under the dead still mosquito netting, he luxuriated in that plush caress. With a faltering voice she beseeched Brahm to beware. She warned him about the vampire.

Is this a joke, he wondered, a story, or does she believe it? Is she playing a game with me? Or is Memsahib mad?

Kalyani and the boy watched the Thomsons leave in the brougham gharri. The tongas that followed them with their belongings to the nearby Banaras railway station raised dust to veil the departure and make it easier for all of them. Varney, left behind by his mistress to protect the boy, barked, and Brahm patted his head to quiet him. "*Yah lijie Varni-ji,*" he said and then went to fetch a bowl of water for the dog, some relief from the miserable heat of the season. He laughed, "Of course, Mister Varney doesn't understand Hindustani. I'll teach you. Take this, this is water. *Pani.* Drink. Don't be afraid."

Jeth: sky and earth had become bitter and ascetic; the Ganga had withered. The only good thing about this time of year, his mother would say, is that it was too hot for the mosquitos. They left the windows open throughout the house as an invitation to any wayward breezes that might pass near.

It was just the three of them—Brahm, his mother, and the dog—left alone in that great cantonment house. Brahm missed Memsahib and didn't like it that his mother, despite the thirteen empty British-style beds, insisted that they sleep on the floor.

If she had known that he was awake, watching her in the darkness, she would have restrained her tears. He could smell the consoling drug and the ember in the red clay chillum was reflected, glistening, in a tear as she sucked in, held the smoke down, and then sighed to let it out. When he closed his eyes he could see his absent mother: the high white collar, soft, the dark bows beneath, soft, and the pink curve of graceful neck above, wisped with strands of reddish hair and her eyes, above the round pink cheeks, pastel green and soft. Her flushed lips parted and he could hear the story and taste their secret drink, the Irish whiskey mixed with warm milk and a swirl of Irish honey gathered up by drunken, angelic Irish bees from fragrant Irish flowers far away. He opened his eyes again to look at his Indian mother, a dark shape in darker darkness on the floor, leaning over, softly weeping. He could hear Mrs. Thomson reading, each English word vivid in his ears. *Chapter four. Jonathan Harker's Journal (continued),* she began in her Jonathan voice: *I shall try to scale the castle wall farther than I have yet attempted. I shall take some gold with me, lest I want it later. I may find a way from this dreadful place. And then away, away to the quickest and nearest train, away from this cursed spot, from this cursed land, where the devil and his children still walk with earthy feet. At least God's mercy is better than that of these monsters, and the precipice is steep and high. At its foot a man may sleep. . . ."* And the child slept in the shadows of precipices on the edges of dark unbottomed infinite abysses.

96 Morning came like the slow opening of great furnace doors. Varney, his nose hot and dry, his tongue dangling out of the ever-open panting mouth, stayed in the corner trying to sleep the day away, prompted only by the most urgent thirst and other bodily necessities to slowly rise and lethargically lumber out the door. Then he'd be back to take refuge once more in the shaded corner and in dog dream until the coming of the vaguely cooler twilight.

That night, amavasya, the darkest night of the month, Bhutnath Kathuwala returned at midnight. "Brahm, wake up! Wake up," his mother said shaking him. As the boy opened his eyes, startled, he gasped at the sight of the storyteller there in the house with them. Eerily iluminated by the paraffin lamp, the skull earring gleamed. Waving his peacock-feather fan with one hand, holding Kalyani's wrist with the other, eyes half-closed, entranced, he rocked back and forth muttering syllables to himself or to some god, "*Phrum phuh phuh prah phat phrah phat. . . .*" His beard, glistening with silver, quivered as he recited. Brahm looked around for Varney but could not locate him in the darkness.

"The ojha's here to help us," Kalyani told her son. The man's tale terrified the child: "They're here. The ghosts are here now. The bhuts, the prets. They're here. Can't you sense it? They weren't here the last time I was in this house. They don't come when the British are here. They're afraid of the British." Brahm clutched his crucifix just in case. "They are the old ghosts of those people violently killed during the Mutiny. There are some new ghosts also, from Amritsar. They're restless and hungry. They don't have children to feed them. You're a boy without a father, and they're sonless fathers. Do you understand? They want you to feed them. That's why they're here—for you. Feed them balls of sweetened rice. Feed them without fear." He tied a small silver amulet around Brahm's arm with a black string. "If you begin to feel afraid, remember the tale of Vijayadatta and Sanjayadatta; tell yourself the story of how Sanjaya saved Vijaya from the rakshasas, how he exorcised the spirit that had possessed the boy. Tell it to your mother too. Recollect his courage and let it be your own." He anointed the boy's forehead, tongue, and stomach with ashes. Kalyani, now adorned with his charms and herbs and diagrams, was anointed too.

When Brahm woke up the storyteller was gone again. His magic did not assuage Kalyani's despair. Still she wept each night and never did she tell Brahm why. All she said was that he needed to know how to take care of himself. It became habitual for the boy to awaken in the middle of each heated night, to hear her nocturnal sobbing and sometimes Varney's growl. He'd crawl over the floors that she'd have swept all day to put his hand gently on her shoulder and not say a word.

Varney barked that night with teeth bared—barked and growled, snarled and howled—but nothing could be seen. "Shhh, Varney. Don't be afraid. There's nothing to be afraid of."

He crawled along the floor to his mother's mat and was alarmed to find her absent. He rose and whispered, Ma, then said it, Ma, then louder, Ma, then cried it, Ma Ma, then screamed it, Ma, Ma, Ma, Ma. . . .

Brahm wept, not for himself, not with the feeling of abandonment, but wept for his mother, certain that the Vetala Raja had beguiled her; Count Dracula had come that dark night to possess her because she was his mother, because she had returned Bram Stoker to this world, and the vampire transformed her into one of the Un-Dead just as he had done with Lucy Westenra, *Lucy Westenra, but yet how changed. The sweetness was turned to adamantine, heartless cru-*

elty, and the purity to voluptuous wantonness. . . . by the concentrated light that fell on Lucy's face we could see that the lips were crimson with fresh blood, and that the stream had trickled over her chin and stained the purity of her lawn death robe. . . . her eyes blazed with unholy light. . . . With a careless motion, she flung to the ground the child that up to now she had clutched strenuously to her breast, growling over it as a dog growls over a bone. The child gave a sharp cry and lay there moaning.

Brahm dried his eyes, caught his breath, calmed himself by petting Varney, and tried to think it through, to consider other possibilities. Perhaps she ran away with Bhutnath Kathuwala, became the itinerant storyteller's consort, following him on the open road from village to village, delivered from the burdens of servitude, utterly free, hearing wonderful stories every night and day, and even smiling.

After a few weeks it was, at least during the daylight, alright that she was gone. That Brahm and Varney were alone in the house changed the routine, of course: they started sleeping in the master bedroom, Brahm in Mrs. Thomson's bed, Varney in the Doctor's. They went through every closet, cupboard, drawer, in the house, Brahm peering and Varney sniffing, taking what they wanted. Brahm began wearing a silk top hat that Dr. Thomson had left behind and Varney wore a paisley cravat. They found enough money (a pittance to the Thomsons, but a fortune to the servant child and his dog) in Memsahib's dresser drawer not to have to worry about food. Brahm arranged to have provisions delivered for a haggled price: chapatis and dal for them (sometimes a bit of chicken or goat) and rice balls for the ghosts. The milk came as usual, and the boy found a bottle of Irish whiskey and the jar of Irish honey to mix with it. Varney learned to like the drink as well, and so the child and the dog got drunk most nights and, just in case, Brahm would set a cup of that wonderful magic drink by the tree in the garden for the restless wraiths.

When Brahm discovered the book under Memsahib's pillow, he let Varney have a sniff of England in the green cloth cover and the leather binding of *Dracula* by Bram Stoker, the smell of Westminster, the aroma of the offices of Archibald Constable and Company at number 2 Whitehall Gardens. "The secret of what has happened to my mother may be somewhere in this story," he thought to himself as he tucked the book under his arm.

They waited and waited and waited for something to happen, for Kalyani to return, for the Thomsons to come home, or, at least, for the rains to come. But nothing happened, no one came. Brahm passed the time by telling stories to Varney, an abridged and caninized version of *Dracula,* an embellished account of the Man-Lion, and what he remembered of Bhutnath Kathuwala's terrible tale of the boy who became possessed and of Sanjayadatta, the brother who redeemed him. Soon he began to invent stories for the dog.

During the night he missed both his mothers. He'd bury his face in Memsahib's pillow to smell her and the scent, the delicious English smells—roses and mint, creams and custard—would conjure up the voice. Sometimes it was comforting: *And there are bad dreams for those who sleep unwisely,* her voice was lusciously sweet and brimming with play: *Be warned! Should sleep now or ever overcome you, or be like to do, then hasten to your own chamber or to these rooms, for your rest will then be safe. . . .* "These rooms, my little Brahm, be at home here and sleep and dream safely here, near me." But sometimes the voice made him genuinely afraid: *I am beginning to feel this nocturnal existence tell on me. It is destroying my nerve. I start at my own shadow, and am full of all sorts of horrible imagining. . . .*

The habitual midnight awakenings persisted, and each time he thought he heard his mother's weeping. "Ma, Ma . . ." But, no, she wasn't there. But, yes, he thought to himself, yes, I hear something. "Varney! Come with me, Varney!" he commanded, but the dog, strangely whimpering, his ears twitching and hair bristling, wouldn't leave the room, wouldn't follow the boy into the dark hallway on the upper floor.

Brahm moved slowly and silently. "Ma," he whispered. Though all of the windows had been left wide open, there was not a breeze in the hot night. *Bless that good, good woman who hung the crucifix round my neck! for it is a comfort and strength to me whenever I touch it. It is odd that a thing which I have been taught to regard with disfavor and as idolatrous should in a time of loneliness and trouble be of help.* He heard it again, the low whimpering, just what he imagined those shadowless female slaves of Count Dracula must have sounded like, then, very faintly, their muted whispers and hushed laughter, slight and silvery, musical like the tingling of glasses. Then, at midnight, the cantonment government house might as well have been Castle Dracula. There were the scratching, grating, and flapping sounds, and what seemed to be faintly rattling chains and clanking bolts, Gothic echoes and horror story reverberations, and a real jackal howled hauntingly in the distant darkness amidst fabulous wolves with white teeth and lolling red tongues, with long sinewy limbs and shaggy hair. And suddenly he could hear the ghastly whisper. *You think to baffle me. You shall be sorry yet. You think you have left me without a place to rest, but I have more. My revenge is just begun! I spread it over centuries, and time is on my side. Your girls that you all love are mine already; and through them you and others shall yet be mine— my creatures, to do my bidding and to be my jackals when I want to feed. Bah!* "It's *him*. *He's* here, *he's* found me. I must escape."

He awoke in the morning in Mrs. Thomson's bed. If it be that Brahm had not dreamed, *he* must have carried him there. That was the only explanation he could offer himself. His own silent thoughts were indistinguishable from those of the book; he didn't know if the words were his or Stoker's: *As I look round this room, although it has been to me so full of fear, it is now a sort of sanctuary, for nothing can be more dreadful than those awful women, who were—who are—waiting to suck my blood. . . . I shall try to scale the castle wall farther than I have yet attempted. I shall take some gold with me, lest I want it later. I may find a way from this dreadful place. Away, away from this cursed spot, from this cursed land, where the devil and his children still walk with earthy feet.*

Despite desperate coaxing, despite the temptation of a piece of mutton, Varney refused to follow Brahm when he departed early the next morning, setting out alone on the dusty road, the crucifix around his neck, the silver amulet tied with the black string to his arms, the walking stick formed from the branch of a tree, and the copy of *Dracula* in his hand.

The black silk top hat, being much too large for the boy's head, came down over his eyes; he tried to balance it, tilted back so that he could see his way. At the gate he turned around to look one more time at the red Irish Setter on the veranda, utterly abandoned, alone amidst the sonless revenants of the Sepoy dead, the childless ghosts of the Amritsar massacre, and the thirsty spectral mistresses of the Maharaja of Vetals. The Lord of the Un-Dead himself would certainly leave the house that night when he, awakened by the darkness, discovered that Brahm was gone. *He* was after the child. *He* would pursue him.

The boy was resolved to find his mother. He'd search the abyss for her. He reckoned that it would not be so difficult to find the easily describable old storyteller magician ("He's in some village—Ballia district I think I heard him say—telling some story and selling his amulets"), and he would certainly be able to help him find his mother.

And, indeed, the storyteller was in a village in Ballia district and, when night came, he set out his charms to sell, and sitting cross-legged in ascetic posture on the platform under the pipal tree near the now dry bed of the stream, he continued an ancient story: *Yes, yes, come a little closer, come now and let me tell you what happened to Govindaswami and his sons Sanjayadatta and Vijayadatta. Let's hear about his son Vijaya, the boy who became possessed. Haha! And let's hear about Sanjaya, the older son, let's hear about his great adventures too.*

4

And taking the anklet he went again on the fourteenth night of the black fortnight to the cemetery where he had first obtained it; and after he had entered that cemetery which was full of Rakshasas as it was of trees, besmirched with the copious smoke of the funeral pyres, and with men hanging from their trunks which were weighed down and surrounded with nooses, he did not at first see that woman that he had seen before. . . . He pulled down a corpse from the noose by which it was suspended on the tree, and he wandered about in the cemetery, crying aloud— "Human flesh for sale, buy, buy!" And immediately a woman called to him from a distance, saying "Courageous man, bring the human flesh and come along with me."

KATHASARITSAGARA OF SOMADEVA (ELEVENTH CENTURY); TRANSLATED BY C. H. TAWNEY AS *THE OCEAN OF THE STREAMS OF STORY* (1880)

Clarimonde entered, took off her clothes, and lay down next to me on the bed until she was quite certain I was asleep. Then she bared my arm; then she drew a gold pin from her hair; then she murmured to herself: "One drop, just one crimson drop—a ruby on the point of this needle. It is because you love me that I must die."

THEOPHILE GAUTIER, *LA MORTE AMOUREUSE* (1836); TRANSLATED BY MARY SHERIDAN THOMSON AS *THE IMPASSIONED LADY OF DEATH* (1900)

The post-orgasmic sense of loss, or indeed the sense of escape or explusion, seems to tie up very strongly with the preoccupations of horror, which are, very often, about the transformation of the body, which are about getting close to death but maybe avoiding it, which are about being out of control of oneself and one's feelings. Sex is about a little madness—how often is horror about madness? Sex is about a little death—how often is horror about death? It's about the body—how often is horror about the body?

CLIVE BARKER, INTERVIEW WITH DOUGLAS E. WINTER IN *FACES OF FEAR* (1990)

20 May 1991

(SEVENTH LUNAR DAY OF THE LIGHT HALF OF VAISHAKH, SAMVAT 2048; GANGA'S SEVENTH).

Before beginning the story of Sanjaya's adventures, my storyteller instinctively hesitates in order to survey his anxious crowd of overlabored, ever-tired village people, gathered tonight for a second time beneath the pipal tree, sitting before and below him, their backs to dry and fallow fields thirsting for rains and aching to give forth rice, potatoes, and onions. He has beckoned the wearied souls, wrapped in thin shawls dusty from summer gusts, to him with the ominous rat-tattoo of his drum and now, to quiet them, to ready them for delectable fears, he pipes shrill notes on the thighbone flute. He holds up the kerosene lamp as if to see them better, but it's really to display his own face—the one clear eye wide open and his smile almost demonic, the silk top hat shining and skull-earring shimmering. There are more women here tonight and a few young girls. The monkey skull, smeared with vermillion, glows by the light of the lantern, a cool lunar flush. "Now let's hear what happened to the good brahmin Govindaswami."

Brahm Kathuwala has spread his shawl out before him to display the collection of mysterious amulets, talismans of every sort, some charm for every different fearful or coveted thing: copper and silvery tubes in which there is holy crematory ash, consecrated in dark rites, other cylinders containing bits of paper or cloth torn in geometric shapes that have some arcane meaning, inscribed by a trembling hand with occult phrases and cryptic syllables in black ink, red blood, and some in dyes invisible; there are gems as well, polished stones veined, striated, flecked, and a little pile of black string, twisted twines of dread and tangled threads of longing. He has not displayed them yet; it's his custom to wait for the second evening until the musty spell of ancient tales has them intoxicated. On the first night these odd charms would make the villagers, always distrustful of strangers, dismiss him as a mere vendor of amulets; they would be on guard, watchful of their money, not so vulnerable to their imaginations, not so likely to be enchanted by the story. The tales themselves, he feels, are his amulets, verbal charms that keep sly evils away and bring uncommon blessings to the heart. They stifle *him*.

Although the heat has wilted the marigolds, they remain on the dais before the storyteller. He smiles at them, gestures casual obeisance to the black shivalingam, and gently touches the crucifix around his neck. He sets the old book and walking stick in clear view. The air is the fevered breath of an afflicted earth.

Before he begins his story he closes his eyes and listens for his enemy. No, the storyteller reassures himself, no, *he's* not here. No, it's safe—*he*'ll not come tonight.

"Okay, yes, yes, come a little closer, come now and let me tell you what happened to Govindaswami and his sons Sanjayadatta and Vijayadatta. Let's hear about his son Vijaya, the one who became a rakshasa. And let's hear about Sanjaya, the older son; let's hear about his adventures too."

The audience is already motionless. Smiling, stopping to light the last of his Charminars and take a slow, deep puff, the taleteller picks up a stone from the cloth, fingering the smooth surface as if to burnish it, then holds it close to the lamp where it glistens like some molten droplet. "With these amulets, no more fears. They banish terror. They protect the wearer from rakshasas and vetals, from prets and bhuts. I'm prepared to part with some of them, if any of you has any need, any fear at all. But we'll talk about that later. Haha! Now let's get on with our story."

Nishad sits still and wholly attentive.

Remember? Vijaya was laughing. Haha! Remember? He had

blown upon the smoldering spear to sharpen it, blazing sharp to enter flesh like a heated nail into butter, to pierce the skin here, like this, into the breast here to bring the blood in the heart to a boil. He raised the flaming stake—remember?—aimed at his father's breast, and let laughter yield screams as he summoned the strength to bring it down, to force it in, in, in and through. Haha!

Thinking it was the end, the father, good Govindaswami, closed his eyes and cried out to God: "Jay Ram! Jay Ram!" Remember! The storyteller laughs and shakes his head as if to call the man a fool: "He should have worn some amulets like these, or a ring like this one—I'd have provided him with some. Haha! Before taking the boy to the cremation grounds he could have adorned the child's delicate neck with these, an amulet like this one here—it'll keep you safe in the cemetery at any hour of the night. I could have saved that boy from

being possessed. Not me, but these amulets I have. Rakshasas, prets, bhuts, vetals, all of these fearful beings have their fears too. They can be kept away."

Nishad wants an amulet. He'll beg for it, beg his father for the money, or beg the storyteller if he stays with them again tonight. "Please stay with us," he mutters to himself as an incantation to make the man come to them again. It's a blessing to have him under their roof. That in itself will keep evil away. He leaves behind something of his fearlessness. Nishad wants to hear the story of the storyteller's childhood, wants it to go on and on, wants the story to keep the storyteller with them. Feeling his father's arm across his back, the hand on his shoulder, he leans forward; for no reason that he understands, the embrace makes him sad. Sadness is inextricably mixed with fear: he is at once afraid of his father's sadness and saddened by his fear. The scratches on his father's face make the man look rather pathetic. Where did he get them? Mitu himself cannot figure it out. He has awakened this morning with a new graze mark—added to the one across his forehead and right cheek, there is now a fine linear scab across his left cheek, reaching back to his ear. He can't remember if he has dreamed of being attacked again last night, if the demon that had scratched his face two nights ago had come, pounced once more, and clawed his face again. "What am I thinking? This scratch is really on my face. No dream will explain it. Something scratched me in the night. I didn't do it to myself—I trimmed my nails—I'm innocent. Maybe a cat or a rat crept in through the window last night. Or a monkey, even a tiger. No. Maybe some insect. It doesn't make any sense," he thinks as he lightly traces the scratches with his fingertips.

"Jay Ram!" Govindaswami cried, but it was not Ram that saved him, no, not God nor any amulet. No, it was, believe me or not, a rakshasa who interceded. He came for Vijaya. There he was. These rakshasas can take on any form, you know: dark, velvety black or luminous, leprous white, or painful crimson, or stale green, or the color of you, or you, or you (he points at Mitu); *immense monsters with tusks studding blood-red rims of dark, cavernous mouths or minute, two-legged insects with needle teeth, bristled skin, and minuscule dots of fire in their eerie eyes. They change from this to that, from a beauty that beckons to an ugliness that sickens. In the cremation grounds they are ghastly, for there, there in the city of dreadful night, the horrible is beauty. There monstrosity is perfection. And there he was: gray skin, dry, pocked and peppered with wet sores, encrusted with molds and spores, bone revealing, barely covered by filthy shreds of burned cere cloth, glassy, eyelidless eyes rolling, lips eaten away, nose disintegrated, scaly scalp issuing sparse wisps and tangles of long gray hair, fine like threads of spiders' webs, and, his body trembling with shooting laughter, the rakshasa cried out to the boy, "Come, my boy, come away, into the death that is our life."*

The voice—a moan, a whistle, a whir, a hum, a growl, no human voice—echoed through the darkness of the cremation grounds: "Ooouuuwhooaa eeeeerraaah bhiiiyaoooo . . ." It called out to Vijaya by a new name: "Come Kapalasphota! Come! You are a rakshasa now! You're my son now. Haha! Come, leave the father, this pitiful man, abandon him groveling and whimpering in the clutch of human fears, pathetic and miserable! Leave the human world, the realm of terror, behind. Come with me, come, come to the land of the rakshasas where fears are turned inside out. Come savor the sweet and terrible ecstasies of our delectable rites! Come and eat with us our soups of human blood and bile with delicious dumpling clots; come to feast on brains fresh fried in the cranial brazier or slow smoked in dark thoracic ovens; come and gnaw on human steaks and ribs grilled over smoldering cadavers, dripping sweet with fat and marrow."

It was not any human mercy that saved Govindaswami. No. Pity is not felt by rakshasas; hunger's all that moves them. The rakshasa had come to take his new son, freshly initiated into that deathlike life. Vijaya, called now by the rakshasa name "Kapalasphota," licking his chops and smacking his lips over the prospect of human viands, dropped his spear into the fire, and the ravenous flames curled, cracked, and devoured it. Laughing loud, turning to enter the darkness, he was trailed by his new, allegiant attendants: the leper hobbling, the black serpent slithering, the Skullbearer crawling on all fours and howling like a dog.

Nishad looks up at his father who, unable to concentrate on the story, has turned to look back for his wife among the other women. He must not feel jealousy, the least manly of all feelings, he reminds himself. "If she's no good, she's no good. And that's all there is to it." The child nudges his father to bring him back, points to the storyteller, forces a smile, and feels a melancholy pity for the man.

The storyteller explains that Govindaswami returned to the temple of Bhairavi to tell his wife and older son, Sanjaya, what has happened to Vijaya. He describes the father's despair and agony with such skill and grace that you'd imagine he had known just such sorrows. It's as if he's speaking of himself, and at the same time it's as if he speaks of each one of them, as if he knows their sadnesses and fears, the pain of their memories and the intractable dread clouding their infinite hopes.

Brahm speaks of the heat and of the dry winds that precede the rains, of parched mouths and sweat-wet skin, fiery nights, and scorched and blistered earth. They dab their brows with their light cotton shawls and *they dabbed their brows with light cotton shawls* the storyteller says. Words bubble in the boil and seethe of the night air of summer. In winter he would speak of shivering flesh, frosted nights, and frigid earth, and his audience would pull their thick woolen shawls tighter around their shoulders. And *they pulled their thick woolen shawls tighter around their shoulders* the storyteller would say.

Stories have a way of spreading. Tales are like diseases. You catch them. They get inside of you like parasites living on your blood. They invade the spine to gnaw their way up into the jellies of the brain. And it's hard to stop them once they've been let loose. Soon everybody in Varanasi had their version of the tale of the boy who became a rakshasa.

The storyteller tells the story of a wealthy merchant in Varanasi who, having heard the sad account of Govindaswami, and having been moved by it to pity for that righteous brahmin, his devoted wife, and their obedient son, invites them to live in his home and be sumptuously honored there. *Govindaswami served as a court priest. His eldest son, Sanjayadatta, excelled at wrestling,* Brahm Kathuwala explains: *assiduously, with all his heart, he studied the shastras of the wrestlers' art and his skill and strength increased each day, each month and year. Wearing a ring like this one, with a stone in it just like this one, he became the champion of Varanasi, the city of great wrestlers. The maharaja of Varanasi always bet on him, and, because he always won, he delighted in the young man, took the pride in him that a father takes in an accomplished son. He called Sanjaya to his court, asked him to be his bodyguard.*

Mitu the carpenter looks around for his wife. It makes him angry, and helplessly sad as well, that she isn't there. He rises, bending forward, and slouches back through the assembly, going to find her, stepping over the crouching people huddled so close together. "Get out of the way Mitu! Where are you going?" He squats down by his own father to ask if he has seen her. The old man points into the darkness. "Shhh, shhhh," people murmur and motion him to move, "Get out of the way Mitu! I can't see or hear a thing."

"What kind of wife do I have? What's she up to? She's no good! Maybe *she* scratched my face. Yes, that's it—she doesn't really care for me. Out of anger she scratched me in my sleep." But then he remembers that, when he had been awakened by the nightmare on the first night, she had been asleep. "Sleeping soundly and looking very beautiful. Oh, she is beautiful when she sleeps. That's even more terrible! She scratched me in her sleep. What was she dreaming? Was she dreaming that she was clawing at my face, trying to rip it away as if it were some mask? Or was she dreaming about someone or something else. Perhaps she doesn't hate me. Perhaps she was dreaming of some demon just as I was doing. In her dream, to protect me and save our child too, she was scratching the demon's face, trying to kill him. Only he turned out to be me! She's a good woman after all. Where is she? Where is my wife?"

When, failing to find the woman, Mitu returns, the storyteller is still talking, his arms spread wide in an illustrative gesture. He's not distracted as he watches the man refind his place by his son—he doesn't need to think to formulate the story; it comes of its own accord. It pours from him by itself, flowing with a momentum accrued over years and years of telling.

Returning home from pilgrimage one heated, murky night, the maharaja and his entourage passed a cemetery. It was as if the funeral fires had inflamed the air; it was as hot as noontime, but dark, so dark with only the most meager measure of the moon, incandescent horns, Shiva's crest, a sliver of silver barely visible through silhouetted branches that night, the stars obscured by black smoke and blacker clouds. And they dabbed their brows with light cotton shawls, held handfuls of that cloth over their mouths and noses to muffle and filter the pungent billow and stench of smoldering flesh, crackling skin, and sizzling fat. Their eyes burned with the vapors of death and their ears with the haunting hooting of owls and the harrowing howling of jackals and hyenas. Amidst the feral shrieks of beasts there were the desperate cries of human supplication from within the cremation grounds: "Help! Help! Help me!"

The maharani laughed over the excruciatingly pitiful supplications of help and, just as the slice of moon penetrated the shroud of branches, the gleam and sparkle of the gold ornament in her nose penetrated the dark diaphanous veil that draped her lovely face. Her earrings jingled as she laughed the delicate laughter of women, laughter sweet and heartless. And "Help! Help!" the man, agoniz-

ingly impaled upon the forked stake, cried with the pain of men: "Help me!"

Though they could not see him, they knew the spectacle and could envision it. The village audience can see it too. *One prong entered the man's back here, under the right shoulder blade, and it came out here, right here between the shoulder and the chest, severing the roots—those veins, arteries, tendons, and nerves that feed the arm. The other prong came out of his chest here. And between the harsh splintered tines, his heart, beating urgently, perversely pounding, refused to stop and release the body to death. And the maharani giggled once more. Her husband, riding next to her, laughed as well. "Help! " the man cried again, and others, but not the bodyguard Sanjayadatta, joined in the royal laughter.*

Why did they laugh! Were they heartless? I don't think so; we might have done the same. In those days, you must understand, *criminals were executed in the cremation grounds. To die like that was to become a bhut for sure. A ghost forever hungry. That was the punishment, not the excruciating death but the horrors to follow death, the unappeasable restlessness and wild hunger, the perpetual filthiness and gross malignity. Why would the maharaja feel any pity for a man who must have been paying for some social misconduct? "May your punishment conform to your crime," he laughed aloud and then shouted out to the tormented one: "May your affliction match your iniquity."*

"Help me!" the voice quavered with misery, and he tried to explain himself: "Yes, I'm being punished for a crime. But it's a crime I did not commit. I'm innocent. But that's not why I cry out. I accept my fate. The ears of destiny are deaf to all our supplications, reasonings, and laments. I cry out not to be saved, not for life, but for death. Why will this racked body not die? Help me. Why does this flesh still thirst? It has been three days since my impalement and still I cannot die. I thirst! I thirst and do not die. Help me. Give me something to drink, please; or if not, give me my death. Water or fire, please, the bowl or the knife, please. Mercy! Quench my thirst for drink and death."

The maharani coldly laughed again, and the maharaja

smiled: "Sanjaya, take water to the man. Quench his thirst. Help him. Ease his pain." "No, not water," the maharani interrupted, "don't take water; better yet, take wine." "Yes," the maharaja concurred, "take this honeyed wine to him that he may drink and ease his pain. Then watch over him, staying with him until he dies. And then come to me and describe his death for me, recount the very moment. Is he afraid or does he surrender? What's the look in his eyes? Does he speak? Tell me. Stay with him until you have a story. Stories of death please us no less than stories of love, especially if they're true."

Mitu can't concentrate. He's trying to tweeze the splinters from his fingertips with his teeth. His heart's pounding desperately. "Where is she? Where is that woman?" Again he rises and, crouching, pushes his way out of the crowd. "Stop moving about Mitu. Sit still! Stop all this commotion. Either stay put or go and don't come back. Make up your mind." It embarrasses Nishad and makes him fear that the others will think that his father's leaving because he is afraid of the story; it's a curse to have a ridiculous father.

Perhaps the maharaja was afraid, afraid to enter the cemetery at night, or afraid of the man, or of his death. I don't know for sure. But turning his horse, he laughed once more and said, "Let's go," and was followed by his queen and entourage, followed to his palace and followed in his laughter. Laughter, haha! Perhaps he laughed to show that he wasn't afraid—that's what some would say. But I don't know. I'm a storyteller—I know what stories are, but I don't know how to explain the things that happen in them. Do we laugh because we're not afraid or because, deep down, we are? I don't know, but I do know that the ones who turned and rode away were laughing. And I know that Sanjayadatta, dismounting, the wine jug in his steady hand, standing by himself there at the entrance to the cremation ground, was silent. He did not laugh.

The scorch of night, the fervid blast of an immense and ancient sacrifice, bellowed from the penumbral arcades of the cemetery. In the dark conflagration shadows skulked; timid dogs or prowling prets, sneaking jackals or uneasy bhuts. Branches moved: vigilant owls or vetals hanging in those trees. Smoke rose from smol-

dering pyres and flames crackled; or were those the hands of rakshasas clapping, the bones around their necks, wrists, and ankles jingle-jangling in mad nocturnal dance? Though he remembered that night when, while he slept, his brother Vijaya was, in a cemetery, transformed and taken, Sanjaya was not afraid. He didn't laugh. He took a deep breath, and the smoky air seemed to give him strength as he walked forward and into the heart of it.

The storyteller hesitates to listen once more for *him*. Just to make sure. Nothing. The Vetala Raja, Betul Rajo, isn't here, not right now, but *he's* always near. Always. *He* comes when least expected.

Still unable to locate his wife, Mitu settles for finding the bottle of toddy and, though he returns to the pipal tree, he doesn't venture back into the crowd but remains squatted down and hidden in the darkness, the bottle concealed in his cotton shawl.

A Dom woman, abandoned by her husband, covering her face in shame over her miserable existence, I suppose, scurried by him, hid somewhere in that hot and massive darkness. She's mad, some say "possessed." And though it was the middle of the night, and though eyes glowed in the gloom (animals or spirits?), there were other human beings in the cemetery that night. A monk with a shaven head, ocher-wrapped, sitting corpse-still in meditation before a fire. A skull still smoking, wrenched from the flames, was set before him as reminder of what awaits us all. They looked each other in the eyes. Somewhere there also was a thief, hiding from the law; he was terrified to be there but just as terrified by the thought of leaving his horrid sanctuary. Fear, placing its fingers on his throat, its shackles around his legs, its rancid breath upon his face, paralyzed him. Mosquitos, refusing the blood of the dead, swarmed thirsty for the living.

And there was a woman there, a beautiful woman with beautiful eyes, glistening beautifully with delicate tears. She kneeled with reverential grace at the feet of the criminal who was impaled upon the stake, the man whose cries had led Sanjaya there. He writhed violently; she softly wept and whispered. The execution site was near a pyre where the body of some family's loved one burned. Unlike the other bodies there, it was left intact—the jackals at night, the crows and vultures in the day, the dogs both day and night were kept away by the presence of that beautiful woman. Beauty is, it seems, as terrifying or repulsive to them as deformity is to you and me.

It startled Sanjaya to see her there, her hands together in a gesture of devotion, bowing to the executed man. She turned her face toward him and he saw those eyes, wide and lustrous, glimmering with tears, and in those droplets were reflections of funeral fire and the flames of what seemed to be her love. That fire too was mirrored in the sheen of her combed hair, parted with pearls, and the gloss of her perfect nails, in the burnished ornaments on her ears, nose, neck, in the bangles on her graceful arms and the exquisite rings on her delicate fingers, and in the ruby that adorned her forehead, the sectarian mark of a devotee in the cult of love. She wor-

shipped her dying husband. The firelight danced a holy dance in sparks upon the glistening red lip. She burned with an ethereal fire that shimmered in beauty, moved Sanjaya's heart, and took his breath away.

There, beneath the writhing, wailing victim of some injustice, the racked body whitened by torment, white blotched and bruised black, she spoke softly to solace him with the serenity of her voice, with tones no less than messages of consolation: "He's come. Someone strong enough to feel pity, brave enough for mercy, has come to help us, someone not afraid."

She greeted Sanjaya with poise, bowed with the equilibrium and refinement of well-bred women as she thanked and blessed him: "I have been waiting. Waiting. Waiting for my husband's death. For only when he dies can I set him on the pyre, crack the skull to free the soul, and then, then I myself can smash and scatter these bangles, discard all ornaments, mount the funeral pyre, and surrender myself to him and death. I ache for that sweet death embrace, for the ecstatic love-fed flames to devour me, every part of me, each limb, my face, this hair, these breasts, this heart, flames to enrapture me with truth and virtue, with the glory of sati, the moment when, by giving myself to death upon my husband's pyre, I deliver us, my husband and myself, his servant who worships and adores him, to tens of thousands of years of blissful union in a heaven where there is only beauty and not a trace of fear. There alone is love pure, cleansed of the fear that, here on earth, is always mingled with it, sometimes hidden, sometimes not. I long for the funeral pyre as the new bride longs for the nuptial bed. There is a union in death unknown in life, the jubilation of eternities. Let jackals gnaw our bones! Let crows pluck out our eyes and fight over our flesh! We'll but laugh, for we'll be gone. We shall, at last, be one, melted together, and whole. I am adorned now for that union. I'm decorated for the rites of love and for those of death. I'm adorned for him, the husband for whom I was born, the one whom I would follow anywhere. I'm ready."

Overwhelmed by the woman's piety, a righteousness tempered by love, passion forged into devotion, Sanjaya, praying in his heart to find such a wife some day, addressed her as Sati, woman of truth, bride of a god: "I've come with wine, an offering to him who suffers and now, also, a libation to honor the one who incarnates all the virtues of womankind. Sati, Savitri, goddess in a human form, I bow to you."

"Pass the wine," she calmly spoke. "Let me give the drink for which my beloved cries out. Let me quench his thirst as the mother does the infant with her milk, as the bride does her husband with the nectar of her kiss, as the sacred river does the embracing banks with her watery body."

The woman was not tall enough to reach her husband's mouth. Standing up, upon her toes, she stretched both arms and legs to hold the wine jug higher.

"Here," Sanjaya said as he came forward, bending over like this. The storyteller rises, takes a few steps back toward the trunk of the tree and then bends forward to imitate the posture of Sanjaya. On the first night of stories, and again tonight, up until this point, he has not stood up while telling his tale. The sudden raising up readies the audience for something frightening. They expect something unexpected. *Here,* Brahm Kathuwala says, and he comes forward, bending over like Sanjaya, and then bowing further and dropping to one knee: *"Here, crawl up on my back. Stand here, upon my shoulders. Then*

you'll be able to reach him. Feed him wine to soothe the soul in anguish, to ease him into the calm and quiet death that waits for him."

"I want to do so; I long for my beloved to take the wine from my loving hands; I ache for his solace. But it's impossible. If I were to place my foot upon your back, my flesh touching yours, in that moment, in that touch, all my virtue, like tears dropping on a scorching iron, would vanish. I would be sullied and unworthy to perform his obsequies, unqualified to give my life for him. There is no way, nothing that can be done. Sorrow abides in love."

Sanjaya smiled: "No, it can be done. All the texts agree—the moment you lay your body down upon your husband's pyre, all sins are absolved. All impurities are burned away in that lustral fire. The fire perfects all that touches it. The impurity will be momentary. If you can bear these transient moments of imperfection, then come,

crawl up upon my back, stand on my shoulders and give this man, despite his torment more fortunate because of you than any man I know, this wine to drink."

Nishad looks around for the father who is concealed in the shadows. "Where is he? Why is he doing this to me? Why can't he stay still and listen to the story? If the story is over and he's not here, the storyteller can't be invited to stay with us tonight." He curses his father for a weakness that he hopes is not in his blood.

And Mitu curses the storyteller: "Because of him, she thinks we're all distracted and taken care of, thinks that she can sneak off without anyone knowing. Damn him." And then, taking another swig from the bottle, he curses Lord Ram for allowing it. Another gulp and he curses his mother for giving birth to him and his daughter for being born—the dowry he has had to pay last year to get someone to take the young girl away has put him into debt. "Mothers, wives, sisters, daughters—they bring misery into the world." He closes his eyes and listens once more to the storyteller. He tilts the bottle into his hand and then applies some of the liquor as a disinfectant to the scratches on his face. It stings; but the pain feels as if it's doing some good.

The woman hesitated, closed her eyes, took a deep breath, listened to the cries of her husband, mere whimpers now, like the delicate mewing of an infant newborn and thirsting, and she smiled the smile of resignation: "I would bear all sins, all punishments for those sins, for my husband. If the act would deliver him or be for his glory, I would be a whore in hell, would clean the hovels of dogs and chandalas, would give myself to lepers. Love and devotion have eclipsed the fear and disgust innate in the human heart."

As she approached Sanjaya, he bent over more, down on his knees like this; and then he stood, holding her on his shoulders like this, with his hands on her ankles to balance her, then moving closer, like this, standing next to the stake upon which the sobbing man was impaled. He closed his eyes. The storyteller steps back toward the dark trunk of the pipal tree. Eerily its leaves seem to slightly tremble. *Her ankles were so delicate in his hands. Their warmth seemed some function of the love this woman so perfectly embodied. Sanjaya breathed and felt a slight sigh. The admiration he felt in his heart for this beautiful woman, his love for her devotion, for her capacity to love, inspired a desire to protect her. He vowed that he would place offerings of flowers and sweet rice at the spot of her immolation. He would install a Sati-stone. He would worship her as long as he lived.*

The impaled man moaned, and Sanjaya bowed his head in sadness for the man whose groans of relief sounded as pained as the sobs of his agony. The wife sighed with love, muffled but passionate moan blending with his. They groaned together and their breath, full and heavy, deep and sad, was in harmony. It grew more ardent.

Sanjaya saw the red droplets on the ground, spilled no doubt, he thought, from lips contorted in pain and desperation, dripping no doubt down the man's naked legs to form rivulets between his toes. Drip, drip, drip. Red drops fell upon the charred black dirt of the cemetery. Drip, drip, drop; a drop fell on Sanjaya's arm. He looked at it. Wine? He raised his forearm to his mouth to lick it.

Blood! the storyteller screams, and the audience jumps, gasps, then falls still and silent at once so as not to lose the line. They're sweating from the heat of the summer night. *Blood! Sanjaya raised up the eyes that had been averted to give lover and beloved the privacy they deserved. He saw it. The wine jug dropped, cracked open, and the wine seeped into the earth. A great gulp of blood blurted and gushed from the man's mouth, streamed through the ripped lips, and the woman sucked it from his chin. Letting out a hideous howl, at once shriek and laugh, yelp and hiss, she flashed her razor teeth, then dug them in again, chewed at the bleeding cheek, gnawed at the nose, gorged out the eye with her finger and sucked it down.*

As Sanjaya jumped back in terror, his knees gave way. Lying stunned in the dirt, his mouth gaping with fright, he saw her clinging to the writhing form upon the stake: one leg, naked, bloodstained, wrapped around his waist; one arm, naked, bloodstained, wrapped around the bruised neck into which her fingernail dug for the vein. She pulled the pulsing vessel through the skin, and it spewed a spray of blood, writhed like a maddened serpent wrenched from its lair and vomiting crimson poisons. Her bellowing laughter fanned the flames that burned in the furnaces of her eyes. She forced the serpent's head into her fuming mouth, sucked on it, swilled the blood from the man's heart, sucked harder and harder, chewed on that vein, and sucked, and her shoulders began to quiver, to surge, her loins, wrapped around him pushed against him, back and forth, up and down, sucking, faster and faster, her whole body convulsing with the succulent ecstasy of it, bangles and anklets ringing, clattering, screeching with the frenzy of her undulous pounding, thrusting, gulping. She sucked, chewed, pushed, pushed, groaned, threw her head back, screamed and shook faster, faster still.

The standing storyteller, eyes closed tight, arms open wide, fingers spread, seems to tremble, to feel the fear he describes. He moans, and Mitu, standing in the back of the crowd, has a lump in his throat. He's sweating and drunk and there are tears clinging to the stubble on his cheeks. When he rubs those tears away with the border of his shawl, the scab lines on his cheeks are scratched and start to bleed. He looks at the fresh, bright blood on the shawl and the sight of it makes him sadder still.

Sanjaya raised himself to his knees, leaped forward, grabbed the one leg of the witch that hung down, pulled upon it, tugged with all his strength, pulled, pulled, wrenched her from her victim's body, now eviscerated, now not screaming, not breathing, but still exuding blood. Now it did not pulse out or spray—it slowly oozed and dripped. The witch struggled in the wrestler's grasp—the blood that bathed her body made it difficult to hold tight. She laughed loudly, a piercing shrill and horrible laughter as she slipped her wet leg from his grip. He fell back, rolled, looked up and saw that she was gone.

Silence. Just the crackling of the pyres. The only movement was the flicker of flames. The body hung limp and slack on the stake. Silence. Death. The storyteller falls quiet for a moment. His mouth opens and he speaks the silence, makes it palpable, makes his silence the vast silence of cemeteries.

Sanjaya raised his arm to bring his blood-stained hand in front of his face. Clots began to form on the trembling fingers that held the anklet, still clasped, still sparkling, the polished gold and perfect diamonds not holding blood on their surfaces. In each diamond there was cold fire and horror.

Silence. *Silence.* Brahm Kathuwala sustains it for a moment, keeping his eyes closed. The village audience is dead still. Then the storyteller opens his eyes and smiles. He sits down, crosses his legs, and continues with soft, modulated, and strangely comforting solemnity. He tells them how Sanjaya has returned to his patron and, recounting the eerie tale of the witch to the maharaja, has given the splendid anklet to him. Brahm Kathuwala explains to them that the maharaja presented it to his wife who was so dazzled by it that she beseeched him to procure a matching one for her.

"You must find the other anklet," the maharaja ordered and, to fulfill his duty to his royal patron, Sanjayadatta, fearless as only the virtuous can be, returned to the cemetery on amavasya, the fourteenth night of the black fortnight. Brahm Kathuwala looks up, through the dark fanned edges of the pipal tree, his eyes searching for the waning moon. There are those among his audience who have felt uneasiness aroused by the dreadful approach of that dangerous night. And as the storyteller speaks they can see what he is describing: the cemetery, the black rotting tree draped with the decomposing corpse of a man executed for some horrid crime, the dance of shadows. The wrestler takes the body from the tree and carries it in his arms. The hoot of a village owl enters the story to join the taleteller in the telling.

"Human flesh for sale!" They can hear the grim proclamation

forged by the storyteller, the loud voice of Sanjayadatta as he walked boldly through the cemetery with the corpse slung over his shoulder: *"Human flesh for sale! Human flesh for sale! Juicy, fat, the bones still full of marrow. Delicious, delectable, fresh flesh for you."*

The storyteller stops, scratches his chin, smiles: "I'm getting hungry myself. Who's going to feed me tonight? And where am I going to sleep?" He taunts his audience with the interruption. "Get on with the story," the old goatherd, as if speaking for them all, snaps impatiently and Brahm laughs to flaunt a detachment from his story. It's a trick of his, a way to make it seem to each listener that he's telling the story for their sake, that he doesn't really want to tell the story, but that he's complying with some wish or need of theirs; that indebts them.

"So, who's going to feed me tonight? And where am I going to sleep? Mitu are your here? Mitu? Where are you Mitu?"

Utterly embarrassed, Nishad can't turn around to look at his father who, in self-conscious pain and drunkenness, waves from the back of the crowd to moan: "Here. I'm here. Yes, I'm here."

"Do I stay with you again tonight? But what's for dinner. Those makhuni last night were so bone dry I almost choked to death. So much for Bihari food!" The audience laughs at Mitu, and he slumps down into a squat waving his hand as if to say, "Don't look at me. Don't look at the scratches on my face. Don't look at the sadness there."

"Tonight I'd like some meat. Some flesh. A bit of mutton on the bone, the bone still full of marrow, the meat juicy and fresh cooked." He lapses into the slightly deeper voice he uses for the rakshasa, *"Delicious, delectable. Haha!"*

"Get on with the story," the old man barks, and the storyteller again laughs. "That's easy for you to ask, but what about my supper. Mitu's a poor man, he can't afford the goat." Nishad's humiliation swells, and the old man himself promises the storyteller a leg of mutton: "But get on with the story."

"Give that flesh to me," a hideous rakshasa, dropping from a tree before Sanjaya, groaned. "Feed me flesh," he drooled, his yellow eyes wide, dripping tears of pus, his nostrils contracting and expanding as if chewing on the odors of that rotting human meat.

He would have snatched it from a weaker man, but the fearlessness of Sanjaya, his arms and neck adorned with amulets just like these, was a fearful thing.

"Let's discuss the price. Bodies don't come cheap now. In the good old days every cremation ground had plenty of executed criminals. But now too many people are obeying the law. It's hard to find an unburned corpse, freshly putrefying. This will cost you."

"What's the price?" the cautious rakshasa asked.

"An ornament to match this one," Sanjaya, holding up the glistening anklet, smiled.

The rakshasa brayed with laughter: "My daughter has one just like it! " And the bargaining began: an anklet like that, diamonds and gold, for the body of a mere human being? No, no, the price is too high; but, on the other hand, a rakshasa can't let flesh pass by. Something else thrown in. Make it an even trade. The rakshasa's proposal: "You take my daughter as your bride. The dowry is that anklet. The body over your shoulder will be food for the wedding guests."

"No, now you've tilted the scale in your favor," Sanjaya smiled. "I'll need something more. So, what else do you have?"

Like a human merchant, the hungry rakshasa pleaded poverty. "I have nothing but my daughter and my son, Kapalasphota, my dear adopted son, a brahmin rakshasa."

Sanjayadatta closed the negotiations: "The boy must be added to the dowry. I'll have your son as my servant, your daughter as my wife, and her anklet as my prize."

The storyteller stretches out the description of the marriage feast of the rakshasas—they dance around the fire, laughing and lewdly cavorting. The cobra from the previous night's story has joined a swarm of serpents to hang like decorations from the tree branch that forms the ceiling of the marriage hall. Brahm Kathuwala makes it an evening's entertainment, as lengthy as the films that entertain the city dwellers. That's the joy of summer tales. In winter they have to be shorter since the audience can't bear to stay too long outside in the cold. But winter has its own advantages for horror: the storyteller can transform the inevitable bonfire into a prop, the cremation pyre, the cooking pit of the rakshasas; the village itself becomes the set, the haunted cemetery.

Over those flames, kebabs of human flesh are roasted. Maggots are the rice of their biryanis tossed with human tongues and eyes, succulent knuckles and chewy noses, grisly gizzards and juicy giblets. Their chapatis, made from a flour of ground up bones, are dipped in raitas that they, the rakshasas themselves, have vomited up after gorging themselves on halvas sweet with thick white spinal milk. No animal flesh is served for such a special feast. Just human meat—flanksteaks and tenderloins marinated in bile and spit, human briskets and brains, tripes, trotters, and lots of ribs, delicious meat of man minced for keemas, samosas stuffed with human liver and kidneys. There are chutneys made of pickled glands. They suck on the gristle and guzzle fermented urine. When any of it drips down their bristled chins, others lick it off, lap it up, belching heady fumes; and if one vomits they fight for the spoils. Or they sneak off into the darkness, stick a greenish, bony, finger down their own swollen throats to bring up from their guts what they've eaten so that they can consume it once again, and again, and again, until there's nothing left to vomit up. These wedding feasts have special treats, of course—human milk taken from the disgorged guts of a dead infant. The bride gets the baby for herself—it's roasted whole to honor her.

What about the intestines? They're not consumed—no, they've saved for decoration, garlands for the bride and groom, and for the honored guests. The rakshasis braid them into their hair—blood provides them with their rouge, and the char of human bone is mascara for their eyes. The genitals of the male corpses are just for the females—they eat the testicles and use the penis as a straw to suck down the draughts of blood that are served up to them in skulls.

The audience laughs just as Brahm Kathuwala expects them to do, and they laugh again over his discursus on aphrodisiacs, his explanation that the males eat the female parts for arousal. "That's how the rakshasa keeps his manhood. Human beings need amulets for that. And so, for example, this amulet, containing as it does a uterine-shaped stone, cures impotence in us." After rattling the amulet so they hear the magic stone within, he sets it down with the other charms he'll sell.

In winter the dancing of the shadows, cast by firelight against the seated audience, becomes the wild wedding dance of rakshasas and rakshasis; at this time of year, just before the rains, in this part of the tale, the storyteller plays upon its being the marriage season; just as what is seen during the day can be turned by the mind in sleep into some nightmare, so what they encounter each day around them, spectacles of nuptial joy, are transformed into spectral festivities by the weaver of nocturnal tales.

Sanjaya recognized the bride, the rakshasi with whom he had wrestled in the cremation ground, and he saw the single anklet that she wore. Her smile oozed with blood-laced spit, her glance was phosphorescent—she recognized him as well and was eager to take him in her arms, to clutch and pull him into her, and scorch him with desire.

The storyteller evokes the music of the wedding feast with his hourglass drum, with his flute, with words of rattling bones, terrible cacophonies and murmurous monodies, the howls of choruses ecstatic. He thumps the earth with his hand, makes strange sounds with his mouth, then gives them a silence they themselves can fill with frightful sounds rummaged from their memories.

The bride began to dance for her prospective groom. . . .

Unable to endure it any longer, Mitu rises, hesitates to seek some balance, then, dizzy, nauseated, and deeply sad, he staggers, stumbles, and wends his way toward the house he has built for his family. He wants his wife, wants to hold her and be held by her. It's strange perhaps that he loves her the most after her escapades. "She's not really cruel. She didn't scratch me. Or, if she did, she didn't mean to do it. The madness makes her seem cruel, her frailty makes a rakshasi of her. Just like drunkenness makes me angry and I think things that I don't really think, well, it's the same with her. But her heart is good and I know that she's devoted to me, that she doesn't want to do what she does. She becomes possessed, that's all." After these disasters, when she'd disappear only to come back disheveled, crying, insisting that she'd been raped by a stranger, he would weep with her. They'd both be drunk. He'd forgive her, hold her in his arms, apologize for being angry with her and for scolding her when she neglected her chores and duties. With all his heart he promises to make life better for her and their Nishad.

The child doesn't see his father leave: drawn into the story world, he attends the wedding, watches the feast from the grim depths of the story forest, observes the ceremonial presentation of the dowry: first the anklet and then the promised servant are given to Sanjaya. He sees the hero's face register recognition as he greets his bride's brother, Kapalasphota, the brother that was once his own—Vijayadatta.

He took an amulet, just like this one, strung on a string like this, and, under the pretense that it was an ornament, a gift for the new brother-in-law, he tied the string around the rakshasa's neck. Kapalasphota trembled. The amulet began to work. And then, through the energy of this amulet, released and enhanced through the power of fraternal love, eclipsed but still present in the heart of Vijayadatta, the young man recognized the courageous Sanjayadatta. Tears doused the fire in his eyes. The smoke made him gasp. He caught his breath, breathed again, breathed and he was free. Yes, these amulets have been prepared just for such things—to free those who've been possessed. Still, despite the power of the ojha who blessed them, they cannot work except on one in whose heart some devotion has been instilled and still remains. The amulets merely activate that devotion.

"Now to the bridal chamber," Sanjaya cried out with an anxiousness that the rakshasas mistook for lust, and when they, having formed their procession, still howling, drooling, jumping up and down, began to march, following the bride, into the darkness, toward a hut that had been built of human bones, Sanjaya signaled his brother— "Run! Run with me!"

Nishad claps his hands with excitement over the escape from the rakshasas, smiles at the imagined vision of their return to the palace of the king. It's just like in the films that he has seen when the videovan has come to the village.

Sanjayadatta and Vijayadatta were greeted by their father, tears of gratitude in his eyes, and by their king, smiling over the anklet for his wife. The king celebrated their return with a magnificent feast—chicken and mutton, biryanis and chapatis, even Chinese food and Continental food, the storyteller laughs, *and whiskey too, imported Scotch whiskey, everything, and speaking of food, I'm hungry, famished, starving to death, in fact. So let me stop my story here. I wish that was the end of it, but, I must be honest with you, it's not. Such happy endings are not typical of life in this world, I'm sorry to say. Unfortunately, that king, Sanjaya's patron, became very ill the very next day. Chills and fever, malaria I suppose. And the only way to save him was by performing a magic rite in the cemetery. And for that a corpse had to be found and used to heal the king. Ah, but that's another story, a terrible, horrible story. And it's a long one too. And it's late now, and I'm hungry, and I'm headed for Varanasi tomorrow.*

Of course they invite him to stay, to tell that story the following
night, and as he rises (saying, "Oh, I suppose I can stay one more night, but I'm hungry right now and must go to Mitu's. Bring my mutton, old man"), pretending that he has forgotten to offer the amulets up for sale, they protest: "Wait—what about those charms and amulets?" Again detachment, as all the ancient sages have insisted, is the secret of success in kama, artha, and dharma, in love and art, in business and commerce, and in religion—in both life and death.

"In this other story," the schoolmaster asks, "is Sanjay there? And Vijay—what happens to him?"

"Of course," Brahm laughs, "they are there. Sanjaya has just begun to be a hero. And Vijaya will be fine, just as the Skullbearer foretold."

When, after selling the talismans and amulets that would keep prets and bhuts and rakshasas away, he arrives at Mitu's little house, the poor drunkard is alone, lying on the floor, breathing as if asleep, but with open eyes. The carpenter sits up suddenly and slaps his hand on the ground. "Why did you say I can't afford a goat? Damn you, Mr. Storyteller! What do you know of my story? What do you know of my family?"

The storyteller sits next to him on the floor, puts his hand on his knee affectionately, and laughs: "Joke, my friend. Little joke."

Mitu says nothing.

"What happened to your face," the storyteller asks. "How did you get those scratches?"

"Why is that your business?" Mitu growls.

"It's not," Brahm Kathuwala answers with a reassuring smile.

"I got them in a dream, a bad dream," the carpenter grumbles. "A rakshasa like the one in your story came into my dream. He did this to me with his claws."

The storyteller laughs more softly, gently now: "I'd imagine that you were looking for your wife. You were crawling around in some bushes trying to find her and the brambles scratched your face."

"Damn you," Mitu shouts. "You know nothing about me or about my wife. Don't you think a rakshasa could do this in a dream. You're the storyteller—don't you believe that the same things happen in life that happen in your stories?"

"Listen," the storyteller whispers, hesitating, closing his eyes and then opening them again to smile almost sadly. "Listen, I understand the problem. Don't think I haven't had my own share of woman troubles. Don't be ashamed. Any man who is truly a man has had plenty of woman problems. This has always been the case. Let me tell you a very old story. Believe it or not I heard it from a marvelous parrot, the parrot that had once belonged to Govindaswami. Oh, but the story of that parrot—that's another story. This story, you'll understand. Listen: *Once upon a time there was a good man, a merchant in fact but he could have been a brahmin or a farmer or a servant or a carpenter like you, or a wandering storyteller like me—woman problems ignore all caste distinctions. He married a wanton woman, a certain Malati, and no sooner had they married than she began to sneak out of his house, to go into the forest outside the city gates at midnight*—(the storyteller looks at one of his watches and then the other) "it's just about midnight now"—*and there she would meet her lover. And you know, of course, exactly what they did. This hadn't been going on very long, however, when one night Sanjayadatta—yes, the same Sanjaya of whom I spoke tonight—spotted the man, Malati's young lover, a man no different than the husband, no different than you or me, a man not wicked in any way but as susceptible as any man to the charms of women. Sanjaya naturally assumed he was a thief, and the man, not wanting to bring shame upon his beloved, did not deny it. "Yes," he lied, "It's true. I'm a thief." Love makes men noble. Now, the treasury house of our king, yes, the same king of whom I'll speak tomorrow night, had recently been robbed and, infuriated by the audacity of the thief, he had ordered Sanjaya to find the criminal and kill him. And so the man was dutifully hanged by Sanjaya on the spot. Love makes men noble with a nobility that is foolish, that is deadly. Poor fellow.* And despite himself, despite his hatred for the adulterer, Mitu, against his will and his sense of right and wrong, feels pity for the hapless man. *Our beautiful Malati, unaware of what had befallen her lover, wrapped in a dark shawl, her bracelets and anklets silenced with black bandannas, slipped from her husband's house, made her way through the darkness. It was almost midnight.* The storyteller looks once more at the watch on each wrist. *At the very place where she thought he would embrace her, she found him hanging lifeless from a tree.* Mitu has tears in his eyes. He feels pity for the woman too. *She wanted to scream, to cry out with anguish, to wail for the dead, but, to muffle the sorrow, she folded the black edge of her shawl over her gasping mouth. Her lover's eyes bulged open. The lips were icy blue. The sadness of passion is greater, I believe, than the sadness born of devotion. Overwhelmed with it, she lowered her lover from that tree, untied the knot around his neck with the trembling fingers that had been anxious to unknot the cords of their garments. She took her lover in her arms, caressed him, weeping with a desire to feel the heat of that body as she held the lifeless head in her hands, raised the frozen face, lowered her own, and closed her eyes to kiss him.* When the storyteller suddenly yells, Mitu jumps, feels his heart in his throat, and listens in horror to the description of the corpse, animated by a vetal, opening its mouth and biting off the faithless woman's nose. The storyteller laughs as he makes Mitu sit back down: *Do you know what that woman did? Can you believe it? To explain her missing nose, she took her husband to the courts, claimed he had mutilated her for no reason, and demanded justice, insisted that her husband be executed for the crime and that she retain all of his worldly goods.*

And, believe me, that would certainly have happened if it had not been for the actual thief, the one that had actually robbed the king's treasury. Hiding from the king's guards in the forest outside the city gates that night, he had seen the whole thing. He appeared at the court and suggested that the king look in the mouth of the corpse of the man that had been executed for robbery. Sanjaya fetched the corpse and pried open the clenched jaws. There it was—the woman's nose! Haha! They cut off her tongue for lying.

"The poor woman," Mitu sighs. "Not to mention the poor husband. And poor Sanjay having to live with killing an innocent man, a poor man. Poor everyone, except the thief!"

"No, I'm afraid the thief was also executed," the storyteller continued: *The king, bowing reverently before the beheading, spoke respectfully to the condemned thief: "May you be rewarded in your next life for bringing justice to my kingdom; and may this exemplary execution, required by the sacred law that protects the royal coffers, deliver you from this life into that one more fortunate."*

The storyteller produces the two amulets: "One for you and one for your wife. Tie yours around your left arm and have her tie hers around her right arm. As long as you are both wearing the amulets she will be faithful to you. Don't be a fool and tell her what they do. Tell her it will make her breasts firm. Then she will wear it constantly."

"I don't like this story at all," Mitu, sitting up straight, announces. "No! What's the meaning of it? What is the idea you are trying to tell me? What is the point of this story?"

"There's no point or idea here," Brahm smiles. "I have no use for ideas. I only have stories. Ideas tear people apart; stories bring people together."

"Still, I don't like this story at all," Mitu, slumping, sighs. "And why are you telling it to me? My wife is not like that woman! My wife is a good woman. We don't need your sex amulets. We are happy with each other. Give me an amulet to cure nightmares. Give me an amulet so I won't get my face scratched in my sleep any more. I could tell you that story, the story of the rakshasa who attacks me in my sleep. Since you like stories so much, I could tell you lots of stories. I know terrible stories, but I know happy ones too. I'll tell you the story of my wife, the story of a devoted woman, devoted to her father, devoted to her husband, devoted to her son, devoted to god, devoted, devoted. . . ."

His story is interrupted by the arrival of Nishad, accompanied by the old man with the roasted goat leg for the storyteller. "How did you get those scratches on your face Mitu?" the goatherd asks. But Mitu answers by telling him to hand over the meat. In this season, just before the rains, the marriage season, the old man has plenty of goats slaughtered, bled, hung, and ready to be sold for the nuptial feasts.

Leaning forward to have a closer look at the storyteller, the old man remembers him, remembers that he's come to the village at various times during the past. He can see a young man, wearing the same hat and amulets, carrying the same book and stick. "Was he with a woman? Yes, I think he was followed by a woman." He remembers buying a ring that did not bring him luck and he remembers his wife scolding him for making the purchase. He remembers what was once a bright fire in the storyteller's eyes.

"This goat I used to call Khataka," he says of the roasted meat. "You are eating an excellent goat, always friendly to the other goats, always cooperative with me. . . ." His voice trails off and he turns mumbling to himself: "Nobody is interested in stories about my goats. Nobody!"

He leaves, still muttering something or other that does not even make sense to himself as he hurries home to listen to All-India Radio, to the nightly news, to hear stories of all India, epic narratives of order and chaos, virtue and vice, hope and horror, ancient tales continuing to unfold.

In the house of the Lingayat, the storyteller's story is being interpreted: "Sanjaya is Sanjay Gandhi."

"No, no," the Lingayat corrects his son: "No. Sanjaya is Rajiv Gandhi. Vijaya is Sanjay. Govindaswami is Nehru, if not Mahatma Gandhi."

The young man shakes his head: "Then why didn't the storyteller simply call Vijaya 'Sanjay?'"

The wise father smiles: "Storytellers like to mix things up. A good story should not be too easy to figure out. The pleasure's in the decipherment."

Watching the storyteller eat, Nishad hopes that he might get both an amulet from him and a continuation of the story of his childhood, maybe even a telling of the adventures in that *Dkakula* book. Brahm pulls the flesh from the bone and chews it, smiling happily, wiping the greasy juices from his lips with his fingers, then tearing off a piece of the chapati that Mitu has supplied, that Nishad's mother has cooked that afternoon, he lets the bread soak up the taste of the goat from those fingers and then follow the meat. The storyteller bites into the bread with lips curling back, then tugging, ripping it, pulling off a piece, then wrapping his lips around what remains in his teeth, chewing slowly. Then he takes a gulp of water and Mitu refills the metal tumbler from the clay pot of well water. "I suppose all the toddy's gone," the storyteller smiles, and Mitu shakes his head ambiguously as he changes the subject: "Why did you say I can't afford a goat? What do you know about me? What gives you the right to make up a story about me? I can afford a goat—I can afford even a damn herd of goats. But why squander money in such a backward way? I'm saving my money for a scooter. A scooter is freedom. It is happiness. I'm saving my money for freedom and happiness, for a beautiful Bajaj, Hamara Bajaj, vehicle of the future. Nishti, get the photograph."

The boy fetches the page of a magazine, an advertisement photograph that is a story in Mitu's heart: *Once upon a time there was a very happy man who owned a Bajaj motor scooter; he drove that scooter everywhere; his devoted wife sat behind him on it, her arms around his waist; his obedient son sat behind her, facing backward, waving to his many admiring, though envious, friends. The three of them were happy, and the motor scooter got many miles to the liter.* "We'll ride to Varanasi, we'll ride to Lucknow; we'll ride to Delhi for Republic Day. And when it's hot like this, we'll ride up to Almora or Simla and enjoy the cool air and beautiful surroundings."

The storyteller sucks the marrow from the broken bones. By the time he's finished and lit a cigarette, Nishad has curled up on the floor and fallen asleep. His mother still hasn't come home. His father, as he starts to clean up from the meal, asks Brahm Kathuwala if he's married.

"I was married, a long time ago," the storyteller says, "but that's another story."

"A love story, I presume," Mitu, still drunk, beams. "I am a man in love with love, though I may not seem so to you. Love is the greatest thing. That is my philosophy, though you may find it strange to hear a village carpenter express such ideas and feelings. Though I do not read, I know stories and my favorite ones are love stories. Radha-Krishna, Sita-Ram, and like that. But Raj Kapoor is my guru in this matter. He lives on in his love stories and in my heart. It has been his films, shown in our village by the videowala every so often—the videovan comes once a month in fact—yes, it has been the beautiful love stories of Raj Kapoor that have inspired me, that have taught me, a humble carpenter, how to dream great dreams. Who can forget Dimple in *Bobby* or Mandakini in *Ram Teri Ganga Maili?* Who cannot have been thrilled with love? Have you seen *Satyam Shivam Sundaram?* Excellent film with a beautiful story and a beautiful philosophy. How did the great Kapoor get the ideas for his stories? Who else but a genius could have come up with the idea of a love story in which the hero never properly sees the face of his beloved? We the audience know the face of the star, the beautiful Zeenat Aman, is beautiful; we have dreamed of that beautiful visage, that voluptuous body, that goddess-like mien. But her lover remains in the dark. And, this is the great part, the beautiful goddess plays the part of woman whose face has been badly scarred. What horror! But I think it is a beautiful allegory about love. It shows us that it is the inner beauty that is the most important thing. I, although I'm a grown man, wept over that love story! Can you believe it!"

The storyteller confesses that he does not enjoy movies: "They leave nothing to the imagination. And it's there, in the imagination, where the real passion and horror, the real beauty and greater virtue, reside."

"No, no." Mitu laughs. "Raj Kapoor has inflamed my imagination and brought it to life and me with it! He is the greatest of all storytellers, the Valmiki of the modern world. Sometimes I imagine talking to Zeenat personally, telling her my problems, obtaining advice from her about my wife. Do you tell love stories?" the carpenter asks. "Real love stories, beautiful stories, not like that terrible Malati story."

"I used to tell the story of a different Malati and of her beloved Madhava who ventured into the cremation ground to sell human flesh that he might have her for his wife. I tell the story of Hidimba, the rakshasi, hideous devourer of human flesh, who, upon seeing the great Bhima, transformed herself into a beautiful woman and fell in love with the mighty hero and suffered with great love for him."

"This is a Raj Kapoor film?" Mitu asks in earnest.

"No," the storyteller says. "This is *Mahabharata*."

Mitu yawns and goes to bed but can't sleep without his wife there. His guts are churned with terrible jealousies; he fears that she's with Moti: "He's a rakshasa alright. He's a thief and maybe a murderer; he himself boasts that he's killed someone. He crows of his friendship with dacoits. But he's a damn liar too, a storyteller in his own right and way; so who's to know what he's done and hasn't done? And what's he doing right now?" The carpenter tosses about on his bed in anguish, trying to push the images of his wife and Moti out of his mind, struggling to replace them with images of Zeenat Aman and himself. Barefoot, the bells of her anklets jingling his name, her gait is dance as she skips toward him singing, head thrown back in laughter, her silk scarf, diaphanous veil over the splendid full moon breasts, waving in the springtime mountain breeze behind her as she comes, closer, closer, her luscious mouth all gaiety and voluptuous song, her dark lashes waving like the wings of joyous birds hurrying to their mates, and the golden soft-focus glow of her flesh illuminates the vision in which Mitu longs to drown himself. He aches to die and does not know why.

Brahm Kathuwala, reclining on the charpoy outside, can hear the pitiful weeping of the carpenter who believes that "love is the greatest thing." The storyteller closes his eyes and whispers to the darkness: "Love is the terrible, thirsty vampire, its revenge just begun, its anguish spread over centuries, with time on its side making us do its bidding and be its jackals when it wants to feed. You know it too, don't you, Mitu? You know that Raj Kapoor has lied to you."

Nishad rolls over, moaning in his sleep.

The storyteller senses the presence of ghosts there in the darkness: is it his mother, Kalyani, sweeping in death as in life, softly singing the song, *"milk from a magic cow, sweet rice pudding from the kitchen of a king, and a golden child?"* Is it Mena, loving in death as in life, remembering without forgiveness? Or is it the carpenter's wife sneaking home? Kalyani, Mena, or the mother of Nishad—she's under *his* power and the storyteller can hear *his* hideously muffled laughter (or is it Moti's obscene snickering?). He hears proclamations in what is silence to the ears of the carpenter: *"Your girls that you all love are mine already; and through them you and others shall yet be mine."*

"Love the Impaler," Brahm Kathuwala says aloud. "Love the Ripper. Spring Heel Love."

The moonlight fails as a black cloud, the first herald of the imminent rainy season, sails across the sky. The storyteller can hear the voice of a woman reading, can hear each word of it: *On the bed beside the window lay Jonathan Harker, his face flushed and breathing heavily as though in a stupor. Kneeling on the near edge of the bed facing outward was the white-clad figure of his wife.* Mina, Mena. *By her side stood a tall, thin man, clad in black. With his left hand he held both Mrs. Harker's hands, keeping them away with her arms at full tension; his right hand gripped her by the back of the neck, forcing her face down on his bosom. Her white nightdress was smeared with blood, and a thin stream trickled down the man's bare breast which was shown by his torn-open dress. The attitude of the two had a terrible resemblance to a child forcing a kitten's nose into a saucer of milk to compel it to drink.*

"Mina," the storyteller whispers. "Mena!"

5

The lady, moans flowing from her throat,
laughing for no reason,
her hair undone,
Wounding with her teeth and nails,
made impudent
by draughts of wine,
Her neck bearing wanton bruises—
having seen the sight of her at night,
how can men not but be
afraid?
For the girl is like a demonness, a pishachi,
drunk on the mead of the bone marrow
and human fat that she has
consumed.

ATTRIBUTED TO BHASKARAVARMAN, (*SUKTIMUKTAVALI* OF JALHANA (THIRTEENTH CENTURY); TRANSLATED BY GODFREY SANDERS (1913)

Gradually her mind gave way. Bare-headed, bare-bodied, with a little hatchet in her hand, she would sit in desolate places. She abandoned her hut and was seen wandering around the ruins in a cremation ghat along the river—dishevelled, red-eyed, grimacing crazily, her arms and legs emaciated. When they saw her like this people were frightened. . . . Women were frightened when they heard her howling voice in the stillness of the night. But more terrible than her words was her wild laughter.

PREMCHAND, *GARIB KI HAY* (1911); TRANSLATED BY DAVID RUIN AS "THE POWER OF A CURSE" IN *DELIVERANCE AND OTHER STORIES* (1969)

It must have lasted many days; it was a strong stench that awakened me. I sat up and looked at Naani; nothing had changed in the tableau of rape: the parted lips and thighs, the palms resting on the breasts. I touched her thighs, the flesh had begun to rot, and as I took my hand away, I heard an eerie laugh like the cackle of a woodpecker. I was alone with a corpse and its mortuary odour. The unseen woodpecker laughed again. Fear gave me the energy to rise and move; I went to the mirror. . . .

O. V. VIJAYAN, "THE WART"; TRANSLATED BY THE AUTHOR IN *THE PENGUIN BOOK OF MODERN INDIAN SHORT STORIES* (1989)

10 August 1947

(AMAVASYA: DARKEST NIGHT OF SHRAVAN, THE RAINY SEASON, SAMVAT 1890).

As the storyteller walked not without fear through the cantonment along the road by which he had left his childhood behind, his heart ached with stories, was engorged and bursting with the exuberant pain of tales. Embedded in each of crores of untold stories, lakhs more were germinating: there would be a burst of tales, an eruption of memories, an explosion of words and sentiment—fragmented images and phantasmal characters would be scattered in the chaos of the night. He would collect and assemble them in the morning, put stories together to be carried from town to town, village to village, and traded for food and places to rest. Because times were bad the sales of charms and amulets would be good.

The clouds had been frugal; a petulant monsoon passed too soon, leaving heavy mud and bitter grime behind. Nature had no rhythm nor order other than that which was desperately imagined or greedily hoped for. Expectations had created a world that brutally betrayed its inhabitants, and earth moaned under infinite burdens. There were murmurs of remorse, rancor, and dread, a mysterious, unidentifiable whimpering in the distance, feminine and hopeless; masculine, nasty detonations incessantly intruded—gunshot and shout, gunfire and furor, shrill and terrible.

Creaking and heaving, the earth, Prithvi, was possessed, and Lord Vishnu seemed to have turned his back on her—all gods were heartless that night, that season and year. Brahmins chanted exorcistic incantations in the face of a feral demonic spirit. Desperate pujas were made, urgently pious vratas performed.

Acrimonious and convulsive northbound clouds strained to rain, grunted with the burden of dirty waters, twisted and turned contortions in what could not be called the heavens. With a spasmodic movement across the stars, cramped postures, raucous moans, flush and delirious, the clouds would suddenly belch, vomit, and spew a bilious rain. Then it would stop. Then again, more like billows of black smoke than clouds, all full of contagion, the sudden-lightning-pierced shapeless shapes were eviscerated, disengorged to spill sparse rancid rains. Then it would stop again. Then sudden thunder was the scream of Tataka, lightning the arrow, her scabrous black skin the pierced envelope of cloud, her blood the fitful storm. Then it would stop once more. It was difficult to distinguish the thunder from the gunfire, the lightning from the flash of bombs.

In stories, ancient and new, the rainy season heralded passionate delicacies, dreaming lovers and dancing peacocks, nectarous cloudbursts and bright blossoming jasmine or lusciously fragrant kadamba. But in reality there was cruelty and hatred, poison and fever. Bloodthirsty mosquitos teemed and the quick quivering of minute wings pierced the ears of those who tried to sleep. The high-pitched hum, the vibration and massive swarm of minute blood-bulging bodies, blood-swollen to the bursting point, agitated the steamed air.

The females carried the malaria and cholera and no one knew what else; people said it was the female snakes that killed so many people this month. Disturbed by the flooding of their burrows, indignant serpents slithered in search of earth dried by the dark, indecent sun of Shravan. Villagers stepped on snakes this month, mistaking them for sticks, dried vines, lengths of discarded rope, or not seeing them at all. Thus it was a month of snake festivals, of fear and propitiation, bile and blood, a time of long shadows. Everyone and everything seemed to need protection.

Shravan was a corrupt and dirty month, leaving lesions on the skin of the earth where fires had been set, holes filled with water, puddles pus-oily with swirls of white in black, of silt in soot, scars of sultry earth's distemper. In her fever, the listless earth was indiscreet. She was lewd and yet lustless.

The storyteller could smell asafetida and chaulmoogra, sulfur and phosphorous, gunpowder and mildew, corruption and death; he could hear death too, hear the crackle of distant fire and crack of artillery, dogs yapping, yowling, yelping, the anxious flapping of dark, unseen wings above him. Screams were muffled by distance. In the practically moonless sky he could see the faint lights of fires from the railway station and the fainter fires from the city of night beyond it, the pale but blinding conflagratory flames of a great sacrifice. He could taste the taste of death, the flavor of terrible tales told, bitter stories of true events, blood sacrifices for the state: in August of 1947 India was a macabre melodrama, a monstrous collection of horror stories. People had listened to gruesome reports of the obscenities of war, fiendish stories of concentration camps in a savage Europe, with a certain condescension and scorn, and now, in the aftermath of Independence celebrations, Partition spawned intractable terrors and proof that horror was universal.

For the last few years the storyteller had often spent the rainy season in Banaras. He avoided Manikarnika, the burning ghat; or, if he did go there, he'd remove the black top hat and silver skull earring in case the Doms might still recognize him and ask for Mena back.

He drank arak, smoked opiated ganja, and traded stories with Arun Patel, the keeper of the shop in Godalia where Brahm acquired the stones for his necromantic rings and mystic amulets, each stone a story petrified. Arun Patel, as if he believed in the magic of gems and fragrances, would polish each stone with a particular perfumed oil to reinforce its power. With the sudden outbreak of violence, the shop had been abandoned in fear. After solemnly boarding up the open front, while locking the final combination lock, Patel frowned at his customer and friend: "Maybe we'll never see each other again." He turned away before Brahm could utter anything sanguine.

The storyteller then fled the perilous city: there was fighting between the Vishvanath temple and the great mosque of Aurangzeb, in Bakaria Kund, and near Harishchandra ghat. Reacting to reports from Bengal and the Punjab, people simply, purposely, and unremorsefully killed each other. To slay a Muslim or Hindu here was a way of executing one there.

Atrociously exquisite revenge by gun, or by knife, pick, shovel, bludgeon, pipe, inflamed the heart, brought ecstasies. Murder was mystical, was real. Power was accessible, ardent, and profound. Any object might realize its potential as an instrument of death: a bank teller with a pencil forced up his nose and into his brain clutched the bars of his window with such force that his corpse could not be pried loose and carried away. The wide-dilated stare of dead eyes penetrated the depths of an abyss.

The blade, bought or homemade, was the sweetest, slickest weapon. It felt the best: to push it in, turn it, and feel the clutch of the victim's hand tighten on your shoulder, then loosen, to hear the defiant scream or despairing groan, then the whimper of surrender, to see the incandescent terror in the eyes, and then the dim emptiness, to feel the pumping blood, wet and warm, then drip, not pulse, becoming cool and dry, was to discover the exuberant magic that is in real blood. Blood darkened beneath the fingernails and accentuated the lines of destiny that marked the hands of killers.

To make his way back to his childhood home in the cantonment, the storyteller had to pass through the Muslim settlement where a pig had been set loose in the mosque. A bookseller's stock, stories of the Prophet (Peace be upon Him), had been burned; a jeweler was beaten and, of course, his gold was guiltlessly stolen. The butcher's eight-year-old daughter was disemboweled and hung on a hook amidst the carcasses of goats and chickens in revenge against the Muslims who had slain a cow at the entrance to the Vishvanath temple. The cruelties of reality were more ingenious that those in any story that could be imagined or told.

Hindus took their revenge for the revenge for the revenge . . . and the ripples of repercussions of repercussions of repercussions . . . formed a gigantic, swirling, sucking whirlpool of virulent blood. Muslim graveyards were invaded, Muslim bodies exhumed and mocked, and Shaitan, deprived of his meat, was angered. The living attacked the dead. Skulls were thrown in the air, kicked, smashed against trees, boulders, or walls (the ground was too muddy to shatter them). Parts of one body—an arm, a foot, a finger, a nose, the genitals—were scattered; parts of assorted other bodies—a leg, a hand, an eye from this one and another from that one, an ear or two or three, and the genitals, or parts of them—were mixed together. Hellish laughter beyond a laughter that might be mustered by any ghoul or demon in any storyteller's story rang out as rotting Muslim corpses were mocked: they wrapped a turban about the slouching head of one freshly dead and a makeshift sari on another decomposing (a man, in death, turned into a woman), and the two were married, placed one on top of the other in a gruesome parody of sex.

The Vetala Raja, Betul Rajo, Brahm presumed, was delighted by these grisly games, this spectacular feast for a festival of death celebrating *his* appalling power and glory; *he*'s the master of ceremonies for the furious debacle in the city of dreadful night, the great crematorium on this night of error and shameless nakedness, of a frenzied dance of death, the sickness and chaos inherent in everything unleashed. And you could hear *his* laughter in the crackle of every fire, and every scream, human or bestial, and in the rumble of military trucks and tanks.

Knowing that *he* was there, that *he* was the only way to explain the world that night, Brahm sought refuge in the Christian graveyard where Mary Sheridan Thomson was buried. As he entered it, he touched the crucifix dangling around his neck amidst the Hindu charms and amulets, protection from the specters that followed him—the Vetala Raja (or one of his emissaries, some vampire or ghoul), some terrorist (Hindu or Muslim), someone on patrol (police or army enforcing the ignored curfew), a dacoit (or just a petty criminal on his own), a bhut or pret (British or Indian), or Mena (her ghost or the still living woman of flesh and blood, no character in a story, but a real woman, alive and stalking him)—it hardly made a difference which of these stories, if any, were true. Unshakable specters followed him there. Though he ached for escape from the story, craved to crawl out of the narrative, off the page, out of the throat, into the void, the storyteller, knowing that it was futile, was resolved to wait, though impatiently, until the end, to be carried toward it word by word, phrase by phrase, episode by episode, forward toward that final period, that minute dot, the closing of the lips, the end that was followed by empty space and perfect silence.

The abyss. He uttered it aloud in English: *abyss.* In the end deliverance and rest were inevitable. There, in the abyss finally faced, horrors might find some resolution or meaning. He longed for the end.

He had come back here to this graveyard before, with Mena, seventeen years earlier, in the year of the Great Depression that had crawled, hungry, contaminated, and febrile, from Europe. He had embraced her here and they had trembled and thrilled with what seemed forbidden and dangerous about the arousal of desire in the place of death. He pulled up the turns of cloth, felt the stretch and yawn of legs, leaned her back against the flame tree, pushed close, bit the lip hungrily, hungrily lapped up the panting mouth, fumbling, anxious, moaning, as ghosts peered lecherously on with eyes of flame that could see through the darkness of the cemetery.

Mena had had a dream in this graveyard on that night, a hallucination that in retrospect had been mantic: *People are throwing bricks, stones, rocks, not just men but children too, and women. There are houses on fire and blood in the streets, blood in rivulets flowing down to the ghats and into the Ganga. Decomposing bodies litter the streets. There are murders, people killing other people and people killing themselves in order to deprive still other people of that satisfaction. The vultures are delighting, wings flapping wildly, crying out threat and exultation. I see a man decapitate a little boy and then five men attack to cut off his arm, then the other arm, then his legs. They burn the wounds with torches. The torso twitches and they laugh as they command it to dance. Cries—"Kill him, kill him"—resound and, wait, look over there: see those three women bludgeoning an old man to death. There's a baby impaled—the stick through the anus and out of the mouth, arms stretched out as if reaching for something. A man witnesses other men, neighbors he knows, cut off his wife's hair; then they rape her. Then they douse her with kerosene and light the fire; her husband whimpers like an infant. There's another figure, Mussalman—he's wearing a topi—he's pissing on the body of a sadhu that he's just killed as another Mussalman looks on laughing. Then, to outdo his friend, the laughing man opens the corpse's mouth and shits in it. It's night and the people have no faces. They're just silhouettes, black shapes in blacker night, until suddenly there's an explosion and in the flash of light the faces appear—wide black eyes, gaping red mouths, silver teeth barred in scream or laughter—golden faces shiny wet with sweat.*

And you . . . where are you? I'm alone and I'm afraid. It was suddenly dark and quiet. Brahm took a deep breath and could taste the smoke and fumes of violence in the air. The only sound was from his feet in the mud, warmed by rotting, oozing between his toes. Occasional gunshot, then the barking of dogs, perhaps a call, a scream, a shout, a laugh, a curse, the howl of a jackal, the spiteful hum of a thirsty mosquito, punctuated ominous moments of silence. Mena's prophetic powers, Brahm now realized, were but an early symptom of the sickness that was to come. Madness is a knowing too much, a seeing too clearly.

Even in the darkness he could locate the grave, and, like a blind man feeling the face of a friend with recognition, he ran his fingers over the carved marble, touching each letter to put the words together again: "Mary Thomson, 1860–1929. May no ill Dreams disturb my Rest, Nor Powers of Darkness me molest." The epitaph, which had been embroidered by Memsahib in black on a white pillow case, had been selected for the tombstone by Dr. Thomson, a choice that would not have been made had he been aware that his wife had not composed it, but unearthed it from a book—it was the epigraph to Kipling's "The Phantom Rickshaw." Dr. Thomson had disapproved of Kipling ever since a heated argument with him in 1888 in Almora over the use of native volunteers in medical experiments.

The touch of the stone, the feel of the Roman letters, the English words, invoked her voice, smooth as the marble beneath his fingertips: "My child, my son, my little one, my Brahma-baba, Brahm, Bram, my little Stokerji." The voice brought comfort to the graveyard refuge from the madly rioting world. Setting her book on the grave, propping it up against the stone, he affectionately mimicked her accent and dulcet intonation: *Should sleep now or ever overcome you, or be like to do. . . .* The guns started again; and the mosquitos. "The book," Brahm thought and could not help but laugh, "the book. Damn the book!" It seemed, in consideration of the world that night, devoid of any real horror and yet, the storyteller surmised, tales of terror and abomination at least stand for something, mean something; in life such events signify absolutely nothing and that's the real horror.

Reclining on the ground, he could picture her still form, the once warm and pliant body beneath him, under the dirt—the raw-boned carcass, its eyeless, noseless, earless skull with teeth exposed as if in perpetual grin. He smiled with the thought of how proud of him she'd be for the purity of his English gothic meditation: throbbing pulpy-gray worms oozily slithering over brittle naked bones and through the lipless gaping mouth. The succulent brain, once the source and store of so many macabre stories, had been consumed. Buried with her in the ground were dreams and stories; she slept, rested and unmolested, absorbed and absolved, amidst the splendid dark secrets of the earth.

The fitful high-pitched buzz of the mosquitos around him, the only other living things in the cemetery, threatened to keep him awake all night, more than the interminable clamor of the distant riots. He
wrapped the shawl around his head and heard her mud-muffled voice percolating up through the earth, filtered by dirt and gravel, "Now, come a little close to me, yes, that's it, be warm and comfortable and safe and I'll read you more *Dracula,* the terrible tale of the Vetala Raja. . . ." He tried to picture her, to conjure her up from the dead, to incarnate the ghost as he knew she would have wished him to do. But she did not come. "Why?" He whispered invitations to her: "Come, come close, let me tell you a story." But the figure forming, thin, dark, swaying in the mists, translucent and undulous, wasn't rosy Memsahib, but was his other mother, dolorous Kalyani, thin and dark, gracefully sweeping, darkly sweeping, slowly twirling in her languorous dance of sweep, sweep, sweeping. She hesitated, daubed the sweat from her face with the border of her light shawl and then turned to Brahm, the man and the child at once and, when she smiled, he opened his eyes and looked away for fear that glistening tears would roll down her memory-shadowed cheeks.

He could hear the machine guns again. In the city people ran from body to body searching for friends or loved ones, turning over an awkwardly fallen corpse only to see a face so brutally disfigured that recognition was impossible. Dogs, caught up in the frenzy, behaved like human beings, deliriously attacking men and each other. A child enchanted by the terrors around him, not knowing why, killed a kitten with a length of pipe and laughed; and then he vomited, then cried.

The storyteller tried not to imagine it, strained rather to stay within the graveyard, picturing it as it had been when he was a child, when it was daytime, after the night and rains—delicate flowers trembled over the dead on well-keep grass; gravestones and tombs were cared for and clean. He struggled to envision the Thomson house as it was then, every room illuminated, smelling of leather and brandy, cigar smoke and polish, newspapers and English pudding, meat and bread, mint and lavender and rose and lilac and . . . fragrances unidentifiable. But memory could not assert itself against the very forces that had dismantled the cantonment: the abandoned houses had but the faintest echoes of laughter gone, tinkling of glasses, the neigh of well-bred horses, stories told, the very edges of the sonic ripples.

The church bell was utterly silent; the telegraph office surrounded by armed guards. Each house, locked up tight that night, contained so many stories, the echoes of every word ever spoken in its rooms. "All houses, after one generation, have ghosts," Memsahib explained to the servant child. "Isn't that obvious? All who've lived there remain in some way, haunting it to the degree that we are unable to resist the manifestation of their stories."

Memsahib was not without company in earth and death: Varney's grave was next to hers, marked by the bronze statue of an Irish setter sent from England by Nigel Thomson with the plaque: "R.I.P. Varney 1911–1922." The dog had, through an understandable misunderstanding, become a god in India. Mrs. Thomson had ordered the servants to place flowers on the grave each week, an activity perceived by local eyes as puja. Once Dr. Thomson had left, the workers at the Dak Bungalow into which his house had been turned, felt compelled to continue the ritual prayers and offerings to the exotic English god. There were faded marigolds on the canine resting place—the god's shrine—even now.

The storyteller remembered the smell of Varney's warm fur, the feel of the cold nose pushing into his neck, and despite the rat-tat-tat of a stick against the stones of the crumbling wall around the cemetery, the rumbling of maimed clouds, more gun racket in the distance, dogs baying, other howlings human or animal, he closed his eyes and tried to sleep and dream, to search for soothing stories.

He often thought of Mena when he could not sleep. The bedtime story that was never told aloud: *Mena,* a love story; *Mena,* a ghost story; *Mena,* a true story.

Once upon a time there was a young storyteller and he crossed the path of a Dom's daughter, a child raised by the burning ghats in the City of Dreadful Night. Her story began with the telling of another story; the prelude was their meeting: he was in the red stone tower that overlooked the cremation site at Manikarnika where her father tended corpses: *It was dawn and I saw her from a distance, from the back, her stride, the tilt of her head atop the graceful neck, the turn of the ankleted feet, the complaisant cling of light cotton to her thigh, and it took my breath away to behold so much life amidst that death. She turned, squatted near the burning corpse, the brightness of her teeth revealed by an uncontrollable smile which now and then she covered with a modest hand. Pulling up the bright shawl—yellow, red, and swirled with orange—she shook her head and earrings rang delicate songs. She shooed the crows and dogs away and joked with two other Dom girl-children.*

When I went down to speak to her, she turned away from me, mistaking me for a mourner, something, I, parentless and childless, thought I'd never be; but now, now I mourn, still mourn for her, not for flesh that may still be or not, but for something else. All memory, if it's true, has, I believe, a trace of mourning in it.

I turned her around and let my smile reveal the truth. I was not in mourning, no, not at all—I laughed in the face of death, laughed with gruesome stories that scared away all dreadful things.

I can't remember anything we said in the early morning any more than I can forget anything we said later in the day. Once upon an afternoon I rowed a boat near the bank at Manikarnika where her father, the Dom, like the voracious crows around him, watched the smoldering cadavers, and I reached out a hand to steady her entry. "Come, come closer," I said; and, "Steady, steady," she answered.

The water was strewn with human ashes—white, gray, black—

and flower petals—white, pink, yellow—and the boat, amidst those delicate fragments of faded, interrupted life, rocked as mother, moody Ganga, flexed, rippled, splashed the steps leading out of her and up toward the flames.

Bodies brightly wrapped as gifts for death rested racked on stone stairs with their usual composure and infinite patience, waiting for the splendid obliteration that the mouth of fire offers. Smoke caressed them gently. Against the solemn parental injunction of the white-haired, flame-eyed man, she boarded the boat, and rocked with the storyteller in it as he rowed, rowed, looking back to the father's angry glower, and swayed and rowed and the muscles of his shoulders shined with sweat in the sun and were taut with the strain of row, row, row, and it took her breath away, that she would be rowed like that boat, longing to row at the same time, at once clutched and clutching

his arms as she might two strong oars and pull as he pulled, then raise, then down and pull, then up, trembling, drop, pull, quiver, again, again, again, and then, then float with him and feel the one gentle motion and rhythmic drift, the restful rocking beneath, and nothing needed to be said. So softly she hummed a wordless song that he could hardly hear it over the soft lap, lap, lapping of the maternal waters against the now haunted boat, the soft knock, knocking of the oars against the boat, rocking, and he softly smiled at the girl.

When the hero heard her name—Mena, Mena—he knew she was the heroine of his story. Mena, Mena the Dom, Mena/Mina, Mina Murray, Mina Harker, O Mina, *Mina was looking tired and pale, but she made a gallant effort to be bright and cheerful,* Memsahib read the English words, fragrant with her mint- and honey-sweet breath, *I took Mina to her room and the dear girl was more affectionate with me than ever, and clung to me as though she would detain me . . .* and he could smell the creamy breath, the breeze on his face, the river sighing and panting, the mother whispering.

The river body was swollen from the rains as suppliant bathers entered her, touching the rainbow-swirled skin dappled with swirls of soot and oil, flecked with bits of this and that, fragments of dream and desire, remnants of memory and story.

"When I can't sleep," Mean interrupted her song, "I imagine

that I'm in a boat like this, drifting toward the sea, and I rock a bit and the ropes of my bed stretch and pull the wooden frame and it sounds like the creaking of a boat and I believe it and I drift and I'm sure to fall asleep before I reach the ocean. I've never seen the sea."

"The heat, the heat," the storyteller murmured, sighed, and let loose the oars to wipe his face and shut his eyes, feel the river's breath, and the unrowed boat turned full circle and "let me row," she said. He taught her how to row. "Now teach me how to smoke," she ordered.

"Oh, yes, yes, I'll be your smoking guru," he laughed. "I'm a smoking expert, you know, a professional smoker. It's part of the storyteller's stock and trade."

"You're a storyteller?"

"Yes," he smiled proudly, "a teller of terrible tales, stories of ghosts and ghouls, of vetals, bhuts, prets, pishachas, and demons," he growled with a mock terrible smile and she demurely covered the mouth opened by laughter with her swirlingly bright shawl and that made him laugh too. "I'm a storyteller like my father, like his father before him, and his father, and his—a line that goes back to the great Valmiki. It's a life of freedom and joy: I've seen the ocean, the sea break upon the shore at Puri, Kanyakumari, and Goa; I've breathed the mountain air of Almora, Simla, Srinagar, and Ooty; I've sifted the sands of Rajasthan through these fingers. I've told stories in all of these places and heard them in more, listened to them in Bengali and Tamil, Malayalam and Panjabi, English and other languages too. Because I'm a storyteller I know places and languages and faces and what dreams mean. Because I know what stories mean, I can decipher the patterns in the flight of birds or the falling of leaves, the messages in the ashes of a fire or the shapes of passing clouds. And, because I'm a storyteller, I know how to smoke. Smoke, you must understand, is one of my props, as essential to ghost stories as skulls and amulets. I blow it out slowly, like this, in curls like this, in billows like this. It can be the smoke of cremation grounds or of tantric sacrifices; it can be a rolling rainy mist mysterious and warm or an eerie winter fog upon a cold river. How beautiful it is, trailing from the small glow, the ember at the tip of this bone-white cigarette, twisting, rising, dispersing itself, delicate, diaphanous, finally disappearing, gone forever. Yes, you must learn to smoke.

How old are you? Fourteen? Fourteen years old and you still don't know how to smoke? Shameful. What kind of parents do you have? Delicious dhumra paan! Sweet, sweet smoke. Tobacco smoke is prana, my child, is joy, is life. In ancient India the wise and holy ones breathed in the smoke of celestial kusha grass. The Muslims say that everyone smokes in Paradise. Smoking is glorious and blessed."

She coughed on the first puff, covered her face, and laughed—"I'm dizzy"—and he scolded her: "No laughing! Smoking is serious business."

He rowed while she smoked, then she rowed while he smoked and then, beyond Assi, beyond Ramnagar, around the bend in the river, they both smoked, letting the boat drift and roll, surrendering all will to the holy coiling currents of the flowing, swelling Ganga, allowing fate or accident, gods or nature, to carry them to wherever they were meant to be.

"Do you only know ghost stories? Don't you know love stories? Radha and Krishna, Sita and Ram, Sati and my Lord Maheshvar? Do you know the story of Sati burning herself, turning the sacrifice into a pyre for the love of my Lord? Do you know the story of Shiva taking Parvati into his body, making her half of him, him half of her, the two of them merged, one?"

"I know all stories. Those god stories, those stories of heroism and love—every storyteller knows those. But ghost stories, tales of bhuts and vetals, these stories, my specialty, are best of all. They take control of fear and bring me food and places to sleep. I get cigarettes for ghost stories! Only women want to hear stories of love. And women don't have anything to give me. Women are poor."

While he waited for her to beg, she remained stubbornly silent. "Would your father burn a body without being paid? So why should I tell a story, without remuneration?" After a cunningly sustained silence, her lips parted: "Give me another cigarette."

"You're a terrible child, a very bad girl," he laughed, "but I'll tell you a story anyway."

"If that's what you want to do," she said dispassionately, taking the cigarette from his mouth, placing it between her lips and inhaling deeply. "Do whatever you want. But I don't like ghost stories. Why would anyone want to be frightened anyway?"

"Love stories are," he smiled, "the really frightening tales. Ghosts stories cure fear; love stories inspire it."

"I'm not afraid," she said.

"Then come close," he began with a smile, "a little closer, come now and let me tell you an old, old story, a love story then, the wonderful tale of the beautiful Malati, the daughter of the minister to the king of Padmavati, and her heroic lover, Madhava, the son of the minister to the king of Vidarbha. Let me tell you of their love for each other, of the obstacles set in the way of desire, and of the means of lovers to overcome those hindrances."

Bhutnath Kathuwala, the storyteller and exorcist, by example, years before, when he sat in the compound of the Thomson household, had taught Brahm to close his eyes as he began to see the figures: "If you can see them as you begin, your audience will see them too. So close your eyes, look at them, the man and woman, picture them—what are they wearing? Where are they? Do you see them? Yes? Try to smell what they must smelling, to see what they are seeing, to hear what they are hearing. What are they saying? Listen, listen. . . ."

While the boat drifted, he told her the story of Malati and Madhava, starting slowly, slowly, then gaining momentum, opening and closing his eyes, gesturing with his hands, acting out the parts for her, making the boat sway with the movement of his arms, the shifting of his weight, made her heart sway too, made her even smile, finally laugh (not at the story, but at the perfection of the way in which he told it); then, in the wake of laughter, he even brought tears to her eyes, then a full smile again, and then the story opened her eyes wide and fixed her vision on him and once upon a time she opened her arms and held him close to her and felt his stories in every part of her; and his words were in her blood.

His descriptions of Malati were portraits painted of her *(blushing cheeks as round as the nectar-full moon with deepset eyes above them—dark darting rabbits, timid and hungry—and soft humid lips, the candied curved of the lower one voluptuously begging to be kissed, trembling with ardent supplication, the white, slightly crooked, teeth poised both to fiercely and gently bite, the curve of the brow stretching to encompass, the flushed breasts aching for caress, the glance sulky and yet divulging sweet sweltering desire, the gait utterly free yet faltering, her feet turned out enhancing the cling of the yellow-orange-red sari to her hip, the fall of her diaphanous shawl, the smell of the laughing jasmine in the full cascade of hair)* and his portrayal of the hero, acted out with exaggerated movements of the eyes, twists of the mouth, turns of the nose, allowed her to paint a portrait of him (she dressed Madhava in a silk top hat, decorated his arms, wrists, and neck with amulets, placed mysterious rings on his fingers; it was not strange to her that the hero of an ancient Indian tale wore a soiled banian. The radiant smile was not strange but perfect, was Madhava's and Brahm's).

The father of Malati and the father of Madhava had been
150 *friends when they were young students together under the tutelage of the Buddhist nun Kamandaki, an expert in the lore of ghosts and all the tantric rites, a magician with powers to see the future, to know how stories ended.* Brahm closed his eyes and saw what he imagined his mother Kalyani must look like now: he shaved her head and dyed a blue sari ocher. *Her youthful beauty had gone unmarred by tonsure and unconcealed by monastic robes. Now, though she was old, though skin was wrinkled, frame bent, knees bowed, loveliness persisted in clear, bright eyes, the eyes of a child, lustrous jewels set in a cracked, corroded base.* The grace with which Kalyani swept the Thomson home persisted in the old woman's movements as she walked with Malati in the love god's fragrant garden.

Kamandaki knew what the plot should be: Madhava and Malati, the children of her former students, were destined to marry. Brahm suspected that his mother might or would, if she could, have picked Mena to be his bride. "Love in stories is all fate," he glossed his narrative. "In life it is all fragile promises and solemn contracts, breaking them, piecing them back together, and trying to keep them."

Now the king of Vidarbha had a friend to whom he could deny nothing—a foul smelling and ugly brahmin, his skin wrinkled and pocked, belly paunched, neck sagging; and this gassy and pathetic old sycophant wished to marry Malati. The king, a loyal friend to his friends and subjects, a man who, like all righteous rulers in ancient stories, like the great Harishchandra himself, gave brahmins anything they asked for, consented to it, and promised Malati to him. Mena could picture the Dom boys, one of whom would receive her dowry, could imagine them grown old and fat, wretched and greedy. They would, like her father, smell sickly sweet of sandalwood and charred flesh; like him they'd have betel-stained teeth, shadowy eyes, and they'd spend their nights counting gold; they'd beat their wives and children and irritably chase scavengers from the burning grounds.

Kamandaki, like you, wanted a love story, wanted the girl to marry Madhava by the Gandharva rite, the riteless rite where love itself is the contract and desire is the priest. "As we might do, my Mena," he wished he could say and make it so.

Kamandaki was the author of the story in which she lived, for which she had been created, and she began it by sending Madhava on errands that took him near Malati's home, and indeed, once the girl had seen him, she became infatuated with the glorious and handsome hero. She had no other thoughts but of him. When there was a sound, her head quickly turned, "Is it Madhava?" and when the slight movement of a leaf in the breeze caught her glance, she turned, startled, hoping he was there. "Will he come for me?" To calm the sickness of love, the wild beating of her heart, the anxious churning in her stomach, the trembling of her limbs, she painted a portrait of him that she might look upon him day and night.

The boat made another full turn and bumped against the bank as Mena smiled and proudly blew smoke through her nostrils. Brahm took up the oars to return them to a river current, telling the story as he rowed, the rhythm of the oars, the strain and flex of his muscles, punctuating it: *Madhava went one day to the Garden of Desire . . . to the temple consecrated to the god who is love . . . the god, bodyless, merciless, invisible, and everywhere . . . Madhava overwhelmed by longing for Malati, his heart uprooted, enchanted. . . . sitting there despondent, he made a garland of jasmine blossoms for her. . . . the garland in your hair . . . the blossoms are, were, little teeth biting with love . . . the smell, the coolness, the delicacy. . . .* Mena, O Mena. . . .

Mena took the oars once more and Brahm described Malati entering the garden of Kama on an ornately caparisoned elephant, surrounded by armed eunuchs, *and there she saw Madhava and sent a servant to purchase the garland he was making. Her glances were nectar and poison to him.*

Again the boat was adrift and cigarettes were smoked and the afternoon seemed too brief for summer. Brahm explained the royal proclamation, the announcement of the wedding day as set for Malati and the repulsive old man who was the king's good friend.

Kamandaki urged Malati to defy her father just as Shakuntala, the daughter of the mythic Mena, your namesake, defied her guardians, just as Sati defied Daksha. The Hindu lawmakers respect the sanctity of a marriage in which love is consummated in secret, by mutual consent, without formal ceremonies.

"Tell me the story of Mena," Mena interrupted, "tell me the stories that Kamandaki told Malati." And as the gray of evening folded itself into a shroud for the burning corpse of the sun with flickering light on the water that mourned for it, with the doleful litanies of crying children, pilgrims, and crows resounding from the banks, he told her those stories within his story within this story.

When it was dark, they went ashore, built a fire with scraps of wood (fragments of wrecked boats, cremation logs that had gone out, broken things, like pieces of stories, that had once some purpose as a chair or bed or building beam), wood that had been washed up upon the shore and dried out by the sun. "Fire's a storyteller," he said. "Agni is the storyteller's god. Listen to the fire, the tongues of flame that hiss, spit, and growl fire's manifold tales. The red mouth wide open. There must be fire in every good story—fire, and water, and earth. There must be both heat and cold."

The fire brought Malati and Madhava back into view, illuminated their features and warmed their flesh. Fire helped the storyteller describe in eerie murmurs how Madhava, to work the secret magic taught to him by Kamandaki, went to make offerings at the shrine of Bhairavi, to propitiate the goddess of terror. *Then, protected by the goddess, he ventured into the ghoul-haunted burning grounds to sell human flesh to the voracious demons there. Only he who can sacrifice flesh and blood, who can endure excruciating pain, can find satisfaction for desire. The mysteries of love are in death and murder, abandonment and sacrifice. Love, in all its forms, is violence, is burning, slaughter, and sacrifice. Madhava went into the place of death to sell human flesh for the sake of love.*

The river bordering the cremation ground was clotted with corpses, and hungry jackals trotted along the banks howling commands to them to drift ashore: "Come now, come a little closer. . . ."

Madhava entered that sprawling burning place, submerged himself in the oily blackness of the night that fumed with roaring pyres and the flame-filled eyes of prowling prets shrieking. The smoldering earth was smoke-cloaked and dusky. Flesh falling from their mouths, human fat dripping down their chins onto their bony bodies (knotted the joints, skin black and cracked, blistered and bleeding), the prets gaped their cavernous mouths and their tongues, like snakes emerging from hollows in the trees, wagged and waved. One ghoul sat upright with a flayed corpse across his knees, its chest opened up; sinking in a finger to pluck out the fatty parts, the human jellies, tugging at a tendon, gnawing on a muscle, the gluttonous pret shuddered with desire distending desire. Bones were roasted on the fire to bubble marrow forth, and they burned their black tongues licking the hot bones. Pishachas had been fighting over a body, dragging it here and there in a tug-of-war that was recorded in the blood smeared in chaotic trails on the earth.

The female ghouls were aroused—guts wrapped around their arms like bracelets, necklaces with pendant human hearts, blood the ornamental lac; they were impassioned, drunk, and frenzied to make themselves more beautifully hideous for their lascivious, screaming lovers.

Madhava heard the screeching from the shrine, the cries of one chosen for the human sacrifice. A tantric sadhu, a Kapalika and his consort, had kidnapped Malati, bound her with chains, and they sang chants to Shiva. The wind blowing through the mouth of a skull made a hissing, laughing sound, mocking the girl who struggled against the bonds. The chains pressed into her bared breasts, bruised the tender thighs that they encircled tight, and cut the fragile wrists. The nectar from the moon in Shiva's hair brought the skulls around his neck to life and they howled curses on the living.

And the storyteller told the entranced girl how the brave hero freed the heroine, killed the priest and his consort and fed them to the ravening ghouls. *Though Malati was rescued from the tantrics, there was now the marriage, worse than death;* but Brahm reassured Mena with descriptions of how he redeemed her from that union with a cunning inspired in him by love.

The teller of tales tried to explain why love in stories is, in the end, after the many tribulations that it causes, always sweet. *But in our life, love is fanged and venomous; it's an affliction.* He spoke of joyous finales, desires satisfied, endings that are truly endings, with no future to threaten them: *Malati and Madhava were together, their union blessed by the king.*

They were together, like this, like this, and he took her in his arms, felt the strong body against his and melted away, Mena and Brahm, Mina and Jonathan, Malati and Madhava, *you and I.*

And in the middle of the night, after the storyteller rowed the Dom girl home with long strokes, with the currents of the Ganga, back to Manikarnika where the bodies burned every hour of the day and night, her remorseless father beat her while her mother watched in a silence that was bitter and sad but wholly resolute.

As he dressed the girl's wounds with wet water lily petals, Brahm took a protagonist's oath, swore he'd sell human flesh in the cremation grounds if that could, as in stories, activate curses on the Dom, torment and then consume him. The heroic speech made the girl laugh, smoke a cigarette, and finally set her heart on following the itinerant storyteller with hopes for the Gandharva's blessings. The Doms told their version of the story of the Dom girl who had been kidnapped by a strange traveler. "Who was he?" the odd man with the English top hat, wearing the amulets and the Christian cross around his neck, they asked each other: "Some sort of sadhu . . . a magician . . . maybe a tribal priest or shaman, who knows?"

"My father's a vetal. He seems alive, but no, he's not. A dead man, bloodthirsty and animated by some restless, demonic spirit. Let me tell you a story now—every time he does the bad thing with my mother, right afterward he beats her and then he runs away for a few days. And then he comes back and is silent and morose. When I hear them in the darkness, moaning, gasping, grunting, I know it will happen. He'll beat her for certain. I thought of that when he was beating me. Why does he do that? Will you do that to me someday? What will you do to me?"

Brahm promised that he would never harm her.

"No matter what I do, no matter how bad I am?"

The words—"I'll never harm you"—made her laugh out loud and choke on the smoke of the cigarette.

"Have I harmed her?" he asked himself, asked Mary Sheridan Thomson in the grave below him. She was a good judge of stories. "Have I kept my promise? Surely I've hurt her; of course, I've caused her pain; I even struck her. But have I harmed her? That's different. Isn't it? I couldn't help what I've done."

There was the sudden, impertinent sound of a motor as the headlights of a truck swept the cemetery, and there was shouting and a great dance of orange light in the sky—a blaze in the cantonment. Flames feasted on the body of an old house, chewed the wooden flesh from the bones of stone. Brahm lay still for fear the men would come into the graveyard, looking for rioters in the present as he was looking for spirits in the past. Lines of time crossed close, stories overlapped. More shouting, the engine gunned and guns cried out, a horn was honking, honking, making dogs bark, again, again, again the clamor and uproar, and the two beams of light once more spanned the moonless graveyard, illuminated swarms of mosquitos and made ghostly silhouettes of the trees, their arms stretched above them, a thousand fingers fanned in fear, and darkness came again, and the tumult of the truck and men became more faint, and the dogs seemed to be running after them in rabid packs in the direction of the house on fire.

Though the graveyard was empty and still, he detected Mena's presence there, sensed the ways in which he had brought her there, and the sound of Memsahib's voice was Mena's, was Mina's: *The fire divided, and seemed to shine on me through the fog like two red eyes. . . . The last conscious effort imagination made was to show me a livid white face bending over me out of the mist.*

In that year, the year of the Depression, seventeen years ago he reckoned, they lived better than most: villagers shared the little food they had in return for his stories; there were even cigarettes. They slept sometimes in shrines; they stayed for two weeks in Chandraprabha, near the Rajdari falls, then Deodari, and the sound of rushing water in the forest of fables cleansed their hearts and washed memories away. He told her stories in the night and tales of ghouls and demons, of haunting and death, would arouse her and her arousal aroused him. And then, holding her in his arms, he whispered: "When I die, burn me my beautiful Dom, break my skull to release my spirit. Do it with these careful hands, these trembling fingers. . . ."

"You don't care that I'm a Dom?" she smiled. "That doesn't disgust you?"

"Wasn't the righteous king, Harishchandra, a Dom?" he smiled back. The storyteller had heard the legend when he was a child, as Bhutnath Kathuwala had rendered it at the Thomson house. It had delighted Memsahib: "The Hindu surpasses the Christian in moral virtue," she declared. "Horror for us is a punishment for the wicked; for them it provides a test for righteousness. They understand the purifying nature of horror and the macabre."

"And now, come now," Bhutnath Kathuwala, the itinerant storyteller and exorcist, had loudly whispered, closing his eyes, beginning slowly, suspensefully, eerily, "now let me tell you the tale of King Harishchandra, famous in the three worlds for his virtue and his generosity. Never had he broken a promise, never would he, never had he denied a supplication. This story is true—ask anyone at Harishchandra ghat, the burning ground named after him, blessed by his former presence there. Listen to his marvelous story."

Close to Memsahib, her arm around him, protecting him, and Brahm sat anxious for the story, feeling it was told just for him.

The sage Vishvamitra, humiliated I suppose because he had been so easily seduced by the enchanting Mena, was jealous of the king Harishchandra's fame as a man of infinite righteousness—untemptable, uncompromising, unseducable. Vishvamitra was determined to demonstrate the king's foibles. "In every human heart there's frailty," he laughed, "and where there's weakness, there is trepidation; and where there is fear, there's vice. Haha!"

Disguised as an impoverished brahmin, Vishvamitra appeared before the king in court to ask if he would be so compassionate as to make an offering to a poor and hungry man.

"Yes, of course," the abundantly generous king smiled.

"What will you give me?" the sage wearing tatters asked.

"Whatever you ask of me," Harishchandra responded resolutely with piety and compassion.

"Your kingdom," Vishvamitra smiled and did not blink an eye.

"It's done!" the great and virtuous king announced calmly, without the slightest display of surprise, disappointment, or distress. Perfect and pure virtue informed all his words and thoughts, his decisions and actions.

Vishvamitra, ruffled by the ease with which the king had displayed his reputed righteousness, annoyed by the royal show of morality, demanded money too, the "customary dakshina."

Still calm and detached, perfectly poised and at peace with himself and his convictions, the king called for his treasury to be opened to the brahmin: "Take what you wish."

"I'm sorry," the disguised Vishvamitra loudly laughed, scornfully smirking, "I'm sorry, but you have no treasury anymore—that, as part of your kingdom, belongs to me now. I'm afraid you'll have to sell something. Ah, but too bad, you don't have anything to sell, no things I mean. And all you have in this world is yourself, your wife, and your young son"—"a boy just about your age," Bhutnath said, pointing to Brahm—*"I suppose you could sell yourself and them as slaves. Haha! Well, on the other hand, there is another way—you could go back on your word, take back the kingdom you've given to me, and send me away. Such a compromise in your morality would certainly be understandable. It would, alas, be human."*

Bhutnath's voice for Vishvamitra was an oily gurgle and gruff hiss that made the skin crawl. The voice of the king was melodic, crystalline, resonant with authoritative reassurance: *"A king must always keep his word," Harishchandra said and announced that he and his wife and son could be bought as slaves.*

"I'll not allow slavery in my kingdom," the angered Vishvamitra shouted. "I am, after all, a virtuous man myself."

Bhutnath Kathuwala told Memsahib and the doctor, Inspector Weston and young Christine, little Brahm, Sanders and his wife, and the others gathered there, guests and servants alike, how Harishchandra went to Banaras and there, in the marketplace in Godalia, he sold his wife and son to a heartless merchant. *He made the child a bearer, the mother a sweeper—all day she swept, swept, sweeping the dust here and then sweeping it there, then back again, and again, pausing only to wipe the sweat from her brow, sweeping as if to assist the god of wind. The merchant beat the woman and her child for no reason at all and the boy longed for his father.*

The storyteller explained that the Doms who bought Harishchandra ordered him to lift the corpses that would not completely burn from the pyres and carry them into the river. *It was his duty to shovel and sweep up the ashes, to clean the burning ghat of the dog shit and crow droppings. A long time passed. Soon they stationed the former king as the cemetery night watchman, ordering him not to permit anyone to enter with a corpse without paying the cremation fee.*

One day the merchant sent the son of Harishchandra to the fields to cut grass for him during the rainy season when, then as now, the serpents crawl out of their burrows to dry out in the sun. It's dangerous in the long grass; it's easy to step on a snake.

Young Brahm knew it was coming, was not in the least surprised that the young son of King Harishchandra was bitten by a krait. And as the storyteller recounted the painful death of the child whose leg was black and swollen, and the sorrow of the mother whose eyes were red and swollen, the ways in which she wailed and mourned for the boy, Brahm hoped that he wouldn't die, not for his own sake, but for the sake of his mother and Memsahib.

The merchant beat the woman for ignoring her duties, for neglecting her sweeping in order to indulge herself in futile mourning and senseless sentimentality, using the death of her child as an excuse to avoid her work.

Embracing the corpse of her young son, weeping warm tears on the pale neck, she lifted the limp body, whispered words of affection in his now deaf ear, then, in anguish broke free, ran, ran from the house of the brutal merchant, ran as fast as she could down toward the river, ran to the cremation grounds to perform the rites for the child she had brought into the world.

Bhutnath related the meeting, after several years of separation, of husband and wife. *He did not recognize the woman whose face was covered with the shawl of mourning; she did not recognize the man whose face had been blackened by soot from the crematory fires, whose hair and beard had been cropped close and singed, whose form was stooped from the many burdens he had been forced to bear. But when Harishchandra spoke, demanding the fee to bring the corpse into the cemetery and place it on the fire, she recognized the sonorous voice, pulled back her shawl and cried aloud, "My lord,* *my blessed husband," and, cradling his dead son in her arms, she fell to her knees weeping before him.*

It was difficult for the foreigners to appreciate the virtue of the king who announced to his wife that, although he loved her with all his heart, and that although his son meant more to him than his own life, he could not permit them into the cremation ground without the customary fee. *"It's my duty," was his only explanation.* It was easier for them to comprehend the anguish of the wife that inspired her to pull the child back from his father's arms, push past her husband, and rush headlong toward the funeral fire. *Tenderly, tears streaming down her cheeks, she placed her child on a freshly kindled, sandal-scented bed of flames.*

When Mrs. Thomson tousled Brahm's hair, caressed him lightly, checking to make sure that he was not too frightened, he smiled up at her and then turned back to the storyteller.

The chief Dom, realizing that the entry fee had not been collected, stormed the burning area, screaming and waving his hands about, enraged with greed. He yelled for buckets of water to put out the fire, then he beat the woman, made her lift the partially burned body of her son, and forced her to carry that small charred corpse away. He drove her out of the cemetery with a whip, and Harishchandra could do nothing but witness the spectacle.

When the people in the streets of Banaras saw the woman, her eyes wide and wild with madness, her unbound hair streaming behind her, screeching with horror, carrying a small, half-burned body in her arms, her robes, her hands and face, black with soot and ash, rushing here, then stopping, screaming, turning, rushing there, not knowing where to go, mad, possessed and terrible, some ran from her, certain she was a rakshasi, a corpse possessed by a spirit hungry to feed on other corpses. "No, no," others insisted, "there are no rakshasis nor rakshasas, no spirits nor monsters in this world. They're created by the fancy of storytellers and poets. This is a tantric witch, a sorceress, a woman of flesh and blood practicing the sinister rites of Bhairavi. The child is her sacrificial offering."

The Doms appealed to the law: "She's just a servant woman gone insane. First she broke into the cemetery without paying the toll.
160 *Then she stole a body. She must be punished. There must be order in the place of funerary rites; if not, there can't be order anywhere."*

The woman was arrested, sentenced to death by beheading, the punishment to be performed by the Doms themselves. The chief Dom handed Harishchandra the sharpened axe and commanded him to proceed with the execution. Bound in chains, forced down on her knees, her head pushed over, her eyes fell focused on the feet of her husband, feet she had once so often bathed. He stood over her, staring down at the wife who had borne him a son, who had devotedly and not without passion served him. He looked at the neck that he had once caressed, at the delicate turn of the shoulders; he heard her soft, hopeless whimpering—and he raised the axe.

Bhutnath Kathuwala was silent for a moment. The suspense was exquisite and Brahm swallowed anxiously.

Suddenly the brahmin who now ruled Harishchandra's kingdom appeared: "Wait," he shouted and with confidence approached the king, the Dom servant, the man of virtue and misery.

"You seem to have fallen on rather bad times, Harishchandra, my friend." Vishvamitra smiled. "Well, I'm a man of compassion, as generous as you. So let me make a proposition. I'll give you the opportunity to take back your kingdom. You can return with your wife, make her a crowned queen rather than a headless corpse,

and rule as you did before. All you have to do is go back on your word. Surely no one will blame you. Everyone will say, 'I would have done the same thing.' Do you want to take back what you've give me?"

Harishchandra stared into the eyes of the brahmin.

Again Bhutnath was silent and still, his eyes closed as if seeing what was transpiring on the ghat. He knew just how long to remain so and just when to begin again, just how to modulate his voice to bring out the dramatic capacities of the moment: *"No," Harishchandra said calmly, with conviction, at peace with himself. "No. A king must never go back on his word. A king must do his duty. And now it is my duty to behead my wife. My personal sorrow makes no difference. Virtue must be maintained."*

The pronouncement had overwhelmed young Brahm, given him gooseflesh and brought tears to his eyes. The happy ending of the story that was then related, the sudden intervention of the gods, the rain of flower petals from heaven, the decree that indeed Harishchandra was the most virtuous of kings and that, as the gods' reward for his righteousness, his kingdom was returned to him, his child was brought back from the dead, and Harishchandra ruled in happiness and prosperity—all this meant no more to Brahm than an obligatory and convenient way out of the more important part of the story. Then, by convention, there was the explanation, the quotes from the *Gita,* the sermon on honesty, compassion, and detachment. But none of this, not the happy ending nor the moral message, was of interest to the child. The horrific scenes of the cremation ground, the description of the boy's body on the pyre, and the mother running through the streets mad—all that was sheer delight.

"I thought it was disgusting," Christine Weston said to Brahm.

"That's because you're a girl," the boy teased. "I thought it was beautiful. I'll tell the story when I become a storyteller; but I'll have vultures and hyenas in the cremation ground; I'll make them try to pull the little boy's body out of his mother's arms. I'll tell it that way to scare and sicken little girls."

And later in this life, Brahm did tell it, adding the hyenas and vultures, recounted it to pilgrims in Banaras, told it near Harishchandra ghat, saying, "the Dom, once king, stood over there, yes, right over there; his wife ran down the bank right there." He sold charms that he said came from the treasury of Harishchandra himself. "When he returned to his kingdom, he gave these stones to all of his subjects to protect them from injustice and unwarranted suffering. If you are virtuous and you wear these amulets around your neck, on your arm or wrists, no harm will ever come to you." He felt that Bhutnath would have considered that a good embellishment.

In his travels from village to village Brahm would often ask if anyone knew of an old storyteller who wore an earring—a little silver skull. No? He wondered if Bhutnath Kathuwala was still alive. Did they know anything of an old woman named Kalyani, Kalyani the sweeper woman of Banaras? No, no, she was lost except in memory: sweep, sweep, sweep, mother Kalyani, alone and as sorrowful as the wife of Harishchandra in her sweeping—sweep, sweep, sweeping the dust here, then there, then back again, then pausing to wipe the sweat from her forehead and cheeks, sweeping as if to assist the god of wind.

Once when Brahm, the itinerant storyteller, and his companion Mena were going to camp in a cremation ground, Mena blocked his entry: "No we can't go in. Smell the body? A body's still burning. You can't go to the cremation ground for thirteen days after the immolation—the ghost is still there. I'm a Dom, so I can go; but you, you can't go in there." She laughed because she didn't really believe any of the Dom lore. But she did not want to sleep there because the burning grounds reminded her too much of childhood and home.

Even when there was not enough food for the villagers to share with them, the storyteller and Mena had enough to eat because Brahm knew how, and taught Mena too, to catch and slaughter, bleed and dress, clean and cook the ubiquitous country crows. A rat in a trap was the lure for the first one and that crow snared, then carefully crucified, became the bait for the rest. Brahm pounded the nails through the black flapping, trembling wings of the breast-up bird, its wild unblinking eyes reflecting the swarming sky, its beak open wide, and its mad squawk and terrible shriek bringing the others lewdly screaming. When they descended to peck their screeching fellow crow to death, it would grab its assailants in fierce upturned talons and clutch and cling and Brahm would then stun the attacker with a blow from his gnarled walking stick and then, with a quick twist of his strong hand, he would snap its neck. Blood dripped over the black tongue from still cocked-open beaks. They caught seven crows that way, and Brahm showed Mena how to pull away the throat feathers, make the incisions, and hang the birds to bleed.

Stepping into the dry pool of clotted crow blood, Mena reached up to take down the birds from the tree branch where they might once have perched. The itinerant storyteller taught her how to remove the small black pin feathers, some of them so fine she had to use her teeth to tweeze them out. Cutting off the wings and legs, and tossing them out for other crows to eat, he saved and dried the heads. Mena watched her lover cut across the birds diagonally, then reach in, with the confident finger that had tenderly explored her own body, to loosen the innards, turn them, crack their spines, and open them wide. Carefully he cut around the vent and yanked out the entrails—the spongy red lungs, the greenish oil sac, and the dark heart that he squeezed between two fingers and sniffed to discern if the bird could be eaten.

After the crows had soaked all day in salt water, Brahm impaled them, one next to another, seven in a row, a naked flock of corpses, and Mena hungrily but patiently turned the spit over the fire, watching the flames reaching up to lick the birds and drink the dark fat dripping from them.

"Whatever we eat, we eat what it has eaten, and I've seen the crows at the cremation grounds pick at human flesh. We might be eating human beings." Then she laughed, shaking her head, "But I'm hungry, so what can I do?"

"Eat," he smiled. "And yes, yes—all lovers are cannibals!"

Sometimes at night he'd sit her on his lap and point out the constellations to her and tell her the myths that connected the random stars and gave them shape and meaning: "There are the Krittikas, the six nurses of the war god, and there, there are the Seven Rishis, Vishvamitra among them. He was, as I have been, seduced by one named Mena. Poor and lucky man! And there's Dhruva who did not know who his father was. There are—are you aware of it?—seven moles on your back, in the exact formation of the stars in the constellation Kumbha, that one there. It's an auspicious sign—did you know that?" She shook her head, buried her face in his neck, and he covered Dhruva with his hands.

Since, because of her family, he couldn't go back to Banaras, he couldn't go to purchase the stones and amulets from Arun Patel; he had to contrive charms of his own from bits of bone and string, from roots he said were rare and magical, and from the skulls of the crows that they had eaten.

Traveling with him from village to village that year, listening again and again to his many stories, she asked about the book: "Is that where the stories come from?"

He told her the story of *Dracula,* reciting now and then in English: *And now for you, Madam Mina, this night is the end until all be well. You are too precious to us to have such risk. When we part to-night, you no more must question. We shall tell you all in good time. We are men and are able to bear; but you must be our star and our hope, and we shall act all the more free that you are not in*

danger, such as we are. And then he paraphrased it for her in Hindi, listened to it transformed, not by him, but by the spirit of the language that the storyteller and his consort knew together.

She didn't like the book: it wasn't the story she feared but the book itself; she smelled it, touched it, opened it up here and there and peered into it, then threw it down in disgust. "There are spirits in it, demons. It's a bad book. Burn it."

"I, myself, wrote it," Brahm smiled. "I wrote it in a former life. If you're afraid of it, it means that you're afraid of me."

The storyteller took Mena to Ballia district, and a child, the son of a carpenter, welcomed them to his village and walked with them, telling them stories of all the terrible things that had happened there that year: dacoits had come to the village and taken their cattle. But far worse than that, a boy, the son of a farmer, had been decapitated and the headless body was hung upside down from the branch of the great pipal tree, and some blamed it on tantrics and others on ghouls and vetals.

The storyteller sat cross-legged on the platform beneath the pipal tree near the rushing stream and his stage was decorated with marigolds and a black shivalingam. "Now come a little closer, come now, and let me tell you an old, old story, the tale of Vijayadatta and Sanjayadatta, the sons of the good brahmin Govindaswami. . . ."

Mena was the only woman in Brahm's audience, and the men

stared at her and the village women in their hovels, huts, and houses gossiped about her: "She's a rakshasi . . . a witch. She's a mad woman . . . a dacoit perhaps. . . ."

As the storyteller told his stories the long footstalked leaves of the pipal quivered even though there was hardly a breeze. "Ghosts live in pipal trees," the villagers said; and Dr. Thomson, Brahm remembered, had always called it the "Devil's Tree."

After telling the story of Sanjaya, the wrestler of Banaras, and the rakshasi, Brahm gave a single anklet to Mena with the explanation that the other one was lost. Though she never wore the ornament, she carried it with her always: "I'll wear it," she promised, "when you bring the matching one from the land of the rakshasas."

After they had been in the village for five days, a dog was found in the fields—its throat ripped out, its gut torn open, and Brahm was certain it was not the tantrics or the ghouls that the villagers had spoken of but that it was the Vetala Raja, Dracula himself, the nosferatu; and he knew that they must flee the village. *He* would come for her because she was with the teller of horror stories, the tales of ghouls and vampires, Brahm, Bram. The words of the count, in Memsahib's reading, were clear. *He* spoke to Mena as *he* did to Mina: *"And you, their best beloved one, are now to me, flesh of my flesh; blood of my blood; kin of my kin; my bountiful winepress for a while; and shall later on be my companion and my helper. . . . When my brain says 'Come!' to you, you shall cross land or sea to do my bidding." And with that he pulled open his shirt,* Mina explained, *and with his long sharp nails opened a vein in his breast. When the blood began to spurt out, he took my hands in one of his, holding them tight, and with the other seized my neck and pressed my mouth to the wound. . . .*

The mosquito bites on her neck made him uneasy. Brahm nursed her through the malarial fever, bathed her after the wracking bouts of diarrhea and vomiting, cleaned her without any feelings of revulsion, massaged her tingling limbs, held her in his arms and rocked her gently, fed her doses of bitter quinine, and told her sweet love stories to help her sleep.

In his arms she began to recover and that reassured Brahm that the Vetala Raja had retreated. He held Mena close to him in Chandraprabha, near the Rajdari falls embraced her as Madhava must finally have enclosed Malati. He wanted to suffuse and permeate her so that he could smell, feel, hear, see, taste the world as she did. His hands on her hips, squeezing as he pushed against her, forcing his breath into her breath, he felt the girl's bones, sinews, tendons, flexing, felt strength and fragility, fear and desire, mortality and life, and, finally, he felt her calm, feverless sleep in his arms.

The love story was interrupted after a year when she miscarried for the first time. He washed the blood from her legs while she cried like a child.

In the beginning, right after the miscarriage, because of the sudden high fever, he surmised that it was a relapse of malaria: she grew pale and could not eat; her eyes were bloodshot and she stopped speaking; she drooled, spit continuously, and would not bind up her hair nor braid it. "Don't touch my hair," she screamed, "a nest for spiders, scorpions, and nightmares. Don't disturb them or they'll bite you. They'll bite me too. Get away!" And then, as if realizing the madness of what she was saying, she fell into a long, long fit of weeping, swaying to and fro, exhausted, seeming neither really awake nor asleep. Suspecting that she might be drunk, smelling her breath, he discovered that it reeked more of ashes than arak. The Vetala Raja, so it seemed, had called her to him.

An old woman in Raiganj village, Kamandaki-like, an expert in the complications of pregnancy, announced that it was the revenant ghost of the miscarried child, tormenting her, forcing her to rave like that, and prompting her to tell Brahm mad stories: *A man came to me and made love to me: his feet were backwards and his eyes were green; he held a cane in one hand and a conch in the other; and he laughed. In front he was fat like that man Malati was supposed to marry, but when I saw him from the back, after he had had his fill of me, he was a skeleton and there were worms crawling over his spine. . . .*

The hag instructed him to take her to the shrine of Bhairavi, to seek help there in pacifying the tormented spirit of that unborn child.

"I'm wicked and filthy," Mena cried, and he'd hold her, saying, "No, no, no." But nothing would soothe her, and she would soil herself and he'd have to wash her.

"I was born with teeth already in my mouth and I sucked blood with the milk from my mother's breast. I've always needed blood to live!" she laughed, and then she'd scream, then weep and weep and weep, then laugh, and weep again. "Doms need death in order to survive."

The storyteller tried to fasten the crucifix around her neck for protection, but, in fear of it, she threw it down, stamped on it, kicked it, then ran away and into another dark spell of long weeping.

In the beginning the fits were seasonal, coming with the dry hot winds of Jeth; then, after the second miscarriage, there were trances each month—she's refuse to wear the menstrual cloth and blood dripped down her legs and she laughed mad laughter. After a few more months she stopped menstruating altogether, and as the seizures occurred more and more often, more and more unpredictably, the storyteller feared that the Vetala Raja had been victorious: *I moved forward to Mina Harker, who by this time had drawn her breath and with it had given a scream so wild, so ear-piercing, so despairing that it will ring in my ears until my dying day. For a few seconds she lay in her helpless attitude and disarray. Her face was ghastly, with a pallor which was accentuated by the blood which smeared her lips and cheeks and chin; from her throat trickled a stream of blood; her eyes were mad with terror. Then she put before her face the poor crushed hands, which bore on their whiteness the red mark of the Count's terrible grip, and from behind them came a low desolate wail which made the terrible scream seem only the quick expression of an endless grief. . . .*

The deliria and trances turned into possessions: first she was a woman who identified herself as "Mari, Mari," and Brahm asked if it was really "Mary," called her "Memsahib," and she laughed, "Yes, yes it's me—(*Mera nam Memsahib*)—you ran away from me and that's why I've come back to get you. Haha!"

He spoke to her in English: "Why can't you find rest?"

"Phairog ma no no no mistar nen! Tohar helloo birg ho," her answer was no language that he recognized.

"Speak to me in English!" he demanded in Hindi, and it made her laugh: "You can't make deals with ghosts."

The possessions were stories: The "mari" was a ghost who, subsisting on fetal blood, caused miscarriages; and once upon a time she was a blood-drinking mosquito, another time a spider, another time a crow that she had eaten, and then a vulture feeding on her own flesh in the cremation ground of her childhood. After those possessions she told Brahm that to be an animal is to always be in fear. Every moment is distressed. Every instant a terror.

"My father's dead and has been burned," she announced one morning without emotion. "He came to me last night and he beat me." And she showed Brahm inexplicable bruises on her legs and arms. Her madness both aroused and repulsed him, made him desire and detest her at once and in equal measure, and the more aroused he was, the more disgusted, and the more disgusted, the more spurred to take her in his arms, to open her mouth, her legs, and heart.

One morning she again begged him to burn the book: "The

vampire escaped from it last night and he came for me to make me drink his blood. I was afraid, but at the same time I wanted it. I wanted it. He crossed from one story into another and wanted me to go back with him. And I wanted it." And, as she described it, he could hear the clear voice of Memsahib beneath him in her grave: *With his left hand he held both Mrs. Harker's hands, keeping them away with her arms at full tension; his right hand gripped her by the back of the neck, forcing her face down on his bosom. Her white nightdress was smeared with blood, and a thin stream trickled down the man's bare breast which was shown by his torn open dress.*

Brahm persistently wondered if Memsahib had really believed that the Vetala Raja was more than a story. He himself believed and yet knew that he could stop believing it, that he had the power to let it be real or not. The power to deliver Mena or to deny her madness was, however, beyond him, the stuff of heroic tales only.

Finally the storyteller took his mistress to the temple of Bhairavi where wild women with matted hair wailed to the fierce goddess on Mena's behalf; but the goddess was deaf to every supplication and, though he did not want to go with her back to Banaras, the exorcists at Pishach Mochan were, by reputation, their only hope.

They entered the city after dark. Night had come, it seemed, too suddenly, as if by ominous eclipse, the sun covered by the gigantic wings of alighting vultures, the flap of heavy wings lifting bulking bodies, the strain on flesh-fed, predatory muscle, flap, flap, wide black wings across the sun, the sinister shade and gloom of vultures' wings.

The magicians at Pishach Mochan seemed to be expecting them. Demonic faces painted on inverted pots, garlanded with flowers, starred at them. The trees were encrusted with nails pounded into their bark, and black ribbons were tied to those rusting nails around each of which the tree bled a ring of shiny black sap. Crows cawed in the naked branches above.

The ojha scrutinized Mena as Brahm enumerated her symptoms. He spent seven days before conceding that the demons who had taken charge of her soul were stronger than he was. He had tried everything: coconuts were offered to Hanuman, and her eyelids were anointed with the oil that dripped slowly from his orange-painted body of stone. A gem was placed in her mouth while the ojha recited mantras: "*Phrum phuh phuh prah phat phrah phat namah . . .* " But the rattle of the syllables, whispered screams and spellbinding incantations, did not penetrate her. She was bathed in the tank and fed opium and small doses of datura to poison the demons, was ornamented with saffron and ash, decorated with amulets (containing splinters from five different trees, each one an arrow). The exorcist wrapped a thread of seven colors (yellow, red, green, blue, white, violet, and black) seven times around her neck—a twisted thread, with seven knots tied in it and seven human ash-filled amulets dangling from it. He seated her in a circle of rice flour, inscribed her breasts in turmeric, with secret names of the goddess and then he called out to the demon in her, cursed, cajoled, flattered, insulted him or her or it or them. He slapped Mena with his left hand and kicked her with his left foot. He spit on her and she sat silent, showing no expression of pain, symptom of fear, nor any sign of anything. Burning the skin at the base of her spine with a heated metal rod, he forced a blister to form, pierced it, drained it, then took the fluid from her body into a little vial that he buried in the ground, then marked the place with a swastika and an inverted pot. Nothing.

"There's an exorcist in Bihar who may be able to help," the defeated ojha explained. "I believe that perhaps your stories have enchanted her. Stories are, you must know, quite dangerous. They can be, anyway. This exorcist is a storyteller too, a bard like you; but his are magic stories and he cures with them. He has stories to frighten fearful spirits and send them far away."

On the road to the village in Bihar she was sullen, quiet, apprehensive of another attack. Begging Brahm's forgiveness, she fell asleep with her head in his lap. He stroked her hair and looked at her, saw more than one possessing soul asleep in her, one that was carnal and heated, full of desire, wet and supple, another that was cool, dry, even cruel, another fierce soul that seemed to watch over those two; and another, the departed spirit of someone he had known before but could not remember, and another, and another. . . . Brahm lifted her head gently from his thigh, set it back down upon the ground, rose, and went to sleep away from her. The teller of ghost stories was, he realized, afraid of her.

She followed him from a distance, and he did not turn to look at her as they walked toward the village that was easy to locate because of the spreading reputation of the storytelling exorcist who was staying there for the season.

Brahm recognized him at once, the old man, gray-bearded, clusters of amulets dangling from his neck and wrists, the peacock-feather fan, lean and shirtless, wrapped only in an unsewn black loin cloth, wearing that earring, a small skull fashioned out of silver. He remembered him, his eyes closed, spreading his arms, sitting in the posture of ascetic on the veranda of the Thomson's cantonment house. Bhutnath Kathuwala. Brahm fell at his feet and addressed him as "guru."

Stroking the younger storyteller's hair, the old man listened to his story: "I remember everything you said, every word of every story. "Listen—*There was a brahmin, good Govindaswami, in this village, my very own. . . . Narasimha growled and shrilled, hissed ecstatic laughter in the twilight (neither day nor night). . . . On the sixteenth day of the great battle, blaze-eyed Bhima, his hair like black smoke from the fires of revenge burning his skull, knocked Duhshasan from his chariot with his terrible blood-stained mace.* I remember everything. Do you remember me? Do you remember the little boy who was entranced by your tales, enchanted by your voice? I've searched for you as if for a father. Do you remember those Angrezi people, Memsahib and the malaria doctor? The Inspector and his daughter? My mother, the sweeper woman? You gave me this silvery amulet, tied it with black string around my arm. Remember?—you had come back to the house after the foreigners had gone away. You came to help my mother. What happened to my mother? Do you know?"

The old storyteller was silent; the young one began again, now softly: "Without you I would not even have known that there was such a thing as a storyteller. I would not have been able to leave, to take to the road. I would have been a hamal, a miserable houseboy. Stories, telling them and hearing them, have been my liberation. I owe you everything, my freedom and any happiness that I've enjoyed."

He placed his bag, the green book, and the silk top hat at the feet of the old storyteller: "This, guruji, is all that I have in the world. I give it to you. Everything. This is my kingdom. I'll serve you." As he spoke, the exorcist looked at the young woman standing nearby and, instinctively understanding that it was because of her that they had come, he motioned for her to move closer and sit down. He took her hand, caressed it, leaned forward, and as he whispered in her ear she closed her eyes and appeared calmed.

Bhutnath Kathuwala picked up the book, smelled it, fanned the pages, laughed, and tossed it back to Brahm: "What would I want with a book? Why would I need a book? I'm a storyteller. Books, books! No good. Books are dangerous, very dangerous, full of infection. I don't like books. That's why I don't learn to read. Reading is bad, very bad. Don't read if you want to be a storyteller. Just listen to stories, stories that are alive and change. The written story is dead. It never grows. Don't read or you'll catch the disease that killed the story in the coffin-book. English book? Yes, English. English is especially bad. We'll have independence some day. Burn the book. Burn everything that is English."

He picked up the top hat, turned it over, looked inside of it: "Why would I want this? It's English too. It's empty." Laughing, he threw it down next to the book, reached for Brahm's bag, looked in. "This is better," he smiled. "This is full. Haha! There's money, everybody needs money. I like money better than books or hats.

"What else would you give me?"

"When I was a child, I heard you tell the story of King Harishchandra. I would be a Dom rather than to deny you anything. I would give you my wife, this woman, my son if I had one, and myself. I would do whatever you asked me to do."

The storyteller ordered his disciple to go away. "Take your hat and book and leave the village. I must be alone with this girl for some time. Go away and stay away for a while. Travel from village to village telling stories and only when you've earned one hundred and one rupees with your stories, then come back and I'll be ready for you. Do you understand? Don't return until you have the one hundred and one rupees, earned by storytelling only."

Brahm bowed to his preceptor and obediently left the village and Mena behind. He knew a jeweler in Daudnagar with whom he struck a bargain: if the craftsman would make some rings for him with stones in them that looked mysterious, the storyteller would sell them in the villages for many times the value of the materials of which they were made. The ornament maker and the storyteller could share the easy profits. Once the jeweler reluctantly agreed to it, Brahm, with the magic rings for sale, wandered from village to village telling stories of bhuts and prets and vetals and selling the charmed rings to protect their wearers from the dead.

The wary jeweler, almost certain that the itinerant would cheat him, was so delightedly surprised with the profits that he gave Brahm an anklet that the storyteller had eyed and fondled—it matched the one that Mena carried.

It was the first time since they had met, since they had rowed together on the Ganga, that the hero of the love story had been separated from the heroine, and he himself was surprised that he missed her, feared for her, prayed and ached for her. In estrangement, he forgave her madness, accepted her weakness, and understood her misery, convincing himself that the demons who possessed her would relinquish her—Bhutnath would drive them out, redeem her true spirit—

and once more he might float with her in the Ganga, smoke and laugh with her, tell her stories about Malati and Madhava, Sita and Ram, Shakuntala and King Dushyanta. He might, once again, seat her on his lap to point out the constellations and tell her the stories that connect those stars, the myths that are the flesh of those sidereal skeletons.

Knowing that Brahm would return, that he would have a hundred and one rupees and no fewer hopes or expectations, Bhutnath waited for him, squatting by the road that led into the village.

As they sat together, facing one another beneath a withering flame tree, the old man, smoking one of the cigarettes from the pack that Brahm had proudly brought him, counted the one hundred and one rupees and then placed his hand on Brahm's knee, looked into his eyes, snuffed out the cigarette in the dirt, and spoke with melancholy tenderness, advising Brahm to let Mena go: "She should not be with you. Your stories are not good for her; travel is not good for her; you're not good for her. Take her away from here. She can't stay here—they don't want her here. Take her somewhere where you can leave her and then abandon her forever. If you don't do this, both of you will die. That's certain. Do you understand? Do this as soon as possible. You, like Harishchandra, have made a promise. You said you'd obey me. Do it without another word."

Bhutnath Kathuwala refused to hear Brahm's protestations, his petition to stay with the old man, to learn tales from him, to follow him on the road and discover the use of stories for exorcism: "The woman's not important now. I want to be your student, your son."

"Go away. Take her with you. Then leave her, abandon her as Harishchandra deserted his wife despite his feelings for her. Suspend all feeling. That's what the storyteller needs to do. Continue to wander, telling stories as you go. Forget her. Listen for stories on the road, and remember the stories you hear and tell them. But, whatever else you do, leave the woman. Leave her or you'll kill her; leave her, or you'll die," he laughed for some strange reason: "The storyteller, no less than the renouncer, must be alone."

Although Brahm promised it, he didn't know if he had the strength to do it, and the old storyteller gave two gifts to his disciple: the silver earring, the little skull that dangled from his ear and glistened by lamplight; and his name—"Kathuwala." "The earring will go nicely with the top hat," he smiled. "You want to look mysterious. And, in time, once you leave her, the name will suit you."

Mena trailed after him from the village in Bihar and he could hear the jingling of the matching anklets. She followed him for almost a year and he tolerated her attacks and possessions (though sometimes he had to gag and bind her to protect her from injuring or killing herself), and she endured the knowledge, unsaid but certain, that he'd leave her. Sometimes it made her laugh out loud; other times it made her weep; at all times he struggled to ignore both the laughter and the tears.

One night by a fire, while Mena dozed, it occurred to Brahm that Bhutnath Kathuwala, long ago, might well have told Kalyani to abandon her child. He could hear the old man's voice: "The boy will be alright; the English madam will care for him. But you, you must leave this house or you will die."

In a village in Ballia district where they had been before the schoolmaster let them stay in the schoolroom that was empty at night and furnished with a charpoy—unable to sleep, the storyteller sat up and lit a cigarette. Mena *Harker was aroused by the quick movement and turned to him with her arms stretched out as though to embrace him; instantly, however, she drew them in again, and putting her elbows together, held her hands before her face and shuddered till the bed beneath her shook. . . .*

They left the village and slept in a shrine at the edge of the rice paddies. She awakened him in the middle of the night with her screaming: "I'm death," she shrieked, and laughed. "Let me dance for you, let me fill you with desire. . . ." As she danced, she struck him, pounded his chest with her hands, grabbed the silver skull and, yanking it, split the lobe of his ear. Blood gushed out, down his neck, and she threw her arms around him, clung, and sucked the wound, lapping up his blood. The terror of the teller of terrible stories was modulated only by his sorrow. He slapped her, pushed her back, thrashed her as her father had once done, and tied her hands behind her back and bound her ankles, trussed her as the Tantric priest had constrained Malati, as the Doms had bound the wife of Harishchandra. And he wept for the first time since his mother had disappeared.

"I believe you, Mena," he said. "And because you're death and beautiful, I leave you. I don't want to die; but you, you dear Mena, make me want to die."

Brahm didn't know what had happened to Mena since he left her; he had stories he could have told about her: horror stories and love stories, stories of heroism and of fear, sad stories and joyous ones; in one she married a rich merchant; in another she became a prostitute; in another she returned to her family and was made queen of the cremation ground; in another she became a mendicant nun or the priestess of Bhairavi; then there were the supernatural stories: she was a churel, a sorceress, a bride of Dracula the Vetala Raja. Or she was dead—in that story her ghost was searching for Brahm, stalking him, and he sensed her presence that night in the Christian cemetery with
the sound of the riots in the distance.

He hadn't abandoned her on the night when he beat her; it was almost two months later when he left. The day had been calm and scented by southern breezes. In the shade of great white clouds, he had told her a pleasant story about Memsahib and Varney the dog and life in the cantonment in the old days. She breathed easily in sleep that night in Chandraprabha in harmony with the soothing sighing of the falls. He stared at her for a long time, smoked cigarette after cigarette and, when the packet was empty, he simply rose and walked away while she slept, so that she might awaken to wonder if he had been a dream. As dream he might be forgiven.

After abandoning her, if sometimes he heard the howling of jackals or hyenas in the night, he would imagine that it was Mena's call. Without Mena, the Dom child, he let his hair and beard grow and began to go to prostitutes. The whores of Banaras knew secrets and stories, comic and terrible, and he loved one simply because her name was Malati—and he didn't mind that she sold herself to other men, that she made love to women too, and that she sometimes forgot his name or did not even recognize him. When she died of cholera, he paid for the cremation with all the money he had and watched the Doms burn her at Harishchandra ghat, sat with four weeping whores to watch the blazing body on the pyre being consumed. In the swirling black smoke he saw Malati (dead), Memsahib (dead), and his mother Kalyani (dead), and Mena (not dead, not alive, but, like a character in a story, eternally Un-Dead).

The crematory fires seemed to consume the entire earth and it took Brahm's breath away. Spark of light . . . skies of fire . . . and Brahm awoke.

It was dawn, the first day of the light half of the month of Shravan. He rose from the surface of Mary Thomson's grave, ran his finger over his teeth and gums, rubbed his eyes, placed the top hat on his head, and looked around him. He listened and sniffed the smoky air and wanted a cup of tea. It was as quiet as graveyards were supposed to be. He felt safe now from the Vetala Raja and from memory; the rioting seemed to have stopped.

He walked past the site of the Thomson house which had, after Dr. Thomson's return to England, become a Dak Bungalow, and he was curiously unmoved by the spectacle of the smokey ruins from the fire set by rioters during the night. All feeling was suspended as he saw the hovering afterimage of the fire-consumed room on the second floor where he had slept near Memsahib. The bed, draped in white mosquito netting, shimmered, then crumbled, and the black cinders of it were blown away, swept up into whispering wisps of spectral smoke. He imagined his mother amidst the black rubble with one hand on her hip, the other holding her broom of reeds—too much to sweep up and yet not enough. "There's nothing left for her to do; she's free now." He wondered if she had ever returned to the house and how Memsahib, arriving home from the hill station, had felt to find the boy gone. "How did she explain it? Did she weep for me?"

Swarming crows waited for still glowing embers to cool so that they might descend to scavenge among the ashes of Brahm's childhood home—the fire an appropriate cremation, the storyteller felt, to release spirits from a dead body, the charred bones of which were now strewn about. It was no less a nocturnal sacrifice to gain blessings for those spirits. The flames had not been those that raged in Memsahib's Christian's Hell but had been those that Brahm Kathuwala knew as the holy, purifying, sacrificial fires of liberation.

The storyteller, turning and walking away as he had done in childhood, set out for the villages to tell his stories, sell his amulets, and confront the Vetala Raja again.

Careful to avoid the army and police patrols in Banaras, he stayed clear of the ravaged heart of the city.

Stopping to rest by a slow curve in a stream, an offshoot of the Varana near Raj Bazaar Road, he looked down at his reflection in the oily water of the dirty rivulet that sluggishly made its way to merge back into the larger Varana, with it to converge with the Ganga, flowing into her and purged by that absorption into that ever-flowing mother, and then after being regestated, being cleansed and purified by offering purification to suppliants, some of its waters would break away to enter tributaries, carrying invisible memories of everything ever reflected in it.

His face shimmered, the top hat, the silver-skull earring, the gray beard: "Who is this man, this reflection in the river of stories? And why does the Vetala Raja not have a reflection?" The storyteller shivered with the uncanny feeling that he was, like the figures in his own stories—like Madhava, Harishchandra, Jonathan Harker, and the sons of Govindaswami—being composed, made up, fabricated not of flesh and bone but of borrowed words and phrases, sentences, paragraphs, and plots. The character, invented, imagined, or real, had been in a village, telling that old, old story of Vijaya and Sanjaya.

My storyteller urgently felt that he had to return to that village in order to finish the story he was telling and to find out what happened or would happen in the stories others told or lived. "What will become of the carpenter, his son, and the faithless wife?" he wondered with a smile as he turned and walked toward the village in Ballia district to take his place on the platform under the pipal tree with its ever-trembling leaves. He knew that they were waiting for him to tell his story.

6

The magician received the corpse joyfully, and honored it with unguents and garlands of blood, and he placed the corpse, possessed of the Vetala, on its back in a great circle marked out with powdered human bones, in the corners of which were placed pitchers of blood, and which was lighted with lamps fed by oil from the human body. And he sat on the breast of the corpse, and holding in his hand a ladle and spoon of human bone, he began to make an oblation of clarified butter in its mouth. Immediately such a flame issued from the mouth of that corpse possessed by the Vetala, that the sorcerer rose up in terror and fled.

KATHASARITSAGARA OF SOMADEVA (ELEVENTH CENTURY); TRANSLATED BY C. H. TAWNEY AS *THE OCEAN OF THE STREAMS OF STORY* (1880)

What's the use of this body—
aggregate of contempt,
abode of repeated deaths?
With its ornaments, its fine
clothing,
its pleasing
sandal scents?
Within it there's shit and the liver,
worms and the bladder,
a tangled net of guts—
While it rots, on its last day,
even crows and hogs
turn their faces away from it.

MUNIMATAMIMAMSA OF KSHEMENDRA (ELEVENTH CENTURY); TRANSLATED BY GODFREY SANDERS (1899)

On the 29th December 1911 Mr. Ishan Chandra Sen, Deputy Magistrate, convicted one Krishna or Kinto Das Babajee, mendicant, in the Magistrates Court, Banaras, under section 290 of the Indian Penal Code of committing a public nuisance by eating the flesh of a human corpse at the cremation and bathing ghat in that town. Mr. Kernath Basu who was one of the witnesses for the prosecution saw the accused exhume portions of a half burned corpse and then eat some of it. . . . Mr. Basu saw this beastly creature eat the vomit of a dog and expose his naked body to the public. Another Hindu gentleman deposed to see the accused eating the remains of a corpse. The Court fined the offender Rs. 15 with the option of 15 days' imprisonment. Such is typical of the Aghorapanthis. They go about nude, smeared with human excrement, with a fresh human skull in their hands, out of which they had previously eaten the putrid flesh, and afterwards scraped out the brain and eyes with their fingers, into which is poured whatsoever is theirs to drink, and to this they pretend to be indifferent whether it be ardent spirits or water. . . . The Aghori is an object of terror and disgust. Hindus, however, look on these wretches with veneration, and none dare to drive them from their doors.

CHIEF INSPECTOR JOHN WESTON, INDIAN IMPERIAL POLICE REPORT ON AGHORIS, JOURNAL OF THE CRIMINOLOGICAL INSTITUTE OF BOMBAY (1919)

21 May 1991

(EIGHTH LUNAR DAY OF THE LIGHT HALF OF VAISHAKH, SAMVAT 2048; DURGA'S EIGHTH).

Despite his son's begging, Mitu won't go to hear the storyteller tonight. He has awakened this morning with fresh scratches on his face, and now he stands looking into the mirror at the network of scabs across his forehead, cheeks, and chin. The scratch across his lip still hurts and, though the pain is slight, it frightens him. It cannot have been his wife, he reasons, for she didn't come home last night; and certainly Nishad wouldn't or couldn't have done this to him. Why hadn't the pain awakened him?

All day, much to his annoyance, people have been asking him about it: "What happened to your face, Mitu," the toddyman, nudging the schoolmaster, laughed—"Love scratches? Fight scratches? Tell me the story."

"Where is she?" Mitu asks the fragment of mirror: the sight of his face there and the pain caused by its silence overwhelms him, makes him feel helpless and weak. It's as though he's dying, being devoured from the inside by some terrible demon from one of Brahm Kathuwala's horrid stories, and he wishes Sanjaya, the brave wrestler of Varanasi, were real and alive, that he'd come to kill his demons, a fiction to abduct a reality, drag it away, make it insubstantial.

The old goatherd won't go to hear the storyteller either: "What's the use of such stories? Why do people enjoy being frightened and disgusted? I appreciated them when I was younger, I suppose, when the storyteller came here long ago. But not now. These tales are for children. There's nothing high-minded about them." Turning on his radio, adjusting the tuner and turning the bicycle-spoke antenna in a futile attempt to cleanse the crackle from the devotional song that is being broadcast, he boasts to himself that he, personally, prefers the purity of such inspirational, spiritual entertainments to the impurities of the sort of fantasy that has drawn people to the pipal tree. "What pleasure is there in horrible stories?"

His neighbors must know the answer, for they are sitting once again in a gathering around the storyteller, anxious to savor the delectable terrors of the evening. There are more women here tonight than there were last night or on the first evening of stories. The marigolds that have been set before Brahm Kathuwala are dead now, drooping and dusty like unfulfilled desires, dried and faded by the summer heat, but still there in the unbaked clay vase, casting a shadow across the platform that, to Nishad, looks like the silhouette of a rakshasa: the vase its neck, the dead flowers its wild hair, the dry stems and withered leaves its grotesque features—the gaping mouth is dotted with curved and pointed fangs and lined with jagged, broken teeth.

The boy has tied the storyteller's amulet around his arm in the same manner in which his father has fixed his own charm. Anxious to learn of what has become of Sanjayadatta and Vijayadatta, the sons of the good brahmin Govindaswami, Nishad listens intently to the continuation of the story: *The king was ill and dying. Then, in the old days, a king's affliction made sick the land; a ruler's disorder disordered the kingdom. The maharani no longer laughed: she wept now for her husband and for herself; fearfully, wrapped in a black shawl, she promised to burn herself upon her lord's pyre, as if that vow would save him.* Brahm speaks slowly and purposefully with the understanding that the villagers need the rest of the story now. They are bewitched. His clear eye surveys them, meets and penetrates their eyes; his mouth shoots barbed words that lodge in their ears. His clouded eye hides in the shadow of the brim of his tilted hat. The storyteller smiles lackadaisically now, a smile at once comforting, seductive, and demonic: *The malarial fever raged in the king and scorched his soul. He was without appetite, the mouth too dry to eat, the tongue too sore, the nausea too violent, and yet, despite not having eaten, his stomach had become bloated. His urine was yolky yellow and thick, almost curdled, steamy and putrid, and there was ominous, rusty-red blood in his excrement. The physicians shook their heads forebodingly during the examination: the skin was a dry sand yellow that augurs death; the long nails, brittle and chipped, a dry bone black that promises pain. His genitals were shriveled. He slept, when he could sleep, in a slight sleep of expansive panic, an apprehension that the weight of his body would squeeze, press, and crush the vessels in his body stopping the flow and pulse of the dark thickening blood. His dreams were grizzle gray. And when he awakened from them, the light stinging his eyes, to a conscious fear no less overwhelming, a feeling that his bones were turning to chalk, he could envision stringy, scarlet-blistered muscles glued by rotten gelatins to those softening bones wrapped with hardening violet veins. He could smell himself: ulcerated sacs and bulging pouches of grit and rot, of plague and slime, green, yellow, and brown. He touched his lacerated lips, cracked and sore at the corners, and felt delicate, translucent peels of skin. There were moans, whispers, and terrible growls deep inside his burning ears.*

The physicians were impotent: none of their herbs, potions, or spells, none of the prayers or sacrifices of the priests, could take hold of the pestilential fever in him. The dark clouds over the land did not rain, nor move, nor give a thing. The maharani, pulled her dark shawl across her face to hide her tears from him.

"There are, of course, rings and amulets for health, stones from deep within the earth that can keep disease away," Brahm carefully explains. "This one, for example, my brothers, cures digestive problems—diarrhea, constipation, gas, hemorrhoids; this one's for the heart, and this for impotence. This one for frigidity. Headache. Faintness. Lethargy. There are amulets for everything. But the longer the disease has been in the body, the tighter the clutch of its claws, the deeper the bite of its teeth, the less influential are the amulets. They must be worn for protection before the sickness, or at the very beginning. The effectiveness diminishes. Better buy them now, before it's too late."

Without breaking the story, without having to elaborate his pitch, the storyteller sells a ring to the toddyman—a bright purple gem said to be a ruby, set in what's claimed to be silver. The schoolmaster, not to be slighted, purchases an amulet—a copper tube dangling on a black string, said to contain sweet-scented ashes from Harishchandra ghat in Varanasi. Blessings accrued by the virtuous behavior of King Harishchandra, whose story has been recounted over those ashes, are shed, by virtue of the telling of that story, upon the one who wears that amulet: "The gods will deliver you from your misery if you are as patient and resolute as Harishchandra."

To establish that he was providing a service to them, rather than money for himself, the storyteller-magician freely gives several charms away to the children—small cylinders rolled from the pliable metal cut from an empty paan masala tin. Nishad holds his tightly in his hand as if it will protect him from the fears this night's stories are certain to evoke. Together with the one tied around his arm, it will guard him from the ghosts that arise from every story told. Stories, he understands, can bring the dead to life; it follows then, he reasons, that they can kill the living.

When the Lingayat asks to purchase the crucifix around Brahm's neck, the storyteller laughs with surprise: "No, it would be dangerous for you. It only works for me because a Christian gave it to me; if I were to sell it to you, that might cause us both great misfortune."

For the last two days, rumors have been spreading through the village: strange tracks, not identifiable as either human or as belonging to any known beast, have been observed in the fields; a dark form, its eyes, according to the tailor's report of what his wife has told him, like pinpoints of fire, has been seen moving in the shadows around the village at dusk, near the mango grove; there's been the faint, distant sound that can't quite be discerned—an eerie cry, at once pitiful moan of despair and threatening shout of wrath. Is it some pret or vetal, some rakshasa or pishacha, churel or bhut? "It's the restless spirit of the toddyman's wife," the washerman confides to his own wife. "That's what happens whenever there's a violent, untimely death. It's inevitable. It's not our fault that she was run over by the truck that night (why was she on the road at that hour anyway?); but still she's tormented and so she returns to beleaguer us."

Others believe that it's the potter's daughter, murdered by her father last year when he discovered her plan of running away with a Muslim boy from Muzaffarpur. It was the arak's fault and nobody ever mentions the crime except the potter himself, in distended, bathetic, and confused confessions, whenever he's drunk. The daughter's restless and vengeful ghost abhors everyone in the village; their torment would be her delight.

It's inevitable that stories of ghosts, fiends, and monsters are

contagious, that they spread through the villages where Brahm Kathuwala tells his tales, and the storyteller capitalizes on this by selling extra amulets to keep away whatever demons and ghosts there are. In expectation of the return of the Vetala Raja, the storyteller is no less baited by the story than the villagers; but "I'm not afraid," he whispers under his breath. "I'm not afraid of *you*." The night is quiet. *He*'s not here.

Brahm notices the absence of Mitu and the old goatherd, and, while speaking, he wonders where they are, hoping for their sake that they do not stray too far away. *Like a disease itself, the story of the king's illness spread and men were greedy for the rumored rewards that would be bestowed upon anyone who could combat the contagion.* The storyteller speaks of avarice, fabricates a quote from the *Bhagavadgita* and recites it in made-up Sanskrit—it warns them that avidity spawns demons, releases terrors in the world, and works a wicked magic. Proverb-spiced sermons, provided they are brief, justify and empower the storyteller's stories. *Greed is a rakshasa, lust his wife, their offspring are our petty fears and little cravings.* These asides infuse his tales with what seems an ancient wisdom (wise precisely and solely to the degree that it is ancient), and they prompt the mind to supply allegorical significance, mysterious, vague meanings that can be strongly sensed but not clearly articulated or explained.

A magician appeared in the court, stood near the king whose throne had been replaced by a cot. Servants worked constantly to replace the silk pillows as quickly as their king dirtied them. "I have the power to heal the king," the magician, after but a moment of looking at the king, boasted with a bow. It seemed not so much a bow of respect to the monarch as a more arrogant bow to himself.

Sanjaya and Vijaya recognized the sorcerer at once—the Skullbearer, naked, smeared with white ashes, pale white as a corpse, the white scar on his cheek, the silver skull ring, the ash-caked beard of serpentine locks, the white garlands of rat skulls and dark rudraksha beads, the milky sloughed skin of a krait his sacred thread. He hadn't changed at all. Not at all. He, however, did not recognize them; the boys whose hands he had read were now the very men he'd said they'd be. Their father, by the way, the good brahmin Govindaswami—remember?—had passed away that year and they had performed the rites for him. Their mother too had died, just after her husband, burned to death. There was something horrible and strange, mysterious, unsolved in that—ah, but that's another story.

Silently Mitu is crawling on his hands and knees beneath the windows of the village houses, stealthily peering into each one in both hope and fear that he might find his wife. Almost every house is empty. The potter, who hasn't gone to hear any of the stories, is weeping in his hut, passively accepting the continuous castigations of his wife; like a kitten licking milk spilled on a filthy floor, he laps up the reproach and disgrace that is poured out around him.

Hearing the music from the nearby goatherd's house (*"Har, Har, Mahadeva! Har! Har! Har!"*), and though the man was certainly too old to be a seducer, Mitu checks on it just to be sure. No, his wife isn't there—of course not. The old man, a widower of some years, illuminated by the smokey light of his kerosene lamp, is lying on his back, dead still, his mouth open, staring at the ceiling or through it perhaps and into the depths of dark, hot sky, as he listens to religious songs on the radio, and Mitu feels a curious envy for him, for the life which, except for his goats, is one of utter solitude. Such isolation, Mitu reasons, must be full of peace. He creeps on tiptoe up to each house and shack. "Where is she? Where is she? She must be somewhere here."

The wife of the village washerman, returning home from the pipal tree, sees him prowling in the shadows and, instinctively gasping with sudden fear, darts back and behind a tree, her heart pounding, certain that it's some demon there, that the rumors that have been spreading through the village are true. "It wasn't the toddyman's wife, nor the daughter of you know who; it was a rakshasa," she'll claim later tonight, after the story. "I saw him with my own eyes. I swear it's true. He had tusks all around his mouth and his eyes were burning coals;

his bright red hair was standing straight up on end. It was horrible. His skin was covered with pox, hundreds of red-rimmed, pus-filled craters, and his finger nails and toe nails were so long they curled around like the tails of pigs. He wanted to eat me alive. He wanted to take me, carry me away from here, to do terrible things to me first. Then he'd eat me alive." But her husband, because of what will happen tonight, because of what will end the story at midnight, won't listen to her; his shock will be too great, the horror so vast that he won't be able to hear a thing.

"I'll need someone's assistance, a fearless man, a hero like those in stories if there is such a man in this kingdom," the Skullbearer said, "a man with nerve enough to enter the cremation ground on the last night of the dark fortnight, and in that darkness to face a vetala, subdue him, and bring him to me for the rite."

Vijaya bowed to touch the feet of his brother upon whom all of the eyes in the court had fallen. The hero received his instructions from the sorcerer: they'd rendezvous in the city of dreadful night where ghosts prowled, hyenas howled, where funeral fires shimmered in bats' and owls' eager eyes.

Two jackals were fighting over a severed human arm, growling as they pulled it this way, lustily tugged that way, resolute in their greed, with the sharp teeth in their clamped and drooling jaws firmly fixed. Frozen in torment, grotesque and miserable, criminal corpses, hung on red-rusted iron stakes and in the bleak black and bare branches of dark trees. The sources of the shadows strewn by funeral fire could not be fathomed, neither could one dare to suppose what sort of gaping throats issued the strident shrieks and roars or the stifled murmurs and moans that echoed through the tenebrous city of death.

The storyteller falls silent for a moment, closes his eyes, moves his lips as if muttering some magic spell or protective prayer beneath his breath. That they can tell that he clearly sees the cemetery and Sanjaya there makes it easier for them to see things too, to picture Sanjaya in the smoke and mist and darkness, bowing before the magician who sits cross-legged like the storyteller, the cranial begging bowl, drum, and trident at his side: *the old wizard smiled at Sanjaya and Sanjaya was unnerved by it, for it did not seem to be the cruel, unnatural smile of the Skullbearer but the kinder, known smile of his deceased father, Govindaswami. What could be the meaning of that? I don't know. Sanjaya didn't know, but the sense of his father's presence made the brave man shudder. Warily he prompted himself to stay calm, not to think of his father, to shut the doors of memory, not to feel anything, to remain detached and in that detachment to receive his orders: "Not far from here there's an ashoka tree, its leaves singed by the flames of the funeral fires, and suspended upside-down in its branches is a corpse. There, in that direction—follow that dark path until you see the light. Fetch the body. Bring it here. Go now. And hurry. Hurry!"*

On the path, through the gloomy hall of towering trees, he heard the wind and deeper, deeper in the darkness the gusts seemed to form muted whisperings—Govindaswami's words: "We may try to hold to things, but finally we must let go, let all things pass by and on, through others, into oblivion. In the end there's nothing, and in that there's rest." Fixing his hands over his ears in case it was the bewitching voice of a bhut, a ravening ghost imitating his father in order to lure him away and steal his heart, Sanjaya didn't hear another word. The storyteller falls silent again.

Nishad is overwhelmed with the excitement of the dread that's being evoked, anxious for the story to move along, to pull him through the dark forests, around the bends and turns of terror, past things unknown, to take him to the horrible encounter, the things inevitable, to get them over with. "Get on with it! Hurry! *Hurry!*"

Mitu can't see where he's going. The mango grove is very dark. Holding his own breath in order to listen, he thinks he can hear breathing there, not far from him, breathing—shhhh—and the sound of leaves being stepped on—shhhh, shhhhh. And he's afraid. *Shhhhh!* He's afraid it might be his wife, alone or with a lover, perhaps the wicked Moti, by consent or by force, or, no, not that, it might be a dacoit, a thief or murderer, or someone murdered, dead, risen, and angry, or a terrible animal of some kind. Maybe it's a serpent languorously crawling out of its grim burrow in the storyteller's tales. He can see it in the darkness: the snake silently uncoils to sway, swerve, and

curve its way across the dry ground, to hesitate, raise up its head and expanded hood, and in the shiny black beads of death—its fearless eyes dots of cold fire—the entire grove is reflected. The head, horrid and exquisite, arches and turns. The supple cobra's eyes, glittering with menace, seek Mitu. The split needle of tongue waves and wags through the front of the fatal, lipless mouth to taste the vapors that lace the heated air, to find traces of him in there. Or perhaps the rumors are true—perhaps it is actually some sort of demon, a rakshasa or a vetal, a bhut or pret. Fear-frozen, Mitu leans back against the mango tree trying to quiet his breath, trying not to gasp for fear. Shhhh. *Shhhhh.*

The faint light at the end of the pathway grew brighter and brighter still and then, by that funereal radiance, Sanjaya saw the dark silhouette moving. A man (or could it be a woman?) was dragging a corpse away from the ashoka tree with the singed leaves.

"Stop!" Sanjaya cried out as he rushed forward toward the thief. "Stop," he shouted as he placed his hand on the rag-wrapped shoulder and pulled the intruder around. The cadaver fell from a fingerless grasp and a single open eye, a hideous moon in a dark night of a face, gazed in terror at Sanjaya. It was, yes, yes of course, the leper. Remember? Do you remember him at the tea stall when

Sanjaya and Vijaya were children? Do you remember? I don't know if Sanjaya did or not.

Yes, of course they remember—the storyteller knows how to manipulate memories, understands the ways in which remembrance is the source of horror no less than it is the source of love; he supposes that just as memory gives life to the dead, and is thus the heart of redemption, so too it burdens life with death, clouds our eyes with death. It can squeeze, choke, and paralyze the heart.

Brahm Kathuwala kindles memories in his audiences: each listener provides Sanjaya and Vijaya, the Skullbearer and the king, the rakshasas and rakshasis, with forms and faces from their own memories. He but provides them with names and a place to be. The dark, wide eyes of memory do the rest.

"Let go of me! Get away!" the leper snarled. "What are you doing? Get away!" There in that dreadful cemetery, amidst the lonely dead, the two living men, the leper and the wrestler, by the light of funeral fire, struggled over the corpse. The leper, though he was old, was strong—leprosy, they say, can give a man an unnatural strength, a demonic potency. Like the flame of a candle sometimes, just before it burns out, so the power of the body swells and magnifies itself just before the surrender. There's a lust just before death, a brilliant, blinding blaze of light on the brink of infinite abysmal darkness.

The leper needed that corpse for a tantric rite by which, it had been promised, a magic cure for his leprosy would be effected. His toes and fingers, his lips and nose, would, he had been assured, grow back. He would be fair again. He would smile and be at ease. He would hold a woman in his arms, touch her tenderly with clean and gentle fingers, and she too would smile and lean over him, kiss his lips with hers, drink his fragrant breath.

But he did not tell this to Sanjaya. No, no, of course not. "Don't interfere. Leave me alone. This is my friend and I must take him," the leper lied as he reached down to clutch the arm of the corpse between his fingerless hands. "It's my duty to perform the funerary rites for him. Get away!"

"No," the resolute and fearless Sanjaya responded, grasping the cadaver's other arm. "I'll not let this dead man go. He's my friend and it is I who will perform the cremation for him. It's my duty. Get away!"

Each one knew the other had lied.

The leper pulled the body toward himself, wrapped his arm around the neck; Sanjaya tugged back on the other arm with such force that the body, ripped from the leper's embrace, flew past him into a heap upon the ground, the pallid face pressed into the burnt black earth. Suddenly the head twisted around and the eyes opened wide. The corpse stretched open its mouth, exposed the broken teeth, the black tongue, and screamed a terrible scream, a hideous howl that verged on a laughter that, in turn, verged back on scream.

The storyteller's sudden histrionic laughter chills the audience. Their eyes are wide, their throats dry, their bodies still. They hear the horror, taste the terror; and it's wonderful. They gasp with the benignly cruel pleasure of this entertainment.

With his hand over his heart, fingers extended and spread, eyes closed tight, the storyteller gasps for air *and the leper gasped for air but could not breathe. He clutched his chest, gasped more and harder, his eyes as wide as the corpse's, gasped, gasped, fell, and moaned. . . . he was dead.* Brahm Kathuwala, his lips slightly open, is silent for moment. His crystalline right eye opens wide and the kerosene firelight illuminates it: *He was dead. Dead.* The storyteller smiles slightly, relaxes his gaze then and speaks softly: *To die of terror. Think of it. All terror is rooted in a terror of death and yet terror itself can kill. We die because we do not want to die; we die of greed, of lust, of all our petty fears and little wishes. . . .*

The philosophical meditation, the return to the sermon on greed, is interrupted by the loud, harsh, honking of a horn. It comes, anxious, impatient, and beseeching, from the border of the village, the place where the drivable road curves back around to join itself and take away whatever it brings. The horn honks again, and again, persistently and irritably announcing something, some emergency perhaps, calling out for help it seems. And Brahm Kathuwala, anticipating his audience's curiosity and apprehension, stops. As if expecting, even planning, such an intermission, he lights a bidi as if to say, "Go, see what it is. I'll wait. One smoke." This distraction from the painstakingly constructed illusion, the shattering of the story-trance, is difficult for him to overcome. He'll have to use it somehow.

Again, and again, the impetuous and insolent sound of the horn: it commands them, "Come here, come quickly, come on, hurry!" Even Nishad, after looking up to the storyteller as if for permission for leave, runs from the gathering place around the pipal tree out toward the road to see what's going on. Mitu, alone in the mango grove, hears it too and is stunned by it. "It must have something to do with my wife," he concludes. "They've found her."

"Some emergency," the Lingayat is certain—someone injured or killed on the road. A bus or truck overturned? Something terrible for sure. The toddyman thinks of the night he lost his wife.

The horn honks again. Again. It's like a demonic groan from Brahm's story, the scream of a mysterious nocturnal beast. Again, again. An unseen hand pushes desperately on the metal bar on the steering wheel: the dauntless tone is sustained, forced upon the night, held hard and with urgency: "Come here, come quickly!"

Nishad is afraid it has something to do with his father. "No, no," he snaps at himself, clutching his new amulet tight. "No, why should it have to do with him?" His mother? "No, why should it have to do with any of us?"

The old goatherd pokes his head out of his doorway cursing: "Quiet! Silence! Let an old man rest! All this racket's going to upset my goats. What did they ever do to you? Have some compassion for an old man and his goats. What's going on here? Quiet!"

"What is it? What's all the noise about?"

"Who's there? What is this?"

Holding his ground beneath the pipal tree, the storyteller lights another bidi. "One more smoke. I wish I had some Charminars." He knows exactly what and who it is: Pradip the videowala with the video-van that he drives through the countryside, from village to village, showing films from the cities. A large screen is revealed when he opens the back doors of the van and he puts the big metal speaker on the roof. He and Brahm crossed paths a month earlier in Bihar, in a village near Gaya, not far from where Lord Buddha attained enlightenment and not far from the village of Mitu's wife.

"How much do you pay to see the film," Brahm asked the villagers in Bihar. Shaking his head with approbation, he tried to convince them that his stories were better than any film. "You don't have to pay for my stories. Of course, for the price of a film or even less, you can buy an amulet or a ring that will help and protect you long after the story's over, long after both the videowala and I are gone. A story's better than a film: a film's the same every time it's shown; whereas a story always changes. It changes for you. You're a part of it, you make it what it is. It's custom-made."

But it's difficult to compete. Young Pradip, full of sparkle and energy, smartly dressed in Western long pants and a T-shirt emblazoned with a likeness of Amitabh Bachchan, has a patter of his own: "Bollywood comes to you, my friends! The wonders of the world delivered to your village! The videovan, rage of America and Europe, entertainment of the future, technology working for you, is here for your pleasure and enlightenment. Enjoy the simple pleasures of village life while partaking of the advanced culture of the big cities." Just as Brahm has his rings and amulets to sell, so Pradip vends Pepsi-Cola and 7-Up, sweets and cigarettes, and also—if you know enough to ask—hashish and whisky, Indian film magazines and foreign magazines with pornographic photographs of women with golden hair.

Brahm had withdrawn from the agon in Bihar and set out upon the road alone, walked to the next village and told ancient stories there. But now, tonight, he decides, he won't give in, won't submit again to technology, won't let the future devour the past.

"We didn't recognize the sound of your horn," the schoolmaster explains with relief and delight. "New horn?"

"New van!" Pradip, surrounded by the men and children of the village, proudly laughs. "Business is good. I'm making everyone happy and I am, thus, prospering. I bring my profits back to my customers. The new van is the latest model now equipped for your pleasure with advanced stereo music! I also sell audio cassettes of film music these days; it will not be any problem if any of you are interested in looking at them after the film."

The side of the van has a poster on it: *KABARISTAN*. Pradip smiles with pride and cheer as he points to the terrifyingly terrified and monstrously mutilated face with bulging eyes and a mouth that's drooling bright red blood: "A hit in Delhi, a smash in Bombay, sold out in Calcutta and Madras! See it tonight, my friends."

The crowd pushes forward to look at the poster and hear his polished pitch: *Come, come closer, and I'll show you the film about the terrible Dr. DeSouza. He is a medical genius. First doctor in Goa to perform a successful heart transplant operation.* Pradip laughs with delight as he motions the villagers to come closer. *But beneath this thin veneer of respectability, great evil lurks. Dr. DeSouza dreams of a formula to bring the dead back to life! He will stop at nothing to realize his dream. And, yes, he needs subjects for his diabolic experiments. Haha! What has driven this great scientist to such perverted and sinister madness? Watch and find out! Come, come closer, gather round, let's see a film, a great film, a masterpiece of horror, scariest of scary films!*

The villagers know Pradip. A year ago he came to show *Ladies' Tailor* and he had warned them that it might be too spicy for the children; just over a month ago he returned and had cautioned them that *Banarsi Babu* might just be too much fun for the elderly. Now he alerts them that *Kabaristan* just might scare them all to death. "It's not a film for those with weak hearts or weak stomachs," he laughs.

"No," the Lingayat says to the toddyman in a muffled voice, "it's a film for those with weak minds."

He's shown horror movies here before: *Sau Saal Ke Baad, Cheekh,* and *Hatyarin*. During the latter, utterly terrified by the story of the beautiful woman who, because of changes in the moon, sprouted long incisors with which she opened the throats of men and drank their blood, Nishad had suddenly jumped up and run home to his mother only to be teased later in the evening by his father for not being more brave.

Now, tonight, Nishad hopes that the others won't think that it's because of fear that he's leaving; but he wants to return to the pipal tree. While he was terrified by *Hatyarin,* he did enjoy (though in a terrible sort of way) the parts he saw; he had, furthermore, utterly cherished *Banarsi Babu* and still imagines the voluptuous, ornamented women joyously singing and playfully dancing on the ghats in Varanasi. Boatmen join in the songs; vendors toss sweets to the children. Nishad can still hear the songs and he hums along with them. But the storyteller, he feels, is his friend and it wouldn't be kind or cordial to leave him without an audience for his story tonight.

Mitu, who has been drawn to the van in hopes of finding his wife or news of her there also withdraws. Certain the deadly snake is in the mango grove, he avoids the north of the village and ventures east toward the river and the village cemetery where his father's body was burned, the cremation ground next to the graveyard where the

casteless ones are buried. There is a small tomb there in which a prosperous Muslim, the last of his creed to die in the village, is inhumed. It would make an ideal trysting place, Mitu thinks. Death, and fears of death, would make it a lovers' refuge. "She's there," the carpenter whispers. "I know it. I can feel it in my bones. She's hiding in that tomb, sighing and laughing in the place of death."

The Lingayat, dismissing the film as something too crass for his taste, opts for tradition over technology, what he cherishes and respects as Indian over what he despises and fears as foreign. While the washerman is attempting to convince Brahm Kathuwala to postpone telling the rest of his story, the toddyman tries to tell Pradip about the storyteller: "Why don't you wait and show us your film tomorrow night? Come along, hear a good story, and then tomorrow we'll all watch your film." The videowala laughs: "Tomorrow I'll be in Chapra, Arah, or Sasaram, or God only knows where. I'm a man on the move. All over the north village people are waiting for their beloved Pradip with his sensational films. Haha! Go listen to your story. These other people are anxious for a film, not some old story, but a film, with music, with real people, in living color! Or, tonight, should I say *deadly* color? Haha! This chilling horror story will thrill you with terror—delectable terrors, enthralling horrors, disgusting and wonderful."

The toddyman, pulled in both directions but finally deciding to return to the tree and to Brahm's story, as if tapped on the shoulder by the crackle of the loudspeaker can't help but turn to look back once more; he stops to watch the opening of the film: *Owls hooted in the Christian graveyard and stuffed bats flew on wires. There was thunder, lightning, rain, and the mad laughter of the evil Dr. DeSouza: "Haha, haha, haha . . ."*

By the time the toddyman finally pulls himself away from the film to push himself back to the scene of the story, Brahm Kathuwala, now standing, has already described Sanjaya putting the corpse over his shoulder to take it to the Skullbearer. He has painted a clear picture of the leper, stricken by a heart attack, lying dead upon the ground. He has conjured up spirits to hover over that mishapened body. Brahm Kathuwala now describes a vetal there, and how he has claimed the corpse of the leper, entered it through the nostrils, filled its lungs, possessed and animated it to make it seem alive again. *With limbs not yet stiff with death, the dead man stood. The disease-distorted face smiled, the mouth drooled, the unblinking eyes blazed,and the dead man, throwing off his shawl, started after Sanjaya, screaming out to him, "Come back, come back with my friend, give me back my friend."*

Over half the audience is gone. Brahm smiles affectionately, with what seems to be a sort of gratitude, at what remains of the gathering around him. "You," he says with a grin, "you the connoisseurs of stories, you are, I know, able to see things with the minds' eyes. You who don't need the crude representations of a film—can you picture Sanjaya? Can you see him now, moving forward, carrying the corpse, here and now, almost reaching the border of cemetery, almost out and free? See him? See him!" The faint music from the film in the distance seeps into the story. There are electric sounds of thunder, screams and howls, drums and dramatic organ blasts.

Suddenly Sanjaya felt the fingerless hand upon his shoulder and heard the mirthless laughter. "Stop! Stop and give my friend back to me."

Perhaps our hero did not know that it was a vetala in the dead body of the leper—perhaps he thought the man had not really died. It seems so, for his courage persisted and he refused to give up the body. "The corpse is mine. It's the body of my friend. It's my duty to perform the rites," Sanjaya lied fearlessly again.

"No, no," the other shrieked. It was not the leper's low, gritty growl but a shrill, sharp cackle. "Haha!" the vetala in the leper's body laughed. Hear him? "Haha!" Hear it! He counted on complicities between the dead: "Let's not fight or argue over this any more. Why not let the corpse himself settle the matter? If the corpse could scream, if he could laugh, then certainly he might answer a question. Let's ask him which one of us he wants to perform the rites for him."

Ever confident, Sanjaya agreed to it and set the body down, propped it up against a rock. The arms hung limp and the head, contorted and awkward with death, tilted lifelessly to the side. Both eyes were open, but while the pupil of one was dilated wide the other

was but a pinpoint.

"Who has the right to take your body?" the storyteller moans in a deep, slow, sonorous, voice. And the eyes of his audience widen in horrified suspense. *"Who shall perform the obsequies for you? Who do you chose? Who do you want to take you?" "Who?" asked Sanjaya; "who?" asked the vetala; and "who?"* asks the storyteller. *"Who? Who?" and the question echoed like the cry of owls through the darkness of the village, the fields and groves.* Nishad hears the owl and it frightens him. Is it real, imagined, or is it from the soundtrack of the film? That, of course, doesn't really matter. Enthralled, the boy sits up straight, swallows, and fixes his gaze on the storyteller.

The mouth of the corpse did not move, but the nasty voice issued from it was sharp and clear: "Whoever feeds me first is my friend. He is my mother and my father. He who feeds me owns me. So feed me! Feed me now! I hunger! Death is all hunger, infinite and horrible appetite. So feed me! Take me! He who feeds me may take me where he wishes. He who feeds me possesses me. Feed me! Feed me leprous flesh, or flesh untainted, either one delicious. Feed meat and blood and life to me. Feed me. Possess me!"

Sanjaya and the vetala in the leper's body, those rivals for the voracious corpse, neither one of them having any food with them to give the starving supplicant, the hungry dead, listened motionless, as stunned as the members of Brahm Kathuwala's audience.

The storyteller, still standing (doing exactly what he, when he was a child, saw Bhutnath Kathuwala do), holds his walking stick up in the air to transform it into Sanjaya's suddenly drawn sword and the audience, like the vetal in the leper's body, thinks it's to slay him, the vetal-possessed leper. *The monster jumped back in vain. Then, in awe and wonder, as if actually struck by the sword, he fell to his knees and watched it—the gruesome spectacle of Sanjaya with that sword slicing into his thigh, through the cloth around his loins, cutting through the skin, across the muscle, turning the blade to plank the meat from his own leg in thin slices, to carve human viands for the corpse. The dead man's neck straightened, the mouth opened and drooled as the swollen tongue stretched forward curling and quivering for the fresh meat. It* *motioned like a finger gesturing, "Come here."* The storyteller's finger becomes that tongue, curling, shaking, pointing. It's as if the ghost of Bhutnath Kathuwala has taken possession of Brahm's body—it's his spirit that moves the finger, his voice utters the words: *Sweet, rich blood dripped around Sanjaya's bent knee, down the trembling calf to form rivulets over the ankle, feeding the scarlet pool beneath his foot. The thirsty earth sucked up the warm blood. The stunned leper bowed in awe and obeisance to the hero and then disappeared, into the darkness, defeated by Sanjaya's greedlessness and courage.*

While the storyteller describes the feeding of the corpse, depicts Sanjaya's own blood on his own fingers as he butchered himself, stripped the meat from his own thigh and pushed it into the ravenous, sucking mouth of the corpse, stuffing it in as the mother crow packs wormy carrion into the beaks of her fledglings, the villagers who have been lured by the videovan watch the evil Dr. DeSouza busy in his laboratory: *there are jars in which human hearts, still beating, gurgle and float; two metal rods with an electric current crackling between them; test tubes and bottles bubbling with vaporous chemicals; a white, waxen corpse has been opened up upon the op-*

erating table, the skin of its abdomen folded and pinned back with spikes.

Mitu, having found the tomb empty, heads for the small hut in the fields that he himself has constructed to give the farmers shelter from the noontime sun of this season. He's proud of himself for having been able to enter the graveyard without any fear of ghosts or spirits. "What is fearful in a story is not fearful in life," the carpenter, though muddled with despair, reflects, "and what's fearful in life is not fearful in a story."

Approaching the hut on tiptoe, Mitu hears the soft noises within it—a breathing, a moaning. "It's her," he whispers aloud, and the image that comes into focus in his imagination is terrible. It chokes and freezes him. He's anguished and afraid.

Dr. DeSouza, searching the night for new victims, is being trailed by a vengeful corpse that he has brought back to life. Its body wrapped in torn and dirty bandages, its arms awkwardly outstretched, the animate cadaver marches slowly but purposefully forward. With a skull in his hands, the wild sadhu sits before the hideous idol chanting the names of Bhairavi. . . .

"This is getting ridiculous," the village washerman reflects as he rises from his place before the video screen, despite having paid for the viewing, to return to the pipal tree. "Ridiculous! What is Mahakali, the terrible Bhairavi, doing in a Christian graveyard. And who is this mummy? He is good or bad? I don't know. And why is the tantric sadhu helping Dr. DeSouza? This story doesn't make any sense. I'll see how the other story is coming along."

Others, now and then, leave the van and return to the pipal tree; still others, then and now, leave the story of Sanjaya to go and see what abominations are being perpetrated by Dr. DeSouza. Passing his brother in the darkness, the washerman asks what's going on in the story that Brahm is telling: "The Skullbearer's waiting for Sanjaya. It's good I suppose, but I'm tired. I've been up since before the dawn—working, working, working. I've got to sleep now. It's work tomorrow, not ghouls or demons tonight, that I'm afraid of. It's my work that haunts me and won't leave me alone. I can't keep my eyes open a moment longer."

Muttering the magic phrases out loud—"Phrum phuh phuh prah phat phrah phat namah"—*incantations to bring Sanjaya back to him with the cadaver, the Skullbearer sat still, waiting outside the mandala, the magic square that he had drawn upon the ground, traced with a white powder milled of human bones. Each corner of the mandala was marked with an urn in which there was blood, congealing and clotting. And midway between those urns, marking the sides of the mandala, there was a pot in which fat burned and the flames danced on the face of the magician.*

The storyteller has strewn the dead marigolds to mark his dais with an area representing the dreadful mandala. He carefully straightens them into lines around the square. *"Phrum phuh phuh prah phat phrah phat namah,"* Brahm Kathuwala chants again, and then again rhythmically, a mantra to bewitch his audience, to draw them into the mandala, to deepen the trance and inspire visions. *"Phrum phuh phuh prah phat phrah phat namah,"* and Nishad can see Sanjaya arrive, carrying the corpse in his arms and standing before the Skullbearer. *"Khphrem mahachandayogeshvar,"* and Nishad sees the sorcerer rise, rejoicing in his heart, smiling, and reaching to embrace Sanjaya.

The corpse was anointed with unguents and oils, turmeric and saffron. The Skullbearer used a razor, first to shave the hair from the body, then to cut the names of Shambara and Bhairavi into the cool, bloodless flesh. He forced rings just like this one on the fingers, licked them so they'd slip on with ease, and then he tied amulets, just like this one, strung on thread like this, around the wrists and ankles of the corpse. He put a gem upon the chest and mustard seeds in the mouth, the nostrils, and the ears. "Now," the magician instructed Sanjaya, "now place the body in the mandala. No, no, turn it, point the head that way, the feet over here. Careful, don't touch the lines. Yes, good. Now there, stay there. Sit down." And Sanjaya obeyed.

The Skullbearer, straddling the corpse, sitting across it as a man sits on the back of a horse, recited: "Phrum phuh phuh prah phat phrah phat namah"; *and then, like a woman riding astride a man in wild sexual intercourse, he leaned forward to rub his chest against the chest of the cadaver, and indecently he kissed the lips of the dead. The ashes on his body marked the corpse just as the sandal unguents on a lover's breast imprint the flesh of the beloved. He sat up again, smiled, and with both hands forced open the mouth of the corpse. Several teeth dislodged from the decomposed gums and fell back into the throat of the dead man. The Skullbearer reached to the side for the charred ladle that had been carved from a human thigh bone, dipped the instrument into a pot of liquified fat, and dribbled his oblation into the mouth of the cadaver.*

A flame burst from the mouth of the corpse—flames like laughter, flames like screams, bright and terrible, and in horror, afraid of the power of his own magic, the Skullbearer leaped up from the corpse, leaped back and ran. But the corpse came alive, rose and pursued him. His mouth was on fire, smoke trailing behind him, and he pounced upon the sorcerer, dragged him to the ground, bit into the magician's neck with a fiery mouth to gnaw and chew and rend the flesh from the bones. The Skullbearer's screams stopped just as Sanjaya, in pursuit of them, arrived. The sorcerer's heart, still beating was plucked from his chest and swallowed whole, and "stop, stop," Sanjaya cried out to the corpse, the vetala within, but his screams were not heard. The vetala's mouth opened wider and fixed upon the neck, twisted off the flesh, and with each bite the animated corpse grew larger and larger. "Stop, stop," Sanjaya screeched, but the vetala dug his head into the open breast, slurped out the entrails, grew still larger, gulped the spluttering blood, sucked, gnawed, chewed, grew larger, larger, large enough to consume a wiggling, writhing arm in a single bite, to slurp down a still kicking and twitching leg. The toes curled in pain. He swallowed the screaming head.

"Stop, stop!" Sanjaya cried. The vetala grew—the Skullbearer was gone, wholly devoured.

The vetala, his mouth dripping with the blood of the Skullbearer, turned laughing to Sanjaya, turned laughing with drunken delight, laughing and belching, turned to Sanjaya like a drunkard to a comrade in the drinking place: "Haha!"

Shaking his sword menacingly, the storyteller says as he rattles the walking stick above his head again, *Sanjaya cursed him furi-*

ously: "What have you done? I cut the flesh from my own body to feed you, and you repay me this way! My king will die now. You've sealed my fate as well. You've killed me, the one who fed you. I curse you. Damn you! May you never find rest! The king will say that I have killed his magician. And if I don't return to the palace I'll be hunted down. Do you understand? Because you've killed this man, I'll be executed, impaled upon a stake or hung to die in some tree in some place of death, to become like you. And my king will die of fever too! Is that what you wanted to do? By this act, you've turned me into yourself?"

"No, my friend," the vetala laughed. "I've saved your king and you. Haha! You don't understand. Haha! Listen. I've saved you because fearlessly you fed me with your own flesh, ignored the pain and faced the terror. Listen! This Skullbearer, unaware that I was present in the corpse, was endeavoring to fix a spirit there, to make a living idol of that corpse, worship it, and in so doing, with the great, dark power that he would have drawn from that act, he would have killed you, paralyzed you first, then slain you, and then your flesh would have been offered to his idol. Then he would have returned to the king and sworn that one of us—a vetala—had killed you. The king, without a cure, would have soon died, and the Skullbearer, using the magic power attained in his tantric rite, would have taken the throne and ruled the kingdom. But, because of what you did for me, I was moved to save you, to help you accomplish your task. Now listen. I shall leave this body and I'll find rest. In a few moments it will drop lifeless on the ground. I'll be at peace. Take the corpse, this filthy body of mine, to the king, set it before him and disembowel it there. When that is done, you'll be able to show evidence of the body of the magician within it—the silver skull ring upon his finger, the scar upon the undigested cheek—tell the king the story, show him the evidence. Be as resolute and courageous as you were when you offered up your own flesh to me. He'll believe you, and you will cure him of his illness. When I release this body there will be mustard seeds in this mouth, these nostrils, these ears. Remove them and take them to the king. Place them on his tongue and, when he closes his

mouth and eyes, all at once, rest assured, your king will be cured. The fever will vanish. Haha!"

All at once, abandoned by the vetala, the corpse fell lifeless to the ground.

Midnight: the old goatkeeper sits up in horror when the devotional song of Mira Bai being sung for him on the radio is suddenly interrupted by a cool and distinct voice: *"Rajiv has been assassinated. Former Prime Minister and AICCI president Rajiv Gandhi was assassinated in Sriperumpudur, Tamil Nadu, forty-five miles from Madras tonight at 10:10 P.M. Mr. Rajiv Gandhi apparently stepped on a remote controlled bomb device which blew him into pieces along with twenty supporters."* The stunned old man repeats what he has just heard to himself, then out loud: *"Rajiv Gandhi has been assassinated, blown into a thousand pieces along with hundreds of devoted supporters."* He leaps up from the charpoy and bolts for the door. "He's dead," he screams. "He's dead!" He runs toward the pipal tree shouting it. "Rajiv's dead."

"What? What is it?"

The terrible story spreads instantaneously through the village. Brahm stops so that they can listen to the goatherd's shocking story: *"Terrorists have killed him. Sikhs and Muslims and tribals from Assam and Tamils and the CIA—they've murdered him. All of them have killed him. We've all killed him. All of us."*

The Lingayat rushes to his house where his wife is crying, wailing so fervently that she can't tell him the story. He searches for the transistor radio. "Where is it?" he shouts, but she answers only with more sobbing.

The news reaches the videovan and, though Pradip's crowd rises in chaotic panic and dismay, the videowala doesn't turn the film off. "What can they do about it?" he reasons. "They'll realize there's nothing they can do about it and they they'll sit back down to see what happens to Dr. DeSouza."

He reckons wrongly. When there's no one left, he turns off the video machine and the motor of the van and walks into the village, joining the shocked and anxious people who appear from their shacks and houses, stammering versions of the story, arguing, questioning, conjecturing, thronging toward the pipal tree.

Everyone, even the poor potter and his wife, crowds around to hear the macabre story. "Turn up the sound," they shout to the Lingayat. "That's as loud as it goes." It's impossible to hear. Everyone's talking at once: "I can't hear! What happened?" "Who killed him?" "What?" "One of his tennis shoes with his foot still in it was found forty feet from the explosion." "His head landed in a woman's lap."

And so the storyteller never gets to finish his story, to tell them how Sanjaya cured his king and how the king adopted him and Vijaya, making them his own sons and heirs to his kingdom. The villagers will never hear, at least not this season, how both sons married beautiful women, wealthy daughters of the kings of neighboring kingdoms, how Sanjaya ruled over the kingdom in righteousness, prosperity, and pleasure. Nor will they see Dr. DeSouza burned to death in the Christian graveyard. They'll never hear or see the ways in which horror can come to an end, resolved into rest, peace, and happiness.

Pradip approaches Brahm Kathuwala: "There's not much point in staying around here. Reality always gets the best of us," he laughs. "Life always ruins a good story or a good film in the end. Haha! I'm driving to Varanasi tonight. I'll be there before dawn. Why not come along with me; take a ride in the videovan?"

Nodding and smiling rather sadly, the storyteller agrees and, without yielding to a temptation to say goodbye to Nishad, he follows the videowala to his van. He watches the young man dismantle the speaker and pack it into the van. He inspects the movie poster: "Is this supposed to be a rakshasa?"

"No," Pradip shrugs. "It's some kind of mummy. The evil doctor in the film has wrapped up some dead body in bandages. Then he brings the guy to life. It's a great movie, a classic. I'll show it to you sometime if you want. I'll show it to you free of charge—why not?"

"I haven't seen many films," the storyteller confesses. "A long time ago I went to see a film called *Dracula,* an English language film. It must have been before 1947, long before you were born, because the theater in Varanasi where I saw it was burned down during the Partition riots. Do you know about *Dracula?*"

"Listen, my friend, I know everything about films," Pradip says as he turns the key to start the motor of the van. "You name it, I know it: *Dracula, Dracula's Daughter, Son of Dracula, The Return of the Vampire, Horror of Dracula.* There are a lot of Dracula movies because Dracula, you must realize, can't be killed—I've seen them all. I learned English from watching those movies, from watching every American movie I could ever see. I love horror films. But you know, better than those English and American horror films, much more terrifying and sublime than any of them, is our own *Dracula,* made in Hindi and in a beautiful Indian style. It's called *Band Darwaza* starring the one and only Anirudh. A masterpiece of horror! It will scare you to death. It will take your breath away. Haha! I don't have it right now, but, for a reasonable price, I can get it."

"I'd like that," Brahm smiles as they turn off the small road that leads from the village and onto the paved highway that will take them through Ballia District to Varanasi.

Brahm asks Pradip for one of the Charminar cigarettes from the packet on the dashboard of the van and the young man gestures for his passenger to help himself.

"How can I deny you anything you might ask of me? You and I, we're like cousins or brothers, even father and son," Pradip continues happily despite the national news. "We're really one and the same, professionally speaking I mean. You tell horror stories and I show them on the screen. What's the difference? It's like the cremation ghats in Varanasi—Manikarnika and Harishchandra. You're like Manikarnika, dealing with the dead in an effective but old-fashioned way; I'm like Harishchandra where they've installed the electric crematorium, dealing with the dead more efficiently, more cleanly, more modernly. Haha! Do you see my point?"

Brahm asks if the young man thinks it will be safe to drive into Varanasi. "There will, no doubt, be riots," the videowala forecasts with seemingly inappropriate good cheer, "just like when his mother was killed. Riots! People want to get in on the fun, shed a little blood themselves, break a few skulls," Pradip laughs. "It'll be bad for our business,

I'd be thinking if I were the kind of guy who looks at the dark side. But I'm a lighthearted fellow. That's why I like horror videos. They teach you how to be happy. They make you realize that nothing should frighten or bother you. There's always something mysteriously amusing about them, isn't there. What's it to me if the world is crazy, addicted to gore, in love with death if it's violent enough, obsessed with horror—not the horror of your stories and my films but real horror, gory and grisly, real death? I'm looking at this as a chance for a vacation, to have a little fun. Let me tell you a story. *There's a woman in Varanasi, married to a landowner who doesn't seem to care very much if she wants a little entertainment on the side. It doesn't bother him as long as it's hush-hush. . . .*

As Pradip tells his story of passionate intrigues in the holy city, Brahm squints his eyes in an effort to see into the darkness ahead of them. Two lights, like the eyes of one of the rakshasas from his stories, heading straight for them, then disappear behind them. He'll stay awhile in Varanasi, he thinks to himself, sleep in the tower at Manikarnika ghat at night, drink a little with Arun Patel, visit the cantonment and find the site of the old Thomson house to see if anything has been built there. He'll go to the graves of Memsahib and Varney in the garden of memories.

"Of course," Pradip loudly laughs, "it must have been the same for you when you were younger. I mean, with the women. You probably had a woman in every village too. We're just alike, you and I, horror professionals that we are. But, you see, it's easier for me with my video than it is for you as a storyteller. I set up my show and it keeps the audience by the van. I've got the husbands hypnotized, frozen dead still in front of the screen while this wife or that wife, whomever I chose, waits fo me in a designated place. I can leave my show, whereas you've got to be there for yours. Ah, technology!"

The headlights of the van illuminate the back of a white-bearded, balding sadhu, followed by a young boy, walking purposefully on the road to Varanasi. The consummately friendly and enthusiastic Pradip pulls over next to them and offers a ride. But, without speaking, the holy man motions him on. The videowala, his van coasting next to the walkers, tries to tell them about the assassination of

Rajiv Gandhi, but without reacting visibly to the story the old man, not breaking his gait, again motions the van away.

"We're like him," the irrepressible Pradip announces with cheerful pride. "Don't you think so? You and I—we're the same; only you're old and I'm young. We're the same; only you're the past of what we are and I'm the future of what we are. And here we are together in the present! Haha! We're holy people—you and I, Manikarnika and Harishchandra—made all the more holy by our wanderings. Oh, the life of the road, the freedom of the wanderer! I feel sorry for my brother—he's not like us: he owns a video store in Varanasi near Durga Kund, the Divine Goddess Video Bazaar. Sure, he makes plenty of money and, much to my convenience, he supplies me with my videos, but he's tied to that shop, a rich slave! Incidentally, he has some excellent porno movies. Not this Indian porn but the real thing, smuggled

in and really dirty. Beautiful stuff. I can show you. Porno masterpieces! No charge for you."

"After I see the Indian *Dracula,*" Brahm smiles.

"Oh, yes, yes, *Band Darwaza,*" Pradip answers excitedly. "I won't forget. I like horror as much as I like porn. Porn and horror, desire and fear, are, obviously, just two sides of the same thing. Both porn and horror get people excited, get the heart beating, the blood flowing, the lungs pumping, and all of that is very good, very healthy. Thank god for porn and horror!" Brahm, smoking another one of the Charminars, is staring into the night again, hardly listening as Pradip tells him his story: *My father never showed porn or horror. Just religious films, culture, you know, Mahabharata, Ramayana, that sort of thing. With a film projector, a bed sheet to set up as the screen, five cans of film, and an old generator, all loaded onto his horse-drawn cart, he'd go from village to village. . . .*

As the young man talks, the storyteller, continuing to gaze into the darkness of the stubble fields, can picture poor Mitu out there desperately searching the heated night for his wife. *Slowly, slowly he reached and placed his hand on the door to the hut in the fields, the little shack that he himself had built so that the farmers might find shelter there, and slowly, slowly he pulled it open, and, as he did, the creak of it was like the hideous scream of a vetala in the night. . . .*

"Hey, old man," Pradip brays as he reaches over to shake his traveling companion. "Are you listening to me? You're awfully quiet. I don't like it when old people are too silent. It makes me afraid that they've died. You're not dead are you?"

The storyteller smiles, lights another cigarette, and the reassured videowala continues his story out loud while Brahm Kathuwala continues his story to himself. "Poor Mitu," he thinks, and "poor Nishad," he sighs, saddened over the end of the tale: *In the morning they found Mitu. He was dead. His face had been ripped away like a mask. The naked skull, all skin and muscle, vessels and nerves, clawed off, stripped clean, its jaws gaping with a silent scream over horrors unknown, stared at the people of the village, looked into their hearts and saw the innumerable terrors, great and small, concealed there.*

The Lingayat, the toddyman, the washerman and his wife, the potter, the schoolmaster, the tailor, the old goatkeeper—all of them and others too—gathered in the cremation ground near the river, adjacent to the graveyard where the casteless ones were buried, to watch the flames consume the body of poor Mitu, the carpenter, to say goodbye. Sadness absolved their fears.

Mitu's widow took their child, the young Nishad, away from the village and back to her home in Bihar. The boy got malaria, burned with fever and shivered with chills. He did not speak for some months.

The first words that came from his mouth were very strange. He spoke them to his grandparents: "Now, come a little closer, come now and let me tell you a story," *the boy softly said, hesitating, closing his eyes and then opening them to smile almost sadly,* "an old, old story, yes, yes a true story, the terrible tale of the boy who became possessed."

The storyteller suddenly laughs aloud, and the videowala, whose story is over, who has fallen quiet and is grateful for relief from the silence, wants to know why.

"Do you ever lose track," the old man smiles, "of the line between what you've seen in your videos and what you've seen or heard or done in your life? Does memory ever jumble videos, stories, and life together? Sometimes I have to wonder—even though deep in my heart I actually know the truth—whether I'm a storyteller or a story told. Do you know what I'm talking about? Do the borders between different worlds ever crumble before your eyes? That's what just happened, that's why I laughed. Real people suddenly became characters in a story I know. Perhaps the other can also happen—characters in a story suddenly becoming real. Count Dracula could rise from the coffin which is the videotape or the film can or the book, could rise up and into our world. Why not? He could be standing on the road just ahead of us, around the turn ahead, his cape spread out behind him, his eyes two glowing dots of fire in

the darkness! Do you understand what I'm saying, or is it just that I'm very old?"

"It's that you're old," the young man answers automatically and then reconsiders. "Well, actually, it's that way for me with videoporn. Sometimes I remember doing it and I don't know whether I've actually done it with the woman or just watched her doing it on the screen with some other guy whose face they don't show you. I suppose that's because I have both had so many women and watched so many porno films. I don't know. But, I can assure you that it never happens with horror videos. That would not be desirable. I wouldn't know what to do if we suddenly ran into Dracula."

"We would kill him," Brahm smiles. "You said earlier that Dracula can't be killed, but you're wrong. He can be destroyed. A woman named Mina described his death in her journal." Then, still smiling, almost glowing, the storyteller recites it in English, something he hasn't done for many, many years: *On the instant came the sweep and flash of Jonathan's great knife. I shrieked as I saw it shear through the throat; whilst at the same moment Mr. Morris's bowie knife plunged into the heart. It was like a miracle; before our very eyes, and almost in the drawing of the breath, the whole body crumbled into dust and passed from our sight.*

“No,” the videowala insists, “in *The Return of the Vampire* they explain that he can never die or be killed. I’m certain of that.”

“No,” the old storyteller argues, “he can die precisely because he, the Lord of the Un-Dead, aches for death. He wants to rest. We have only to give him that gift. Listen to Mina again: *I shall be glad as long as I live that, in that moment of final dissolution, there was in the face a look of peace such as I never could have imagined might have rested there.*

“That’s a good end to the story,” the videowala smiles, “and the right time to end it. We’re almost in Varanasi, almost back to real life!”

7

There is a half-moon in the sky today which will disappear shortly after midnight, said the storyteller. I'll select a tale which will end before the moon sets, so that you may all go home when there is still a little light.

R. K. NARAYAN, *GODS, DEMONS, AND OTHERS* (1964)

The sentimental taxonomies of classical Indian aesthetic theory elucidate two literary sentiments that are the functional equivalents of horror and macabre. Horror, the bhayanaka-rasa, *the aesthetic realization of the universal human emotion, or primary, congenital feeling of fear or terror, arises, according to Bharata, "from hearing hideous laughter and other terrifying noises such as the hooting of owls and the howling of jackals, from seeing ghosts or being alone in an empty house or in a forest; it also arises from seeing or hearing about the death or captivity of those one cares about. It makes the hands tremble, the knees shake, the mouth dry and the heart beat fast"* (Natyashastra *6. prose after 68, and 69–72). The macabre, the* bibhatsa-rasa, *is the aesthetic realization of innate, natural feelings of disgust or revulsion: "The macabre has disgust as its single basis," Dhanamjaya explains, "It arouses anxiety by means of worms, stench, and vomit; it causes trembling by means of blood, entrails, bones, fat, flesh, etc.; and, in the case of renunciation, it inspires genuine revulsion in respect to hips, thighs, breasts, etc. It is physically expressed by contortions of the mouth and nostrils and other grimaces; and the affects, in the case of this sentiment, include frenzy, nervousness, fear, and so forth"* (Dasharupa *4.80).*

LEE SIEGEL, *CITY OF DREADFUL NIGHT: A STUDY OF HORROR AND THE MACABRE IN INDIAN LITERATURE* (1991)

There are many books written by Westerners about India, some flattering, some not. Reading these books, I have often felt that Westerners who glorify India and Westerners who denigrate her both write from essentially the same understanding—the understanding of the outsider who creates a fiction and then proceeds to analyze this fiction as if it were reality.

JAYATHI MURTHY, GONE JUNGLI IN *INDIA CURRENTS* (1992)

29 May 1991

(THE FULL MOON BEGINS TO WANE; FIRST LUNAR DAY OF THE DARK FORTNIGHT OF JYESHTHA, SAMVAT 2048; NARADA JAYANTI)

DELHI. *The death roll in poll related violence touched the 200 mark with 42 more deaths reported today as fresh violence erupted in curfew bound Varanasi and Meerut.*

(Hindustan Times)

The shoot-on-sight curfew is still (except for several vaguely announced hours each day around noon) in effect, and we're incarcerated like Jonathan Harker in Castle Dracula: *When I found that I was a prisoner a sort of wild feeling came over me . . . the conviction of my helplessness overpowered all other feelings.*

When we arrived from the cantonment this afternoon, the elderly, sullen servant explained that we could not go out again until tomorrow morning at ten o'clock. Sweat has dissolved the edges of the yellow mark of devotion smudged on his forehead, his eyes are gloomy, and his breath is laboriously forced back and forth across frowning, wrinkled lips. When I ask how long the curfew will last, he gravely shrugs his shoulders. The air cooler grumbles discontentedly, the ceiling fan quivers nervously, and the ash from my cigarette, catching a small, whirling current, does a pirouette on the dusty green linoleum floor.

"I don't want to be here," I think and then, thinking about what I'm thinking, I'm glad I'm here to feel the feeling of the phrase—"I don't want to be here"—it expresses a sentiment essential to horror's manifold texts.

"What if," I write, "I have to spend this entire visit to India in this house, unable to go out except briefly at midday, unable to find my storyteller and collect the ghost stories and macabre lore, prevented from my proposed explorations of the cremation ghats and Muslim burial grounds, unable to visit the places in Varanasi where, I plan to argue, fear and disgust are resolved in stories and myths, dramas and rituals? Shall I take it as an outer augury or inner warning that I'm not meant to write a scholarly study of horror and the macabre? The project, like the tombs and mansions of horror, is decomposing. There are cobwebs and the smells of mold, rot, and infection. Are the soldiers patroling the streets to keep me in, separated from what I want to see? Shall I trick them by writing a fable instead of making the study? What's the difference? Shall I allow myself the regressive pleasures of storytelling, sparing myself and others the pontifical tribulations of analysis? Perhaps I'll throw out the scholarly manuscript or, more spectacularly, burn it, yes, cremate the text, let it transmigrate and take on another body, yes, haha, anoint myself with the funerary ashes and sing a song of horror."

While Cheryl reads Christine Weston's *Indigo,* I read the week's worth of English-language newspapers that the servant has brought to me for the second time today. Why does he want me to see this?—it's all horror and the macabre: "Ex-minister of Jammu-Kashmir Shot Dead"; "Two More Candidates in the Punjab Shot"; "7 Militants Shot . . . 18 Dead in the Punjab"; "Director General of Doordarshan Shot—Fear Grips Electronic Media"; "26 Die of Cholera"; "Girl Found Hanging from Ceiling Fan"; "Noted Criminal Lawyer Shot"; "Heat Wave Kills Nine in Rajasthan." And there, published again and again, is the photograph of what remains of the young girl they're calling Dhanu or Thanu, "the human bomb," her body reassembled without the torso, without one of her arms, without the back of her head, without her soul. What remains of her legs is naked and spread on the sheet like the opening limbs of a lover. Her jewelry has been stripped from her and her hair has come undone as if from lovemaking. The eyes that looked into his eyes are closed beneath the vivid, unsmudged forehead marking. The expression is almost peaceful.

The electricity, strained by the air coolers, air conditioners, and fans of a city that was not meant to be cool or modern, goes out. Our air cooler is hushed, our overworked fan slows down, slower, more slowly, and stops to rest with a certain melancholy fatigue. The black telephone, like an ominous prop in some horror story or murder mystery, doesn't work. The toilet doesn't flush. Suddenly there's an unexpected surge—the fan starts to turn, one, two, three rotations, and then it slows again and eerily stops. No, no electricity. Beware of hopefulness; expect terror.

A militant heat breaks through the doors and windows and forces us to lie down and remain still as it demands surrender and laughs at us. It binds and gags us and takes what we have. The sun is

a merciless terrorist, staring down upon our house with a fevered leer, ecstatic with the pleasure of violence. It's 122° in Rajasthan and over one hundred here. The fire, if one had faith, could be understood as sacrificial. Is the brutality of nature seeping into the hearts of human beings, or is it the other way around?

Tonight, this first fading of a full lugubrious moon, a moon melting in the boiling, black fluid of night, we've been sitting out on the roof-veranda that overlooks the deserted street, smoking duty-free cigarettes, drinking duty-free scotch, and watching for the occasional advent of the trucks full of dutiful soldiers (fearful boys and bitter men), their uniforms and berets the same dark drab brownish green as the canopied vehicles. Here they come, around the corner. The rifles in silhouette have become the rigid appendages or erect antennae of a strange nocturnal beast with luminous searching eyes and a diesel growl echoing ominously as it sniffs the heated air for human flesh. Then the lumbering primordial monster howls: "currrrfffewwwww." Its prey—an excited child running, a daring boy on a bicycle, a defiant man limping—scatter in thrill-tempered panic.

An owl, perched as a portent on the frayed electrical wire that crosses our field of vision, stares at us with disturbingly enormous eyes. Suddenly it swoops and vanishes into the darkness, transforming itself unwittingly and instantly into symbol as it spreads its wings to dive from wire into text: in the owl all beings vault into oblivion.

For a moment of relief from the torrid night air, Cheryl's taking a trickling shower in the dark, and, drained, listless, and alone, I stare at the momentarily empty street, listen to the water splash, close my eyes, open them, light another cigarette, and begin again to envision the storyteller that I'm supposed to meet, the person I've come to Varanasi to find, the man who "will explain everything I need to know about horror and the macabre in India."

Brahm wakes up on the first day of Jeth in the tower that overlooks the constantly burning pyres of Manikarnika. Ashes, a floating veil of human remains, petal-studded, cling to the rippled body of Ganga in repose, the place he enters her to bathe. She opens up to him with infinite lapping suppleness to lick and wash him clean. He remembers his mother pouring the bucket of water over him and also Memsahib coaxing him into her spacious British bathtub.

Arriving in this city of dreadful night just before dawn, over a week ago, on the morning after the assassination of Rajiv Gandhi, he was dropped off at Chowk by Pradip who had exuberantly extorted a promise that, yes, he'd come to his brother's video rental shop to see Band Darwaza, Hatyarin, *"and, I will do my best to secure some great American films like* The Vampire Returns *in which Dracula is shown to be immortal as I have contended, always returning no matter how he has been killed in whatever previous movie.* He *cannot be destroyed. The old film, the old story, the old book, has to kill him off so that it can end. Obviously. The new film or book, however, has to bring him back to life so that it can begin. Also obvious." He switched to a cheerful English— "I will also show you some very beautiful American porno, old man"—and then back to Hindi with tricky smile— "that should bring back a few memories, a few spicy stories."*

As the videovan pulled away, the immaculate light of what seemed a Vedic dawn beginning to inflame the dark sky, the primeval blackness that had covered the land on that night of murder, the storyteller stared at the forebodingly mutilated face on the poster on the side of the van, and the bulging eyes mockingly and mawkishly gawked back. Brahm smiled: it was impossible not to feel a bit of affection for the brash entrepreneur; they were after all, as the young man had insisted, in the same business—vendors of horror, capitalizing on the apprehensions of their audiences by making those fears a source of entertainment. The gaudy horror of fictions, told or shown, inflated by rhetoric or technicolor, was a pleasantly fearful distraction from the real horror which, whether manifest or latent, informs our lives.

Though he's unable, because the curfew is still being en-
forced, to move freely into the town, it's safe enough by the river for
him to walk all the way to Assi and back along the empty expanse of
stone stairways on the city side of the low and sluggish Ganga. The
 ghats are so exquisitely beautiful to him that he aches with feeling.
He sees a young man rowing a woman in a boat and can hear their
faint laughter across the water.

He has slept each night in the open tower amidst other wandering pariahs, sonless widows, feckless renouncers, petty crooks, and two very dirty Americans (or are they British like the Thomsons?), *a young man and a girl who smoke ganja and inject each other with "brown sugar." The girl has diarrhea and no modesty. When the man tries to buy the storyteller's silver skull earring, Brahm shrugs his shoulders and adopts a quizzical expression in a pretense of not knowing English. Afterwards the foreigners speak freely in front of him, certain that he doesn't understand the utterances that are mingled with the other sounds in the tower—snoring and coughing, whimpers and whispers, moans and prayers.*

The foreign man mouths macabre and self-aggrandizing clichés, vain but voluble injunctions, and petty perceptions: "You can't accept your life until you've confronted death. That's why we're here—to see, hear, smell, taste, and feel death, to get acquainted and make death our friend. In America we're afraid, we hide death. But here, in India, they put death on display. Like someone forcing a kitten's nose into a bowl of milk, India pushes your face into it—death." He repeats the word with forced relish and a self-consciously demonic glee: "Death." The girl placidly nods, closing her eyes slightly as if to suggest an understanding of, or agreement with, the young man's inflated epiphanies.

Brahm eyes the traveler's Rothman's King Size Cigarettes, smells their fragrance even through the aroma of human flesh roasting in the fires on the ghat below. . . .

30 May

(SECOND LUNAR DAY OF THE DARK FORTNIGHT OF JYESHTHA)

> MEERUT. *The death roll in the poll related violence rose again in the curfew-bound township here today. An irate mob set two persons ablaze near Makbara Aabhu Diggi at noon resulting in the instant death of one and severe injuries to the other.*
>
> (Hindustan Times)

Last night on television, during the twenty minutes of electricity, a murdered politician from Gauhati was immolated. Cremations are prime-time fare on Doordarshan this season.

This morning, with the news that the curfew had been lifted during the daylight hours, we went straight to the river, down to Assi ghat and then, by boat, past Harishchandra, the site of the electric crematorium, we were rowed to Manikarnika ghat, and directed by the boatman to the two-story tower where, he explained, we would have a fine view. "Tourists," he elaborated quite gleefully, "always enjoy burning bodies. Tourists love death! All of them come here and all of them go to the Taj Mahal. What is Taj Mahal? A tomb! Death in India is a number one tourist attraction! Haha!"

Fire and water, Agni and Ganga: one corpse burning, another soaking in waters veiled with ashes and cooked by the fire of sun and pyre—incessant birth and death, the hectic heat of fecundity and decay. Intensifying, as if intent on bringing this dirt-spiced stew to a boil, sacramental fire waits for the corpse that's trussed and wrapped in white. Another body is gaudily garbed in bright crimson silks, costumed as a celebrant for the great cotillion of death. Silent corpses and fitfully yapping dogs are everywhere.

The mood on the ghat has very little to do with the fear or disgust that I'm so anxious to observe. It's all very matter-of-fact and business as usual. It's like the railway station: people bid their friends and loved ones goodbye; the oily smoke of the pyres is no different than the coal smoke of the train engines. The dead, passengers to unknown places, pull out. Black smoke curls and unfurls into the heated haze. Goodbye, goodbye. . . .

A young man approaches with a prominent smile to ask where I'm from, to politely chat for distraction from the conflagrant heat of summer, to explain, as he duly feels it's his duty to do, these funerary rites to an apparent tourist. "One body, three hours," he says with curious cheer. "Look, look there. They are throwing that part of the body

into the Ganga. Pelvis! It must have been a woman. The woman's pelvis doesn't burn. I don't know why. It goes into the Ganga whole and uncooked. Always. With the men, it's the chest that doesn't burn. Woman, womb; man, heart. Always."

"Where are the women mourners?" I ask.

"Women aren't good here. They cry. There shouldn't be crying here. The men cry too, of course, but only after they get home. That's where the women are—crying at home. See those women there—Dom women, low caste people. Working, not mourning. Do you like my Varanasi? All of Varanasi is a burning ground, my brother," he smiles proudly.

When I explain that I have come to Varanasi to learn about bhuts and prets, about ghosts, ghouls, and goblins, to gather the lore that comprises the romance of the cremation grounds, he laughs and claims that there are no prets in Varanasi, only bhuts: "A pret is an evil bhut. And nothing can be evil in Varanasi. Varanasi turns evil into good, poison into nectar, and fear into hope. Actually prets and bhuts are very much alike, but they have a different diet—bhuts will eat ghee, curds, and things like that. Prets want blood."

I have my own understanding: the preta is the spirit of the dead person before the obsequial rites are performed, the terrifying and repugnant ghost that remains in this world tormenting us as a guilt-laced memory if the funeral rites are not done or if they are done improperly, if we do not care for our dead as if they were still alive. The pretas, our fears and regrets, hunger and need to be appeased. The young man laughs and then repeats his own explanation word for word: "There are no prets in Varanasi. . . ."

We descend the bank, approach the river, turn our backs to the fresh corpses, the tirelessly flaming pyres, and the young man, and we walk.

Noon is mercilessly fiery.

I turn to look back at Cheryl. And then I turn again.

I spin around—"oh no, no"—I'm stunned by the suddenly frightful sight of her: the bright red and sweatless face, eyelids closing and peeling lips darkly trembling. Taking her hand I feel the hot dry skin, the twitching of muscle and fizzle of nerve beneath it. She's breathing heavily, uncomfortably, and says, "I'll be alright," a certain sign that she's not. I look into her eyes, opening them with my thumb tips, and see pupils dilated wide despite the brightness of noon, and she's mumbling about being dizzy and nauseated. I panic over what might be sunstroke. "Hold on to me, hold on," I repeat, desperately trying to mask my anxiety with reassuring tones as I lead her up the blazing bright stone steps: "Hold on."

At the summit of the stairway there's a small vegetable market, shaded by a low burlap canopy, a tent black with grime that shelters merchants vending dirty potatoes, dry onions, and dark vegetables. We have to stoop under it as we push forward to find water. "Hold on, hold on. You'll be alright. Don't be afraid."

Cheryl's asleep now. So's the old servant, curled up on the floor and so strangely still that I find myself creeping over to see if he's still alive. The pacemaker implanted in his chest is visible through his bare skin and, through the closed, wrinkled eyelids, I see his eyes moving with dreams.

It's stifling inside and blazing outside. But, feeling closed in, I go out to walk, walk, not sure where, looking down at the ground: tracks crossing in the dry dirt, cigarette filters and bidi butts, chunks of dirt and dust, bits of tire, the sole of a slipper, fragments of cloth, paper, rock, brick, wire, twine, twigs, betel spit, ashes, turds, dry grass, dust, a dry and toxic sea of dirt, its nauseating roll so slow that it can't be readily observed. But it is felt. I'm adrift. The surface shifts with the traffic, with the shuffle of feet and tires, the drag of hooves and paws, with the rude blow of the lu, those hot winds of Jeth, and beneath the whisked, chimerical surface, hard earth seems ready to crack from the heat and explode like a skull in the funeral fire. The ground is a kind of story, a text that I try to read, translate, and interpret. The street asks me what I'm doing here.

Suddenly afraid that I'm being too lackadaisical about Cheryl, I rush back to the house to find her still sleeping. As I hold the febrile wrist and feel the all-too-rapid pulse beneath my wet fingertips, sore eyelids and parched lips languorously open: "I'll be alright," she promises.

Night and curfew. The servant has disappeared after locking us in. Between the stars and myself there are wires crisscrossing in the sky, at this angle and that to form a chaotic etching of stretched, twisted, frayed, broken lines. The owl is back and perched on the wire from which dangle twigs and twine, straw and string, random strands of evidence of past winds. What omens can the night bird discern in the darkness that is its home?

I sit outside writing to avoid getting into bed and having to turn out the lights and offer my blood to the mosquitoes (did we remember to take our malaria pills?) that, right now, are waiting patiently, hiding silently, until we try to sleep; then, if even only one toe is exposed, they dive, buzz, land, pierce, inject, and suck. And so Cheryl and I are wrapped in our bleached, cere-white sheets like corpses on the ghats. Once you fall asleep, you can kick away the covers—it doesn't matter what bites you or drinks your blood, as long as you don't know about it.

. . . on the morning of the storyteller's arrival, before the curfew had been announced over the loudspeakers atop the grumbling green army trucks that were just beginning to enter the city, arousing summer dust and fear, he had walked straight to Godalia, down into Vishvanath Gali, then right and into Kalika Gali toward the jewelry and curio shop of his friend, Arun Patel. He'd have tea with

him and they'd smoke together peacefully, almost happily. The homeless one would feel at home.

The streets were thronged with people gathered in curiosity or dismay or panic, asking question after question or arguing or conjecturing about the identity of Rajiv's assassins. Rising unaware of the violence in the south that night, oblivious to the passions of Chitralekha, alias Thanu, alias Dhanu, "the human bomb," devoted or obedient souls, emerging from their homes early for the morning ritual bath in the Ganga, were confronted yet again with the terror that both energizes and cripples their society. "There are sure to be riots," the pedestrian prophesy, echoed through each cramped and clamorous congregation of souls.

Patel's shop was boarded up as it had been years before during the riots over Partition. The same combination locks were in place, dangling from the rusted chain across the bars and planks. A fragrant Mr. Roshanlal, proprietor of the adjacent oil and perfume stall, recognizing the storyteller standing there, staring at the now signless stall, and seemingly disoriented, offered the visitor tea along with an explanation: Mr. Patel had died some months before. Exactly how many months, he was not quite sure. In stories, Brahm reflected, you either arrive just in time (just when your friend is on his death bed, moments before his death, so that in his dying breath he can whisper some important utterance into your anxious ear, something that gives his death and your persistent life some new significance), or you arrive just afterward (moments too late, ironically, poignantly, or tragically, a day or so late—a week at the most; that has dramatic resonance). But "some months" (let alone "I don't remember exactly how long ago it was") was absurd. There was no story, no dramatic climax, no aesthetic sentiment, no meaning. Mr. Roshanlal resolutely offered the customary commentary: "At least he died in Varanasi. . . . He had lived a full life. . . . He really had nothing left to live for, what with his wife dead and his children gone. . . . Who can say what is for the best and what is not? . . . We shall all miss the kind and generous Shree A. R. Patel. . . ."

Looking a last time at the locks, the storyteller was strangely struck by the realization that, now that Patel was dead, no one on earth knew the combination of combinations. The chains and bars might be cut, but the locks were locked forever. There was something oddly pleasing about that thought at that moment, so pleasing that, silently turning, Brahm smiled as he walked through the labyrinth of galis, down, down toward Manikarnika. Looking at the watch on his right wrist ("about twenty past ten") and then the electronic one on his left ("9:09 AM"), he quickened his steps, pushing his way through the clustered crowds of people as he walked, and it occurred to him that with age he thought less and less about death, that rude interruption that so frightens younger souls, less about death and yet more and more about time, its elusiveness, elasticity, and mysteriousness. He hurried as he was late, some months late for the funeral of Arun Patel. . . .

31 May

(THIRD LUNAR DAY OF THE DARK FORTNIGHT OF JYESHTHA)

> NEW DELHI. At the eastern edge of Menda Tola village in district Gadhchiroli, Maharashtra, a 14-year-old boy who worked as an agricultural laborer to support his invalid father and two younger sisters, was found hanging from a tamarind tree, tied by a small white towel to a thin branch. The right eye was missing and the fingertips had perforations for draining blood. "Its *Narbali*" (human sacrifice), cried out the little group who witnessed the sight. There was neither anger nor much remorse, only fear.
>
> (Nalini Singh, *Indian Express)*

Anxious to meet the man I had been told about in Delhi who might act as my research assistant and introduce me to the storyteller who specialized in tales of horror and the macabre, I left right after breakfast. Feeling better, but still weak, Cheryl stayed at home.

Young men, released from their houses by the lifting of the curfew, were out walking and holding hands. Horns, bells, and buzzers, of bicycles, scooters, rickshaws, and an occasional car, seemed to call and answer each other with honks, toots, rings, clacks, and howls like the crows, cattle, and dogs of the day.

Opening the door for me, a lean boy with bath-wet hair and a freshly applied mark of ashes on his forehead directed me to be seated by the open window that looked out over the Durga Temple, where quarrelsome monkeys, scrambling nervously over the rooftops, hissed nastily at each other. Animals seem to live in perpetual fear; do they feel disgust?

The mold-dappled and peeling green wall was decorated with an illustrated calendar: there above the days of May (this being the last) Bhairavi Kali, the terrible mother, held the head of Brahma in one hand, a sword in another, a skull bowl, brimming with a broth of blood, in another. Her fourth hand was open and empty. Garlanded with entrails, she stood upon the corpse of an unconscious Shiva and laughed with a mouth that dripped with blood. Which god would come with June?

As if expecting me, showing no signs of curiosity, wonder, or surprise, the man entered with a hospitable smile. Rising to greet him and tell him my name, I handed him the letter of introduction from our mutual acquaintance in Delhi. Apologizing for any inconvenience that I might be causing him by appearing unannounced, I explained that I hoped he might be able to help me with my project. "Our friend told me that here, in your house, he once met a storyteller who specialized in ghost stories and tales of terror. I would like to meet him if that is at all possible."

"Yes, yes, his name is Brahm, Brahm Kathuwala, Mr.Storywala, professional bard of sorts. Old man. A very good friend of mine. It will be no problem for you to meet him. I'll arrange everything. He speaks English very, very well, better than I do."

"Does he tell stories in the traditional way, horror stories? Does he tell them in the villages?"

"Oh, yes, yes, absolutely. Very traditional. He is also an ojha, and he can perform some very good exorcisms for you if you wish. All the foreign scholars always want to see possession and exorcism."

"I'd like to travel with him on some occasion in order to hear him tell his stories in a traditional way, in a traditional setting."

"Of course, of course. This is for your Ph.D. dissertation?"

"No, no, a book. I'm writing a book about horror and the macabre in India."

"A novel?"

"No, a scholarly study [I wince at how pretentious it sounds]. I'm interested in the ways in which fear and disgust are transformed and resolved in Indian literature and religion."

"Mr. Brahm will be excellent. He knows every ghost and monster story. He even knows your English ghost stories like *Dracula, Frankenstein,* and what-have-you."

"When can I meet him?"

"Tomorrow night. Kindly be here at eight o'clock."

. . . *over sixty years earlier the storyteller had stood in this very tower, staring through this stone portal, taken refuge from the Vetala Raja here and looked down toward the pyres and seen her there among the dead, the tentative tilt of her head and graceful turn of her neck, the complaisant cling of cotton to the muscular thigh and the voluptuous, prankish smile and frisky dark eyes, the bright yellow shawl swirled orange and crimson and billowed by the dry winds of summer. And, as they say in stories, it took his breath away.*

He watches the Doms work the pyre, wondering which ones might be her relatives, which ones might be old enough to remember her or him. A corpse, its muscles suddenly shrunken by heat, its bones strained to crack, seems to struggle against the ropes that bound it to the sandal log. Mena-like, a young Dom girl laughs as she shoos a hungry yellow dog away from the flaming cadaver. It cowers, growls, and drools.

Once upon a time Brahm saw Mena through two bright and hungry eyes; this girl is obscured by the haze that has come and progressed with age. With only one clear and shining eye it's difficult to discern how close or far away things are in space or time. The heat cracks the skull and the cadaver lies still, surrendering to the ravenous flames and timelessness.

Failing eyesight allows him to see Arun Patel upon the pyre, shrouded in silk and flame. The storyteller watches the body burn, the smoke rise in gushing curls, turn into feathery flurries that are dispersed into the vastness of sky, and he bids Arun Patel a sweet goodbye. It's him. All the dead, after all, are the same, each one death itself offering to be burned away, involuntarily volunteering to scout out oblivion. "I'm here, Patel," he whispers, "here in Varanasi to join you in the abyss, to die in Varanasi."

The storyteller turns from the paneless window. Several pariahs are playing cards and bickering in hushed but rapid grumbles; the foreigners are sleeping and a tantric sadhu, his face covered with ashes, is rummaging their packs for exotic treasures. Exposing betel-red broken teeth with a wily smile, he removes a packet of cigarettes, cocks his head to the side, and tosses a smoke to Brahm who then secrets it in his bundle.

The sleeping girl, wearing a single anklet, her leg exposed in a way that amuses the others gathered in the tower, reminds the storyteller of Christine Weston somehow, a dirty Christine (and that would bring a reprimand from Inspector Weston), but a Christine nonetheless—the pink cheeks, ruddy blond hair, and the green eyes, at once wonderful and terrible. She was forbidden and desirable. There had always been an excuse for the accidental or unconscious rubbing against her or bumping into her. When things had been bad with Mena he'd recollect Christine Weston, imagine the white breasts, pink nipples, and wisps of golden hair around a pubis that must have smelled like lavender and sweet cream. Christine, Brahm thinks, must be dead by now, inhumed in some Christian tomb, the fragrance of lavender and cream turned to the odor of mildew and must, far away in the place where she was born. . . .

1 June

(FOURTH LUNAR DAY OF THE DARK FORTNIGHT OF JYESHTHA)

> CHANDIGARH. In the biggest shoot-out till now in this state, militants massacred about 125 train passengers in Ludhiana district late tonight. A statewide red alert has been sounded.
>
> *(Sunday Times).*

I was anxious all day about meeting the storyteller. I had already constructed him in my imagination and wanted now to compare my creation with the man, my words with his flesh and blood. Cheryl was still feeling too listless and nauseated to come with me.

I arrive at my informant's house before eight: "Where is he?"

"Don't worry. We will meet him at the Baba Kinnaram Ashram. It is the Aghori ashram," my smiling informant, a householder Aghori himself, explains.

The hangout of Aghoris was an obviously important place for me to do fieldwork: they, the "fearsomely fearless ones," are reputedly the spectacularly macabre heroes who understand liberation as a confrontation with all terror and a conquest of all disgust. They are said to go about naked, carrying skulls from which they eat human flesh. Shit and gold, piss and milk, evil and good, all are the same to them. They sit on cadavers to meditate and laugh ecstatically in the face of death.

Adorning the gates of the ashram are large plaster skulls, gigantic kitsch reminiscent of the greasy cranial decorations outside the haunted houses at the amusement parks of my adolescence (that period of my life when I understood horror and the macabre, when I drew pictures of winged and taloned eyeballs pierced with spikes and bleeding).

The skulls are apotropaic tokens of horror as are the enormous fruit bats hanging happily in the tremendous tamarind tree. Horrors keep horror away. Other than the plaster skulls and real bats, there are few signs of the macabre and no evidence of antinomian or tantric practices. All that has, it seems, been dissolved in bourgeois norms and modern sensibilities.

Anxious to meet my storyteller, I, for his sake, endure the puja—the drums and horns, the tirelessly devout bowing to the burning log and the glossy photograph of a teenage guru, the anointment with ashes from Harishchandra ghat and the exchange of pious felicities. I'm given a packet of the sacred ash as a souvenir.

"Is he here?" I ask impatiently. "Will he be coming soon?"

The pujari, circuitously explaining that, no, he hadn't been around for a long time, suggests that I go to Vishvanath Gali, that the storyteller often stays with another householder Aghori, a certain Mr. Patel who is the proprietor of a jewelry and curio shop there.

As we walk home, my informant, sensing my disappointment both in the banalization of the gruesome tradition and in the absence of my storyteller, tells me a story himself: *Once upon a time Baba Kinnaram was sitting by the river, on the ghat next to the funeral pyre. Because he was hungry, he called out to a passing fish and that fish jumped out of the Ganga and onto the pyre to cook itself for Baba Kinnaram. Great is the power of the fearless one! Once you have overcome fear and disgust you can do anything! The Aghori wished to listen to some music while he ate his meal, so he called out to a corpse that was floating by that spot on the river. It happened to be the body of a famous musician. Baba Kinnaram unwrapped the body and woke up the dead musician who all at once floated up into the air. When he floated back down he was playing the sitar. Bats,* *enchanted by his music, descended from the sky with him, and those very bats remain nested in the tamarind tree in the ashram. Good story?*

"Do you know any ghost stories or horror stories?" I ask.

"That was a horror story," my informant insists with a frown.

"It didn't seem very horrifying."

"That's the point," he smiles proudly. "Through the power of Baba Kinnaram all fear is vanquished. What is fear? It is desire turned inside-out. The ashes that you were given tonight make it impossible for you to be afraid. You will feed these ashes to your wife so that her sickness will go away. Put the ashes on her forehead, her tongue, and on her stomach. She will be cured."

. . . Brahm has sold enough amulets and charms in the village to be able to afford to take a rickshaw to the cantonment. There is now a tall hotel, concrete, glass, metal, walled and landscaped, where the Thomson house once stood, and the site of the storyteller's childhood is guarded by a uniformed gateman.

Brahm's driver joins the other rickshaw boys in the line outside the gate to the paved drive into the hotel grounds and Brahm squats across the road from it, lights at last his Rothman's King Size cigarette, and tries to sift through the smokey memories of the charred rubble on the morning after the fire and reconstruct the Thomson house there as it once was—to picture the entry, the vestibule decorated with the mounted heads of jackals (trophies of a British hunt), the stairway up to the landing, the hallway to the room where Memsahib had read stories to him each night. The home has no more substance than the houses of story, than the House on Haunted Hill, Castle Dracula, or the Lankan palace of the demon king Ravana.

"Brother," the old man, a snake charmer, calls from behind him, "Give me one of those cigarettes, brother." The storyteller explains to his fellow performer, who now squats next to him with a languorous python wrapped around his neck, that it's his last. "Same old story," the snake handler laughs and, stroking the neck of his indolent viper, moving his finger along the grain of the smooth scales, asks Brahm his business.

"Storyteller."

"You won't make much here, brother. You know English? French? German? Japanese?"

"English," the storyteller says, switching into that tongue with a smile, "The grass is green, the rose is red, and the night is dark. Haha!"

*"Yes," the snake man says in English, "You are a fine gentleman." And then he slips back into a fluid Hindi: "These tourists are probably not interested in the great stories of India—*Mahabharat, Ramayan, *and so forth. Too long. Too much time. Tourists are in a hurry. But perhaps you could be a guide, going with them to Sarnath and telling stories of Lord Buddh. But let me give you some professional advice—get rid of this foreign hat—they don't want that. You must have a turban, something very, very Indian. Be typical. That's my advice. Your gray beard, like my own, is excellent, very typical. The amulets, rings, that earring, walking stick, also very good. But the hat, no—dispose of that hat. Likewise the foreign book. The hat and book aren't typical. What stories do you tell?"*

"Ghost stories—bhuts, prets, vetals. Tales of terror."

"Maybe it's not possible for foreigners to understand. Possibly they would pay to hear the stories of our gods. I don't know. The richer a man is, the more tightly he guards his wallet—these tourists are difficult. Take my own trade for example: snake charmer, from a family of snake charmers, an illustrious family that in the past entertained in the durbars of the great Moghuls, before that in the court of the Maharaja of Banaras, and before that in the palace of the great Vikramaditya himself. But the past is past. Nowadays no one cares about these things. People don't have time to stand around watching a snake charmer. It's all changed. It's all television and films now. My brothers still try to perform on the streets. After showing all the snakes, they can, if the police haven't chased them off, sell maybe three or four or five protections against snake bite for one rupee each. And for that they must risk their life catching the cobras. They make a little extra selling the venom, but it's a difficult existence. The old way—traveling snake charmers, bear handlers, magicians, storytellers—the old way is dying out. These things will vanish with you and me, brother. It's a new world. But I'm adapting to it, making the best of it. I've given up on Indian audiences. I come here for the tourists. I need only one snake, my beloved, my baby, this beauty, raised by me and devoted to me. She's friendly and well-behaved, faithful and graceful, and she only eats once a month—I buy the plumpest chicken I can find for her from a farmer who lives not so far from here. And in return for this single meal, she makes a lot of money for me by posing with the tourists. There are photos of her beautiful body displayed in homes in America, Europe, Australia, Japan, all over the world. I ask them for one hundred rupees to pose with her; then they always say fifty, and then I get no less than sixty and they're happy and I'm happy. I'm happy because it's easy money and little work; they're happy too because they've been scared out of their wits and come through it alive and laughing. Yes, they're willing to pay to hold the snake, to wrap it around their necks, and they'll pay precisely because they're afraid of snakes. They get a photograph to show that they are not frightened by what really terrifies them. Haha!"

The serpent flicks its tongue and the storyteller can see two small reflections of himself, one in each of the python's glittering eyes.

"Do you tell snake fables?"

"Serpents crawl through many of my stories. They bring a touch of fear, a bit of suspense. I've told the story of Garuda devouring the snakes to prevent them from consuming the nectar of immortality."

"Perhaps you'll tell it to me sometime?"

2 June

(FIFTH LUNAR DAY OF THE DARK FORTNIGHT OF JYESHTHA)

> NEW DELHI. The third and final round of polling for the tenth Lok Sabha ended today with 23 persons reported killed in separate incidents of violence in part of Andhra Pradesh, Gujarat and U.P.
>
> (Hindustan Times)

The heat makes it impossible to accomplish anything at all. I go to Vishvanath Gali to get a lead on my storyteller from the curio vendor, only to learn that Patel died some time ago and no one around here seems to know what I'm talking about when I ask about an itinerant bard. No, no one has ever seen anyone wearing an English top hat. I'm getting sucked in—people are starting to appear sinister, and I begin to suspect they're hiding something, fearfully keeping me from the storyteller. Perhaps they imagine that I'm Count Dracula, the foreign Vetala Raja, here to take my revenge.

As I walk back via Manikarnika, objects are turned by my gaze into symbols out of control: tower, river, funeral pyre, corpse, crow, sandalwood, smoke, ashes, the dirt under my finger nails, the shit under the sole of my shoe.

I go to the Sanskrit Department at Banaras Hindu University in hopes of finding Professor Pandey, supposedly an expert on *rasa,* on the codified aesthetic sentiments in classical Sanskrit literature, as I want to talk to him about the *rasas* of horror and the macabre, to ask him the crucial question: "Why do people relish what is distasteful to them? Why do we enjoy in the context of art what in life is fearful and/ or disgusting? How do the classical Indian theoreticians answer that?" He's not there, but I'm directed to his home and assured that he will be delighted to receive me.

Professor Pandey, wiping the perspiration from his round, dark face, smiles as he evades my questions: "Nothing in Varanasi is fearful or disgusting. No, what must be difficult for you to understand is that there is no fear in Varanasi. Everyone comes here to die. Elsewhere people are afraid to die, so they come here and the fear is gone. And there is no disgust in Varanasi, for everything in the City of Blessed Light is pure, purified by the Ganga, purified by the funeral pyres, purified, you see, by fire and water. Purified, purified, purified!" He laughs: "Varanasi is the city of burning and learning; body cooks, read books!"

I tell him about the storyteller, an old man who wears a top hat, a British hat. But Pandey has never heard of the storyteller and says that he has never seen anyone in Varanasi in a top hat.

I ask him if he has seen the posters for the film *Roohani Taqaat*—I'd like to see it, to see if traditional styles of horror and the macabre, the sentiment as it is manifest in the *Malati-Madhava* or in Sanskrit poetry, is latent or manifest in the new Indian examples of terror.

He's uninterested: "I don't go to films. I don't watch television. The last time I went to the cinema was when I was a small boy, just after Partition. It was the year the movie theater in Caitganj went up in flames." Again he laughs: "It was blamed on Muslims, but in fact—I have it from reliable authorities—the film had become jammed in the projector. The projectionist, a pious Hindu, was drunk and the projection booth caught fire. Some of the people in the theater, thinking the smoke and flames were simply part of the effect, part of the action of the film, stayed to watch and they, together with the projectionist, unconscious from his liquor, were burned to death. Mass cremation! I, myself, fortunately escaped and I have not gone to a film since."

Professor Pandey speaks for an hour on the different kinds of mango available in Varanasi at this time of year. I take it as a nonsequitur until he suddenly remarks: "There are, from Lucknow, heart-shaped mangoes that are so deliciously sweet that it is almost disgusting. Perhaps there are things that are so horribly disgusting that they are almost sweet. Unfortunately I cannot think of any examples at this time."

There is a moment of silence, and then he advises me not to write about the *rasas* of horror and the macabre. "They are not important. Write about the sentiments of love, heroism, and peace. They are important."

. . . the cantonment graveyard has vanished into thin air, and with it English roses and epitaphs which, if read together, form a mysterious poem about memory and affection, penitence and hope, about love, heroism, and peace. Where the cemetery once was, where Brahm has come again and again for refuge and recollection over the years, is now the site of Varanasi Arts and Crafts. Silks and brocades, brass, copper ware, and ivory are sold over the ossuary where Memsahib previously rested. Travelers' checks are cashed, tours to Sarnath are arranged, and false promises are made.

The storyteller loiters in front of the shop until he's certain that her ghost no longer lingers there, that she is not waiting for him.

Naturally apprehensive that this scruffy and eccentric old man might scare customers away, a salesman comes out of the emporium to shoo the storyteller along. Brahm tries to ask him if he knows what has happened to the cemetery, but the salesman, who has no idea what he's talking about, no awareness that, yes, this was once a graveyard and that the bones that have rested there have (all except Varney's) been moved to St. Mary's Church graveyard, shouts at Brahm, "Get away, stay away, don't come near this place."

After Independence local authorities had decided that one Christian graveyard was quite sufficient since fewer Christians would be dying in Varanasi. Varney's bones had been left in the ground. The statue of the Irish setter, having become a living idol, Kuttadevata, had been protectively stolen and solemnly installed in a shrine in a small farming village in Ghazipur district. The pujari at the shrine, inspired by his devotion to the dog he said was Shiva's, now tells pilgrims fabulous tales of the dog-god's exploits. "Come close," he says, "and I will tell you the story of how Kuttadevata chased the vetal away from the house of a village carpenter. The man, born under an unlucky sign, had always been beset by problems—money problems, family problems, woman problems, every problem. But now there was a new problem, the biggest problem of all. His village was haunted by a bloodthirsty vetal. It appeared to the man at first in his dreams, and then it would wait for him in the fields at night. The man would have been devoured by this monster if it had not been for the grace of Kuttadevata who protected the carpenter because he, like you, had once come as a pilgrim to this very shrine. So, come a little closer, and let me tell you the story of the haunted carpenter and the dog god. . . ."

3 June

(SIXTH LUNAR DAY OF THE DARK FORTNIGHT OF JYESHTHA)

> RAIPUR. A 10-year-old girl, Miss Kanchana Sukhoo, was allegedly sacrificed at a temple in the hills near Basmunda village in the South Bastar district recently. Tribals in Bastar believe that by offering human blood to the goddess they can curb epidemics and get a good harvest. The culprits, including the priest, beheaded Kanchana and buried her head and the rest of her severed body at separate places.
>
> (*Times of India*)

Last night, awakened by Cheryl's scream, I jumped up—something was in our bed, some sort of animal. Her shriek sent it—what was it? a monkey, a cat, a rat, a mongoose? what?—scurrying out through the bars across the glassless window. I saw the scampering shadow, smelled the feral scent, and, with a shudder, rubbed my hand across the dirtied sheet.

My informant is suddenly out of town. Our water cooler no longer works even when there is electricity. And Cheryl is sicker: there are blotches on her legs and lips and she complains of losing the feeling in her hands and feet; there's a tingling radiating up her arms. And, without the courage to express our fear, we both pretend to take it lightly.

I read to her to comfort her and myself and, as I do, she dozes off . . . *when the storyteller arrives back at the red tower adjacent to Manikarnika, the foreigner accuses him of stealing something from his pack: "Look at that hat, that cross around his neck, the book he carries! He's a thief and I'm calling the cops. Where did he get that book? Look at what it says on the side of the book*—Dracula. *He can't even speak English, so he sure can't read—he's a fucking thief. And those watches, two watches, where did he get the watches? He stole my stuff. I know it—he's a fucking thief! I'm getting the police!"*

Brahm smiles calmly. His cloudy eye frightens the girl; and his gnarled walking stick, she surmises, could be a deadly weapon. Her fears are not in vain: one of the card players, only half joking, whispers to Brahm in muffled Hindi, "Should we kill him?"

The question makes the storyteller laugh and shake his head, no, no, it will be alright. "Have you ever read this book, Dracula?*" Brahm suddenly asks the foreigners in fluent English as he opens the book for them, and both his command of the language and the question itself startle them into silence.*

"Be very careful my young friends," Brahm, now modulating the storyteller's voice, using his craft to frighten the travelers, warns. "In your country, these are just stories, fanciful tales, a source of amusement; but in our land, in India, ancient as she is, these things are real. The vampire king, the Lord of the Un-Dead, the one we call Vetala Maharaja, lives, is as real as you or I, and he thirsts. You have no business here. This is the place of death; the mourners who come here to grieve for their departed loved ones are not out of place. But you, you are out of place, like Jonathan Harker at the Borgo Pass. Go to the cantonment, stay in a hotel there. You will be happier, safer, out of reach of the Un-Dead One who questions the reason for your presence here. You are intruding here. You are trespassers in the City of Dreadful Night. You are characters from another story, out of place in the plot of this one. This story is a dangerous one, all horror and the macabre—beware of it. Return to your romance, your comedy, your little satire."

No, this isn't believable. Despite the fact that I met the two Americans today in Varanasi, that they are sleeping each night in the tower, despite the fact that, coincidentally, the girl's name is Christine and that she wears a single anklet, despite the fact that they are real and very clear in my mind, they seem no more than fictions or ghosts next to the storyteller. They are, as the storyteller himself says, out of place in the story. How do I integrate and quicken them? By making her afraid? By making them leave the story?

The girl is terrified, the man infuriated: "He's not only a thief, he's a liar too. He's a madman, fucking possessed—Dracula, Un-Dead, vampires. I'm getting the cops." And with that they (she in fear, he in disgust) exit the story; and Brahm smiles with satisfaction over his cultivation of the power to frighten with words. Memsahib would have been proud of him. . . .

4 June

(SIXTH LUNAR DAY OF THE DARK FORTNIGHT OF JYESHTHA CONTINUED; THE DAY IS, ACCORDING TO THE ALMANAC, A DANGEROUS ONE [SAMKASHTHI])

> ALLAHABAD. Squeeze a lemon and collect the juice in a copper bowl. Mix 100 gm of pure honey in it. Add 50cc to 100cc of fresh blood drop by drop and stir with a copper spoon. Finally pour in water and drink the potion. No, this is not the recipe for Dracula's continental breakfast. It is a unique, though bizarre, therapy given by Dr. R. C. Gupta to patients suffering from incurable diseases. The iconoclastic doctor shot into prominence last year when he offered a blood-soaked sandwich to one of his interns, Dr. Rautela. While a nauseous Rautela was hospitalized, horrified college students went on strike.
>
> (Dilip Awasthi, *India Today*)

Cheryl feels well enough to come with me this evening, to take a boat from Assi. "Come, *saab*—boat ride, see burning ghats, very nice. See bodies, dead bodies—one body, three hours. Very, very nice." I insist that he leave us at Dashashvamedha, that "no, no, no," we don't want to go to the pyres of Manikarnika. Weak from the heat that persists despite the evening (my head pulsing, feeling my body exude, pores open and dripping like bad pipes broken by the heat; the cotton cloth on my back and arms clinging like bandages sticking to gaping wounds), I struggle to haggle over the price of the ride.

Lepers, crouched and lumped on the steps of Dashashvamedha ghat, transported here, depicted now, are utterly and necessarily transformed by utterance and print. Flesh is rendered into inky metaphor. It's the sin of the storyteller and his redemption.

They're waiting. Not for us, though it almost seems so. But they're waiting, and what are they waiting for? They're lined up, touching and on top of each other, overlapping and intertwined into a chain of bruised flesh strung from pole to pole beneath the rust-crusted railing that you'd reach for, that you'd hold on to for support and balance, if it didn't mean getting too close. *"Saab! Saab! Baksheesh, saab!"* the lepers moan in antiphony. The litany of misery, the call for alms and

mercy, is sung by mouths disease-distorted, some lipless, some tongueless, some wordless, is chanted in syncopated groans and dreadful threnodies. We push our way through the crowds, purposefully, as though we really had somewhere to go, vehemently repeating, "no, no, no," to the dolorous lepers no less than to the ardent hawkers, straight for the stairs, up to and through the market, past the gaudy shrines of gods who do not feel. "No, no, no," echoes automatic and don't look into their eyes or they've got you. There are leprous couples waiting there, bodies sabotaged by a disease so audacious that it withholds its pain, husbands with their wives—or are they lovers?—one with feet to push the other's cart, one with hands to extend for the other's alms. Boundaries between text and world, literature or film and life, are carefully marked in and by horror and the macabre. One leper sings a hymn of praise to some distant god, sung to move that deity—Bhairava Shiva, I think—to soften the heart of a passerby: *"Saab, saab, baksheesh, saab!"*

"When we had the Asian Games in Delhi, Mrs. Gandhi forbid lepers on the streets. They were arrested on sight and taken away. This was because she didn't want people to automatically think of lepers when they think of India. She didn't want people to think of India as a horrible place," a man with whom we later found ourselves seated in the Yelchiko Bar near Godalia was to explain. He would ask: "And the lepers? Do the lepers of our holy city trouble you?" We drank Indian Scotch and ate meat pakoras with ketchup and I wondered what was the right answer to his question.

"But, listen, Mrs. Gandhi was wrong. Foreigners enjoy seeing lepers. It is one of the reasons they come to India. Why disappoint them? Besides, the leper is a holy man, just like a sadhu in every way. He wears rags, begs, and is set apart from society, without attachments to this world. Leprosy is a sadhana. The leper, more than any other man, more than you or I, knows the worthlessness of the body and the meaninglessness of this world. The body of the leper, because of the disease, appears to be covered with ashes like that of a sannyasi." Both are simultaneously, and yet differently, in perhaps opposite ways, images of abjection and holiness, objects of revulsion and reverence. The leper is an unintentional Aghori, a Kapalika against his will, all the more saintly for not knowing it. A holy man without the sanctimony, he suffers for our sins.

At the top of the stairs, as the market haphazardly begins to form itself, there's a man with a booth from which he sells charms, amulets, bones, skulls—rodent, bird, cat, dog, monkey, and human skulls, one of which wears sunglasses and has a cigarette in its lipless mouth. Why is it always a cigarette?

I buy a monkey skull that's marked with dirt and vermillion; its jaw and front teeth missing, its enormous eye sockets staring into abysses unseen by the living. Five hundred rupees and now he wants to sell me a human skull; but I show no interest. "I know," he laughs, "you already have one on top of your neck! Good joke?"

. . . at dawn the storyteller joins the other suppliant bathers in the waters of the Ganges near Dashashvamedha ghat, and next to him a brahmin recites the Gayatri mantra to celebrate the splendor of the sun, asking it to purify his visions, and hymns of praise are muttered, and Brahm feels cleansed and curiously pleased even though he does not believe that gods are as real as ghosts, spirits that at least once upon a time were clad in real flesh and warmed by real blood.

The lepers are already posed along the railing up the stairs from the water into the marketplace. And climbing the steps, passing them quickly, Brahm sees an old woman displaying her cracked and toeless feet, the unknowing bride of the terrible leper from Brahm's story with the chalk-white finger stumps on the coal-black hand reaching through the oily fold of dark wrappings. He knows her through his stories, the macabre mistress formed of both memory and imagination, horrid living idol of all that men find disgusting or fearful in women. Her leprosy is childbirth, menstruation, moodiness, jealousy, obstinacy, tears, and the cloy of love. And, over the clamor of the already busy ghat, the storyteller can hear faint fragments of the wordless song she hums with a pain that is not so unbeautiful. No. Brahm suddenly stops, turns, his heart pounding, his stomach churning, three steps down and he whispers it: "Mena?" The mad, disfigured woman, accustomed to being mistaken for someone else, someone once known, lost, and unresolved, turns cackling and stretching out the hand for a charity that is propitiation. Some ghosts still have shreds of flesh clinging to them.

Brahm stands between the sun and her and the drape of his shadow makes her cower. "I won't harm you," he says as he drops the two-rupee note into her battered bowl. He takes the lit cigarette from his lips and places it in her mutilated mouth. She inhales deeply, blows great clouds of smoke from her nostrils and shivers with pleasure. . . .

5 June

(SEVENTH LUNAR DAY OF THE DARK FORTNIGHT OF JYESHTHA; BUDHA'S EIGHTH AND SHITALA'S EIGHTH)

> PANDHARPUR. Eleven pilgrims died and 29 were injured in a stampede near Pandharpur this morning when an elephant accompanying the Gajanan Maharaj Palanquin went berserk, creating horror and panic among the crowd.
>
> *(Times of India)*

I can't conceal my anger from my informant, and, although he can't conceal the defensiveness and nervousness that my exasperation causes him, he insists on reassuring and commanding me to be patient. Enumerating the elaborate measures he is taking to find the storyteller for me, he insists that he'll inform me when Brahm Kathuwala has been located. "Until then, enjoy Varanasi, City of Light!" He wants to know if the ashes have cured my wife yet.

"No? It's because of the monkey skull you purchased. Get rid of the skull. I am warning you. It's good to be a little superstitious; have you noticed that in horror films, monster tales, and ghost stories, it's always the people who laugh at the superstitions, who don't believe in them, that get killed by the monsters? Bury the skull somewhere far away. It will be most effective if you bury it at midnight on amavasya. If you wish, I will consult an astrologer for you in order to determine when and where it is most effective to perform this. Listen, I'll tell you a story, a real horror story: You know the little Kali shrine behind the Monkey Temple? Mataji there was given the skull of a certain business-
man. The old skull that she had there, the one she used for her puja, started bickering and fighting with the new skull, and soon Mataji became sick. You could hear those two skulls bickering sometimes at midnight, cursing each other. But when she put the new skull outside, she got better." My informant laughs: "My children, I don't know how, got that skull from her. For a joke they brought it home without telling me and they put little blinking lights in the eye sockets to frighten me. My son became very, very ill, just like your wife. But when my daughter returned the skull, my boy was cured."

Despite the fact that I've kept the skull, Cheryl seems to be feeling better again, well enough to come with me to see the horror movie, *Roohani Taqaat*.

I suppose it's because she's the only woman in the entire theater that every head is turned away from the screen to look at her. The movie is all sex and death, bats and owls, monsters and fiends, a confabulation of mythologies (Shaitan and Kali), demonologies (mummies and spirits), and sensibilities (prurience and puritanism). It brings back childhood: I enjoy horror movies in which you can see the zipper on the monster's costume, in which the knees of that costume get baggier as the movie goes along. Mummies moan, devils shriek, vampires hiss, Tantric sadhus invoke demons, women scream, the audience howls, laughs, argues, jabbers, hoots, cheers. It's chaos. A boy next to me addresses me in English: "Excellent film! Very blood curling! You are enjoying it very much?"

Tonight on the veranda we wonder about the flashes of light in the distance: "Is that lightning? Fireworks? Bombs? A riot? What's going on?"

. . . *there, near Harishchandra ghat, two dead dogs are floating in the tremorous river, and two young children are lackadaisically playing amidst them in the lacy membrane of grime adhering to the shimmering surface of the holy water, laughing at those bloated buoys. The storyteller watches the boys splash the bobbing carcasses as he eats the delicious, heart-shaped Lucknow mango, nature's sweet consolation for all the other discomforts of this sweltering season.*

Taking off his hat and leaning over the smooth water to let Ganga lick the sticky sweet juice from his hands, the storyteller, noticing his reflection there, his earring a luminous sparkle in the dark sheen of the billowy river surface, sees Bhutnath there. He senses that he has, in some very real sense, become the old man, not like him, but him incarnate, taking his place in the world and telling his stories. And in the water, behind Bhutnath, his mother, Kalyani, is undulously reflected, her blue sari almost invisible in the azure ripple of Ganga water lapping and pulsing against the stone step in the swelling cadence of the mother's song: leaves of betel, pierced with clove, la la la all the gods of Kashi and the lonely sweeper woman. . . . *Her hand comes tenderly to rest on Bhutnath's shoulder—he can both see and feel it. She had gone away with the ojha, Brahm realized, and suddenly it seemed obvious, so startlingly obvious: yes, Bhutnath was his father. Yes. Of course. Why else would he have given him the earring? Why would he have given him the name, his name? Why has that, in all these years, never occurred to him? And even if it isn't true, he reckoned, it makes a good story. Brahm Kathuwala smiles: "At last, now that I am old, so very old, I've found my father," he laughs. "And, at last, he's with my mother."*

The storyteller washes his hands and the ghosts disappear in the gentle churning of the divine waters. The aqueous dungeons of memory are sealed, the dogs are silent, and the children are laughing still. . . .

6 June

(EIGHTH LUNAR DAY OF THE DARK FORTNIGHT OF JYESHTHA)

> BOMBAY. Tall, dark, and bat-like, the black-caped figure strides regally down the corridor. The camera zooms in. The eyes glow red, like traffic lights. The two veins protruding from his forehead look as if they are about to burst. The two canine teeth stretch down to his chin. It's Count Dracula in his Indian incarnation. . . . Suddenly the industry is churning out horror films by the dozen. The deluge came two years ago. Interestingly, most of the converts to the world of the mud-dipped ghosts are Punjabi film makers. "I switched to horror films when terrorism came to Punjab," says Mohan Bhakri. . . . There is, it seems, no business like the horror business.
>
> (Madhu Jain, *India Today)*

At the little Kali shrine Cheryl playfully takes down her hair with Mataji so that they can pose together, disheveled and mocking mad devotions, for a photograph with the idol of the terrible goddess. The little crone tries to teach Cheryl how to smoke hashish from the chillum. Cheryl's name makes Mataji laugh.

"Churel," the old woman repeats with a grin, referring to Indian witches with long nails, long, loose blond hair, hideous creatures who take on beautiful forms, who appear captivatingly lovely except that their feet are turned backward. "Churel! Haha!" Usually they are the ghosts of barren women, causing impotence or death, haunting cemeteries or places where people have died violently, seducing travelers, holy men, pilgrims, farmers coming home late from the fields, and male visitors to the cremation grounds. "Churel!"

The shrine of Bhairavi Kali, which has become a kind of creche for the giggling children of the poor who jokingly tease me and the churel, is our refuge from the sudden and unexpected rain. At first the enormous monsoon droplets evaporate the moment they hit the hot, red-washed cement floor; and instantly the desiccated earth sucks them into herself. But then, asserting itself, the rain begins to triumph: the droplets bounce on the concrete, then form pools, and soon the road in front of the shrine has become a stream.

The rain quiets the incessant motors, bicycle bells, scooter horns, and cars honking. An old woman forges through the rain and mud, hiking up her sari almost lewdly above her knees so that the cloth won't suck up the torrent of filthy water.

When we arrive home, after the rain lets up, I ask the servant if my informant has come by. No. No, of course not.

The servant, out of what seems a genuine concern about Cheryl's health, tries to explain to me about *"nazar,"* the evil eye, and *"tona,"* witchcraft: Has someone been able to get hold of any of her hair, or a fingernail perhaps? Is some evil magic being done against us? No. I try to reassure him. No.

Cheryl was moaning in her sleep tonight. I touched her in order to calm her and it made her flinch. Her eyes suddenly opened wide.

"It's alright," I say, "there's nothing to be afraid of." And I'm afraid.

. . . the storyteller sits smoking, protected in the shade beneath the stone relief of dread Bhairavi, two of her four arms raised above him—one wielding her sword, a head in one of her lowered hands, a skirt of severed arms, a garland of skulls around her neck. She has often defended him from the Vetala Raja, the Lord of the Abyss, who, counting on the frailty and fears of women, backs off from her as from garlic or asafetida, a crucifix or a trishula; he retreats from her as from a mirror.

Watching a fitful flock of crows fighting over a bone with dried, dark morsels of some sort of putrefied flesh still clinging to it, the storyteller considers the great difference between city crows and country crows, a different species to be sure: the one tasty, the other rancid; the one aggressive but good humored, the other at once fearful and nasty. When he rises they disband upward, squawking as if they are aware that he has killed, cooked, and eaten crow.

He has considered going to both the Baba Kinnaram Ashram

and to Pishach Mochan but now decides against it: "It's too hot. And, after all, there's no point in it. There's no going back. All the old ones are dead and gone now. All my friends are ghosts."

Walking through the streets as aimlessly as a leaf, a twig, a bit of refuse, or an offering floating on the surface of the Ganga, he stops, amused, in front of the poster on the side of the goddess shrine for the film playing at the Lalita Cinema in Bhelupur: Roohani Taqaat *(the two o's formed of laughing, flame-haloed skulls). The ad is English: "BLOOD CURLING HORROR!" [surely they mean "curdling" Brahm thinks] "FRIGHTFUL H-O-R-R-O-R!"*

Perhaps it's the poster peeling under the merciless heat that inspires him to keep the promise of visiting Pradip's brother's shop, The Divine Goddess Video Bazaar, near Durga Kund. There's the din of the wedding procession. . . .

The videovan parked in front indicates that Pradip is there, and he jumps up delighted to see the old storyteller, excitedly introducing him to his brother Sagar: "He tells horror stories in the villages. Ghost stories and dracula-type monster tales. He doesn't appreciate video. We have to introduce him to its wonders and delights."

It is, of course, true: in his peregrinations, the storyteller has developed an enmity toward video, has learned to avoid the villages with too many electrical wires leading into them and too many television antennae on their rooftops. An antenna means there's a television set and a television set means a VCR and a VCR means disinterest in Brahm's tales of terror. "You're the past," Pradip had said in the van on the night Rajiv was assassinated: "I'm the future and the future always wins over the past. That's not good or bad, happy or sad—it's just the way things are. We have to let go of the past."

"What will you watch, horror or porn?" Sagar asks the old man as he hands him the cold Campa-Cola that his peon has just fetched. "Anything you want, free, no charge, we'll watch it right now."

The storyteller, pointing to his cloudy left eye, falsely protests with apologetic explanations that his failing eyesight makes video-watching vain. And that's not why he's visiting the shop. He has come, he says, to give a small gift to Pradip: the silver skull earring.

The young man smiles wholeheartedly as he lets the old man hold the ice against his ear lobe and then pierce it with a disinfected nail. His brother and the peon wince. There's a large drop of dark glistening blood. Then, as he fastens the clasp of the skull, the story-teller tells the videowala that it would be good for business to wear it when he shows horror movies: "You want to look mysterious."

"Why are giving this to me?" Pradip asks.

"I'm letting go of the past."

"I don't believe you," Pradip laughs.

"You're right," Brahm smiles. "You should never believe a storyteller." He hesitates, then lightly laughs. "Never believe a story-teller unless you want to enjoy yourself. . . ."

7 June

(NINTH LUNAR DAY OF THE DARK FORTNIGHT OF JYESHTHA)

> RAIGANJ. In a chilling display of medieval obscurantism, a 10-month-old boy was sacrificed to appease goddess Kali in Malibari village about 30 km away from here. The child's father Bibhisan Burman (35) allegedly agreed to offer his son for sacrifice at the behest of a tantrik, who is now absconding. . . . The beheaded corpse of the boy was found under a heap of banana leaves and flowers near a pond. An elevated ground flanked by bamboo bushes located some distance away from the pond is traditionally worshipped by the villagers as their "debosthan" (god's place). The altar here was blood splattered and rice and flowers lay scattered on it—a sign of a prayer having been conducted.
>
> *(Hindustan Times).*

Cheryl's sickness—the nausea, diarrhea, and cramps, the chills, fever, and tingling in her limbs, the dry mouth, nervousness, and stifled breath—stuns me as it reveals what horror and the macabre are about.

There's no water except what's in the bucket that the old servant painfully and dutifully strains to carry up the stairs for us so that we can use it to flush the toilet. The feel of my own grimy skin, the smell of our own shit, urine, and perspiration, the sound of Cheryl's wretch and moan, the sight of the old man wheezing as he struggles with the bucket, the taste of ashes, sicken me as they reveal what horror and the macabre are about.

The pig outside and the monkey skull on the table in front of me reveal it too. So too the mysterious nocturnal animal. It came through the window again last night and entered our bed. I was armed with a flashlight, but it was too fast for me and escaped. We never see the real objects of terror; they're always in the peripheries of vision, eternally penumbral.

I'm consoled by the fact that this, *this,* isn't a horror story, that there is, in fact and fiction, a distinction between story and reality. It's easy to imagine what might happen to Cheryl if this were a horror novel: her eyes would widen and fill with terrible light; ghouls and goblins would dance around her; snakes and scorpions might break from her mouth or womb. But, no, she smiles and tells me that she's feeling better.

It's as if it had never rained. Everything is bone dry and hot again. And my informant seems to be doing nothing to find the storyteller for me.

Cheryl, because of the illness, has, she tells me, been having nightmares—dreams of a demon under the bed, a dream about Rajiv Gandhi and another about the girl who assassinated him, another about me, and a frightening dream about the storyteller we're supposed to meet.

. . . tonight on the river, the lights shimmering in the rippling currents, Brahm smokes, looks into the black yawn of sky and forms a constellation there with a star from this stellar configuration, and another from that, and a lone star, nervously twinkling, from here, another from there—an irregular circle of seven sidereal jewels. He calls the new constellation Mena's Anklet and later tonight, in his dreams, Mena will dance, her anklet bells echoing through the heavens, and her footsteps will measure out the mansions of the sky. . . .

8 June

(TENTH LUNAR DAY OF THE DARK FORTNIGHT OF JYESHTHA)

> NEW DELHI. For decades India was the world's main supplier of human skeletons. In 1985, however, the Indian government banned the sales amid rumours of grave robbing.
>
> *(Science)*

When I angrily and impatiently insist that I have to find the storyteller, that if I don't meet him within a week I'll be leaving Varanasi, my informant, apparently to appease me, suggests that we go to a village in Ballia district where he suspects the man might be staying.

There's blood on the road. An army truck has rammed at full speed into the back of a bullock cart decapitating the animal. The driver sits by the headless beast and the demolished wooden wagon and weeps.

On the way to Ballia there is cane, palm, mango, eucalyptus, pipal, nim, and I'm dazzled by how much remains green and defiantly alive despite the blistering blaze of summer. Makeshift villages sprout up on, along, and around the paved roads: paan and chai stalls, huts and hovels, charpoys and stools, piles of things—bricks, lumber, pipe—and everything is covered with dust.

There are children everywhere and travelers, shepherds and sadhus, pony boys and goatherds, pigs and dogs, cows and buffalo, and we pass a rickshaw in which a woman rides: she's wrapped in a bright silk sheet, a sari perhaps, so that only her feet can be seen. Who is she? Why is she hidden? In town I saw a corpse wrapped like that, being taken to Harishchandra ghat in a rickshaw.

When we arrive in the village children swarm around the taxi. A man with a face that's badly scratched stares through the window at me with a quizzical glower. It's clear that several of the villagers know my informant; he disappears with them, leaving me to sit on the edge of the platform under the pipal tree near the now dry bed of stream. The children stare at me as they cautiously inch closer and closer. Suddenly, "booo!" I shout and they scamper, at once giggling with delight and screeching with fear.

My informant returns to explain that, no, they know nothing of the storyteller. No storytellers have come this year. But there was a videovan, an "Open Air Theater," and they saw a scary film called *Kabaristan*.

I'm afraid to drink the water that's offered to me in the clay bowl, but finally my thirst is greater than my fear or revulsion, and there's nothing else to drink. I gulp the water desperately.

Furious with my informant, certain that he has tricked me into paying the seven-hundred-rupee taxi fare so that he can conduct some personal business in the village under the pretext of helping me, I refuse to speak to him during the long ride back to Varanasi.

My eyes close and I imagine a story about my storyteller and in it *the storyteller imagines a story and in it Sanjaya, the wrestler of Banaras, stands before the slowly opening door of the abandoned palace*. Within stood a tall old man, clean shaven save for a long white moustache, and clad in black from head to foot, without a single speck of color abut him anywhere. He held in his hand an antique silver lamp, in which the flame burned without chimney or globe of any kind, throwing long quivering shadows as it flickered in the draught of the open door. The old man motioned Sanjaya in with his right hand with courtly gesture: "Welcome to my house! Enter freely and of your own will!"

At the end of the story, Sanjaya and Vijaya, in an abandoned Dak Bungalow in the cantonment, pry open the lid of the great, earth-filled box with their kukri knives. Under the efforts of both men the lid began to yield; the nails drew with a quick screeching sound, and the top of the box was thrown back. *Lying within the box atop the moldy earth lies the Vetala Maharaja,* deathly pale, just like a waxen image, and the red eyes glared with a horrible vindictive look. The eyes saw the sinking sun, and the look of hate in them turned to triumph. *Sanjay's dagger flashes, lowers, sweeps to shear through the throat as Vijaya's comes down and into the heart with the twist, a pry, and a jab*. It was like a miracle; almost in the drawing of a breath, the whole body crumbled into dust and passed from sight, and in that moment of final dissolution there was in the face a look of peace. . . .

Brahm bids goodbye to the Maharaja of Vetalas, Betul Rajo, King of the Vampires, Lord of the Un-Dead, Count Dracula, the nosferatu conjured up by the mad Irish Memsahib so many years ago, raised and infused with living death, with Un-Deadness. And at that same moment, without realizing it at the time, I say goodbye to my storyteller.

Brahm Kathuwala has been inspired by the Count, kept alive and awake by him. He already misses the terror. It's eerie and uncomfortable to say out loud that his great enemy is not real, is but a specter of foreign imagination. The ghosts of Mena's miscarried children vanish with him. And Mena's face, no less than his, takes on a look of peace in that moment of final dissolution. . . .

9 June

(ELEVENTH LUNAR DAY OF THE DARK FORTNIGHT OF JYESHTHA)

> DELHI. Dr. R. Joshi, of the Department of Psychiatry at the All India Institute of Medical Sciences, speaking at today's meeting on terrorism, explained that in order to understand the motivations of Thanu, the assassin of former Prime Minister Rajiv Gandhi, we must not think simply in political terms but in psychological terms as well. "Many lost souls," he explained, "want to be mentioned in newspapers. The degree of exposure you get from an act of violence overtakes the fear, the pain, the thought of death, or even rational thinking."
>
> *(Illustrated Weekly of India)*

My informant and his son arrive with great smiles, and the boy presents me with two Hindi comic books, copies of the series *Dabal Seekret Egent 00½:* one entitled *Drakyula Balak;* the other *Bhutmahal.* As I look at the green humanoid monster with red eyes and sharp fangs and pointed fingernails on the torn cover, he speaks: "Here are some excellent samples of Indian horror stories for your research. My son found them for you. We are working very hard on your project."

"Yeah, yeah, thanks," I say and then ask if I'm ever going to meet the storyteller. He tells me to be patient and it makes me impatient. He claims that he has sent his son to the hostels in Varanasi where people go to die. "He's old and might be in one of them. Or perhaps he has already died. In that case you won't meet him. But let's not look on the dark side of things. Have you looked for him at Pishach Mochan? He might, assuming that he is not dead, very well be there."

. . . though Brahm, as he bathes in the Ganga, remembers Memsahib's voice quoting some English poet, he cannot for the life of him remember the poet's name: "Who shall tempt with wandering feet the dark unbottomed infinite abyss and through the palpable obscure find out his uncouth way?"

After all these years, the storyteller is finally able to answer the question, to say that yes, yes, he'll do it. He has no fear of the abyss. No fear, no disgust. All such feelings are suspended. . . .

10 June

(THIRTEENTH LUNAR DAY OF THE DARK FORTNIGHT OF JYESHTHA)

> BANDA. Amid the sound of conch shells and the breaking of coconuts, a 47-year-old woman of Banda District stepped on the funeral pyre of her husband on Monday. She was dressed in her wedding finery and wore a huge tilak on her forehead while around her the crowd roared and priests chanted mantras. All efforts to persuade Kesaria to give up her immolation attempt were of little avail. Instead there were angry murmurings from the 10,000-strong crowd of villagers which had gathered at the funeral site to watch the sati. According to the District Magistrate, Dr. Shankar Dutt Ojha, the elders of the village had spared no effort to promote the event as a devout happening.
>
> *(Times of India)*

I go to Pishach Mochan on the chance, and in the vague hope, that *he* might be there. The servant, assuming that I'm going there to get a cure for Cheryl, approves.

Those who grieve for the unfortunate pishacha souls come

here to turn them from goblins or hungry ghosts into ancestors. There are several large pipal trees, "Devil Trees" studded with nails and spikes from which bleak black ribbons hang loose in the breezeless summer air. Inverted pots are transformed by paint and propitiatory offerings into the heads of terrible demons decapitated by Bhairava Shiva.

I talk to an officiant whose function here seems to be to answer the questions of pilgrims and tourists, suppliants and penitents. Pishachs, he explains, the vilest, most repugnant and malignant of the demonic and malefic orders, enter the body through the anus if one doesn't do the proper ablutions after defecation; they are the spirits of those who have been killed violently, in accidents or crimes. And all politicians, he says, become pishachs when they die.

"Has Rajiv become a pishach then?"

"No, no, he became a bhut, because he was a victim. That girl

who killed him. She has become a pishachi."

"But you said that pishachs are the spirits of those who've died violently."

"Yes, if you are afraid at the moment you die. If there is terror, you become a pishach. Rajiv was not afraid. He has become an ancestor. He is at peace. But not the girl. Her spirit still haunts the earth. She's afraid and angry, hungry and lustful."

"I've heard of a man, an ojha, a storyteller who wears a hat, a foreign hat. He tells stories about bhuts and pishachs. I've heard he sometimes comes here. He's called Brahm Kathuwala."

The man didn't seem to know what I was talking about.

. . . Mena had told Brahm to burn the book; Bhutnath told Brahm to burn the book; and he remembered hearing Dr. Thomson arguing with Memsahib: "Burn that damn book. It's become an obsession. It's begun to take over your life." And surely his mother must have wanted to destroy the book that separated her from her son by binding him to the plump pink woman who possessed them both. Even the snake charmer has advised him to get rid of it.

Opening the text, resting the silver crucifix between the cover and the first page (which is inscribed "To my mother who, from an early age, by reading to me and telling me stories, instilled a love of books and an appreciation of the sublime, the supernatural and the macabre, in me. With warmest affection, Nigel. 22 July 1897"), and he sets the book on the fire, and as the crematory flames begin to turn and curl, crackle and blacken the pages, to consume the words and release the spirit, Brahm Kathuwala turns and walks away.

He expects to hear screams, but the book burns in silence. In silence the ashes scatter. . . .

11 June

(FOURTEENTH LUNAR DAY OF THE DARK FORTNIGHT OF JYESHTHA)

> VARANASI. Miss Sneh Lata of Sonapur was found hanging from a ceiling fan in the Sonapur home of her father who subsequently informed authorities that the girl had been depressed of late due to a breakdown in matrimonial arrangements.
>
> *(Hindustan Times)*

Cheryl feels better, and, because for three days we have had no shower, no water except the stagnant liquid said to be water in the bucket with which we are supposed to flush the toilet, we return to Clark's Hotel in the cantonment to have a swim in the pool there. We do this despite the advice of the servant that we should not, that we should bathe in the Ganga instead. The Ganga is, by its very nature, pure; a hotel pool is, by virtue of the foreigners who have swum in it, polluted.

Deaf to my commands that he slow down, the motor rickshaw driver speeds up, honking madly and gunning his engine, shoots in between two trucks, faster he swerves, darts, careens, faster he zips under the railway bridge, cursing a buffalo, shaking his fist at a taxi, almost hitting an old woman, faster, faster, and as we overtake a boy on a bicycle the handlebar of the bike catches on the rickshaw and the boy is thrown onto the ground, into the traffic. "Stop! *Bas! Bas!* Stop!" In terror I shout that the child has fallen beneath the tires of the hurried, charging trucks and careening cars. "Stop!" But my cry only makes him increase his speed, curse out loud, and almost hit a dog. "Stop! Stop. Stop. . . ." It ceases to matter. . . . and we pass the butcher shops in the Muslim market where the flies swarm around the meat and viscera that dangle from dark iron hooks.

Drinking beer by the swimming pool we talk to an English couple on an around-the-world trip. They too arrived the day of the Gandhi assassination. They are disgusted with India and afraid of her, truly afraid. "Our journey has been an utter nightmare. Everything has gone wrong. What are you doing here?"

"I'm doing research. I'm trying to write a book about horror and the macabre in India."

The man laughs: "That ought to be easy."

. . . the storyteller is struggling to remain in control of his story. He feels himself fading. There's a shortness of breath, a fatigue, a blurring of vision. He thought he had overcome fear, but no, he's afraid again, truly afraid that either death (if, by any chance, he's real) or I (if he's really only a character in a story) have taken from him the power to determine the end, the way and mood, the place and time, of his death. He struggles to push that death beyond and outside the end of his story. . . .

12 June

(AMAVASYA, THE DARKEST NIGHT OF JYESHTHA; SHANI JAYANTI; [AT ONCE INAUSPICIOUS AND AUSPICIOUS — A TRANSITION])

> CALCUTTA. Sudipa Pal, 17, a ninth standard student, fed her parents and grandparents sweets mixed with poison after testing them on a pig. When they were dead, she tied all of them with electric wire and connected it to the mains to make it look like a mass suicide. She eliminated them in the expectation that they would hinder her relationship with her tutor Randhir Bose, 51. She showed no signs of remorse. Appearing for her tenth standard exams shortly after, she scored distinction marks.
>
> (Ramesh Menon, *India Today*)

This is the night that in the literature is the dreadful nocturne on which heroes venture into the cremation grounds to face their fears, destroy their demons, and vanquish revulsion. This is the night. . . .

We spend the evening in the Yelchiko Bar drinking Indian Scotch to pass the time until midnight. Having now given up on ever meeting the storyteller, that specter of imagination, I tell Cheryl that I'm going to burn my scholarly study of horror and macabre in Indian literature. Burning the book, she laughs, seems a bit melodramatic, the kind of thing that happens in fiction. "But nobody really does it. Do they?"

We leave the bar at eleven o'clock. The electricity is out (of course) in the town and the flicker of kerosene lamps, a candle here and there, faintly illuminate a paan vendor here, a flower seller there, a leper, a holy man, a drunkard. . . . There's the smell of incense and excrement, the sound of bhajanas and bickering. The doorway to the Vishvanath Temple is open but closed to us as foreigners.

Cheryl is holding my hand, and it gets darker and darker, shadows, dark profiles in darkness almost as dark, passing, some animals, some people, I keep saying "Manikarnika" and am pointed by murky faceless, unknown forms, shrouded in gloom, in one obscure direction or another, darker, darker, feeling our way, slipping in mud, ooze, shit . . . cows, oxen, goats . . . the growl of a dog, something scurrying, scratching—we are unsure. Low beams and buttresses—"don't hit your head!"—sudden stairs—"watch your step!"—we almost fall, inching and shuffling our way in fear of holes, drains, ravines, abysses opening . . . holding on to Cheryl, pulling her through the tenebrous maze, darker, darker, and suddenly there's a shape, and "Manikarnika?" I ask, and his or her hand clasps tightly around my forearm to pull me along without saying anything, and I'm pulling Cheryl and the ghost says, "steps," a whisper, a growl, and then it pulls, and it could be Dracula, the Maharaja of Vetalas, tugging us into the crypt. Stairs— *"ek, do, tin, char"*—"four steps, Cheryl," and darker still and then suddenly a golden glow, people slumped on the ground and, silhouetted before that crematory, incandescent light, fantastic roofs, and a voice in English—"straight"—and the eidolon of night disappears as we move forward now able to make our way down toward the river, drawn like moths to flame, the holy fire of unholy death. Discovering an empty stone pavilion, we sit together and watch the bodies burn, and our eyes are full of fire, our nostrils of smoke, our ears of crackle and whisper, our hearts of an eerie melancholy, and our hands touch unaware of the presence of others . . .*above Manikarnika ghat, above the dark pavilion, above the real world, looking down at the fires consuming the corpses, the storyteller, Brahm Kathuwala, knew the end was at hand. . . .*

13 June

(FIRST LUNAR DAY OF THE LIGHT FORTNIGHT OF JYESHTHA)

> MADRAS. The assassin of former Prime Minister Rajiv Gandhi, identified till now as Thanu, was Chitralekka hailing from Chavakachery in Jaffna peninsula in Sri Lanka, informed sources said today.
>
> *(Times of India)*

Gangadashahara begins today: ten days during which the farmers prepare the paddy fields for the coming monsoon. One begins to wait for the rains, to watch for them: the earth is parched, the Ganga low, and the other rivers, streams, tanks are completely dry. And Cheryl's feeling better. The rains will come, the world will be renewed.

The storyteller listens as the boy explains that his father is bringing an American professor to talk to him. He's writing some sort of book about bhuts, vetals, prets, something about tales of terror and the tradition of storytelling. The storyteller lightly laughs—yes, yes, he knows some stories. The boy insists that the storyteller stay put, sitting on the steps near Harishchandra ghat.

I had given up. I was certain there was no storyteller, no one even slightly resembling the construction of my imagination, fed by my own hopes, by the enthusiasm of my friend in Delhi and the assurances of my informant in Varanasi. The project was useless. He was no more real than Count Dracula.

"Hurry please, I have a scooter waiting outside. Please hurry," my informant says with uncharacteristic excitement and urgency. The scooter rickshaw races toward the river where my informant's son is waving his arms to get our attention. We follow him down to the ghat.

I can see the top hat. *The storyteller is smoking. He looks up at the foreigner with curiosity and is introduced to him in English: "This is Mr. Brahm Kathuwala . . . and this is Professor Lee Siegel."*

"At last," I smile. He is older and more frail than I imagined.

And later the old storyteller of Banaras, sitting cross-legged in front of me, hesitates, closes his eyes and then opens them again to smile almost sadly.

And, yes, then he begins to tell me a story, *an old, old story, a true story. . . .*

Acknowledgments

The visit to India described in this book was made possible by a Senior Research Fellowship from the American Institute of Indian Studies and the Smithsonian Institute. Further research was supported by a Fujio Matsuda Scholarship from the University of Hawaii and a grant from the Joint Committee on South Asia of the American Council of Learned Societies and the Social Science Research Council, with funds provided by the National Endowment for the Humanities and the Ford Foundation. The Rockefeller Foundation generously rendered me the luxury of beginning this project in residency at the Villa Serbelloni in Bellagio.